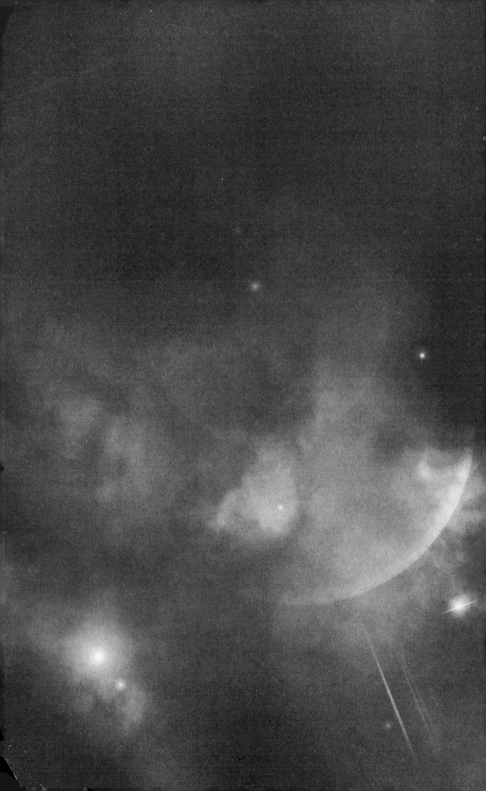

ZODIAC

ROMINA RUSSELL

razOr
bill

An Imprint of Penguin Random House

An Imprint of Penguin Random House
Penguin.com

ISBN: 978-1-59514-741-7

Printed in the United States of America

11 13 15 17 19 20 18 16 14 12

Interior design by Vanessa Han

For my parents and sister,
the stars who guide my universe.

Y para mi abuelo *Bebo*, gracias por compartir
el mágico mundo de los libros conmigo.

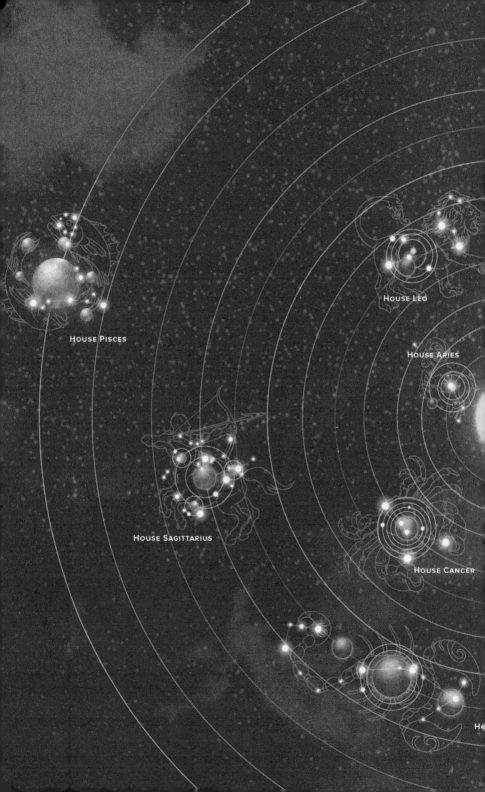

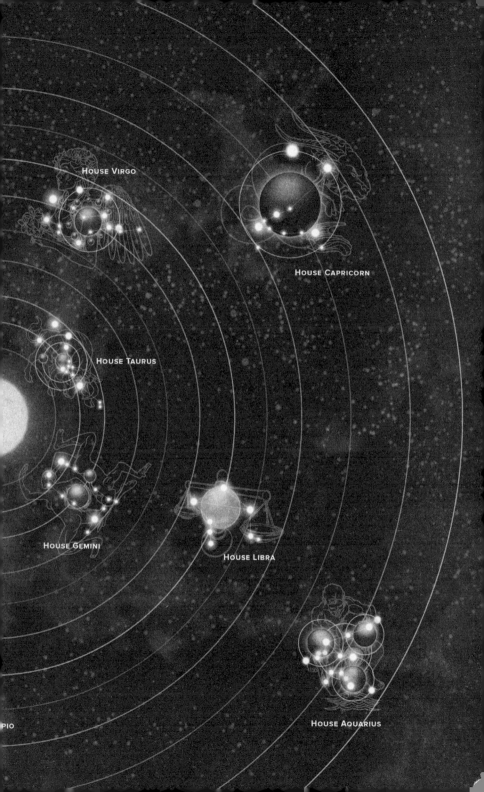

THE HOUSES OF THE ZODIAC GALAXY

THE FIRST HOUSE:
ARIES, *THE RAM*
CONSTELLATION
Strength: Military
Guardian: General Eurek

THE SECOND HOUSE:
TAURUS, *THE BULL*
CONSTELLATION
Strength: Industry
Guardian: Chief Executive
Purecell

THE THIRD HOUSE:
GEMINI, *THE DOUBLE*
CONSTELLATION
Strength: Imagination
Guardians: Twins Caaseum
and Rubidum

THE FOURTH HOUSE:
CANCER, *THE CRAB*
CONSTELLATION
Strength: Nurture
Guardian: Mother Origene

THE FIFTH HOUSE:
LEO, *THE LION*
CONSTELLATION
Strength: Passion
Guardian: Holy Leader Aurelius

THE SIXTH HOUSE:
VIRGO, *THE TRIPLE VIRGIN*
CONSTELLATION
Strength: Sustenance
Guardian: Empress Moira

THE SEVENTH HOUSE:
LIBRA, *THE SCALES OF*
JUSTICE CONSTELLATION
Strength: Justice
Guardian: Lord Neith

THE EIGHTH HOUSE:
SCORPIO, *THE SCORPION*
CONSTELLATION
Strength: Innovation
Guardian: Chieftain Skiff

THE NINTH HOUSE:
SAGITTARIUS, *THE ARCHER*
CONSTELLATION
Strength: Curiosity
Guardian: Guardian Brynda

THE TENTH HOUSE:
CAPRICORN, *THE SEAGOAT*
CONSTELLATION
Strength: Wisdom
Guardian: Sage Ferez

THE ELEVENTH HOUSE:
AQUARIUS, *THE WATER*
BEARER CONSTELLATION
Strength: Philosophy
Guardian: Supreme Guardian
Gortheaux the Thirty-Third

THE TWELFTH HOUSE:
PISCES, *THE FISH*
CONSTELLATION
Strength: Spirituality
Guardian: Prophet Marinda

~~THE THIRTEENTH HOUSE:~~
~~OPHIUCHUS, *THE SERPENT*~~
~~*BEARER CONSTELLATION*~~

CANCRIAN FOLK TALE, ORIGINS AND AUTHOR UNKNOWN

BEWARE OCHUS

Once upon a Guardian Star,
When the Zodiac was new,
A Serpent stole in from afar,
And trouble began to brew.

Twelve Houses fell in disarray,
Until the Snake drew their focus.
Their discord he promised to allay,
He told them his true name was Ochus.

Trust in him the Houses did,
But cross them he would in the end.
Their greatest magic Ochus hid,
A wound even time could not mend.

Now we guard against his return,
For before setting off he did warn us,
To one day see our Zodiac burn,
So now we must all *Beware Ochus*.

PROLOGUE

WHEN I THINK OF HOME, I see blue. The swirling blue of the seawater, the infinite blue of the sky, the brilliant blue of Mom's gaze. Sometimes I question if her eyes were really that blue, or if the blue of House Cancer colors them in my memory. I guess I'll never know, since I didn't pack pictures of her when I moved to Elara, the largest moon in our constellation. All I brought was the necklace.

On my brother Stanton's tenth birthday, Dad took us nar-clamming on his Strider. Unlike our schooner, which was built to cover long distances, the Strider was small and shaped like a clamshell half, with rows of buoyancy benches, clam-cubbies for the nar-clams, a holographic navigational screen, and even a diving board that stuck out from the front like a tongue. The vessel's underside was coated in millions of microscopic cilia-like legs that scurried us along the surface of the Cancer Sea.

I always loved leaning my head over the side and staring down at the tiny whirlpools that occasionally formed, swirling in various hues of blue. As if the ocean were made of paint rather than water.

I was only seven, under the legal deep-diving age, so I stayed topside with Mom, while Dad and Stanton dove down for nar-clams. Mom looked like a siren that day, perched on the peak of the diving board as we waited for the guys to surface with their spoils. Her long, light locks spilled down her back, and the sun glinted off her ivory skin and orb-like eyes. Lying back on my springy seat, I tried to soak up the heat and unwind. But I was always aware in her presence, always ready to recite facts about the Zodiac at her command.

"Rho." Mom leapt gracefully off the platform onto the carved clamshell floor, and I straightened my spine as she approached. "I have something for you."

She drew a pouch from her purse. Mom wasn't the type to buy gifts or remember special occasions; those responsibilities usually fell to Dad. "But it's not *my* birthday."

A familiar, far-off look fell over her features, and I regretted saying it. I opened the pouch and pulled out a dozen nar-clam pearls, each one a different color, all strung together on a strand of silver seahorse hair. Each pearl was spaced equally apart and bore the symbol of a different Zodiac House, inscribed in Mom's delicate calligraphy. "*Wow*" was all I could say as I slipped it on.

She flashed me a rare smile and sat on the bench beside me. As always, she smelled like water lilies. "In the early days," she whispered, her electric stare lost in the blue of the horizon, "the original Guardians ruled the Zodiac together."

Her stories always eased my nerves, and I settled into my seat, closing my eyes so I could focus on the sound of her voice. "Yet each of the Twelve prized a different strength as the key for keeping our universe safe, which caused disagreements and rifts between them. Until one day, a stranger arrived promising to restore balance. The stranger's name was *Ochus*."

Every Cancrian child knew the tale of Ochus, but Mom's version wasn't the same as the poem we had to memorize in school. The way she told it, the story sounded less like myth and more like a history lesson. "Ochus appeared before each Guardian in a different disguise, claiming to possess a powerful gift—a secret weapon that would turn the tide in that House's favor. To the philosophical Aquarian, Ochus promised an ancient text that contained answers to the Zodiac's most profound questions. To the imaginative leaders of Gemini, he promised a magical mask that would create enchantments beyond the wearer's beliefs. To Capricorn, the wisest House of all, he promised a treasure chest filled with truths amassed from worlds older than our own, worlds accessed through Helios."

I opened my eyes to see a blonde curl blowing across Mom's forehead. I felt the urge to brush it back for her, but I knew I shouldn't. Mom wasn't *cold*, exactly, just . . . distant.

"Ochus instructed each Guardian to meet him at a secret location, where he promised to deliver his gift. Upon arriving, each of the Twelve were shocked to learn the others had also been summoned. Their shock only grew as they each described the Ochus that had visited them: The Cancrian Mother had encountered a sea snake, the Piscene Prophet saw a shapeless spirit, the Sagittarian

Guardian met a hooded wanderer, and so on. As no two had seen the same stranger, the Guardians distrusted each other's accounts. While they argued, Ochus silently slipped away, taking with him the Zodiac's greatest magic: the Houses' trust in one another. All he left behind was a warning: *Beware my return, when all shall burn.*"

"He stole our trust, and we've never gotten it back," I said, reciting the moral my teacher taught us. I'd just started school a week earlier, and wanting to impress Mom further, I went on. "Ochus was the Zodiac's first orphan. He didn't have a House to belong to and was jealous of the ones in our galaxy. That's why on Cancer we look out for each other and make sure everyone has a home."

Mom's brow dipped. "You mean, *All healthy hearts start with a happy home?* Rho, you know better than that. In our lessons, I've taught you about great individuals who came from broken homes, like Galileo Sprock of Scorpio, who developed the first hologram centuries ago, or renowned pacifist Lord Vaz, House Libra's revered Guardian." She looked hurt. "If you're going to let your teachers brainwash you, then maybe you're not ready for school."

"No—it was just something I heard," I assured her. Mom was always worried about the Cancrian school system *brainwashing* me. It's why she didn't enroll me when I was five like the other kids in our House. She decided to tutor me herself instead.

I waited for her expression to clear and didn't interrupt again. I knew Mom was only looking out for me, but I liked playing with kids my age too much to go back to her homeschooling.

"The *point*," she went on, "is our ancient Guardians chose to fight one another instead of admitting they were afraid of the same monster." When I met her gaze, her expression turned hard. "You will face fears in your life, and people will try to take them from you. They'll try to convince you what you fear isn't real, that it's just in your head—but you can't let them."

Her reflective eyes drank in the blue around us, until they shone brighter than the sky itself. "*Trust your fears*, Rho. Believing in them will keep you safe."

Her stare was so intense that I had to pull away. Whenever Mom got this worked up, I'd wonder if she was just having one of her strange spells—like the time she meditated on the roof of our bungalow and didn't come down for two days—or if she had seen something in the stars.

Instead of meeting her eyes again, I surveyed the water. A trail of bubbles broke the surface, and I arched my neck to look for Dad and Stanton. But neither emerged.

"Let's take a dip," said Mom suddenly, her tone light again. She leapt up to the diving board, and in one fluid motion, she was in the water. Dad always said she was a secret mermaid. I threw on his navigational glasses to follow her movements underwater and watched her spin gracefully around the Strider. Seeing her swim was like watching a ballet.

Just as her head broke the surface, so did Dad's and Stanton's. Dad raised his net filled with nar-clams onto the diving board, and I dragged the day's catch into the boat. Still in the sea, Dad and my brother pulled off their facemasks. In my periphery, I thought I saw bubbles frothing in the water again.

"This thing's too tight." Stanton fussed, undoing the top of his suit to free his arms. I ducked as he tossed his wet mask into the boat. It landed with a squelch. I was just about to lose the glasses and jump in with them, when a black mass broke through the sea's surface.

The snake was five feet long, with scaly skin and red eyes—but I knew from Mom's lessons its power was in its poisonous bite.

"There's a Maw next to you!" I screamed, pointing at the sea snake. Stanton shrieked as the Maw shot toward him and—before my parents could reach my brother—the snake sank its teeth into his shoulder.

Stanton cried out in pain, and Mom dove to him, swimming faster that I'd ever seen anyone go. She hooked a hand under his healthy arm and pulled him toward Dad. I just stared, too terrified to think of a way to help.

Through the glasses' special lenses, I could see the snake was orbiting us, waiting for its poison to spread and immobilize its victim, so it could feed. Its glowing red eyes can cut through darkness, which is where Maws are supposed to live—in the Rift, hundreds of fathoms down. I didn't think they ever came up this high.

As Dad carried Stanton into the boat, Mom's bright blue eyes flashed and her lips curled. I'd never seen her look like that: so furious and *feral*.

Then she vanished beneath the surface. "Mom!"

I turned to Dad in desperation, but he was bent over Stanton, sucking out the Maw's poison from his shoulder wound. I found Mom again in the water: She was leading the Maw away from us, but the snake was gaining on her. It was going to strike.

I couldn't move, I couldn't even scream; all I could do was watch. My hands gripped the side of the Strider, and I wasn't sure if my body could take much more of my heart's beating. Then Mom stopped swimming and turned around to face the snake.

Something silver glinted in her hand. It looked like the blade Dad used to pry open the nar-clams—he always brought it with him underwater, and she must have grabbed it from his belt before diving in. When the Maw lashed out with its mouth to bite her, Mom raised her hand and sliced the snake in half.

I gasped.

"Rho!" called Dad. "Where's Mom?"

"She's—alive," I said, breathless, "and coming back." Seeing Stanton's pallid and unconscious figure, my panic resurfaced. "Is he—?"

"I got the poison out, but we need to get him to a healer," said Dad, starting up the Strider and steering it toward Mom. She pulled herself up by the diving board and landed lightly in the boat. As soon as she was in, Dad went full speed.

Mom sat beside Stanton and rested her hand on his forehead. I expected her to tell Dad how she sliced the Maw in two, but she just sat there in silence. I couldn't believe how brave she'd been. She saved us.

"What in the name of Helios was a Maw doing in the shallows?" mused Dad to himself, his eyes glassy and his breathing still heavy. He didn't speak again after that, reverting to his quiet nature. I helped Mom sort the nar-clams into clam-cubbies, and when we finished, we sat with Stanton.

"Mom, I'm sorry," I muttered, the tears falling before I could stop them, "I didn't know what to do. . . ."

"It's okay, Rho," said Mom, surprising me by reaching out to adjust the pearl necklace so the Crab was centered on my chest. "You're still young, so of course the world seems scary to you." Then she looked at me—looked *into* me—and everything outside her bulletproof gaze grew blurry.

"Hold onto your fears," she whispered. "They're real."

1

TWELVE HOLOGRAPHIC SYMBOLS DRIFT DOWN the Academy hallway, gliding through people like colorful ghosts. The signs represent the Houses of our Zodiac Solar System, and they're parading to promote unity. But everyone's too busy buzzing about tonight's Lunar Quadract to spare them a glance.

"You ready for tonight?" asks my best friend, Nishiko, an exchange student from Sagittarius. She waves at her locker and it pops open.

"Yeah . . . what I'm not ready for is this test," I say, still watching the twelve signs drift through the school. Acolytes aren't invited to the celebration, so we're hosting our own party on campus. And after Nishi's brilliant idea to bribe the dining hall staff into adding our new song to their lunchtime playlist, our band was voted to play the event.

I dip my fingers in my coat pocket to make sure I have my drum-sticks, just as Nishi slams her locker shut. "Have they told you why they're making you retake it?"

"Probably the same old reason—I never show my work."

"I don't know. . . ." Nishi scrunches up her forehead in that uniquely Sagittarian *I'm-curious-about-everything* way. "They might want to know more about what you saw in the stars last time."

I shake my head. "I only saw it because I don't use an Astralator for my predictions. Everyone knows intuition isn't star-proof."

"Having a different method doesn't make you wrong. I think they want to hear more about your omen." She waits for me to say something more about it, and when I don't, she pushes harder. "You said it was black? And . . . *writhing?*"

"Yeah, kind of," I mutter. Nishi knows I don't like discussing that vision, but asking a Sagittarian to suppress her curiosity is like asking a Cancrian to abandon a friend in need. Neither is in our natures.

"Have you seen it again since the test?" she presses.

This time I don't answer. The symbols are rounding the corner. I can just make out the Fish of Pisces before they vanish.

"I should go," I finally say, flashing her a small smile so she knows I'm not upset. "See you onstage."

✦ ✦ ✦

The halls still swarm with restless Acolytes, so nobody sees me slip into Instructor Tidus's empty classroom. I leave the lights off and let instinct guide me through the black space.

When I've reached the teacher's desk, I feel along its surface until my fingers find cold metal. Though I know I shouldn't, I switch on the Ephemeris.

Stars puncture the blackness.

Hovering in the center of the room, countless winking pinpricks of light form a dozen distinct constellations—the Houses of the Zodiac. Larger balls of colored light swirl among the stars: our planets and moons. In the midst of it all burns a ball of blazing fire: Helios.

I slide a stick from my pocket and twirl it. Amid all the sparkles in the glittering universe, I find the churning mass of blue, the brightest point in the Crab-shaped constellation . . . and I miss home.

The Blue Planet.

Cancer.

I reach out, but my hand goes right through the hologram. Four lesser gray orbs hover in a row beside my planet; if connected, they look like they would form a straight line. That's because the Lunar Quadract is the only time this millennium our four moons will align.

Our school sits on Cancer's closest and largest moon, Elara. We share this gray rock with the prestigious Zodai University, which has training campuses on every House in our galaxy.

I'm forbidden from activating the school's Ephemeris without an instructor present. I steal a last look at my home planet, a whirling ball of blending blues, and I picture Dad at our airy bungalow home, tending to his nar-clams on the banks of the Cancer Sea. The smell of the salty water engulfs me, and the heat of

Helios warms my skin, almost like I'm really there. . . .

The Ephemeris flickers, and our smallest and farthest moon disappears.

I fix on the black spot where the gray light of Thebe was just extinguished—and one by one, the other moons go dark.

I turn to inspect the rest of the constellations, just as the whole galaxy explodes in a blinding blast of light.

The room is plunged into total darkness, until images begin to appear all around me. On the walls, the ceiling, desks—every surface is covered in multicolored holograms. Some I can identify from my classes, but there are so many—words, images, equations, diagrams, charts—that I can't possibly take them all in—

"Acolyte Rho!"

The room is flooded with light. The holograms disappear, and the place is back to being a plain classroom. The Ephemeris sits innocently on the teacher's desk.

Instructor Tidus towers over it. Her old, plump face is so perpetually pleasant that it's hard to tell when I've upset her. "You were told to wait outside. You have been reminded of this before: Acolytes are forbidden from using the school Ephemeris without an instructor, and I can't imagine what you'll need a drumstick for during your testing."

"Sorry, ma'am." The stick goes still in my hand and joins its twin in my pocket.

Hanging behind her is the only disruption to the room's white walls, white ceiling, and white floor. Large letters in blue ink, bearing the Zodai's favorite precaution: *Trust Only What You Can Touch.*

Dean Lyll barges in. I square my shoulders, surprised to see the head of the Academy present at my exam. It's bad enough being the only student forced to take this test twice. Doing it under his curt supervision will be unbearable.

"Acolyte, take a seat until we are ready to proceed." The dean is tall and thin, and unlike Instructor Tidus, there isn't a pleasant thing about him. So much for Nishi's theory that they want to hear more about my vision.

I slide into a chair, wishing the room had a window. Mother Origene, the Guardian of our House, landed less than an hour ago with her Council of Advisors and the Zodai Royal Guard. I'd love to catch even a passing glimpse of them.

My friends and I are graduating this year, so the Academy has already submitted our transcripts for consideration at Zodai University. Only the top Acolytes in our class will be accepted.

The university's best-ranked graduates get invited to join the Order of the Zodai, our galaxy's peacekeepers. The best of the best are recruited into the Guardian's Royal Guard, the Zodai's highest honor.

When I was younger, I used to dream about being in the Royal Guard one day. Until I realized it wasn't my dream.

"Given that our moon is hosting tonight's celebration," says the dean, "we'll need to make this quick."

"Yes, sir." My hands itch for my sticks again. I step into the middle of the room as the dean activates the Ephemeris.

"Please give a general read on the Lunar Quadract."

The room plunges into darkness once more, and the twelve

constellations come alight. I wait until the whole Zodiac has filled out, and then I try accessing my Center—the first step to reading the stars.

The Ephemeris is a device that reflects Space in real time, but when we're Centered, it can be used to tap into the Psy Network, or Collective Conscious—where we're not limited to the physical realm. Where we can read what's written in the stars.

Centering means relaxing my vision so much my eyes start to cross, like looking at a stereogram, followed by calling on whatever brings me the greatest inner peace. It can be a memory, a movement, a story—whatever most touches my soul.

When I was very young, Mom taught me an ancient art the very first Zodai used to access their Center. Passed on from long-forgotten civilizations, it's called Yarrot, and it's a series of poses designed to mimic the twelve constellations of the Zodiac. The movements align one's body and mind with the stars, and the longer you practice, the easier Centering is supposed to become . . . but when Mom left, I gave it up.

I stare at the four gray orbs floating next to Cancer, but I can't relax my vision. I'm too worried Thebe will vanish again. My brother, Stanton, works there.

We Cancrians are known for our nurturing natures and strong family values. We're supposed to put our loved ones ahead of ourselves. Yet one after the other, my Mom, my brother, and I abandoned Dad. Abandoned our home.

"Four minutes."

I pull my drumstick from my pocket and pirouette it on my fingertips until the movement relaxes me, and then I start to play my latest composition in my mind, the beat growing louder with every rendition. Eventually, I can't hear anything else.

After what feels like forever but might just be minutes, my mind begins to rise, elevating higher, toward Helios. The lights of the Crab constellation start to shuffle, adjusting their place in the sky. Our four moons—Elara, Orion, Galene, Thebe—move to their future positions, where they'll be in a few hours, for the Lunar Quadract.

My instructors can't see the movement because it's only happening in the Psy Network, so it's confined to my mind. Skill level and ability determine what and how much a Zodai can see when Centered, so visions of the future are unique for each of us.

Once the stars in the holographic map have realigned themselves, their trajectories leave faint arcs in Space that fade fast. Using an Astralator, we can measure these movements and plug the numbers into equations—but if I have to solve for x, the Lunar Quadract will be over before I can predict it. And, as Dean Lyll pointed out, we *are* in a rush. . . .

I concentrate as hard as I can, and soon I pick up a faint rhythm reaching me from afar, echoing weakly in my ears. It sounds like a drumbeat—or a pulse. Its beat is slow and ominous . . . like something's coming for us.

Then the vision appears—the same vision I've been seeing for a week now: a smoldering black mass, barely distinguishable from Space, pressing into the atmosphere past the Twelfth House, Pisces. Its influence seems to be warping our Crab constellation out of shape.

The problem with digging so deep inside my mind without using an Astralator is there's no way to tell apart which warnings are from the stars and which ones I'm manifesting myself.

Thebe vanishes again.

"There's a bad omen," I blurt. "A dangerous opposition in the stars."

The Ephemeris shuts off, and the lights come on. Dean Lyll is scowling at me. "Nonsense. Show me your work."

"I . . . forgot my Astralator."

"You haven't even done the arithmetic!" He rounds on Instructor Tidus. "Is this a joke?"

Instructor Tidus addresses me from the other end of the room. "Rho, the fact that we're here at all right now should indicate how crucial this test is. Our most important long-term planning depends on precise star readings. How we invest, where we build, what our farms grow. I thought you would take today more seriously."

"I'm sorry," I say, shame spreading through me as swiftly as Maw poison.

"Your unorthodox methods are failing you, and now I expect you to do the math, the way your peers do."

Even my toes must be red. "Could I go get my Astralator?"

Without answering, Dean Lyll opens the door and calls into the hallway, "Does anyone have an Astralator for an unprepared Acolyte to borrow?"

Even, measured footsteps approach, and a man marches into the room, something small clasped in his hands. I suppress a gasp of surprise.

"Lodestar Mathias Thais!" booms Dean Lyll, reaching out to touch fists, our traditional greeting. "Wonderful to have you back on our moon for the celebration."

The man nods but doesn't speak. He's still shy. The first time I saw him was almost five years ago, when he was still a student at Zodai University. I was twelve and just starting at the Academy. I missed the singing surf of the Cancer Sea too much to get more than a couple hours' sleep those nights, so I'd spend the rest of the time exploring the city-sized, enclosed compound we share with the university.

That's how I discovered the solarium. It's at the very end of the compound, on the university side, a wide room with windowed walls that curve to form a windowed ceiling. I remember walking in and watching in awe as Helios came into view. I closed my eyes and let the giant orange-red rays warm my skin—until I heard a noise behind me.

In the shadow of an elaborate moonstone sculpture, carved in the shape of our Guardian, was a guy. His eyes were closed in deep meditation, and I recognized his meditative pose instantly. He was practicing Yarrot.

I came back the next day with a book to read, and he was there again. Soon, it became a ritual. Sometimes we were alone, sometimes there were others. We never spoke, but something about being near him, or maybe just being near Yarrot again, soothed my nerves and made it easier to be so far from home.

"That's a marvelous Astralator," says the dean, as the Lodestar holds it out to him. "Give it to Acolyte Rho." I swallow, hard, as he turns to me for the first time.

Surprise registers in his indigo blue eyes. *He knows me*. Warmth spreads through my skin, like I'm being bathed in the light of Helios again.

The Lodestar must be twenty-two now. He's grown—his lean body has a bigger build, and his wavy black hair is trimmed short and neat, like the other male Zodai. "Don't drop it, please," he says in a mild baritone, a voice so musical my bones vibrate.

He passes me his mother-of-pearl Astralator, and our hands brush. The touch tingles up my arm.

So low only I can hear him, he adds, "It's a family heirloom."

"She will return it to you when her exam concludes—and in one piece." Dean Lyll doesn't look at me. "Her grade will rest on its safe return."

Before I can say a single word in his presence, the Lodestar turns and takes off. Great—now he thinks I'm a mute.

"Again," says the dean, impatience coming through in his clipped tone.

The Ephemeris takes over the room. Once I'm Centered and the moons have aligned, I gently hold out the cylindrical instrument and point it at the fading trajectory arcs. Cancrians have excellent memories, and mine is good even by our standards, so I don't need to write the numbers down. When I've taken all the measurements I need—enough to make a prediction about tonight—the dean shuts off the Ephemeris.

I'm still making calculations when the timer goes off. When I finish, I realize the dean was right—there's no opposition in the stars.

"The math looks good," he says roughly. "See how much better you do when you follow instructions and use the right equipment?"

"Yes, sir," I say, even though something is still bothering me. "Sir, what if using the Astralator is shortsighted? What if I didn't see the omen this time because the disturbance isn't near our moons yet—it's still at the far edge of Space? Wouldn't the Astralator be unable to account for a distance that far?"

The dean sighs. "More nonsense. Oh well. At least you passed." Still shaking his head, he yanks open the door and says, "Instructor Tidus, I will meet you at the celebration."

When we're alone, my teacher smiles at me. "How many times must we tell you, Rho? Your clever theories and imaginative stories have no place in astrological science."

"Yes, ma'am." I bow my head, hoping she's right.

"You have talent, Rho, and we don't mean to discourage you." She moves closer as she speaks, until we're face to face. "Think of your drums. You first had to master the basics before you could compose your own riffs. The same principle applies here: If you practice daily on your tutorial Ephemeris with an Astralator, I'm certain you'll see vast improvements in your arithmetic and technique."

The compassion in her eyes makes me feel ashamed that I've put no effort into getting better with an Astralator. It's just that her insistence on daily practices reminds me too much of Mom, and I like to keep those memories walled off.

But disappointing Instructor Tidus hurts as much as remembering.

◆ ◆ ◆

I race to my dorm-pod to change, too crunched for time to find the Lodestar and return his Astralator. I'll have to search for him after the celebration.

The door unlocks at my touch, and I swap my Academy blues for the brand new space suit—black and skintight—I bought myself as an early birthday present. Nishiko is going to flip when she sees me.

Before heading out, I consult my Wave, a small golden device shaped like a clam. Cancrians believe knowledge is like water, fluid and ever changing, so we carry with us a Wave—an interactive way of recording, reviewing, and sending information. The moment I open it, holographic data blooms out and streams all around me: news headlines, messages from friends, updates to my calendar.

Earlier, when Instructor Tidus turned off her Ephemeris, I caught only a brief glimpse of the holograms in her room. But it was long enough for one of them to register.

"Where do we come from?" I ask.

The large holographic diagram from earlier materializes in the air, larger than all the others. It represents an ancient exodus from a world far away and lost to time, a world called Earth.

Archeologists think our earliest ancestors came from there, and the drawing depicts them arriving at our galaxy through Helios— though no one believes that's really how they got here. As the Wave runs through our history, an image of the twelve constellations materializes. Only in Instructor Tidus's hologram, there weren't twelve.

There were thirteen.

2

"RHO!" NISHI'S FACE BLASTS THROUGH all the data, and I jump back a few feet.

"I know, I know, I'm coming!" I call back.

She reaches her hands out like she wants to strangle me, and she looks so real I almost duck—but her holographic fingers go right through my neck.

The Zodiac's traditional hand-touch greeting evolved when it grew hard to tell hologram from human. Our teachers are always reminding us that holograms can be manipulated and forged, and those who have fallen victim to identity fraud have lost fortunes, even lives. But it's such a rare crime that the axiom *Trust Only What You Can Touch* has become more superstition than real warning.

The holograms disappear as I stuff the Wave up my glove, grab my instrument case, and pull on my helmet. When I leave the

Academy, I'm semi-weightless in a subzero climate, facing a dusty gray expanse where a crowd is beginning to form around a crystal dome stage. The crystal is pitch-black, so no one can see inside yet.

I look up at the sky; our three other moons are lined in a row, bright as beacons. My vision from the Ephemeris still haunts me, and for a moment Thebe's light seems to flicker. I shake it off and make for the dome.

In our moon's weak gravity, I bounce out in long, flying leaps. The crowd around me is a sea of shapes and colors, an array of space suit fashion on full display. There are designer suits that sparkle with precious stones, gimmicky suits that do things like project holograms into the air, functional suits that light up in the dark, and more.

The farther I get from the compound, the thicker the night grows, its blackness interrupted only by the glimmer of glow-in-the-dark fabric or a holographic helmet. I steel my gaze on the crystal dome ahead, dazzling like a half-buried diamond. Once I've reached the small side door, I Wave Nishi to let me in.

"*Helios*, can you breathe in that thing?" As soon as I cycle through the airlock, Nishi holds me at arm's length to scan my outfit. "It's about time your body came out of hiding and saw some action."

I take off my helmet and shake my blonde curls loose. Deke whistles appreciatively from the other end of the dome. "Show the men of the Zodiac what we're missing, Rho."

I blush, already wishing I was back under the helmet's shell. "I *date*."

Nishi laughs. "If by *date* you mean endure a male's company for fifteen minutes of stuffing your faces before you're already Waving one of us to come rescue you—"

"Yes, that's exactly what a date—"

"We get it, Rho, no one's good enough for you."

I stare at Deke, my mouth half-open with indignation, but he ignores my glare and turns to Nishi, holding something out to her. "I got them."

"You didn't!" Nishi springs over and inspects the four finger-sized bottles of bubbling black tonic in Deke's hands. "*How?*"

I recognize the Abyssthe immediately. It's a drink the Zodai take to improve their performance in the Ephemeris.

Centering requires an extreme amount of concentration and consumes a ton of mental energy because it requires a person to reach down into her innermost self and listen to the thing that connects her to the stars—her soul. Abyssthe helps lengthen the feeling so that a Zodai can read the Ephemeris for a longer stretch of time.

The three of us have taken it once before, for Instructor Tidus's lesson on Macro Reads, under her supervision. Its sale is closely regulated, so it's very hard to get. A smug smile steals over Deke's features. "Nish, a true Zodai never reveals his secrets."

"You totally stole it from the university's lab," she says, plucking a bottle. Abyssthe is produced in House Sagittarius. Nishi told me that if taken outside an Ephemeris setting, the tonic has a mood-altering effect, making a person feel light-hearted and less inhibited.

Deke hands Kai and me the other two bottles. I'm not sure how I felt about Abyssthe when we took it in class—the brain and body buzz was nice, but the disorienting effect lasted so long I started to panic it would never wear off. They only sell it to people seventeen and older on Cancer . . . which is what I'll be in just a few weeks.

"What will it feel like this time?" I ask Nishi. She's the only one of us who's taken it recreationally before. Sagittarians don't believe in age restrictions.

"Like *you're* the Ephemeris," she says, already opening hers and taking a whiff. I smell a hint of licorice. "You feel your mind broadening, like it's expanding into infinity, the way Space swells out from the Ephemeris. Everything becomes tenuous and dreamlike, like you're Centered, and there's this body high that's like being . . . weightless."

"Which we pretty much are on this moon anyway," Deke points out.

Nishi rolls her eyes at him. While most people study on their own planets, Sagittarius is one of the more widespread Houses because they're natural-born wanderers. Sagittarians are truth-seekers who will follow a trail of knowledge to whatever end—having fun the whole way.

"How long will the effects last?" I ask, shaking the bottle. The Abyssthe bubbles and froths, like it's half liquid, half air.

The peak dropout point for students at Zodai University is when they get to Galactic Readings in the Ephemeris, and they're required to dose themselves with Abyssthe almost every day for a month. I read that students who've had prior experience with

Abyssthe tend to endure it better and have a greater chance of graduating.

"It'll wear off by the end of our first set," Nishi assures me. "And *no*, it won't affect your drumming," she adds, guessing my next question. "You'll still be *you*—just a more relaxed you."

Nishi and Deke down theirs in one gulp, but I hesitate and meet Kai's gaze. He only joined the band two months ago. Since he's a year younger, he's never tried Abyssthe before, and his eyes are round with terror.

To take the attention off him and ease his fear, I wink and drink mine. With a worried smile, Kai nods and takes his, too.

The four of us stare at each other. Nothing happens for so long that we start laughing. "Someone marked you for a sucker," says Nishi, snorting, pointing at Deke.

Then, one by one, we fall silent.

Abyssthe begins with a body buzz I can feel down to my bones, and it makes me wonder whether the crystal dome has detached itself from the moon and is now floating into Space. Nishi was right: My consciousness is tingling, like I'm Centered, but the universe I'm diving through is actually my mind. My head feels so sensitive that it tickles when I think.

I start laughing.

"Countdown: five minutes!" booms a disembodied voice. It's Deke's pod-mate Xander, who manages the sound for our shows from his studio.

We all jump, and I unpack my drum kit, the Abyssthe making it hard to focus on anything in the physical realm. It takes me way too many attempts to fit four spindly metal pegs into their holes on the drum mat, a bouncy bed beneath my feet that has a plush burgundy chair at its center and a crescent of holes arranged around it.

When the pieces are in place and I sit down, the mat lights up and round metal plates unfold from the ends of each rod I've planted. They look like lily pads blossoming on tall stems.

"*Lily pads*," I say out loud, laughing. If metal is starting to remind me of organic life, I must miss home more than I realize.

"Rho's delirious!" shouts Nishi, collapsing in a fit of giggles on the floor.

So is Nishi, if she's risking damage to her imported levlan suit—but the words that come shrieking out of me are: "No, I'm not!" I pounce on her, and we play-wrestle on the floor, each trying to tickle the other.

"Yes, you are!" calls Deke. He's stuffed both feet into his helmet and is hopping around the dome, declaring the exercise an "excellent workout" every time he falls.

"She can't be delirious!" blurts Kai, who hasn't spoken more than a few sentences our whole bandship.

Nishi and I pull apart and stare at him. Even Deke stops hopping. Then Kai shouts, "Delirious isn't real if you can't touch it!"

We all explode in howling laughter, and Deke takes Kai under his arm and scruffs up his hair. "My boy! He talks!"

Kai slips out of Deke's hold, and Deke chases him around, until we hear Xander's booming voice again: "One minute!"

We scream and scramble for our instruments.

I plop onto the plush chair and fit my feet into a pair of metal boots with pedals built in. Two stacked plates—*lily pads*—bloom from the tip of my left foot, my hi-hat, and the largest plate of all, the bass drum, emerges from my right boot, along with a pedal-operated beater.

I've tuned each pad to sound exactly the way I want, so I whirl my sticks in my hands in anticipation, while Deke positions his holographic guitar across his chest. He runs his lucky pick—a crab-shark tooth—through the color-changing strings, and an angry riff wails out. Even though it's a hologram, his guitar operates on technology sensitive enough to trigger sound when Deke makes contact. It's the same with Kai's bass.

"Sound check!" calls Deke.

I roll my sticks across each pad, and then I press hard on the pedals in my boots. The bass drum reverberates menacingly throughout the dome. Nishi joins the percussion next, her voice throaty and soulful. Once Deke and Kai come in, the melody of Nishi's song is haunting against our heavy and complicated compositions.

We only run through a few bars, enough to make sure everything's working right, and then we go deathly silent as we wait for the crystal to turn clear. The nerves of playing are stronger than Abyssthe's buzz, and soon I can't tell apart the tonic's effect from my own restless anticipation.

Xander's voice cuts through the heaviness: "Academy Acolytes! You have been excluded from the big celebration, but you still deserve a good time! On that note, and performing now for your plebian pleasures, I present to you the incredible *Drowning Diamonds*!"

The blackness lifts, making the crystal window so clear it's barely detectable, and the dome's lights blast on, illuminating the night. Outside, hundreds of Acolytes are soundlessly rising and falling in the air, trying to jump as high as they can. Some are flashing holographic messages in the sky, all directed at the same person.

Marry me, Sagittarian siren!

I've been pierced by your arrow, Archer!

Wander my way, Truth-Seeker!

As a Sagittarian, Nishi doesn't share our Cancrian curls and light eyes—her locks are straight and black, her skin is a creamy cinnamon, and her eyes are amber and slanted. Add a sultry singing voice to her exotic beauty, and she's pretty much stolen every Cancrian guy's heart at the Academy.

Cancer has the widest range of skin colors in the galaxy—something I've always loved about our House. Back home, I had a sun-kissed golden tan, but after being on Elara so long, I'm now pale and pasty. What we Cancrians all have in common is our curly hair—which spans every shade but is often bleached from so much sun exposure—and the color of our eyes, which reflect the Cancer Sea.

Cancrian irises range from the softest of sea greens, kind of like mine, to the deepest of indigo blues . . . like Lodestar Mathias Thais's.

Nishi flashes her adorers a winning smile and does a slow turn to show off her sexy red suit, the levlan twisting with every curve of her body. She waves me over so I'll join her, but I shake my head vehemently.

I hate the spotlight—I only agreed to be in the band because as a drummer I can hang farthest back, hidden by my instrument. Deke and Kai aren't crazy about being front and center either—it's a Cancrian thing—so they tend to migrate toward either edge of the dome while they play.

In the distance beyond the crowd, a freighter lands to refuel at our spaceport. The Academy/university compound now has armed Zodai standing guard at every entrance, checking people's identification as they file in to hear our Guardian's speech. It's hard to believe I've been on this moon almost five years, and soon I might be leaving it forever.

We won't find out if we've been accepted to the university for another month. This could be our last show here.

The Abyssthe's influence briefly grows stronger, just for a moment, and I feel myself slightly spacing out, like I'm Centering.

In that second, I see a shadow flit across Thebe. When I blink, it's gone.

"All right, *diamonds*—time to *drown* this place in noise!" shouts Nishi, her voice amplified in the dome and playing through the speakers of every helmet watching.

Another wave of soundless cheers ensues outside, holographic messages flicker, people soar higher off the ground, fists shake in the air—it's time. Nishi turns and winks at me. That's my cue to start us off.

I count four beats with my sticks, and then I come down hard on the snare and cymbal, simultaneously slamming on the bass pedal, and—

I blast backward as an invisible surge of energy smacks into me, hurling me off my chair. I hear my friends also taking tumbles.

My body trembles uncontrollably on the floor from the fiery pulse of electric energy. Once I stop seizing, I pull myself up.

I wish I hadn't taken the Abyssthe—it's making everything wobbly, and I can barely stand upright. As my vision begins to clear, I only have time to register the sight of our three moons, glistening like pearls strung on a string, when I see it: a fireball bursting through our Crab constellation, burning a path through Space.

With a scream, I realize I already know where it's going to land.

3

WHEN I OPEN MY EYES, the dome is dark. All I remember is a fireball . . . and then the world went white.

I reach out and feel pieces of my drum set scattered across the floor. "Nishi? Deke? Kai?" I rise and pick my way through the rubble of stuff, toward the others.

"I'm okay," says Nishi, her back against the wall, head buried in her hands. "Just . . . dizzy."

"A-live," spits Deke from somewhere behind me.

"*Holy Helios,*" I whisper, scanning the scene outside through the crystal window. The sight is terrifying. The crowd of Acolytes that was jumping and cheering moments ago is now floating unconsciously a few feet off the ground. Whether they're passed out or worse, I don't know.

Chunks of metal, plaster, and other materials clutter the air, swimming along with the limp bodies. The debris looks familiar.

I try to see what's happening by the compound, but I can't. The window is fogging up fast.

A high-pitched noise grows louder, and I catch a crack creeping down the side of the crystal. As I watch, the fracturing spreads into a spider web of lines, and when the whinnying pitch reaches a new high, I realize what's about to happen.

"RUN!"

I reach for my helmet and toss Nishi hers. Deke grabs his, and I cast my gaze around the room, realizing I never heard Kai answer.

He's still passed out, his body a small heap. I shove his helmet on his head and pull him up. Hooking a shoulder under his arm, I take him with me through the door Deke is holding open.

Deke comes through last—right as the crystal window blows.

Nishi screams, and Deke shoves the door, slamming it shut just in time. Shards of crystal stab the other side.

As soon as we're on the moon's surface, the lower oxygen lightens my load. I try using my helmet's communication system, but it's not working. Since the dome is blocking our view of campus and the compound, I signal to Deke and Nishi that we should go around.

When we reach the crowd, the sight is so devastating my vision blurs, like my eyes don't want to see more. It takes me a moment to realize I'm sobbing.

Bodies are everywhere. Floating past each other peacefully, three or four feet above the ground. None of them have woken up.

A pink space suit no bigger than Kai drifts past my head, the person light enough to rise higher than the others. I reach for the girl's leg and pull her closer. Where a face should be, there's only frost.

Her thermal controls stopped working. . . . She froze to death.

Shaking, I look around at the suspended space suits surrounding me.

They're *all* dead.

Everything within me goes so cold, my suit might as well have stopped working, too. I suck in lungfuls of oxygen, but still I can't breathe. There are too many bodies here . . . more than a hundred . . . more than two—

I can't.

I can't count. I don't want to know.

A generation of Cancrian children who can never go home again.

It's only when I see Deke and Nishiko move in my periphery that I look up. They've both turned and are surveying the damage behind us, at the compound, their gloved hands gripping the sides of their helmets like it's the only way they'll keep their heads. My gut clenches with dread, and I already know what horrors await if I turn to look.

I know the debris in the air isn't all from Elara's surface.

There are papers and notebooks and bags. Chairs and desks and books. And other bodies . . . bodies not wearing compression suits.

Faint shadows move in the distance.

Squinting, I see a small trail of people bounce-jumping toward the spaceport from the far side of the compound.

I decide not to look back. Right now, I need to get my friends and myself to safety—and to do that, the suffering has to stay behind me. I have to wall off the pain.

If I turn around, I might not be able to.

I nudge Deke and signal to the spaceport. Through his helmet's visor, his face is pale and wet. He takes Kai off my shoulder, and I get Nishi's attention, and together we follow the other survivors.

The spaceport's floodlights are dark, but when we reach the edge of the launchpad, there's a man directing us with a laser torch. When he sees Deke carrying an unconscious Kai, he motions for us to climb into the small mining ship parked in front of the hangar.

I help Deke get Kai on board, and when we've cycled through the airlock, we gently lay him down on the deck and remove his helmet. Then I yank off my own and take deep gulps of air.

We're alone in a cargo hold full of spherical orange tanks of liquid helium from Elara's mines. Frost webs the dark walls, and our breath makes puffs of vapor. The other survivors must have gone deeper into the hangar, toward a larger passenger ship.

The man who was guiding us emerges through the airlock and rushes up to Kai. His compression suit bears the insignia of the Zodai Royal Guard. When he takes off his helmet, I see a pair of indigo blue eyes.

Lodestar Mathias Thais.

Gently, he listens for breath, checks Kai's pulse, and peels open an eyelid. "This boy has fainted. Can someone pass me the healing kit?"

I reach for the large yellow case hanging by the airlock door and hand it to him. When his eyes meet mine, he holds my gaze an extra-long moment, the way he did forever ago in Instructor Tidus's room. Only this time, the surprise in his face doesn't warm my skin. I'm not sure I'll ever be warm again.

He rifles through the vials and packets, then breaks some kind of glass ampoule under Kai's nose. It must be wake-up gas, because Kai jerks up, swinging a punch.

The Lodestar dodges. "Relax. You lost consciousness, but you're going to be fine."

"Lodestar Thais," I say, my voice rough, "what's happened?"

His brow furrows, and he blinks like I just did something unexpected. Maybe he really did think I was mute.

"Please, call me Mathias." Even now, his voice is musical. "And I think it best that we wait to discuss," he adds, looking pointedly at Kai.

"Mathias," I say, a hardness in my tone that wasn't there before, "*please*—we have to know." When I say his name, color rushes to his face, like a match sparking, and I wonder if I've offended him. Maybe he was just being polite offering his first name. "Lodestar Thais," I say quickly, "does it have to do with Thebe?"

"Mathias will do." He turns from me and surveys my friends. I follow his gaze. They look as broken as I feel, and yet they're staring at him just as defiantly.

When his eyes meet mine again, I say, "We don't deserve to be kept in the dark after everything we just saw."

That seems to convince him. "There was an explosion on Thebe."

I turn my head so fast, everything spins. Somehow, I knew it the moment I saw the fireball. I knew it would land on Thebe.

Stanton.

My insides twist like sea snakes, and I snap open my Wave to reach my brother, but there's no connection. I try checking the news and my messages, but nothing's coming through. It's like the whole network has gone offline.

"Rho, I'm sure he's all right," says Nishi, massaging my back. She's the only one of my friends who's met Stanton before. The only one who knows how much he means to me.

Mathias stares at me questioningly but doesn't ask.

"What about the people on Elara?" I whisper. He shakes his head, and I'm not sure he's going to answer.

"The pulse killed the power in their suits . . . everyone outside froze to death." He takes a shaky breath before going on. "Pieces of Thebe entered our atmosphere and crashed into the compound. It's . . . hard to tell how many survived."

Something jolts our ship and knocks me into a helium tank.

Deke helps me up and we all look around apprehensively as the metal hull creaks and the orange tanks bump together. The vibrations intensify, building into a tremor, until the ship is quaking from side to side.

"Shockwave from the explosion!" Mathias calls over the noise. "Hold onto something!"

Nishi shrieks, but Deke steadies her. I grip a handrail and close my eyes. If *we're* having moonquakes, what must be happening on Thebe? Close to three thousand people work at the moon base there.

Stanton told me they have shelters—please let him be in a shelter right now. . . . He has to be in a shelter right now . . . *please.*

With one last convulsion, the shaking ends as abruptly as it started. I watch Mathias move his lips, speaking soundlessly to someone we can't see. Only the Zodai can communicate that way. When his invisible conversation is over, he says, "A meteoroid may have struck Thebe. This ship is launching now. We're heading home to Cancer."

4

THE TRIP WILL TAKE TEN HOURS.

Mathias moves us into the crew's bunkroom, where we're belted into oil-stained hammocks that stink of mildew, while he goes to the bridge. When we're alone and buckled up, I can't look my friends in the face. Somehow, seeing them will make the bodies on Elara real.

Every House has a different outlook on death. We Cancrians send our dead into Space, toward Helios, the gateway to the afterlife. We believe those who pass on with settled souls are at peace and gone for good, while the unsettled soul lives on in the stars as a new constellation.

The hope is that one day, the unsettled soul can return to live again on Cancer.

I picture the girl in the pink space suit. Where will her soul go? I chase the thought from my mind by trying to Wave Stanton and Dad, but there's still no connection. I wonder if Dad even knows what happened. He doesn't watch the news, and his Wave is so old he sometimes has to open and close it twice to get the holographic menus to pop out.

G-forces press us down as we lift off Elara. The ship's engines rumble, loud and ferocious, but I can already hear the ocean's everlasting breath. Maybe Stanton wasn't on Thebe. Maybe he's home right now, waiting for me. The last time we spoke, he told me he was visiting Dad soon.

The hull of the mining ship groans and creaks as we accelerate upward from the moon, leaving the past five years of our lives behind.

"It's okay, Nish," says Deke, squeezing her hand. She gives him a weak smile, her eyes rimmed red and puffy.

At last, the engines cut off, signaling our escape from Elara's gravity, and in the sudden quiet, my ears tingle. Gripping my Wave, I unclasp my belt and float out of the hammock, weightless. So do the others.

"I don't understand why Mother Origene didn't warn us," says Kai, speaking his first words since waking. He tries Waving his parents, but there's no connection. "The stars must have shown signs."

"To see a meteoroid that big, I doubt you'd even need an Ephemeris," says Deke, scrolling through his Wave contacts, trying to get through to anyone on Cancer. "Any telescope should have caught it."

I've been wondering the same thing. The Guardian has two main duties: representing her House in the Galactic Senate and protecting her people by reading the future. So what happened?

"Rho."

Nishi's whisper is so frail, it's the first thing about tonight that seems real. "The omen you saw during your test, the one you've been seeing when you read my future for fun, the one you won't talk about"—she chokes back a sob, tiny weightless tears slipping from her amber eyes and scattering through the air—"could it be . . . *real?*"

"No," I say quickly. Her expression hardens with distrust, which hurts because Cancrians don't use deceit. "It *can't* be," I insist, spilling my evidence: "When I saw the black mass today, at my retest, even Dean Lyll said it was nonsense. He made me use an Astralator, and it confirmed—"

"*You saw it again today,*" says Nishi, like she hasn't heard a word past that admission. "You've been seeing it for days, and then you saw it again today, and now *this*—Rho, take another look in the Ephemeris."

"Why don't one of you look, you're better with an Astralator—"

"Because we didn't see a dark mass in our readings."

"I failed and had to take the test twice, Nishi," I argue, my volume rising. "My reading was *wrong.*"

"Oh, really? So nothing bad happened tonight then?" Her voice breaks, and more tears slip into the air, like tiny diamonds.

I look over at Deke, hoping he'll disagree with her. After all, he's always the first to dismiss my reads as silly stories.

Only he's not paying us attention. He's just staring at his Wave blankly.

He couldn't get through to anyone.

"Okay," I whisper with a sigh. "I'll do it."

I scroll through my Wave and find my copy of the Ephemeris. It's just a tutorial version, so it doesn't have all the detail of the Academy's, but it still works. Stanton gave it to me last year, for my sixteenth birthday. When I whisper the command, the star map swells out in a holographic projection the size of a puffer fish. I relax my vision until my eyes cross, and then I reach into my pocket for my drumsticks.

Only they're not there. Like everything else I own, they're gone. My eyes burn.

"I'm sorry, Rho, I shouldn't have asked," says Nishi, hugging me in midair. "Just forget it."

"No, you're right." My voice comes out steady and determined. I give Nishi a squeeze back, and then I face the map again. "I have to do something. I have to help—if I can."

I summon up one of my usual melodies, sans sticks—but the music reminds me too much of our show. I can't find anything in me to call on.

A blaze of blue flashes through the cabin's small window, and I look up from the map to the real thing.

Even from this far, after so long of only seeing it in the Ephemeris, Cancer is breathtaking. Ninety-eight percent water, our planet is painted every shade of blue, streaked with barely perceptible slices of green. Cancer's cities are built on massive pods that float calmly on the sea's surface, like giant, half-submerged anemones. Our largest structures—buildings, commercial centers, schools—are secured with anchors.

The pods that hold the most populated cities are so vast that whenever I visit one I forget I'm not on land—except when a shift in the planet's core triggers powerful ripples. We have security outposts in the sky, reachable by aircraft, and a handful of underwater stations that have never been used. They were mainly built for protection, in case life above water is ever threatened.

My home is my soul: Cancer is my Center.

I turn back to the star map, and I gaze into the blue orb as though I could see every detail, down to the tiny whirlpools of color that fleetingly form on the sea's surface. The longer I stare, the deeper and wider the map seems to grow, until I'm Space-diving through the stars.

All around me, millions of celestial bodies ascend and decline, and as their paths shift in response to distant events like gamma bursts and supernovas, they leave faint arcs in the sky. They almost look like musical notes.

Music of the night, Mom said the ancients called it.

I look to the side of Cancer. Thebe is gone. Then I survey the moons we have left—and all three begin to flicker.

Like any one of them could be next.

Pulse pumping, I pan away from our House and search beyond the twelfth constellation, where the omen appears. It's not there.

Has it finally disappeared? Or has it moved closer?

I scan the whole solar system, desperately searching for a hint of the writhing blackness, a sign of the opposition in our stars.

Nishiko glides over to me. "You see something. What is it?"

"I . . . don't see the omen anymore. . . ."

As soon as I leave my Center, the map shrinks back down to the size of a puffer fish—the way it's appeared to the others this whole time.

"*But?*" she asks. "Why do you sound bothered by its absence?"

"Because I still felt the sense of danger, only I couldn't see the source. And there's . . . something else." I dread speaking the words, but I have to. Maybe if I'd spoken up earlier, we would have had warning. If I'd just told Instructor Tidus—

"What else? Rho, tell us!" Nishi squeezes my shoulder urgently.

"Sorry—I didn't mean to keep you in suspense, I'm just—okay, listen. Earlier today, at my retest, I saw . . . I saw Thebe's light flickering, and then it vanished. Like, disappeared from the map."

My three friends exchange awed looks. Deke is the first to turn away. "Rho, this isn't time for one of your tales."

"Deke, you're my best friend. Would I really be messing with you after what's happened?"

He glares at me but doesn't say anything. He knows I'm right.

"And what'd you see now?" whispers Nishi.

"Thebe is gone . . . and our other moons have started to flicker."

None of us speaks. My friends are still caught in the gravity of my revelation, but I'm thinking of Instructor Tidus. She was the first grown-up since Mom who saw any potential in me.

Please let her have survived the blast.

Kai floats away from us, to a corner of the bunkroom. "I hope you're wrong," says Deke, following Kai and offering words of comfort.

"Maybe you're not wrong," whispers Nishi. "The omen and the

flickering of the moons could be connected. Did you see anything else?"

"Nish, I don't know anything," I whisper back, growing unexpectedly angry. "None of what I saw was real. The Astralator *proved* I was wrong. I have no clue what you expect me to do."

Deke frowns at us from across the room. "What are you gossiping about now, Nish?"

"I'm being serious," she says. "I don't care how, but Rho saw a threat, and we can't ignore that."

"It wasn't in the stars, it was in my head," I say, my words fueled by more hope than certainty.

"What about all the tragedies in the news?" she asks. The last couple of years, there have been a slew of natural disasters in the Zodiac. Mudslides in House Taurus. Dust storms and drought in the Piscene planetoids. Forest fires raging out of control on a Leonine moon. The past year alone, millions of lives have been lost.

"Maybe it's the Trinary Axis again," whispers Kai, like the thought itself is dangerous.

"Don't even say that," snaps Deke. "Events go in cycles, Kai, that's all. It's nature."

We fall silent, and I wonder if we're all still thinking about the Trinary Axis. A thousand years ago, the axis started a vicious galactic war that raged out of control for a century. When we studied it at school, it seemed unreal—just as unreal as the bodies on Elara.

"Those terrorist attacks in House Aries," I say, "and those suicide bombers on the Geminin space freighter—that's not nature's way."

"Fringe fanatics," says Deke, sounding just like Stanton. "We've always had our share of lunatics."

Nishiko draws me to the far end of the bunkroom, darts a wary glance at Deke and Kai, then whispers in my ear. "What if there is an enemy? Think about the timing of the blast."

"You mean the Lunar Quadract?"

"Almost every Zodai and high-ranking government member in your House was on Elara tonight to hear your Guardian's speech—"

"And our moons were at their closest conjunction," I say, completing her thought. I chew on my lower lip as the full magnitude of her theory sinks in. If someone planned this, they really thought it through. A well-timed blast in exactly the right place, and our moons could crash into each other like marbles.

I feel myself blanch. I don't want to consider this. Cancer has no enemies. Humanity has been at peace for a thousand years. "This was a tragedy . . . no one could have orchestrated it."

Nishi frowns at me. "You've been seeing an omen."

"Yes, and the experts at the Academy who teach classes on this stuff don't find my methods reliable, so neither should you."

Nishi's voice rises higher, and now Deke and Kai are listening again. "Rho, they just don't understand your methods, that's all! I know you've been taught to trust your elders, but on Sagittarius we're raised to question everything—it's the only way to get to the truth of a thing. You and our instructors are being blinded by prejudice right now. You're so distracted by *how* you got the right answer that you're missing the point that you are *right*—"

An alarm blares across the room, and an automated voice echoes through the ship: "Debris field ahead. Brace yourselves."

A heavy object jolts against our hull, and Nishi and I grasp hands just as the retro engines fire, flinging all of us to the ceiling. We must be flying through Thebe's rubble. "Grab something and hang on!" I shout, wrapping my fingers around a handrail.

The engines thunder so loud, my teeth vibrate. We hear the thuds of more space rocks striking our hull, and we cling to our handrails while the ship veers in every direction, blowing our bodies around like seaweed in a riptide.

Kai looks green, so I pull myself over to him and tug on his elbow. "Come on!" I call over the thunderous rumbling. "We have to belt in."

As the ship rolls and swerves, I help him into the nearest hammock and squeeze in beside him, hooking the belt tight across our ribs. An especially large chunk of debris slams our hull, and Kai clutches my hand so hard, I wince.

The ship keeps lurching unpredictably, the wreckage so extensive it feels like we've been bumping through it for hours. After a while, Kai starts singing an old Cancrian seafaring song:

"The wind she blows from north to east.
Our schooner flies ten knots at least.
So ever forward we shall roam,
Until the sea shall bring us home. . . ."

I join in, flat and off-key. When Deke's voice seeps in, he meets my gaze for the first time. His eyes look like dying stars, nebulas of turquoise whose lights are fading.

Now I'm the one crushing Kai's hand.

We sing the song so many times that Nishi memorizes the words. After so much crying and shouting, her voice is nothing more than a soft purr, but it's still beautiful. Gradually, the rest of us drop out so we can listen to her mournful tune.

The ship's trajectory starts to smooth out. When the engines cut off, Nishi's voice fades away, and we wait in tense silence.

"All clear," the automated voice announces.

I take a deep breath, free my fingers from Kai's grip, and undo my belt. When I'm in the air, Nishi's already by my side. "Let's find the Stargazer and tell him what you saw." *Stargazer* is the Sagittarian word for Zodai.

"He told us to stay here," interrupts Deke.

"Nishi's right," I say, taking her hand and digging into my pocket for my Wave. "Besides, I want to know what's happening."

Nishi and I zip up to the hatch in time to barge right into Lodestar Mathias Thais. With a frown, he motions us back into the bunkroom. Inside, dim light falls across his face, shadowing his cheekbones. "We're making a course change."

"The other moons?" I ask, my breath catching. "Did something happen to them?"

He stares at me, and I get the sense he's observing me for the first time. He looks for so long, I begin to feel uncomfortable, but I don't turn away. The same instinct that helps me read the stars seems to be whispering to me now. If I want him to treat me like an equal, I need to act like one.

He swipes the Wave from my hands and opens it. I don't protest. He scans the holograms surrounding him and pulls up the

Ephemeris. When the spectral Space map blossoms out, he asks, "You can read the stars with this?"

He sounds so doubtful that I blush. "Not very well. It's just a tutorial version."

He tips his head to one side, searching my face, continuing to float in the same steady position. "Your reading's correct," he says, his voice stony. "Our four moons have collided, and the rubble is streaking through our atmosphere. In the next few hours, it will strike our ocean and cause planet-wide tsunami waves. We can't land on Cancer."

The edges of my vision darken. I feel like he's sucked the light from my world with his words.

Everything that happened tonight was almost endurable at the thought of setting foot in the Cancer Sea, of sleeping in my old room, of hugging Dad and saying all the things I never said. I take a ragged breath, and Nishi steadies me with her arm. Dad—Stanton—the Academy—*home*—everything I know is sinking away.

I'm Centerless.

Mathias clears his throat, and I realize he isn't finished. Lowering his eyes, he whispers, "Our Guardian Origene is dead."

5

THE SHOCK ROBS ME OF speech and thought, almost of breath itself.

My mind is blank.

My classmates and teachers, maybe my brother and Dad, now Guardian Origene—so many of our people lost in one night. I feel as if their screams are still echoing through the universe, filling my head with their voices.

Nishiko and Deke are as frozen as I am, and the three of us listen to Kai's quiet sobbing like it's an alien language we've only just begun to learn.

Mathias continues in a low baritone. "We'll dock at a satellite called Oceon 6. Admiral Crius is there, organizing our House's disaster response. He's Guardian Origene's Military Advisor, and he's ordered all surviving Cancrian Zodai to report, and that includes you Acolytes."

"Who'll be our Guardian now?" asks Kai.

"We'll find a new one. It's our first priority." Mathias turns to Nishi. "You're Sagittarian?" She nods. "See me after we dock. We'll try to arrange your transport home."

He gives the rest of us another steady inspection, and I guess we must look like lost souls, because his eyes soften. "Wherever we are, whatever happens, Cancer sustains us. She is our Center. Find her now in your hearts."

"What about the people living on Cancer?" I ask, my voice cracking.

When he answers, I get the sense Mathias is trying not to panic us. "The Lodestars foresaw the tsunamis, and the evacuation has already begun. Even now, dive-ships are transporting islanders down to our underwater stations, which are deep enough to remain stable."

His dark indigo eyes swirl like whirlpools of the Cancer Sea. "Of our House's three thousand Zodai, fewer than four hundred have survived. Everyone who's left is on their way to Oceon 6, same as us."

Kai sniffles, and Deke looks ill. "How do you know all this?" asks Nishi. "We couldn't connect to anyone on my Tracker or their Waves."

The Sagittarian version of a Wave is a Tracker. Since they're such nomadic souls, the Tracker is a wristband that projects holographic data and also functions as a locator. It's so Sagittarian families can track their loved ones across the Zodiac.

Mathias speaks softly. "I don't use a Wave. I have my own communication system."

"The Ring?" asks Nishi, her innate curiosity irrepressible. We've all seen the Lodestars on campus whispering into invisible microphones, but none of us know how it works. It's technology that's exclusive to the Zodai.

"Since we have so few Zodai left, and as you are what remains of the pool of candidates, you might as well learn as much as you can, as fast as you can." He spreads his right hand and shows us his Ring. It's just a plain steel band—or so it seems. On closer inspection, there's a faint flickering glow around it.

"It looks like steel, but it's metallic silicon. Like an Ephemeris, the Ring acts as an extrasensory antenna for picking up Psynergy. Only instead of using it to read the stars, the Ring uses Psynergy to link my conscious to every Zodai in the galaxy—what's called the Psy Network."

"I read that a person's Psynergy signature becomes visible in the Psy Network," says Nishiko. "What's it look like?" Just like in class, while the rest of us are trying to process the current lesson, her questioning nature is already pushing us toward the next one.

"It's different for each of us. As you know from your studies, Psynergy is a combination of your psychic energy—which determines your ability to do things like read the stars and access the Collective Consciousness—and your astrological fingerprint. Your fingerprint is on your birth certificate, and it's a snapshot of Space at your moment of birth: the location of the stars, the rotation of the planet, the pull of the moons, an infinite number of factors. Since there can never be two of the same fingerprint, every Psynergy signature is unique—but it can still be veiled or altered in the Psy."

"Why does that matter?" asks Nishi.

By now, Deke would be groaning audibly and begging our teacher to ban Nishiko from speaking for the rest of the lesson—but he doesn't seem to be taking any of this in. He looks how being Centerless feels.

"It matters for the same reason falsified holograms matter: You can't be sure who you're talking to. The better you are at Centering, the easier it will be for you to distinguish people's signatures so you can be certain of who's listening. We Zodai are only human, so the Collective Conscious can't help but reflect our flaws." Mathias is showing remarkable patience, especially under the circumstances.

"If it's like reading the Ephemeris, how in the world will we see a signature?" asks Kai. "It's hard enough just seeing the stars move."

I'm surprised to hear the interest in Kai's tone, since he looks as defeated as Deke. Then again, I probably do, too. Maybe we all look exactly the same—like corpses who are inexplicably still breathing.

"Even stars leave faint impressions of their trajectories in the Psy," says Mathias. "Those small, fading lines are enough for an Astralator to measure a movement's unique astrological footprint. Similarly, a person's consciousness also leaves its mark. Have you taken Abyssthe in your classes yet?"

The word is a dagger. It stabs us all in the gut, so that not even Nishi can answer. We just nod.

"Abyssthe uses your mind as the receiver of Psynergy, same as the Ring. Both work by activating parts of your brain normally dormant, and they can help you stay Centered."

A memory escapes the wall that blocks out my early years. Beyond Centering, Mom's training also involved memorizing everything there is to know about each House of the Zodiac— traits, constellations, histories. But she only brought up Psynergy once.

She told me Psynergy is the magic that makes star reading possible. She said the brain is most susceptible to Psynergy in children, while it's still forming, and that's why she had to make me work as hard as she did.

Mom was certain if I practiced every day, I would one day be able to assert myself fully in the astral plane and see more than any other Zodai. By the time I was five, our lessons were lasting up to ten hours a day.

Two years later, she disappeared. For a while, I kept practicing, even harder than when she was around. I thought if I impressed her enough, she would give us another chance. I thought I could locate her on the star map and convince her to come home.

I bite down on the inside of my lip, shoving the memory deep into my subconscious, somewhere it can't touch me again.

Mathias turns to go. "There's an observation turret two decks up, and the captain has given permission for you to visit if you'd like."

A little later, Deke and I press our faces against the thick, scarred glass of the turret, looking out at Cancer. We've already passed the moon rubble, but every now and then we catch chunks of rock flaming through Cancer's atmosphere and crashing into the ocean. From this distance, it's hard to make out the tsunamis that must be wracking life on our pods and islands. Cancer appears the same as ever, eternally blue and changeless.

"That moon rubble will form a ring," says Deke. "We'll be a ringed planet."

"So now you're reading omens?"

"Not omens. Physics." His turquoise eyes droop at the corners, and he has a puffy, rumpled look. "Our tides will change."

Our tides nourish the shores around our islands, and every sea farmer knows three-quarters of our planet's creatures live near shorelines. If our tides shift, what will happen to the plants and fish that feed the rest of the ecosystem? How will Dad's nar-clams survive?

"Nishiko says people become gods after they die," I whisper. "That's what Sagittarians believe. They celebrate death, like it's a happy event."

"Ask her how she feels about it when her own turn comes."

He sounds so cold, but I have to remind myself it's actually pain. He's hurting as much as the rest of us.

We Cancrians believe those who pass on with settled souls move into Empyrean, a paradise of blissful tranquility reached through a portal in Helios. Some Houses don't believe in Empyrean at all, and others think it's a canal from one life to the next, a kind of rebirth. Nishi's people believe Empyrean is a real planet full of mansions and banquets and dancing in the streets.

Even though it feels like a betrayal to my people, the truth is, I don't know what I believe.

"There. That's Oceon 6." Deke points toward a wheel-shaped satellite floating above our northern pole. It looks like a pinprick of light in an Ephemeris, but it's growing larger. "The Lodestar said the wheel's constant spinning creates centrifugal force in its outer rim to simulate gravity. They were on the far side of Cancer when the moons collided, so they didn't feel the effects."

I don't know what to say to all that, so I don't say anything at all. After a while, he whispers, "When we get there, they'll have survivor lists."

I hook an arm around his elbow. "Where were your sisters when it hit?"

"At the factory, probably." Deke's family produces a line of pearlescent paint from fish scales that's very popular, especially among artist circles on House Gemini, where imagination is prized above all.

"Your island's got hills," I remind him. "I'm sure they made it to your parents' house on higher ground." His parents recently retired and gave the company to their children. Deke lets his twin sisters run it however they want. He looks up to them the way I look up to Stanton.

"They won't find another Guardian," he says, changing the subject. His crabby mood is growing contagious. "We have too few Zodai, and qualifying is too tough. And then what?"

"Then the most senior Zodai in Mother Origene's Council of Advisors will step in until they find one," I say, pulling the fact from my sea of repressed memories.

Guardians are the spiritual leaders of the Zodiac, and the position is always a lifetime appointment. On some Houses, like Virgo, the Guardian is also the government—Empress Moira rules her whole constellation—but Cancer is run by consensus. Our Holy

Mother acts as an arbiter and advisor to our governing body, and she has an equal vote with the rest of our House's representatives.

"They say a Guardian has to embody the noblest traits of our House," says Deke. "Compassion, loyalty, selflessness . . ."

"Brooding, clinging, self-absorption," I add, trying to lighten the mood.

"The Guardian also needs to be a natural at reading the stars. To protect us. You know how rare that is?"

I close my eyes. "Come on, Deke. They'll find somebody."

The automated voice speaks through the ship's intercom: "All passengers, return to crew quarters and prepare for landing."

My elbow still linked with Deke's, I pull him away from the view.

Back in the smelly bunkroom, Kai has stopped crying, though he's still gloomy. Nishiko has cleaned her face and braided her dark hair. I haven't even thought of my hair.

Growing up, I was always jealous of Stanton, who kept his blond curls close-cropped. So when I got to the Academy, I chopped mine off at the chin. My curls have been growing back ever since, and now they fall to my breasts. I usually keep them pulled back in a bushy ponytail or tucked beneath the gray hood of Stanton's jacket . . . the one I took with me when I moved to Elara.

Back then, it fell to my knees. Now it's just the right size—and gone forever.

I strap into the same seat as the start of the trip, barely recognizing the girl I was ten hours ago. The world was a mess of horror and confusion, but even in the face of what we were escaping, at least we were moving toward light and not darkness. The light of Cancer.

Home is on Kalymnos, a small coral atoll in the Northern Hemisphere. Our airy bungalow faces the inner lagoon where we keep our nar-clam beds. At night, bioluminescent microbes glow pale green in the water, creating constellations to rival the night sky. I grew up tending the beds alongside Stanton. We took turns driving off the hungry hookcrabs, but it was Dad alone who beaded the young nar-clams and harvested the pearls by hand.

I never wanted to leave. Becoming an Acolyte was the hardest decision I've ever made. Dad and Stanton didn't understand—they knew how much I loved the fresh air and the Cancer Sea. But it wasn't for my sake I left. . . . I did it for Dad.

He's always been quiet, but after Mom took off, he barely spoke. Stanton could always find a subject to engage him with, but Dad's shyer around me. It wasn't until I was eleven and found an old picture of Mom that I understood why.

I looked just like her.

So I applied to the Academy. If I couldn't bring her back, I could at least free Dad of her memory.

The ship gives a sharp lurch on touchdown, and something jabs into my hip. I peel open my compression suit and dig into an inner pocket. *Mathias's Astralator.*

"All clear," says the automated voice. We unbuckle and float out of our hammocks, still weightless. Since we've docked at the hub, we won't experience the wheel's fake gravity until we reach the rim.

In the hub, we meet a row of officers in the same dark blue uniforms of the Cancrian Royal Guard. They're floating at attention in zero gravity, and I wonder how they keep so straight and still when they exchange the fist touch with Mathias.

One of them says to him, "Admiral Crius wants to see you and your party at once."

"Very well." Mathias grabs onto a stationary rope hanging from a steel bar that wraps along the ceiling. The moment he grips it, the rope heaves forward at a brisk pace, pulling him forward through the air. He turns and waves for us to join him, and we each take a different rope. The Zodai follow along behind us.

Since we're lined up in a row, my friends and I can't compare theories on what this meeting could be about. The station smells of ammonia, and the low-wattage lighting makes everything look beige. When the steel bar dead-ends, we let go of the rope and load into a monorail car. Soon there's a rush of speed. This must be the express train to the rim.

The farther out we go, the more centrifugal force I feel, and it's nothing like gravity. It's more like a carnival ride that's slinging us against the right-hand side of the train. When we reach our destination and I try standing up, I feel like I'm slanting into a strong wind.

Mathias catches my elbow when I almost slip. "You'll get used to it," he breathes in his low baritone.

I've never been so close to his face before. I trace the smooth lines of his jaw and cheekbones with my eyes before catching myself and looking away.

He guides each of us out of the vehicle, and when we resume our procession, our feet clomp along the carpeted deck with something like real weight. It's the first time since the crystal dome's imitation gravity that I feel the full force of my body, and its presence seems foreign to me.

Admiral Crius is waiting for us in what looks like a lecture hall that's been converted into a disaster-response room. A dozen blue-uniformed Zodai are working on slick screens, and an enormous holographic map of Cancer rotates in the air overhead, blinking with red warning lights. Crius gets up from his desk and gives Mathias a fist bump, then frowns at the rest of us. He's a broad-chested man somewhere in his mid-forties, with pepper-colored curls and crinkles around his mouth and eyes. His expression, like everyone else's, is grim.

"You must be Acolyte Rhoma Grace," he says to me.

I stiffen. Deke and Nishiko turn and stare at me, and I try to remember which of the many rules I've broken. "Yes." In a fuller voice, I say, "My name is Rho Grace."

"Come with me, Acolyte. You as well, Lodestar Thais. As for the rest of you, these officers will see to your needs."

The Admiral turns on his heel and strides away, and Mathias nods that I should follow. I give Nishi a questioning look, but she seems as confused as I am.

This can't be about the Academy's test again. This is about Stanton.

Or Dad.

The weight of my bones is too much for me to carry, and my

throat fills with what tastes like acid. I've already lost the only two homes I've ever known—I can't lose what's left of my family.

I peel off my black gloves and stuff them—and my Wave—into a pocket of my compression suit. My helmet is already clipped to my belt.

Fortunately, we don't have to travel far. The Admiral leads us into a space no larger than Instructor Tidus's classroom, where two other people are present.

The elderly white-haired lady's expression is both warm and sad, but there's a sinister snarl on the stout bald man's face. Mathias closes the door and stands in front of it, ramrod straight, hands at his sides, eyes forward. I can't read his expression.

Admiral Crius examines me head to toe. "Acolyte Rhoma Grace. You have been brought before what is left of Holy Mother Origene's Council of Advisors to face judgment. Tonight, your mother, Kassandra Grace, has confessed to treason."

6

TREASON.

The word sounds strange, unfamiliar, unconnected to my life. "I don't believe you." It's almost a snarl. "Betrayal is not in our Cancrian nature."

The stout man's scowl deepens, but it's Crius who says, in his clipped military tone, "Neither is abandoning our loved ones, yet she left you."

After everything I've experienced tonight, I didn't think I had anything left to lose.

I was wrong.

I've not thought about Mom for so long, I never considered what I'd do if I learned she was alive. Despair swims through my veins, and I swivel around and lock eyes with Mathias. The indigo blue of his gaze never looked so explosive, not even when we were escaping Elara. But does he care what happens to me, or is he revolted he showed me pity in the first place?

The desperation makes me feel like I'm falling further and further away from myself, from this moment, from memories of my life. It's like I'm being sucked into a black hole, removed from the reality I thought I knew, only as slowly and painfully as possible.

"Kassandra Grace has been sentenced to summary execution," continues Crius in his wintry way, every word pulling me deeper into the abyss. "If you stay, her name will stain yours. You will be shunned by your House, separated from your friends, and you can never be a Zodai."

I'm so far gone that I barely hear him when he says, "We are here to offer you a choice."

Hope flickers like a small flame, burning bright against so much darkness. "A choice?"

He gives a curt nod. "Denounce her. We'll transfer you to work for us on House Aries, at the Planetary Plenum. You can start a new life for yourself."

The admiral lays his Wave on the table in front of me and says, "Press your thumbprint at the bottom, and you'll be transferred without delay."

I stare at the clam-shaped device, the small sensor in its mouth shining like a pearl.

Shock is like lightning—it only lasts an instant—but its replacement is hot, prickly shame. I would have preferred death on Elara to this *choice*. Whatever my mother did, I know my answer. There is no choice—not for me.

"I belong on Cancer, with my family." My voice is strong, and it makes me stronger. "Thank you for your offer, but I decline."

The admiral's brow dips so low, it forms a wall between his eyes. "You understand you'll be forced to live isolated from Cancrian society, forbidden to return to anything or anyone you know?"

"I understand," I say, opening my mind to memories I've been blocking out for a decade. They're surprisingly well preserved and untarnished. I can't believe I've found Mom again.

"Will you please let me see her? Under our laws, she's allowed a final visit with family."

He shakes his head. "That will not be necessary. We have never met your mother, nor do we know where she is. This was a test, which you have passed."

Confusion flits through my features quickly, followed by relief: *Mom's not a traitor, I can have my life again.*

And then anger.

Another test.

The white-haired lady takes a rickety step, leaning heavily on a cane. "I'm Agatha Cleiss, and this is my colleague, Dr. Emory Eusta." She offers her hand, but I don't exchange the traditional touch.

Her lips stretch into a sad smile. "My dear, forgive us. We've tricked you in a most barbaric way. This terrible tragedy has forced us to act in a cruel manner, and this lie was the quickest route to the answers we sought. If you'll take a seat, we will explain."

I bite hard on the inside of my lip, now angrier about the apology—it'd be easier to storm out of here if she didn't seem so genuinely sorry.

The bald man beside her looks so real that only when I see his arm pass through the corner of a shelf do I realize he's a hologram. Since Dr. Eusta shows no sign of a time delay, he must be transmitting from nearby.

I sit down on one of four cushioned chairs surrounding a square table, where a tray of water and sandwiches has been laid out. The sight of food makes my stomach rumble.

Crius sits across from me. His sallow skin has a fatigued grayish cast, and his mouth twists in a skeptical frown. "Have some refreshment."

"No, thank you," I say, over my stomach's renewed protests.

Agatha lowers her gnarled body into the chair next to mine. "Why do you think you were tested twice at the Academy?"

"Because I failed the first time."

She smiles sadly again, and her misty green-gray eyes grow distant. Across from me, Admiral Crius takes a dark stone from his pocket and lays it on the table. It's smooth and oblong, and though it appears dull black at first, the longer I gaze at it, the more brilliant colors I see within its depths. Viridian blue-green, aqua, indigo, amethyst, even a scattering of crimson. And it's not dull at all. It's glossy slick.

"Black opal," says Dr. Eusta. "It holds Guardian Origene's Ephemeris."

"As far as we can tell," adds Agatha, "it's in perfect working order. We don't know why it failed to show the approach of this catastrophe."

In this room at least, my theory about Astralators being insufficient is irrelevant. The Guardian and her Council are so good at foreseeing the future, they can interpret what's coming from simply observing the stars' movements. They don't need an Astralator to tell apart what's real from what's imagined. That kind of natural Sight takes decades to develop.

Crius gives a voice command to switch off the lights, and we're enveloped in cottony blackness. Now I'm thoroughly confused.

"Touch the stone," says Agatha.

It's a strange request, but I do it. From the moment they brought out the opal, I've wanted to hold it.

When I lift it in my hand, the stone feels warm. I roll it around my fingers, sensing tiny clefts in its smooth surface. The imperfections are so slight, they're barely perceptible; but the moment I discover them, a shadowy mass begins to form in my mind, like I'm unscrambling a code.

The longer I brush my fingertip along the ridges, the more defined the shadow grows, until I recognize the configuration of bumps as part of a constellation.

Cancer.

As soon as I identify the image, a light fountains upward from the stone, and I shriek as it scatters through the air, filling the room with stars. The others stand in shocked silence, but it's not the stone's power that's stumped them—it's mine.

The opal is projecting a hologram of the universe. A large hologram, ovoid in shape, it's the finest and most detailed Ephemeris I've ever seen. I stand inside its nimbus of light and spread my fingers, letting stars sparkle over my skin.

"You've discovered its key," says Agatha, the amazement in her tone less than encouraging. "The ridges on the stone shift their shape every time the Ephemeris shuts off, so the lock changes. The key is always an incomplete map, so only those most familiar with our solar system could even hope to fill in the blanks and open it."

"You mean that was another test?" I ask flatly.

Dr. Eusta's hologram moves through the Ephemeris like a pixilating shade. "Yes. And so is this."

Agatha rests her hands on the head of her cane and locks eyes with me. "Holy Mother used to say the future is a house of a million windows. Every Zodai sees a different view of the stars, so everyone's reading is different. Some readings conflict. Some are wholly wrong. And some . . . may be deliberately misleading."

"We want to hear your reading of what happened to our moons," says the blinking hologram of Dr. Eusta.

"You want me to read Holy Mother's Ephemeris?" I ask. The amazement in Agatha's tone was nothing compared to mine.

I can't believe they're asking for *my* interpretation. "I'm not well trained—I don't use an Astralator. I was the only one in our year who failed the Academy's test—"

"Take all the time you need," says Agatha, like she hasn't heard a word of my protest. She and Admiral Crius sit back and wait, while the holographic Dr. Eusta floats around, like another celestial body on the spectral map.

I blow out a hard breath and look around. I've never seen the Zodiac in such detail before. The soft glimmering lights rotate through the air with much higher resolution than even our planetarium's Ephemeris at the Academy. Black holes, white dwarfs, red giants, and more, all shining in brilliant definition.

It's only now, inside this luminous representation of our world, that I realize I never lost my Center. Like Mathias said—*Cancer sustains us.*

Home is within me, no matter where I go, no matter what happens to our planet or our people. As long as my heart is beating, it's playing a Cancrian tune.

Always.

The thought fills me with such a strong sense of self that I feel large and invincible. In spite of everything the universe strips from me, it can't take what's inside my head and in my heart. Those things are mine forever.

The room grows so quiet, I can hear my exhalations. I stare at the blue orb of Cancer, its surface bluer than in any Ephemeris I've looked through before, and I keep staring until I feel my soul drifting skyward. In the astral plane, I see the rubble field where our moons once orbited. And as I'm watching, the debris begins to flicker.

My pulse picks up as I move closer. This map is so large that it's the first time I can see what's really happening when a moon flickers. It's not fluctuations in the Psy Network, like I'd secretly hoped.

In fact, the moons aren't even flickering. I wasn't seeing them vanish—I was seeing them get swallowed by something black and writhing, something thicker than Space. The tarlike substance is still there, guiding the rubble's movement, like a puppeteer pulling invisible strings.

It's Dark Matter.

"No meteoroid did this," I whisper.

"Of course not. That was only a rumor," mutters Dr. Eusta. "Our astronomers have already confirmed no foreign body struck our moons. No telescope or satellite registered any object. We can't find any data because as soon as the explosion happened, every device in Thebe's vicinity stopped working . . . which you know, since the power outage even reached Elara."

The pink space suit burns in my mind. Like it's been branded there.

I let the pain scorch my brain, welcoming it. I never want to forget the people we lost tonight. They are why I need to help, if I can. I take a few steps back, looking at the Zodiac as a whole instead of focusing on one constellation at a time.

The first thing I notice is a flickering in House Leo. Then I notice another flickering in Taurus. These flickers are feeble, though. They don't seem like threats—they're more like ghosts of flickers past. The Psy Network is showing me that Dark Matter touched those Houses, too.

"It's a pattern," I say, piecing it together out loud as I go. "The Leonine fires, the mudslides in House Taurus—these tragedies . . . they're all connected."

At these words, my interrogators lower their eyes, and I get the sense they're communicating with each other silently. They're going to dismiss my readings as nonsense, just as the dean did. Only I won't let them. Nishi was right: I can't ignore my visions if there's a chance they can help.

"We are not asking about the past," says Admiral Crius, once they've finished conferring in the Psy. "Now answer our question: What caused our moons to collide?"

I force myself not to flinch at the violence in his voice. Then I say, "Dark Matter."

They don't bother with the niceties of hiding their disbelief—this time, they say what they're thinking out loud, to my face.

"*Dark Matter!*" Dr. Eusta sounds halfway hysterical. "Are we done here now?" he asks the other two. "She's wasted enough of our time, don't you think?" Admiral Crius seems inclined to agree.

"Where do you perceive Dark Matter?" asks Agatha, staring at the rubble. I point to where I see it, but she only sees black Space.

She closes her eyes and touches her Ring. When she opens them again, she turns to the men. "Dark Matter is the only substance strong enough to suck the life force from a planet . . . and knock out our energy systems. If it's now starting to appear in the Ephemeris . . ."

Admiral Crius shakes his head. "It can't be."

"But if it *is*," insists Agatha, "that means it's being manipulated using Psynergy. Only a powerful Zodai could wield Psynergy that way."

Crius suddenly leans forward, grips my wrist, and glares into my eyes. My whole arm throbs in agony from his crushing hold. He's checking me for lies. The violence that's been so close to erupting from him strangles my veins and suffocates my skin, but I refuse to even blink.

"So it's true," whispers Agatha when the admiral pulls away from me in defeat.

"*Lights on,*" he says.

When the room brightens, the Ephemeris still glows, speckling Agatha's wrinkled face with bits of color. Her lips are moving very fast, and I realize she's talking through her Ring. Crius whispers hasty notes into his Wave. They glance at each other mysteriously, and each gives the other a slight nod. Then Agatha draws herself upright and smiles at me. "I think we are ready to proceed."

She takes the opal from my hand and lays it on the table. Instantly, the Ephemeris winks out, and Dr. Eusta's hologram stops pixilating. Holographic screens start to beam out from Crius's Wave and hover in the air above us. Each file bears the photo of a uniformed Zodai, but I'm too jittery to read the words.

"Since the beginning of time, our Lodestars have been predicting the birth of each new Potential," says Agatha, her voice soft and soothing . . . like Mom's when she'd settle in to tell me a story.

"Your astrological fingerprint is on that long list, and so you are one of the many Potentials we have been watching. By the time you arrived at the Academy, you had already studied everything you could about the Houses of the Zodiac, and it was noted by a few of your instructors that you had a keen interest in our world—and a hunger to learn that could rival a Sagittarian's. You carried a tutorial Ephemeris in your Wave to read your friends' futures on your own time, *for fun*. You even knew Yarrot, something only taught to the most advanced Zodai in our House.

"You worked hard in your classes, and your only difficulty was using the Astralator. What you didn't realize was that after putting so much work into your Centering technique and spending so much time reading the Ephemeris, you'd become a natural. Like us, you don't need an Astralator."

Admiral Crius jumps in before Agatha's words can sink in, gesturing at the holographic data crowding the air above us. "These files belong to the candidates we've selected as Advisors. They will be beamed to your Wave, as well as the surviving members of the Royal Guard. You'll see one of your comrades on that list, Lodestar Mathias Thais."

I inhale sharply and turn around, only now remembering that Mathias is here. Even before seeing him, I already feel a rush of relief to have a familiar face nearby.

Except when I look, Mathias isn't looking back. He's staring ahead, eyes forward, like he's determined not to listen to our conversation. His demeanor is completely different from before, when he was drinking in every word, as if the exile in question was his and not mine. I don't understand what's changed.

"Lodestar Thais would make a much better Advisor than me, if that's what you're thinking," I blurt.

"Excuse me?" Admiral Crius leans forward, and his expression makes me tremble. "Are you under the impression we want you to be an Advisor?"

"Oh . . . no. Of course not." Suddenly the thing I want most in the world is to melt into my seat cushion.

Crius stands, and so does Agatha. Dr. Eusta floats over, and all three of them look down at me. "Rhoma Grace," Crius starts, his tone making me wonder if we're back on the subject of exile. "Please forgive our cruel methods."

Then—to my extreme shock—he and the others give me a deep bow.

"The stars revealed a portent that some of us found implausible, but it seems we must accept it. As of today, we honor you as Guardian of the Fourth House, our beloved Cancer."

7

BEFORE I CAN EVEN REACT, the black opal is thrust into my hands, and I'm ushered out of the room and into the arms of two women waiting outside the door.

I'm half led, half carried along the dim passageways, flanked by the group of officers that met us at the hub when we first landed. I notice Mathias doesn't come with me this time.

Oceon 6 is a maze of corridors and sealed doors, and by the time we arrive at our destination, I have no idea how we got here. While the women deposit me in a spacious and cold room, the officers stay outside, probably standing guard.

"I'm Lola, your Lady of Robes," says the taller of the two. She's wearing a Cancrian-style draped dress in periwinkle blue. It reminds me painfully of home, where wardrobes and architecture cascade and have a watery flow. "And this is Leyla . . . m-my little sister."

The humanity in her voice is what makes me look up. Lola seems to be about twenty, with a head of thick red curls hiding her small face. Beside her, Leyla smiles shyly, and with a jolt, I realize she's younger than me. She can't be more than fourteen.

"I was apprenticed to Mother Origene's Lady of Robes," continues Lola, "and I was in the middle of my training when she . . ." Her face pulls together, and she casts her gaze to the floor. When she's calm, she makes a small bow. "We are green, but we will do our hardest to serve you, Holy Mother."

I want to speak, but there's something monstrous in my throat, and I'm afraid of releasing it.

Unlike her older sister, Leyla's red curls are pulled away from her face, exposing a pair of round sapphire eyes. She seems to understand what I need and says, "Lola, let's let Holy Mother rest."

They bow to me, and as their dresses swoosh past, I smell a hint of the Cancer Sea in the folds of their fabric. "Can I see my friends?" I whisper, my voice a hoarse rasp.

Lola's already in the hallway, but Leyla's on the threshold, so she hears me. She turns her sapphire eyes to mine and says, "I'm so sorry, Holy Mother. We are under directions to keep you isolated and protected until the threat is identified."

She's just confirming what I already know.

I'm alone.

When the door shuts, I look around the room. I must be in the sleeping quarters of the top-ranking Lodestar posted on Oceon 6. There's a bed in one corner, a private bathroom, and a desk that's been converted into a makeshift vanity for me. I should use this time to shower, find clean clothes. I should be trying to unlock the stars' secrets in the black opal, to figure out how to keep our people safe.

But this room is too empty.

It doesn't have my toothbrush or my drumsticks or the exotic seashells Dad used to bring me back from his dives to the seafloor.

I'm empty.

I'm being asked to give everything, when I have nothing left.

I curl into a ball on the bed. Then I bury my face in a pillow, and I let the monster out.

✦ ✦ ✦

By the time I'm done crying, my eyes are mere slits. I'm still in my compression suit because it's so tight-fitting that I couldn't squeeze a shirt and shorts underneath.

I undo my messy ponytail and pull my hair up into a large puff that sits on my head, like a rat's nest. I don't care how I look. I don't care if I'm proving I'm not Guardian material. I didn't ask for any of this.

There's a knock on my door. "Come in!" I call eagerly, shooting up from bed. If anyone can work her way around rules, it's Nishi.

I'm so thrilled to see her, I throw my arms around her neck the moment she comes through the door. "Nish, I knew you'd—oh!" I pull away quick, like I've touched something scalding.

In fact, what I touched was Lodestar Mathias Thais.

"I'm so sorry," I say, every part of me burning with Helios's heat. "I just—I mean, excuse me." I spin around and press my hands to my cheeks, trying to cool down and hide my mortification. It's not helping that my mind keeps replaying the moment on a loop. Or that my skin still tingles from our close contact.

"Don't apologize," he says softly. When I turn back around, his face is as scarlet as mine.

"I've been sent to deliver a message. Admiral Crius has transmitted the candidates for your Council of Advisors to your Wave."

My *Wave*.

I frantically dig my fingers into the pocket of my suit and pull out my gloves, my Wave, and—"Your Astralator!"

I give the mother-of-pearl device to Mathias, who cups it in his hands like it's a small bird. "Thank you."

I open my Wave and try hailing Dad and Stanton. There's still no connection. I try Nishi's Tracker next, but the signal seems to be scrambled so that it's impossible to communicate with anyone. I have a feeling Crius is behind this—and I'm betting his justification is my protection.

"Once you've selected your twelve Advisors," says Mathias, as though there'd been no interruption, "you must designate one as your—"

"*Guide*, I know," I say, shutting off my Wave. Mom's lessons were thorough, at least. "When a Guardian younger than twenty-two is selected, she must have a Guide who can train her in the ways of the Zodai."

He falls silent.

Then I say, "I want you."

His face flushes all over again, and—realizing how that sounded—I quickly add, "*To be my Guide!*"

I've never seen a face go from red to white so fast. Something flares in Mathias's eyes, like shock—or worse, *refusal*. He looks straight ahead, not meeting my gaze, and says, "One of the more experienced Advisors would be a better choice. I'm new to the Royal Guard, unqualified to teach you."

"Then we'll make a perfect pair, since I'm unqualified to lead."

"I still have a lot to learn about being an Advisor. It would be best if we each found our own mentors."

"Mathias." At the sound of his name, his eyes travel down to mine. For a moment I can almost kid myself that we're bickering about an afterschool group and not the leadership of our House.

I take an uncertain step toward him. "We're running out of familiar faces. I'm only asking for your help. And . . . if you can spare it, your friendship."

He bows. "As you wish, Holy M—"

"What I wish," I say loudly, before he can finish, "is that you use my name. Rho." If Mathias ever calls me *Mother*, I will die.

"*Rho?*" he repeats, like it's a dirty word.

"I'm sorry you don't like it," I say, crossing my arms. "But I called you Mathias and not Lodestar when you asked me to."

Another stare-off.

Then, "As you wish."

"Thank you."

"In one week," he says, picking up the old thread again, "there will be a ceremony and dinner in your honor, where you will be sworn in as our House's new Guardian . . . *Rho*. It's important you select the rest of your Advisors before then. During this week, I will also be training you."

"What about my friends?"

"They have been given lodging on the base. They will be trained as Zodai, along with every surviving Acolyte."

The word *surviving* is a punch to my gut. "I want to see them," I say, my breathing shallow.

"I will try to arrange it." He looks at me like he might say more, but instead he bows abruptly and strides to the door.

"Mathias?"

He stops and turns. "Yes?"

"I can't do this."

Speaking the words out loud, something hard and heavy shifts in my chest, allowing more air to reach my lungs. Like I've just removed an obstacle clogging my airways. I'm still as inadequate as I was seconds ago, but admitting it makes me feel like less of a fraud.

"The stars don't lie," he says, his soft baritone lacking its gentleness. "You've been chosen for a reason. Search your heart, and you'll find it."

His words of encouragement are as Cancrian as it gets, but they only make me feel worse.

I heard it in his tone, saw it in his eyes, sensed it in his demeanor. Mathias doesn't trust in me either.

✦ ✦ ✦

The next day, I return to the room where I was made Guardian, and I sit with Crius, Agatha, Dr. Eusta, and Mathias, while they introduce me to eight people—the rest of my Advisors. They fill me in on procedure, traditions, expectations. . . . Thanks to Mom, I already have a basic understanding, but it's still a lot to process.

In the afternoon, I join Mathias for our first Zodai lesson. We meet in a room filled with plushy mats, towels, and refreshments. Lola found me stretchy pants and an oversized shirt to wear for my training sessions.

Mathias is lying on his back on one of the mats, a strip of abs visible below the hemline of his shirt. Lola walks me to the threshold, and I catch her gaze straying to his bare skin before she leaves.

"First we'll focus on refining your Centering technique," says Mathias, once we're alone. He sits upright. "I think the best way will be using Yarrot."

I swallow, hard. "Yarrot doesn't work for me." He freezes, and we do that thing where we shut up and stare. After watching for so many years, we're each still a complete mystery to the other—but we don't ask those questions yet.

Looking into his eyes, I wonder what he sees. Sometimes the blue grows so soft when he's watching me that I think he might care. Other times, like now, the indigo darkens, and I feel like all he sees is a little girl in grown-up shoes.

He rises to his feet. "I used to practice every day on Elara."

"I remember."

This time the stare is more familiar. As if beyond being Guardian and Guide, we could also be those two people who watched each other grow from afar—only now brought together, forced to grow up even faster.

"Maybe we could try one or two poses," I cede, shrugging as if each movement won't be a knife slicing my chest. Then I sit on the other mat and slip off my shoes.

I don't get back to my room until late, every muscle in my body sore and aching. At first I could barely pull off the easiest positions and kept losing my balance, but by the end it was as though I'd never stopped practicing. Every arc, stretch, and sweep of movement was etched inside my mind, like the dancing of my drumsticks, or the swirling of Cancer in the Ephemeris—everything felt connected, like it's all part of a grand choreography designed by our stars.

We cycled through all twelve poses until I could hold each one for fifteen minutes without breaking a sweat.

When I get to my room, I'm supposed to open the black opal and Center myself, to see what effect the Yarrot has—but I collapse in bed, exhausted, and I don't wake up until morning.

✦ ✦ ✦

Three days have passed, and it's nighttime, I think. Oceon 6 has no windows, and its alternating periods of artificial light confuse my sense of chronology.

Everything's confused. I'm still in shock.

Yesterday, I awoke in a frenzy, thinking I was late for class. Then I remembered. The Academy is gone. So are my instructors and friends. Maybe even my family. My old life is a sand castle that's been washed away in the Cancer Sea's new tide.

This other life feels surreal. I'm beginning to think the Advisors only chose me as Guardian because I'm young and easy to control, since they spend our morning meetings debating strategy among themselves and ignoring my suggestions. The way Mathias eyes me only strengthens my doubts. He keeps saying it's my duty to play the part—but he doesn't say it's my rightful place.

Everyone else on this base looks at me like I'm their savior. I just wish they would tell me what I'm supposed to do.

This morning, Crius told us he found the real cause of the explosion on Thebe—a critical overload in a quantum fusion reactor. What he and Dr. Eusta want to know is how it happened. I keep telling them we already know how—Dark Matter was the trigger. But Agatha is the only one who believes me.

The question isn't how—it's *who*.

Crius wants more answers, and he made me read the Ephemeris for most of the meeting. Mathias made me read it again this afternoon. But both times, I couldn't See.

We've lost twenty million people, a fifth of our population. It's a number too large for me to understand.

What I do understand is that Deke's sisters drowned. Kai lost his parents. Dad and Stanton haven't been found. I'm too full of the past to see the future.

Tonight is the first time I get to be with my friends since we arrived. Wave communications finally started working again, so I spoke to Nishi for hours yesterday, filling her in on everything that's happened since we parted. She was breathless for most of the conversation. It felt strange to share a laugh with someone again— the past three days, it's been all bows and *Holy Mothers* from Lola, Leyla, and the Lodestars, and then a bunch of barking and bossing around from Mathias and my Advisors.

Sagittarians don't bow to their Guardian—they say doing so implies every soul is not equal—so thank Helios Nishi isn't fazed by this stuff. For her part, Nishi told me that she, Deke, and Kai have been grouped together with the other Acolytes who survived . . . the Acolytes who didn't come out to our show.

After she said it, guilt choked both our vocal cords for a while. If we hadn't organized the concert that night. If I'd heeded the warning signs in the Ephemeris. If we'd just stayed indoors . . .

They might have died anyway, a small voice reminds me. The pieces of wreckage that struck the compound killed just as many people as the electric pulse did outdoors.

Nishi said she and the guys have been in Zodai training all day, every day. A Lodestar Garrison trains them in the mornings—while I'm in with the Council of Advisors—and Agatha trains them in the afternoons.

They had to take Abyssthe yesterday, and Kai panicked and refused. Deke was the only one who could convince him that it would be fine, that he wouldn't pass out and wake up to the destruction of our world.

I Waved Deke a few times, but he didn't answer. When I asked Nishi about him, she grew cagey and said he's dealing with loss his own way. I just wish I could help.

This morning, Mathias told me he arranged for the three of them to eat dinner with me in my room tonight. The excitement of seeing my friends is so massive, it doesn't leave room for anything else. I've been distracted all day, and I could tell Mathias and the rest of my Advisors are starting to lose their patience. I'll need to manage something impressive tomorrow.

The moment she's in my room, Nishi and I spring into each other's arms. Squeezed together, we laugh until we're crying, and then we laugh again.

Like all civilian refugees on Oceon 6, she's wearing laboratory scrubs borrowed from the scientists, but she's rolled up the sleeves and added a belt at her waist, so she still manages to look sexy. When we pull away, I turn to hug Deke, but he's not there. Instead, Kai approaches me slowly, without meeting my gaze. He bows. "Holy Mother."

I crush him into an embrace, and I don't let go until he returns it. "Kai, I'm so sorry about your parents," I whisper into his ear. His hold tightens, and his breathing grows heavy, so we stay locked together a while longer. When we're done, he looks at me like I'm Rho again.

"Where's—"

"Holy Mother." Deke bows at me from the other end of the room, his back against the wall and eyes looking straight ahead. It's a Zodai stance, the same one Mathias assumes sometimes.

"Deke—" I move toward him, but he edges away.

Nishi marches up to him. "You're seriously acting this way? She's still Rho, our best friend—"

"Nish, it's okay," I say, even though it isn't.

Shaking, I pull out a chair at the table Lola and Leyla laid out with drinks, fruit, and an assortment of seafood. Kai sits across from me. Soon, Nishi takes the chair next to mine, and once we've started eating, Deke slips into the last seat, his eyes never straying from the tablecloth. He loved his sisters as much as I love Stanton. Of course I understand.

"There are eighteen girls and thirty-three guys, and we're split into two bunkrooms." Nishi is rattling off a lot of the same information she told me yesterday, but I know she's just trying to lighten the mood. "Most of the others are young, between twelve and fourteen."

That's probably why they didn't come to the party. I stab a piece of fruit with my fork and stuff it into my mouth, even though I'm not hungry. "How does the training work if you're all at different levels?" I ask through the food, trying to latch onto safer subjects.

"The three of us, plus a fifteen-year-old named Freida, are in the advanced group," says Nishi, passing me her napkin so I can wipe the fruit juice trailing down my chin. "Everyone else works with Stargazer Swayne, who teaches more basic stuff."

"When are you going home?" I ask her. It's hard to believe there are people in the universe who can still do that.

"They don't really have the ships to spare right now. Since there will be representatives from other Houses coming to your swearing-in ceremony, I'm hitching a ride with the Sagittarian envoy."

The thought of Nishi leaving me to do this alone is unbearable. Now that I'm with her, I don't even know how I made it this far. After tonight, I can't go back to the loneliness of the past few days.

"Did you read anything in the stars today?" she asks, her voice lower. Kai leans into the table, eager to listen. Deke stays still, staring at the table.

I shake my head. "Lately, I can't . . . concentrate." My voice breaks. At this, Deke's head tilts slightly, and his eyes almost look up.

"Of course you can't, Rho," says Nishi, surveying me with her sharp amber eyes. She squeezes my hand. "You're human, you can't block out everything that's happened to you and your House." In a whisper only I can hear, she adds, "It's okay to feel your pain before walling it off."

I wipe a tear before anyone can see.

In what feels like barely any time at all, there's a knock on my door, and the officer outside informs me it's the base's curfew. Kai hugs me on his way out. He seems to have reverted to his non-speaking ways—he didn't say a word the entire night.

I look down when Deke passes me, not wanting to feel the pain of his rejection again. But he stops in front of me. I chance a peek, and he offers me his fist for the hand touch. It's not a hug, but I still take it.

When she's the last one left, I grab Nishi's hand. "Can you stay a sec?"

She's the only person who trusted in my visions, even when I didn't, so she's the best person to consult now. She pokes her head out and tells the officer, "Holy Mother needs me a few more minutes. I'll catch up." When she closes the door behind her, there's a gleam of excitement in her eyes. "What is it?"

I dive right in. "Back on Elara, I saw something . . . strange. I'd activated Instructor Tidus's Ephemeris, and when she turned it off, a series of holograms drowned the room. They were diagrams that looked like the usual stuff we all have on our Waves—history of the galaxy, layout of the stars, facts about the universe. Only her version of the Zodiac included an unnamed constellation. *A Thirteenth House.*"

Nishi's eyes grow wide. Cancrians can be very skeptical, often because we're so quick to get our hopes up that our first instinct is to protect ourselves; but Sagittarians will accept even the most incredible truths, as long as they trust the source.

"Instructor Tidus wouldn't have kept that fact stored on her Wave if she didn't believe it was real," says Nishi, her reasoning soon out-speeding mine. "That means there must be evidence somewhere of a Thirteenth House, enough evidence that she would trust it . . . and something that big will surely have a trail."

"Follow it," I whisper, darting a glance at the door to make sure we're not overheard. I don't want to panic anyone until I have all the facts. "Find out what you can."

"Is this about the omen?"

I nod. "It's always out past the Twelfth House. And I was thinking of the way the Dark Matter showed up in Leo and Taurus when I read the black opal that first night. The stars showed me something that wasn't the future—it was the past. So what if the omen they keep showing me isn't an omen—what if they're pointing to who's responsible?"

Nishi looks entranced by my theory. She whispers, "*The Thirteenth House.*"

I nod. "We need to be certain."

She gives me a quick hug before bouncing to the door, probably already mapping out the ways she'll tackle her search.

"We will be."

8

THE DAY OF THE CEREMONY, my Advisors are busy making arrangements, so I train with Mathias in the morning. He's teaching me what he says will be one of our hardest lessons: communicating through the Psy Network, the way the Zodai do.

He gives me my very own Ring, and as soon as I slip it on my finger, I feel a new energy seep into my skin, like the metallic silicon is bonding with me on a psychic level. An intense inner buzzing pulses through the area, as if my finger's taken a huge swig of Abyssthe.

"Communicating in the Psy doesn't require Centering because the Ring's core is a pool of Abyssthe," says Mathias. We're in our normal training room, standing on a Yarrot mat, facing each other. "The Ring attracts Psynergy to you."

I inspect the thick band. The fact that Abyssthe is such an important tool for the Zodai makes me feel even guiltier for using it the night of the attack. "Sounds like the Ring does all the heavy lifting."

"Try it out."

"Now?" I blurt. He nods, and I hold my hand out in front of me, wondering how I activate it.

"Reach inward toward the buzzing you feel in your hand," he says, guessing at my thoughts. "When you tap into it, you'll access the Psy. Only this time, there's no Ephemeris to direct the energy for you, so you'll need to control it yourself." Noting the obvious confusion in my expression, he adds, "By telling the Psy where you want to go."

"Will it feel like . . . taking Abyssthe without an Ephemeris?" Admitting to illegal behaviors probably isn't the best way to convince Mathias I'm a good choice of Guardian.

"Sort of," he says, eyeing me curiously. "When you drink Abyssthe without an Ephemeris, you're attracting Psyngery to you, but you're not channeling it into anything. This Ring uses the Psynergy from Abyssthe to connect you to all the other Ring-wearing Zodai across the galaxy. We are the Psy Network—the Zodai's Collective Conscious."

It sounds confusing, but I've always been better at diving into something new than understanding its mechanics. "So once I access the Psy Network, do I just think of the person I want to talk to?"

"Sure. Or you can ask the whole network a question, and anyone tuning in will hear. Try it out."

I close my eyes and reach deep inside, into the portal of energy pulsing through my ring finger. When I reach it, I feel like I've touched something icy and liquid. The substance spreads through my insides, rippling outward in waves, until I feel myself pulled in by the tide and swept away from the present, into black Space.

Only this Space isn't filled with orbs of dancing light, but rather silhouettes made of smoke, some floating in place, some zooming like bullets, and all of them popping in and out of existence everywhere I look. My guess is they're the other Zodai who are entering and leaving the Psy right now—and the figures grouped together must be communicating with each other.

I float closer to one of the shadows. I pick up a faint whispering, but I can't hear the words.

Mathias.

I hear myself say his name in my head, but not out loud. I must be speaking soundlessly, the way the Zodai do.

Only nothing happens. Mathias's voice doesn't respond, and the smoke figures around me don't react. The longer I stay in the shadow world, the more dizzying and disorienting it grows, until everything is spinning. Breathless, I open my eyes, and the solar system of souls whirling around me vanishes.

The first thing that feels different is the orientation of the room—I'm staring at the ceiling.

"How are you feeling?"

The musical voice sounds closer than usual. Twisting my neck, I'm met with Mathias's indigo blue eyes. For some reason, we're lying on the floor, his arms reaching out to me at awkward angles. One hand is under my head, the other on the small of my back. Like he was protecting me.

"Did I fall?" I whisper.

"My fault," he murmurs. "Most people get dizzy their first time. I should have mentioned it."

Even though we should stand up, neither of us moves. The space between us is so small that his breath blows on me like a light breeze. I gaze at the barely perceptible cleft in his chin, remembering how he would grow a light stubble there during exam time at the university. Now that he's older, he keeps his skin smooth. I feel the crazy urge to reach out and touch him.

Mathias looks away first. I shift to liberate his hands, and he sits upright. "I'm sorry there's been no word on your family, Rho."

I sit up, too. It's one of the rare times he's used my name since I asked him not to call me *Holy Mother*. That night, he said my name like it was just a word. Now he whispers it, like it's a secret. "Do you know anything about yours?"

"My mother works at the Planetary Plenum, so she and my father are spending most of this year at House Aries. I spoke to them before we left home." His voice grows quiet, and he reaches into his pocket, pulling out the mother-of-pearl Astralator. "When the moons collided, my sister died on Galene."

My throat seems to shrivel up and wither, and I can't speak. All this time we've been training together, and I never asked.

"This was hers," he says, holding up the instrument.

"I-I'm so sorry, Mathias."

He shakes his head and puts it away, turning to face me on the mat. "Let's go again. Only touch the Ring with your other hand when you enter the Psy. It will function as an anchor and help keep you grounded."

I nod and close my eyes, staying seated this go-around. I place my left hand over my right and twist the Ring around my finger, until I've dipped into the icy energy, and I'm pulled into the Collective Conscious.

This time, the world feels steadier—like I'm standing on land instead of floating through Space. I approach the nearest shadow, something about it drawing me closer.

Rho.

It's Mathias.

I hear you, I say back.

That's impressive. Some Zodai can take years to send their first message.

How did I know this smoky figure would be you? I stare at the wispy mass, its shape shifting constantly, like it doesn't have a true form.

The physical proximity helps, but it's also because we've formed a connection. I'm your Guide, so you're drawn to my Psynergy signature, as I am to yours.

I open my eyes. I've left the shadow world, and I'm back in the room with Mathias, holding the Ring. He's staring at me in disbelief, and I watch his lips move without making a sound. *Rho, are you still in the Psy?*

I hear his words in my mind. *Yes.*

Speaking through the Psy from the physical plane is really advanced. "Most beginners can only access the Psy when they are most present within it," he says, finishing the thought out loud. I pull my hand off the Ring.

He watches me, his expression mysterious. "Agatha said your mother trained you from an early age. What exactly was she teaching you?"

I feel like a flying bird crashing into an invisible wall. Soaring through today's lesson, I was finally beginning to feel some semblance of accomplishment for the first time since being made Guardian. Mathias's question makes me feel sixteen years old and small again.

I pull out my Wave from the waistband of my tights. I try calling Dad and Stanton.

"Rho, I don't want to pry. It just seems like what she did had an impact on your ability to manipulate Psynergy . . . and knowing what it was could help me Guide you."

I shut off the Wave and stuff it back in my band. It's not that I disagree with him—it's just that I hate remembering. I don't know how most people's memories work, but mine is merciless. The moment I pull a thread from the Mom years, the whole yarn unspools. And I can't afford to let her to distract me now. Not when Dad and Stanton are still missing.

Mathias starts to reach for me, and I know he's going to pat my back or squeeze my shoulder or do something else that should be comforting, only it won't be. I don't want his pity. So I twist my Ring, and I disappear into the shadow world. An instant later, a new silhouette pops into existence, and immediately I feel Mathias's presence.

Somehow, it's easier to talk in here, where I don't have to hear the words out loud. *I don't like to remember. It's not that the training was traumatic, exactly. . . . It was exhaustive and endless, but you can't call it torture. It's just . . . it's because I . . .*

You miss her.

He's right, but I don't say so. Instead, I try to catalogue some of the things Mom and I studied, careful to stay in the shallow end of my memory pool, without digging too far into any particular moment. So I won't have to see her bottomless blue eyes or hear her storytelling voice or smell her water lily scent.

First it was memorizations. Ever since I was a baby, she would read to me about the Zodiac, until it became all I knew. What each constellation looks like, the name of every star and planet, the operations of the different Houses—all stuff that's in the Acolyte textbooks. Then when I was four, she started teaching me Yarrot.

In the murky and abstract surroundings, it's easier to make the memories feel like stories Mom told me once, rather than real things she did. *By the time I was five, I could Center myself, and I was seeing things in the Ephemeris. I was . . . terrified. I didn't understand how I was doing it, and I didn't know what was real and what wasn't. I would get nightmares from the visions every night. I stayed awake at all hours to avoid sleep. I was a kid, and I was afraid to be inside my own head.*

I'm so sorry, Rho, whispers Mathias softly.

The nights I woke up screaming, Stanton would come into my room to calm me. He'd tell me stories until I fell back asleep, stories he'd make up on the spot. Whenever he ran out of plot twists, I'd join in, and we'd keep going until our hero either got married or died. That's how we'd know we reached the end: Deaths we declared tragedies, weddings comedies.

I open my eyes and take my hand off the Ring. Mathias joins me back on reality. "My mom had this theory that people can see more when they're younger, when their soul is purest. She said that's when we're most susceptible to Psynergy, and that if properly trained from an early age, a person could develop a natural ability to commune with the stars."

I take in a deep breath and exhale a sigh. "I guess it halfway worked because I'm faster at Centering than the other Acolytes, and my reads are right a lot of the time. But since Mom taught me to use my instinct, I'm way behind with an Astralator, and I can't always distinguish between the Psy and my imagination."

He looks away when I say the word *Astralator*, probably thinking of his sister. "Well, you're a pro with the Ring. The more often you use it to communicate, the more familiar you will become with people's Psynergy signatures, and that will help you identify anyone misrepresenting themselves."

It sounds like another version of *Trust Only What You Can Touch*. "Why do people manipulate the Psy so often?"

His eyebrows pull together, and he pauses for a moment. "Think of it this way: In this realm, the rules of science govern us. If you throw a ball at the ground where there's gravity, the ball will bounce."

I nod.

"In the Psy, there are no rules. You're floating through people's minds, and we don't work in black and white. In the brain, everything is relative. Most of us don't intentionally try to misrepresent anything—but the lies we tell ourselves, the truths we repress, the things we conceal in the physical realm . . . they inform reality in the Psy. Even in an abstract dimension, ideas built on flawed foundations will fail."

I get the impression the only way I'm going to understand what he's saying is with more training. "Let's go again—"

Mathias tilts his head, like he's listening for something far off. "Sounds like we have to cut this short," he says, his lips twitching. "You have more important business to attend to before tonight's ceremony." Then he walks off without another word.

"Mathias!" I call after him. "What business? Who was just talking to you?"

"Hello, Holy Mother."

I turn to see Lola and Leyla, their hands locked in front of them and wide smiles on their faces.

✦ ✦ ✦

Back in my room, Leyla sits me down in the desk chair, facing the dusty round mirror. "*Makeover?*" I ask for the fifth time. "You're telling me *this* trumps my learning how to communicate in the Psy?"

"Today it does, Holy Mother," she says, wresting my curls from the hairband they're twisted around. "Representatives from every House are coming to see you."

"Why can't I greet them in my new uniform?" I ask, referring to the Zodai-style blue suit the sisters presented me with yesterday. They took turns sewing it; on the sleeve, instead of the three gold stars of the Royal Guard, they embroidered four silver moons.

I was so moved, I begged them to name something I could give them in return, and after rounds of refusals, Leyla finally said, "We want you to trust yourself." It was a strange request, but then, Leyla is strange—in a wise-beyond-her-years way.

"You wanted me to trust myself, and I think the suit you made me is the way to go." I put as much authority into the words as I can. "Representatives from the Zodiac are coming because our House is in a state of emergency—what will they think if I show up dressed like I've come to have a good time?"

Leyla stops working, and her sapphire gaze meets mine in the mirror. "They will think the Cancrian people are still here, and no matter what else happens, we will live on, in you."

I take her hands in mine, and for a long moment I don't look away from her young face. I've never felt less qualified to lead—or more determined to work harder.

Once I've bathed, Leyla sits me down, turns me away from the mirror, and brushes a few styling products into my locks before spritzing them with a glossing dry-spray. Immediately, the long, wet strands begin to shorten and curve. Next, she applies light, velvety makeup to my skin. She spends more time on my cheekbones and eyes than anywhere else. Once she's moved on to lipstick, Lola arrives with my clothes, and I'm pulled to my feet and helped into a white dress.

White is the traditional color for a Guardian to wear at her ceremony, in respect for the Guardian who's passed. It reminds us it's a bittersweet occasion. White is also the color of a bride's wedding dress, so it symbolizes a Guardian's commitment to House Cancer.

Guardians are allowed to form families, but Mother Origene never did. In public appearances, she'd say she was married to the stars.

"Now for the pearl coronet," says Lola, opening an antique jewelry box and removing a glittering headpiece outlined with white pearls. One of Cancer's sacred symbols, the Crab, sits at its center, formed from millions of tiny diamonds, each one refracting the light so that the crown sparkles radiantly. She sets it on my head, and only then do they let me turn around.

I've never seen the girl reflected back in my life.

My hair hangs nearly to my waist, and in place of the usual bouncy curls there's a sea of glossy, golden waves that are soft to the touch. I feel like I could run my fingers through them without obstruction. My skin is creamy, with hints of bronze in my cheeks to set off my cheekbones, and my lips are painted a rich, reddish plum. But the most startling change is in my eyes: Using liner and sparkly shadow, Leyla made the pale sea green come alive. They're the largest feature on my face.

The dress is made of a silky fabric so fine that when I move, the threads glisten like liquid. Two thin straps beaded with tiny silver pearls hang from my shoulders, the neckline cutting across my chest in a soft V shape and revealing more cleavage than I would normally show. The material is comfortable but tight, draping down to the floor, and it cinches my waist with a light belt of tiny silver pearls.

"How did you do this?" I ask, watching the girl in the mirror mouth the same question. She can't be me.

"Holy Mother, when was the last time you looked at yourself?" asks Leyla, smiling proudly.

Before I can answer, there's knocking. It must be Mathias picking me up. Lola pads to the door, and I grip the desk, a rush of nerves racking my chest. For some reason, I'm terrified of him seeing me like this.

"I need to talk to Holy Mother. It's important."

At the sound of the voice, I run to the door—no easy feat in four-inch heels. "Nishi? What is it?"

"*Holy Helios!*" She gasps on seeing me.

I grab her hand and pull her inside. Since there's so much traffic in and out of the base today, there are no officers posted outside my door. Nishi is still ogling me. "You look amazing!"

"Thanks! Did you come to tell me something?"

"Yes—right—it's about . . . *Thirteen*."

I turn to Lola and Leyla. "Thank you so much. I never could have pulled this off without you." I trust the sisters, but I don't want to get them in trouble; so until I know what Nishi has to say, I'd rather not involve them.

Once they're gone, Nishi hits a button on the flint Tracker around her wrist, and red holographic text sparks out. "Do you recognize this poem?"

I scan the text. "Of course. 'Beware Ochus'—it's a Cancrian children's poem. Ochus is a snake monster our parents threaten will come get us if we misbehave."

She nods, and the poem transforms into song lyrics. "On Sagittarius, we have a lullaby that warns of a wanderer named Ophius. On Virgo—"

"They have a fable about a talking serpent in a garden," I say, hearkening back to Mom's lessons and hoping Nishi will get to the point before we're interrupted.

"Aquarius has a parable about twelve numbers that live harmoniously together, inside a clock, and the villain who ruins everything is—"

"Thirteen," I finish, aghast.

There's a knock at the door, but I don't answer. The last two times I've read the black opal, the Dark Matter showed up again, just past the Twelfth House. I need to know what it means. "What are you saying, Nishi?"

"I'm saying they're all the same entity." She's now whispering in case whoever's at the door can hear us. "I think there used to be another House in the Zodiac, and for some reason, it vanished from the night sky . . . and over time, it's been erased from history."

There's more knocking. "Hurry," I urge Nishi.

Her voice drops so low I have to read her lips to follow what she's saying. "The only evidence now is in the guise of story and myth, stuff no one will take seriously. I know we Sagittarians can be conspiracy nuts at times, but Rho, if someone from the Thirteenth House is behind this, and all these tragedies are part of a trajectory—from the disasters on Leo and Taurus to what's happened to your moons—they're also altering history to cover their tracks. That means they've been planning this for a *very* long time."

"A group of people?" I guess.

She shrugs helplessly. "So far, all I have is a name: *Ophiuchus*."

9

"OPHIUCHUS," I REPEAT, SOUNDING THE word on my tongue.

"It's the name of the Thirteenth House. Do you think your Advisors would know anything about it?"

I gaze at the beauty products littering the room, thinking. My gut tells me my Advisors will dismiss our theory. Most of them already have no faith in my leadership; if I point an accusatory finger at a childhood monster, they could *all* give up on me. Even Mathias.

I recall a sunny day on the Strider with my family, seeing bubbles in the water twice, and both times not saying anything. My silence gave the Maw time to attack my brother. Then I flash to the flickering I'd been seeing before the Lunar Quadract. I didn't trust myself enough to speak up, and Thebe exploded without warning.

What a strange moment to understand Leyla's advice.

Rho?

Mathias's voice calls out to me faintly, as if from a long way off. Instinctively, I touch my Ring, and the sound grows clearer. *Everything okay? he asks. Is there a delay?*

All good. I'll meet you there, I say, moving my lips soundlessly.

"You have a Ring!" squeals Nishi, yanking my hand closer for inspection. "We haven't gotten ours yet, but I'm dying to try it out, though I hear it's super hard—"

"Nishi, you're *stellar.* No one but you could have dug up so much that fast. You're right about consulting my Advisors. I'll see what I can find out, and I'll Wave you after the ceremony."

"Something else," she says, whispering again. "The Dark Matter you've seen by the Thirteenth House and on Leo and Taurus—it's not the stars showing you a pattern. I read that once Dark Matter consumes any part of a planet, it remains in that area of Space forever. So you're seeing everywhere it's been."

I frown. "Then how come it doesn't always show up?"

"Dark Matter is supremely hard to tell apart from normal Space. If there's even the slightest interference, it can become obscured . . . but it's still there. You're just not seeing it."

"Thank you." I hug her tightly. I wish Nishi could come with me tonight, but Admiral Crius said only government officials are allowed. It seems wrong to go through the most significant ceremony in my life supported by a roomful of strangers. I should at least get to have a friend.

Nishi gives me the Sagittarian salute for good fortune, steepling her fingers together and touching her forehead. Then she opens the door to leave, and a sea of excitable voices floods the room. For a moment the halls of Oceon 6 sound like the ones of the Academy on the night of the Lunar Quadract . . . then the door shuts out the noise.

Alone, I face the mirror one last time. I still don't recognize the girl's face or the woman's body or the fancy clothes. I'd much rather stay in here and research Ophiuchus the rest of the night. I wish I'd at least asked Mathias to wait—now I have to go to my own ceremony alone.

"Rho?"

This time, the musical voice is calling from outside the door. "C-come in," I say, my mouth like sandpaper, one singular thought cycling through my head: *He waited.*

When the door swings open, the swarm of voices rushes in again—then it goes away when Mathias's eyes meet mine.

It's like I've drawn a deep breath and plunged my head underwater. The hallway clamor grows muffled, and the edges of the room blur, until all I'm aware of is him. The black hair, the pale face, the midnight-blue gaze.

Eons later, when my Wave starts humming with calls, I realize I don't know how long we've been staring at each other. I only know that any second he's going to tell me we need to go, we're running late, my Advisors are waiting. Instead, he steps inside the room.

The little hairs on my arms tingle, reminding me of the cilia-like legs of the Strider. Then I wonder why I'm thinking of cilia now, when a five-year-long fantasy is coming to life: The beautiful boy I watched in the solarium is finally looking back.

When Mathias is in front of me, I grow leaden, like the centrifugal force anchoring my feet to the ground has doubled. I read his profile among the files Crius sent me: He's twenty-two, and his family has served in the Royal Guard for seven generations. From the age of eight, he attended the Lykeion on House Aquarius, the Zodiac's most famous prep school for future Zodai, and at the university on Elara, he graduated first in his class.

The humming of his Wave joins mine, and I wonder how many calls from the Psy he's ignoring.

"You really make that crown shine," he whispers, his throat so dry I can hear him swallow. He offers me his arm, and I think I might float away if I touch him.

I loop my hand through and realize I've been holding my breath. His face is so close that there's nowhere to look but into his eyes, twin orbs ablaze with the blue light of Cancer. I try to remember why I dressed up, or why we're going anywhere at all.

"We shouldn't keep them waiting longer," he murmurs, in a tone less assertive than his usual one. He gently guides me forward, and incredibly, my legs still work.

"Would"—I clear my voice of its roughness—"would you mind putting my Wave and the black opal in your pocket?" I hold out the two devices I don't go anywhere without.

Mathias stuffs them in his suit, and we pick up speed down the hallway. I hold my coronet to keep it from slipping as we hurtle through passages, until we reach the double doors to the dining hall, which has been converted to host tonight's ceremony. "You're late!" says Admiral Crius, scowling.

Agatha hobbles up to me with her cane, her face alight with pleasure. "You look beautiful, Holy Mother." Dr. Eusta just nods. It's the first time he's shown up in person instead of sending his hologram.

"Let's get inside already," barks Crius. "The Matriarchs are here, as are representatives from every House of the Zodiac." Cancer is managed by the Matriarchy, the eldest Mothers of our twelve founding families. Crius points to Mathias. "Hang back with us. Let our Guardian walk ahead, alone."

Before I can argue, the doors open to a collection of round tables, decked out in lavish fabrics and silverware, seating an array of vastly different people. Even though I've never met an Aquarian before, I recognize their representative by her glassy eyes, narrow face, and ivory skin. She's sitting next to the representative from Scorpio—he's thin and long-faced, and to his suit he's added strange pieces of technology that are probably his own inventions. Some representatives couldn't make it and are floating above the tables as visiting holo-ghosts.

Ghosts are holograms projected from too far away, and since their signals travel at lightspeed, there's a time lag. They can't hold normal conversations because they're always a step or two behind, so they can be funny to watch. In this case, they're just observing and not doing much.

Written across the air are the names of each House and the strength it brings to the Zodiac. Legend says that the first Guardians were actually Guardian Stars, each watching over its own constellation. When the Zodiac foresaw the first people arriving through Helios, each House gave up its Guardian, and the twelve stars fell to earth and became mortal.

Each brought with them the knowledge of a survival skill, so that our Houses would always have to work together, as equals, to ensure our galaxy's eternal existence. They're hovering over our heads:

ARIES: MILITARY

TAURUS: INDUSTRY

GEMINI: IMAGINATION

CANCER: NURTURE

LEO: PASSION

VIRGO: SUSTENANCE

LIBRA: JUSTICE

SCORPIO: INNOVATION

SAGITTARIUS: CURIOSITY

CAPRICORN: WISDOM

AQUARIUS: PHILOSOPHY

PISCES: SPIRITUALITY

I wonder what thirteenth survival skill Ophiuchus represented.

As soon as the crowd sees me, they rise to their feet and stare. I try not to think of how many eyes are on me by focusing on the floor and setting one foot in front of the other. When I get to the end of the room, there's a long table behind which my remaining eight Advisors are standing. Admiral Crius rests a hand on my shoulder, and I stop moving. We pause at a sand basin filled with clear salt water.

Crius fills a crystal glass and raises it in the air. "Rhoma Grace, you are here to swear your life to House Cancer. If you make this solemn oath, you swear to place the lives of Cancer and the Cancrian people ahead of your own. You swear to be a Guiding Star of the Zodiac, to work alongside the Guardians of the Eleven Houses, and to always be a champion of House Cancer. Above all, you swear to do whatever it takes to ensure our galaxy's survival."

From the moment I was made Guardian, I never considered that I could walk away from the role. I'd like to claim it's because I felt a strong sense of duty from the outset, but it's really because I was afraid I didn't have a choice. Maybe that makes me a coward.

On some level, I was secretly hoping Crius and Agatha would recognize their mistake and strip me of the title so that someone better could take over. But the past few days—watching how my Advisors work, training with Mathias, writing my speech for tonight—I realized something. For me, the Guardianship isn't about swapping my life as an individual for a lifetime of service to other people. For me, it's personal.

What happened on Elara happened to House Cancer, but it also happened to *my* school, *my* friends, *my* teachers. The damage even reached my home planet and maybe my family. This is as personal as life gets. I'm not in this role because I'm different—I'm here because I'm like every Cancrian everywhere. I know what it feels like to lose everything.

And whether I'm Rho the person or Rho the Guardian, the same goal guides me: I want to save Cancer, and I want to make sure we never suffer like this again.

"I swear it," I say, the room so silent that my voice carries and lingers.

"With a sip of the Cancer Sea," says Admiral Crius, "your oath will be sealed."

He hands me the glass, and I take a deep gulp, the saltiness burning my nose and throat. I try not to cough.

"May the stars of our Crab constellation welcome you with a smile, Holy Mother Rhoma Grace, Guardian of the Fourth House, Cancer," says the admiral in a deep, carrying voice. Then he bows to me for the second—and probably last—time, whispering under his breath, "Holy Mother."

The rest of the room follows suit, the whispered salute like a sacred chant, and for a few seconds all I see are the tops of forty people's heads. And one face.

A guy my age with white streaks in his blond hair is still looking up, watching me. His expensive coat bears the Libran symbol, the Scales of Justice. When we lock eyes, he winks. Then he bows lower than all the others.

"Holy Mother will now swear in her Council," says Crius. My

Advisors march over and join him in a line. The admiral goes first.

I turn to him and say, "Admiral Axley Crius, you are here to swear your loyalty to your Guardian and House Cancer. If you make this solemn oath, you swear to honor, advise, and protect your Guardian, and to always act in the best interest of House Cancer."

"I swear it."

Agatha pledges her loyalty next, followed by Dr. Eusta and the others. Being the youngest, Mathias goes last. "I swear it," he says, his blue gaze glued to mine, "on my Mother's life."

It's the strongest oath a Cancrian can make.

I'm so moved I forget what comes next. "Holy Mother would like to address all of you present now," says Crius, nudging me forward on his march to the table. I'm left alone with the whole room's attention. I used to have nightmares that began like this—until I discovered what real nightmares are like.

"Thank you all for coming to House Cancer's aid," I say, reciting from memory the speech I wrote with Mathias and Agatha. "I'm pleased to share with you that the tsunamis have ended, and our rescue efforts continue to uncover more survivors." I find my eyes straying to the Libran, who's the only person in the room smiling. Every time I look, he's already looking back.

"The issue now is that our ocean lies restless, pulled in too many directions by the orbiting moon rubble, which is stirring up savage storms. We won't know what the consequences will be to marine life. For now, people are returning to their island homes to rebuild and save as many species as we can. Technicians have begun to repair our satellites and power grid, so communications should be up soon. Our people, our wild species, and our land will adapt. *We will survive."*

Low clapping breaks out, a gesture meant to show solidarity from the room without overpowering my voice. The Libran whistles. A few people turn and glare at him, and I realize I'm smiling.

"As my first official order as Guardian, I am scattering our Zodai Guard to the far-flung posts around our House and galaxy so we won't all be caught in one place again." More clapping. My Advisors and I agreed this would be the wisest move for now, at least until we know more specifics about what caused the explosion. "I look forward to meeting with every one of you tonight. Thank you."

I'm seated at the center of the table, flanked by Admiral Crius and Agatha. Mathias is near the end, so we can't talk. Or so I thought.

You dazzled them.

My Ring grows warm as I receive Mathias's message—and so does my face. *Thank you,* I send back. *I'm going to work hard to be worthy of your oath.*

You already are, Rho.

"You were spectacular," says Agatha, pulling me out of my head. I'm pretty sure my cheeks are still burning.

"Thank you, for everything," I say, taking her hand.

"I am truly sorry for the way we deceived you on your arrival," she says, her gray-green eyes growing misty, as I've noticed they do when she's feeling something deeply. "Heart, mind, and soul. Those are the areas we test."

"What do you mean?"

"When you chose your mother over yourself, we knew you had the heart of a Guardian. When you unlocked the black opal, we knew you had the knowledge and desire to uncover more truths about our universe." She smiles at the growing bewilderment on my face. "And when you saw the Dark Matter, we knew you were a pure soul."

The last one sounds too much like something Mom used to say. That the best seers have the purest souls. "How . . . how did that tell you about my soul?"

"Because only someone very true to herself could see so clearly in the Ephemeris. Remember, when you are Centered, you are accessing your soul. People with tormented souls can barely see beyond their own torment. Your sight is clear because you are honest. Bad things have happened to you, but when it came time to act—when you were tested—you chose to forgive. Even the person who hurt you most."

I blink a few times to fight the burning in my eyes. This is not where I want to be when I cry.

"You have no idea how rare that is, Rho," she whispers. "The Zodiac is entering a dark time, and you will face more difficulties than the rest of us. My hope is that no matter what you experience on your Guardian's journey, you never lose that innocence." She closes her eyes and touches my forehead, a Cancrian blessing. On Cancer, it's tradition for a mother to bless her daughter the day she grows out of her childhood.

"May your inner light always shine," she whispers, "and may it guide us through our darkest nights."

I use my napkin to dab the tears from my face. "Thank you."

A flurry of waiters materializes, and our plates are filled with all kinds of exotic foods. Many dishes have been brought by our guests, so there are specialties from across the Zodiac. I'm only midway through my dinner and about to reach for the Libran fried larks when Admiral Crius makes me part with my plate. He moves me to a small table in a semi-blocked-off corner of the dining hall. I'm now supposed to sit here and meet privately with representatives from each House of the Zodiac.

Up first is the representative from House Capricorn. Guardian Ferez sent his Wildlife Advisor to meet with me, a man dressed in a black robe, the traditional clothes of their House.

Capricorns are considered the wisest people in the universe—as well as the tallest and shortest: Half the population looks like Advisor Riggs—tall, soulful, dark-skinned—while the other half is short, talkative, and ruddy-complexioned.

After we exchange the hand touch, Advisor Riggs tells me House Capricorn is transporting an ark with a team of scientists to aid us in our marine-life rescue efforts. He doesn't bother to sit down. The whole exchange probably lasts less than a minute.

I meet with the Virgo Advisor next, who does sit. She tells me Empress Moira—who's also the Zodiac's foremost Psy expert—has dispatched twelve ships of grain to our House. I'm still in shock at Virgo's generosity when the Advisor hands me a note from Moira herself, who was close friends with Mother Origene.

Please bid my reverent farewell to your beloved
Holy Mother. Origene's compassion taught me the
meaning of friendship. Knowing her has honored me,
and her loss leaves a void in the soul of the Zodiac.

While I'm reading the note, a new representative takes the Virgo Advisor's seat. I don't look up until I'm finished, and then I see the Libran envoy. Close up, his smile is more of a crooked smirk. The kind that makes it hard not to smirk back . . . and also the kind that makes a guy seem too pleased with himself.

Nishi would call it a *centaur smile*. It's a Sagittarian expression for a guy who uses his charm and good looks to distract a girl from his less appealing side.

"You're young," I blurt, surprising myself by giving in to a combative impulse.

"I thought you'd be tired of hearing that by now, my lady." The Libran's voice is warm and playful, the type that sounds the same when it's serious and when it's not.

The stronger my urge to smile, the graver I make my expression—so I'm practically glaring when I ask, "Did Lord Neith send you because you're my age?"

"He didn't send me, my lady." His piercing, leaf-green eyes are so lively, they seem to be holding their own conversation with mine. "I volunteered."

He offers me his hand for the traditional touch, and balling my fingers into a fist, I reach across the table. Then he presses a soft kiss on my skin.

Shocked, I inhale sharply and mumble something that sounds too much like "Ohrrgh" to have been anything else. My blood buzzes where his mouth touched me, as if his lips were bathed in Abyssthe.

"My name is Hysan Dax, and I've come to deliver a tanker of fuel, a gift from Lord Neith and House Libra."

As he rises to go, I snap to my feet, too. "Why did you volunteer?"

Hysan stares at me, his expression growing serious—or as serious as it probably gets. When the flashy outfit, blond-white locks, and symmetrical dimples fade, I spy something else in his eyes . . . *secrets*. Lots of them.

"I saw a new star rising in the Zodiac, blazing so bright it burned blackness." He moves close enough to drop his voice to a whisper. "I wanted to see if the blaze was real . . . or just a trick of the light."

I feel my face getting hot, and I wonder if the golden glow of Hysan's skin radiates warmth, like Helios, or if the heat is in his words. "And what's your verdict?" I ask, even though Nishi would say I shouldn't flirt with boys who smirk like that.

"I've never seen its rival."

His lips twist into his centaur smile again, and this time I can't resist returning it. "I'm at your service, my lady." He bows deeply. "Always."

When he leaves, a representative from Taurus takes his place. He has to introduce himself twice to get my attention. Their Guardian promises a line of credit to help us rebuild our floating pod cities.

When all the representatives have left, only the Matriarchs remain. Now that the Houses have donated what resources they can, the Council and I must distribute them among the Matriarchs.

Even though our House is ruled by consensus, the Guardian has sovereignty regarding all matters involving the other Houses, which extends to emergency relief contributions.

The dining hall has cleared out, and Admiral Crius gathers us at one of the round tables. Only my top Advisors stay for this meeting—Crius, Agatha, Dr. Eusta, and Mathias.

All twelve Matriarchs are in attendance. Two passed away in the tragedy and have already been replaced with the next-eldest Mothers in their family lines. Mother Lea from the low-lying Meadow Islands is the most outspoken of the group. Her lands were submerged by waves, which overloaded their sea-oat fields with salt.

Cancer's only pure water comes from rain cisterns and desalination vats. A lot of people depend on the grain from the Meadow fields, but they need fresh water to rinse away the excess salt—and their cisterns are full of brine, their desalination vats washed away in the flood. Mother Lea jabs her finger at the tablecloth. "There's no time to rebuild the vats. If we don't plant our oats this month, we'll miss an entire harvest. Holy Mother, we need five tanker ships of fresh water."

"Mathias," I say, "what's the plan for the freshwater supply House Aquarius sent?"

He pauses before he speaks, fusing with the Psy. These past few days, I've just begun to realize how much activity goes on behind his quiet face. "All freshwater stores are being diverted to our refugee camps."

I look at Mother Lea, knowing she's not going to like what I'm about to say. "I'm sorry about the sea oats, but for the time being, we have to adapt. What can we grow in salty ground?"

Her face is just about to explode when Crius bangs his hand on the table, and I jump a foot in the air.

"Honored Guardian," he says, his gruff tone not fully masking his fear, "we have an emergency."

Mathias and my Advisors rise, and as I stand to join them, I see the anger in Mother Lea's eyes turn to despair. While the others march off, I stay back and say, "Save your seed, Mother Lea. Keep it dry for later. We'll miss this season, but we'll plant sea oats again. Don't lose hope." I know it's not what she wants to hear, but good fortune is hard to come by these days.

I race down the hall after the others, the train of the white dress whipping behind me, and when I get to the door of the lecture hall where we hold our Advisor meetings, Mathias is waiting. "Before we go in," he says, "I need to tell you something. I received a message tonight, while you were meeting with representatives from the Houses. I know the timing is terrible, and I should probably wait, but I also know you would want to hear this news immediately."

Instead of speaking, he closes his eyes. At first I think he's doing it to be dramatic, and I nearly throttle him, but then my Ring grows warm, and I close my eyes, too. A picture forms in my mind, an image of people not on Occon 6.

Dad is standing in front of our wrecked bungalow on Kalymnos, his clothes tattered. And beside him, wearing a glorious grin that's completely at odds with the destruction, is Stanton.

I love the image so much that I don't want to open my eyes, not ever again. I look for so long that something starts to feel wrong: my knees are rubbery, the floor is wobbly, and everything's spinning—

When I'm back on reality, Mathias's hands are on my waist. "I'm sorry, I shouldn't have shocked you like that—"

"Mathias," I whisper, the tears now freely streaming down my face, washing off the makeup and the nightmares and the days and nights of worrying. "Thank you."

His indigo eyes grow so dark they're almost violet. "Your brother wasn't on Thebe. He was visiting your father, and they were both rescued at sea."

Without thinking, I hug him. He hugs me back, and when I pull away, he's smiling. I haven't seen a smile on his face until now. It softens his features, making him look like the boy he used to be, the one I used to dream about finally being brave enough to talk to one day.

I just never imagined *one day* looking like this.

"Can I Wave them?" I ask.

"I doubt they still have their Waves, and even if they did, the grid isn't up yet—but I'm trying to find a way."

The door to the lecture hall opens, and Admiral Crius barks, "Get in!" Mathias and I scramble inside.

"Let's consult the black opal," says Agatha the moment we've joined them. Mathias hands it to me from his suit pocket, and I feel the ridges along its side, until I see the Bull forming in my mind. House Taurus.

The star map blooms out, filling the room with wispy, flickering lights. As soon as I step into its holographic glow, I lock my eyes on Cancer to reach my Center. The Ring makes it easier, thanks to the Abyssthe in its core, and soon music notes fill the solar system.

Radiant gases, luminous dust, asteroids, quasars, ethereal clusters of fire. I look around, to the place beyond the Twelfth House. The Dark Matter is still there, pulsing.

"We received a message from House Pisces," says Crius. "They've spotted a portent in the stars. An urgent warning for Cancer about more storms on the way. But it's indistinct, and they're asking us to confirm."

"Of course, the message could be counterfeit," Agatha points out. "The Psy is not always reliable."

"Tell us what you see. We trust your skills have been improving, thanks to your Zodai training," says Crius, though I don't hear much trust in his tone.

I think back to my conversation with Nishi. I know what telling the truth will cost me—maybe even more now than I did a few hours ago—but I've taken an oath to place Cancer's life ahead of my own. Staying silent would be cowardly. I need to find the truth: Our survival depends on it.

"Ophiuchus," I say. "I see Dark Matter in the Thirteenth House, the constellation Ophiuchus."

10

FOUR SETS OF EYES STARE at me like I've gone crazy.

Mathias speaks first. "It's a myth. A story handed down for so
many generations it became the source of the Cancrian children's
monster, Ochus." He sounds like he's repeating what someone's
whispering to him in the Psy. "The constellation was said to take
the shape of a snake."

"His other names are Ophius," I say, "and Serpent, and 13 . . ."

"So you're blaming the Zodiac's *boogeyman*?" Dr. Eusta grunts
impatiently and turns away. "Oh, good, and we just made her
Guardian."

"*Look*," I say, raising my voice, "I swore an oath to protect Can-
cer, and that's what I intend to do, no matter where it takes me.
Right now, attackers from House Ophiuchus fit the clues. The Dark
Matter is showing up exactly where the Thirteenth House used to

be. If Leo and Taurus are part of a pattern, then whoever is behind this isn't finished yet."

They all stare back at me blankly.

Admiral Crius rubs his jaw. "I know the myths as well as anyone, but with all due respect, Holy Mother, I can't see how this relates to our situation." He's doing his best to show me proper reverence, but I think he's reached his limit.

"Perhaps we should consult the astronomers," says Dr. Eusta. "With their telescopes, they might see something we've missed. Begging your pardon, *Holy Mother*."

"I'm not mad. Do everything you can think of. Even if I'm right, I don't know how we stop the attacks. Consult everyone, and I'll continue reading the Ephemeris to see if the threat from Pisces appears."

Everyone sets off in a different direction to gather information, and I remain in the lecture hall, reading the Ephemeris. Here is where I feel I can do the most good for my House. Centered among the stars, my heart and mind open to calls from home, I feel most connected to Cancer and best able to lead us.

I'll stay here as long as it takes to read the stars' secrets.

✦ ✦ ✦

An hour later, there's still no sign of the threat seen by Pisces. I check messages on my Wave, hopeful to find a note from Dad or Stanton, even though I've been told the odds.

Nishi sent me something. I tap on her message, and an image of a half-starved man trapped in the coils of an enormous winged serpent beams out. Loose flesh hangs from his skeletal frame, and he seems to be screaming in agony—it's clear the serpent is winning.

Her message scrolls out along the bottom in bright blue text: *Ophiuchus's glyph was a staff with two serpents intertwined—the caduceus. On Capricorn, there's an old kid's story about a famous alchemist and healer named Caduceus who was banished by Lord Helios for a terrible crime. He'd dared to discover a way to conquer death.*

Holy Helios.

Nishi doesn't think Ophiuchus is a group of people from the Thirteenth House.

She thinks it's one man—and he's immortal.

✦ ✦ ✦

I've lost track of time.

I'm still in the lecture hall, lying on the floor and gazing up at the holographic stars. The map's evanescent light nearly fills the small room. Its constant motion lulls me.

Mathias says we can't perceive Psynergy directly, only the trails it leaves in space-time. He says the Ephemeris transcribes Psynergy into visible light. Transmuting the metaphysical into the physical sounds a lot like alchemy. . . .

I raise my bare foot, and a million stars wash over my toes. My crown and heels are resting next to my Wave, beside me on the cold floor.

Mathias's training helped me realize that the instinct that informs my reads in the Ephemeris is my brain interpreting the Psynergy it's picking up in the Psy. When I did Yarrot early on in life, I tuned in to the innermost version of myself, and at such a young age, I was mostly ruled by my needs, whims, and instinct. So when I applied the same method to the Ephemeris, I began to read the universe that way, internalizing its moods and imagining scenarios to go along with my reads—sometimes wrongly.

Centering myself for the hundredth time, I feel my soul soar up, toward the glowing light of Cancer.

Eyes crossed and mind floaty, it's hard to tell apart the things in my brain from the portents in the stars. It's like diving deep underwater, where sunlight never reaches, and seeing the strange and fantastical creatures that lurk there. Everything seems half-real, half-imagined.

I guide the Psynergy where I want it to go—Cancer. Home is where I'm focusing my read. I feel the energy congregating around the planet's orb, making it glow brighter than the rest of Space. Once I'm as Centered as possible, I fuse my mind with the Psy, and I listen for the sounds of Cancer, opening my mind to messages carried by Psynergy.

In the Collective Conscious, I pick up fear, worry, depression. I feel shivery and cold, and I realize the glow around our planet is fading . . . like it's losing health. Next to us, one of the Gemini twin planets starts to dim, the same way as Cancer. I think it means illness has moved into our House . . . and it's going to spread. I'll need to alert Dr. Eusta so he can diagnose it properly and contact House Scorpio for inoculations.

Out over the Cancer Sea, I pick up our marine species' distress, their migration patterns off, their internal sensors confused.

I try digging deeper, to use the Psy to access the actual land, to commune with the planet's core—but all I get for my troubles is a migraine.

I pull back and take a wider view of the Zodiac, surveying the twelve constellations as a whole. The Fire Houses—Aries, Leo, and Sagittarius—are lit up, the glow of Psynergy engulfing them like a blazing flame.

War is coming.

A light wind seems to brush past me, and in my gut I know it's heralding more storms. Not just for Cancer.

I touch my Ring and close my eyes. Immediately, the swirling lights are replaced with gloomy shadows, and the whole room seems to plunge into a deeper night.

I've never asked the communal mind a question before, but tonight I feel like I can. I'm not sure when the confidence crept in—when I took the sacred Guardian's oath, when I learned Dad and Stanton are alive, or when I told my Advisors about Ophiuchus. But it's there.

While confidence doesn't change anything real, or turn me into a better Guardian, it's no less powerful a drug than Abyssthe. It makes me feel larger and more capable than I am—which can be a self-fulfilling prophecy.

Is the Thirteenth House real or make-believe? I ask the Psy.

The network awakens. Thousands of intellects come alert, and composite ideas whisper and churn like waves in a deep ocean. Short stories, lullabies, and poems emerge—the childish chronicles from every House—not as words on a screen, but the same way I read the stars. The essence of the words—their meaning itself—fills my mind.

More brains join the fusion, completing and complicating the picture in my mind. The Collective Conscious is literally building an answer to my question in the Psy. The process is like constructing anything else—a house, a ship, a weapon—only here, it's the creation of a concept.

The longer I remain plugged in, attuned to the Zodai's answers, the more contradictions that arise, as the scores of minds communicating begin to hit areas of disagreement. I sense curiosity, tension, debate. Then more answers come like a tempest.

Now the picture in my brain begins to split—like I'm arguing pros and cons with myself, only there are many more minds involved. On the one hand, Ophiuchus originated as a morality tale that was then twisted into a dozen different forms by the long-ago Guardians of each House, so that each version would best speak to their people. On the other hand, there is a sect of hardcore conspiracy theorists across the Zodiac who go by the moniker *13* and believe Ophiuchus was real.

According to members of 13, Ophiuchus was the original Guardian of the Thirteenth House—since history tells us the original Guardians were named after each House. The theorists claim that when the first humans arrived and the Guardian Stars fell to earth, Ophiuchus was the only one who resented his new, lower place. When he discovered the fall had cost the Guardians their immortality, he set about getting it back.

He betrayed the other Houses in the process, and when he was found out, the Guardians banished him, far away from our solar system.

Unfortunately, they couldn't kill him because he had already made himself immortal. But could any of this be real?

Some believers claim Ophiuchus started out as a brilliant healer, full of compassion for mankind. They say he was searching for death's cure to protect all people—not just himself—and that the other Guardians misconstrued him. If that's true, what would drive him to murder now?

I let go of the Ring, and I'm back on the floor beneath the glimmering Ephemeris. I want to tell Nishi what I learned in the Collective Conscious, but before leaving I consult the spectral map one more time. Staring into the lights' depths, I feel my way into the view of the Psy that only the Ephemeris can show—the view from the stars.

As soon as I'm Centered, the room darkens, as if the Dark Matter were spreading. I spring to my feet and whirl around, searching for the cause—until I see it.

Dark Matter has swallowed House Virgo.

As I watch, the cloud of blackness expands to the double constellation, House Gemini. There are *two* attacks on the way.

I start to pull out of the astral plane, but then I hear whispering in my head, like someone is trying to communicate with me in the Psy. Except that kind of communication only works through the Ring—and the metallic silicon isn't warm, nor is the buzzing in my finger calling to me.

This voice is coming from the Ephemeris. Which is impossible.

I follow the sound, as if I'm an object in Space being sucked by its gravitational pull. The voice is coming from Helios. I reach a hand out to the burning mass and dip my fingers in its yellow light.

Then I vanish.

11

I'M NOT IN THE SHADOW WORLD, and I'm not in the Ephemeris. . . . I'm in a kind of passage through Space. Objects are whizzing by me—meteoroids, stars, debris. Everything is moving too fast, like I'm in a slipstream.

Who are you?

The commanding voice booms through the wind tunnel, and an inhuman coldness grips my heart.

Rho Grace. Guardian of the Fourth House, Cancer.

There are stories about the original Guardians that say they didn't use Rings to communicate through the Psy. The stories claim they could manipulate Psynergy without external aids. After all, they were once part of the night sky.

Ophiuchus? I chance.

The instant I speak the name, I glimpse a face. A face from my childhood nightmares.

Colorless, hairless, with eyes as black as the night—the thirteenth Guardian has features carved from ice. He flutters in the wind like a clear flame. *You are a child. A girl. How dare you look upon me? How did you access this dimension?*

I heard a voice . . . coming from Helios.

Impossible! I glimpse a hand reaching toward me through the darkness. Then his whole body blinks into view, solid and glassy. *You are a mere mortal. You could not have heard me. Now I will learn the truth for myself.*

His hand is so close I almost dodge—then I remember. He can't touch me in here.

Why did you attack—

But I never get the rest of my question out. His frosty fingers close around my head and squeeze.

I scream as his icy grip burns through me. This can't be happening—it's not real, he can't be touching me—

And yet, I can sense him probing through my thoughts, reviewing my memories. I struggle against him, but he's like a block of ice. He pulls me in closer, and I see his tongue melting and refreezing in his mouth.

So you are on my tail, are you? His touch infects me with winter, and I feel every organ and muscle within me frosting over.

Let go of me!

Shockingly, he does.

You are no threat. They will never believe you. He glares at me, his eyes like black holes. *Even still: Speak of me again, and you will die.*

I'm trembling so hard, I can barely feel my fingers as I reach around the floor blindly with my hand, trying to grip the black opal. When I find it, I shut the Ephemeris down.

Once the starry projection blinks off, the phantom vanishes, and the room is gray and ordinary again. I rub my head. The pain where he gripped me is gone.

I have no idea how any of that happened—but there's no time to wonder. I have to warn Virgo and Gemini they're next.

Speak of me again, and you will die. The ice man's threat clangs through my skull.

But whatever the risk, I can't let Ophiuchus ambush them the way he ambushed us. I have to tell the other Houses what's coming.

Opening my mind to fuse with the Psy, I touch my Ring and launch the urgent alarm. *Wake up! Virgo and Gemini are in danger! Ophiuchus was behind the attack on Cancer, and he isn't finished!*

Harsh squeals scramble my thoughts.

What's wrong with the Psy? I can't sense the communal mind. It's like it's not there anymore—but my Ring is heating up.

A voice hisses through the chaos of psychic noise, like a gravelly breath of wind. *I warned you not to speak.*

I gasp. Ophiuchus is in the Psy—any attempts I make to access it will make me vulnerable to him. I try to yank off my Ring, but it's stuck.

Bitter laughter grinds through my mind. *No one will believe you, little girl. And now you're going to die.*

With a hard pull, I wrench off the scorching Ring and throw it to the floor. Still barefoot, I grab my Wave and flee from the lecture hall, where half a dozen Zodai are working the nightshift. I must look wild, because they turn and gawk.

"Where's Mathias's room?"

As soon as I say the words, I realize Mathias is the wrong person. He's not going to be easy to convince. I'll need backup. "Actually, where's the girl from Sagittarius, Nishiko Sai?"

I follow one of the Zodai as she leads me down a bisecting corridor, to the girls' bunkroom. As we run, my thoughts tangle. If Ophiuchus strikes me here, he could kill everyone on Oceon 6. He could even attack our planet. I can't let that happen.

But I can't let him silence me either, or more innocent people will die. The Houses *must* be warned—immediately.

The Zodai leads me to one of the spokes of the wheel-shaped satellite. Nishi's quartered in a storage hold that's been commandeered as a dorm. About twenty folding cots are wedged into the space, and the light's almost too dim to see who's who.

While the bewildered Zodai waits near the door, I tiptoe among the sleeping bodies, searching for Nishi. Finally, I spot her black hair spilling across her pillow, and I shake her awake.

"Huh? Who is it?"

"Nish—it's me. Hurry."

My voice is like a shot of wake-up gas because she shoots up, sleep forgotten, and follows me outside.

"That research you've been doing, is it with you?"

"Always." She touches the heavy Tracker on her wrist.

"Beam me anything new you find, okay? I'm going to need it."
I unfold my Wave and mate it with her Tracker for a download of
what she's found so far. "The blast on Thebe was definitely triggered by the Thirteenth House."

Nishi's eyes go wide. "You saw that in the stars?"

"Virgo and Gemini are next. I have to warn them." I shut
my Wave and glance at the Zodai, who's watching us in confusion. Should I tell Nishi about Ophiuchus's threat on my life?
The memory of his hatred blows through me again, and I feel
queasy. I peek up at the ceiling, half expecting to see a rain of
fire.

Nishi follows my gaze. "What is it, Rho?"

The Zodai is eavesdropping, and since I don't want to spread a
panic, I turn and face her. "Please take us to see Advisor Mathias
Thais, quickly."

Nishi frowns. "You want me to come, too?"

"Please. I need your help."

We sprint down the corridor at top speed, and I try to sort
through the chaos in my mind. Two things I know for certain. One,
Ophiuchus will strike Virgo and Gemini very soon, and I have to
warn them. Two, he's determined to stop me from speaking up,
which could mean striking me here.

I can't Wave the other Houses because holograms can be faked.
I can't use the Psy because Ophiuchus will kill me before I get the
words out. There's only one option left.

I see the answer in my mind, but I don't want to face it. After
everything that's happened, home is where I want to be.

I've never left the Crab constellation, and I have no special skills outside the Psy—the one place I now have to avoid. I've *no* business traveling through Space.

But I have to draw Ophiuchus away. The only way to save home is to leave it.

12

MATHIAS ANSWERS ON THE FIRST KNOCK.

When he opens the door, his dark hair is mussed and his collar's undone, like he passed out in the middle of working. Nishi and I dart in.

"Before you disagree, hear me out," I start, breathing hard from our run. "I was just reading the Ephemeris when I saw a warning for Virgo and Gemini. And then—when I was leaving—I heard this voice, and it's just what Nishi and I thought! Someone from the Thirteenth House caused our moons to collide—"

"Slow down," says Mathias, cupping my shoulder firmly. "What—"

"I can't slow down. He's going to strike Virgo and Gemini next."

"Who?"

"Ophiuchus."

Mathias's expression settles into an uneasy grimace, but I refuse to see it.

I describe everything I saw in the Ephemeris: the Dark Matter around Virgo and Gemini, the voice inside Helios, the phantom made of ice and wind . . . but I hold back his death threat. Mathias—I mean, my Advisors—will never let me go if they know someone's trying to . . . to murder me.

"I have to warn them," I say, shaking my head to refuse the desk chair he pulled out for me. He keeps his hand on my shoulder, and it feels like the only thing anchoring me to the ground. "I can't wait another moment—"

"Rho, settle down."

The soothing quality of Mathias's voice is different from what it was when I showed up. The more upset I get, the calmer he becomes. This is going exactly how I *didn't* want it to.

I take a few breaths and make my voice as even and sane-sounding as I can. "Please, Mathias, I'm asking you to trust me—"

"Where did you leave your shoes?" The way he asks the question, it's clear he isn't listening.

The fact that being barefoot makes me less trustworthy to Mathias is so ridiculous that I'm suddenly angry. The current of emotion takes control of my vocal cords, and I can't hold my feelings back. "I know you don't think I should have been made Guardian."

His whole face slackens like it's been slapped. Even Nishi edges along the wall, like she doesn't want to be contaminated by the conversation. What I'm going to say next will only make it worse, but even if it costs me his friendship—a friendship I fought hard to earn—I can't let Mathias ignore my warnings. Not if it means more people will die.

"You thought it should have been you."

His face flushes dark and he backs away, letting his hand fall off my shoulder. "We each have our duty, Guardian." His voice comes out low and taut. "I know mine."

My heart hammers its dissent to what I've done. I want to take back what I said and beg his forgiveness. But there are too many lives in my hands to stop and worry about my own.

"If that's true," I say, "then as your Guardian, I'm asking—I'm *begging*—you to *trust me*. Nishi, could you show him your files?"

She unpeels herself from the wall and goes through all the literature with him on her Tracker. The whole time, Mathias reads the red holograms with stony eyes, and I realize I've gone about this wrong. Angry Mathias is no better than skeptical Mathias.

"If Ophiuchus is immortal, why haven't we heard from him before?" he asks. "Why has he waited all this time to get his vengeance?" His hardened tone means I won't get anywhere with him fast.

I glance up at the ceiling, half expecting Ophiuchus to blow it apart and send us floating into soundless Space. Every minute, he gets closer to his next attack. Time for plan B.

"Mathias, it's fine if you don't believe me, but I need you to find me a ship. Something with an autopilot that even someone who's never flown could fly."

He snaps his gaze from me to Nishi, gauging how serious I am by her reaction. When she doesn't contradict me, Mathias turns and pours me a glass of water from the carafe near his bed. "You've been up too many hours, Rho. This was an emotional night, and you're not thinking straight."

I brush off the glass he offers me. "You're not hearing me! I'm going to change into my compression suit, and by the time I return, I need a ship. I'm leaving immediately."

"Take it easy." Mathias sets down the water and digs into a bin. He pulls out a pair of socks. "Sit down."

"No."

He pivots me around by the shoulders and pushes me down on the bed.

"Mathias, stop—" My protest dies in my throat when he kneels and starts sliding the socks on my feet. His hands are warm and gentle, and when he's done, he meets my gaze. His blue eyes are soft, and I know this time I'm looking at my friend, and not the Zodai who doubts me.

"Please say you believe me, Mathias."

He doesn't look away, and as I watch the transformation in his eyes again, I realize the person Mathias is fighting is himself. Like me, he wants so much for us to be on the same side in every situation.

But we're not.

"I believe that you believe," he whispers.

The thing I'd been trying to avoid since being named Guardian is now unavoidable. I will always have Mathias's allegiance and protection . . . but I don't have his trust.

"Let's consult Admiral Crius," he says, standing up.

"We don't have time," I argue, also rising. "He'll laugh in my face."

Mathias starts moving his lips, conversing through the Psy, and I wring his hands in panic. "Stop! Ochus is in there. He'll hear you."

"All right. Relax. I'll use my Wave." With a patient sigh, Mathias takes the clam from his pocket, unfolds it, and calls my three most senior Advisors. I hope this way is Ochus-proof.

Ten minutes later, Crius, Agatha, and the holographic Dr. Eusta meet us in the lecture hall. I've changed into my skintight black compression suit, my Wave and the black opal in my pocket. I pick up my Ring from the floor and stuff it in with the rest.

My hair is still long and wavy like a mermaid's, the way Leyla styled it, and I find myself wishing I could have said goodbye to her and Lola. I packed the Zodai suit they made me, along with the velvety makeup and glossing hair spray. Mathias's distrust tonight made one thing clear: When selling the unbelievable, appearances matter.

I waste the first five minutes of the meeting having to insist Nishiko be allowed to attend. So far, she's the only person who believes me, and I need an ally. When we're all seated, I repeat what I told Mathias. I show them Nishi's research, and I tell them my plan.

Only Dr. Eusta laughs. Crius snarls, and Agatha wants me to consult the Ephemeris once more . . . but I can't face that monster again.

"This ice phantom," says Crius. "You say you touched him?"

"I did. I felt his skin." I don't mention that he tried to crack my skull.

"And how does one touch a phantom?" Dr. Eusta's hologram asks. "I think the salt water you drank at the ceremony is addling your brain."

I throw up my hands. If my instructors had taken my test results seriously the first time, we might have saved lives. I can't let my Advisors' distrust condemn the people of Virgo and Gemini. I won't stay silent anymore, not when speaking out can make a difference. No one here can help me now.

In a nervous voice, very unlike her usual assertive one, Nishi speaks to my Advisors for the first time. "You should listen to Rho. You may regret it if you don't."

Mathias scrutinizes her, then me. I'm so furious with him that I'm trembling. Does he really think I would be going through this if I wasn't sure of what I saw? How can he swear his allegiance to me *on his Mother's life*, and a few hours later turn his back when I need him the most?

He's just like Dean Lyll, Admiral Crius, Dr. Eusta. . . . They don't take my readings seriously because they don't take me seriously. They don't respect me. *Mathias* doesn't respect me.

He seems to read the emotions in my eyes, because he turns to my Advisors and—to my bewildered relief—says, "Would it do any harm to alert the other Houses? Just to be safe?"

Dr. Eusta shakes his head, only it's more of a jerk. "That would completely undermine our credibility."

I have to make a deliberate effort not to hit something. "We

Cancrians are people of honor," I plead. "Twenty million of our citizens have just died. How many more will die on Virgo and Gemini if we don't warn them to take precautions?"

Crius crosses his legs. "The Houses don't have a history of mutual trust. When they hear this overblown tale, they may suspect us of treachery."

I feel the short hairs on my neck standing on end. "Look, you chose me to be Guardian. My job is to read the stars, and I have. We can't wait longer."

Agatha rests her cane across her knees. "Mother's right. We must take her word on faith. Let's send the alert."

I blink, stunned by her support, by the sudden reversal of the tide. She touches her Ring and moves her lips, and I spring over and grip her hand. "He's in the Psy. He'll hear you!"

She stares at me, wide-eyed. "Then how do you propose we do this?"

"An encrypted Wave," suggests Mathias. "Or we could send a hologram."

"They won't believe a hologram." When she says this, Nishi looks directly at Dr. Eusta.

"Exactly," I say. "*Trust Only What You Can Touch.* Holograms can be counterfeit, and encryptions aren't foolproof. I have to go in person to prove my warning is real."

"You'll go *yourself?*" When I nod, Agatha leans back in her chair. She seems to be studying me with new interest.

"Impossible!" barks Crius. "Our people need you here. We'll send someone else."

"Who?" I ask. "Which one of you believes what I'm saying?"

For a minute, no one speaks. Anyone could read the doubt on my Advisors' faces.

"I'm the one who saw Ophiuchus. I'm the only one they'll believe." When they still look doubtful, I stand up and say, "I need a ship with an autopilot."

"Out of the question!" roars Dr. Eusta.

"I agree. It's far too risky," says Agatha, and now the tide's turned back against me.

"Do you think I want to leave home?" I snap, for the first time sounding semi-hysterical to myself. I take a deep breath and with my eyes closed say, "We can't stand by while Virgo and Gemini are attacked." I turn to Mathias and make my voice deeper and steadier. "Advisor Thais, I order you to find me a ship that I can take to the other Houses, alone. *Please.*"

He glares at me, and while we stare, no one interrupts. Then he starts speaking soundlessly, and as the others begin to do the same, Nishi pulls me aside. "Don't leave me behind, Rho. You said I could help."

I reel her in for a tight hug. "Nishi, I do need your help. I need you to spread the word."

Beneath her tangled hair, her amber eyes grow wide. "How far?"

"Start with my Advisors. Keep trying to convince them, but don't stop there. Tell everyone you can, in as many Houses as possible, because we're all in danger. Try contacting members of 13—they won't help your credibility with the rest of the Zodiac, but they'll have more information than what we know, and maybe there's something that can help us. Send me everything you find out."

Her eyes shine with tears. "Stay safe out there."

I nod. "Take care of Deke. And Kai."

Crius drums his fingers on the table. "If you insist on this mad journey, we'll tell the people you're raising disaster relief funds. We don't want to incite mass panic."

Anxiety lines Agatha's face. "Come back to us soon, Mother."

"I think you're all insane." Dr. Eusta's hologram blinks and vanishes.

Mathias strides to the door and swings it open for me. "I've commandeered the fastest ship on the dock. A visiting bullet-ship. It should be fueled and ready by the time we reach the hub."

"We?"

He steps forward, until I'm swallowed by his shadow. "Your training isn't finished. And besides, you'll need a pilot."

This flight could be suicide. I can't let Mathias come with me.

"I'm sorry, but I'm doing this alone."

His indigo eyes flash. "There are no self-flying ships. Either I go with you, or you don't go at all."

I bite my lip. There's no other way.

"Welcome aboard."

13

WHEN I WAS EIGHT, Stanton used to give me rides on his sail-board. I remember the feel of the board pressing against my belly as I lay on it, sprawled between Stanton's feet, while he danced around, manhandling the sail.

One day when he wasn't looking, I took the sailboard out by myself. I almost couldn't lift the heavy sail, but as soon as the wind caught, I went zooming across the water. Salt stung my eyes, and I felt free and—for the first time in my short life—*young*.

It was only when my foot slipped and the sail slapped down in the waves that I looked back toward home. Kalymnos was a thin black line on the distant horizon, and every second, the offshore wind was carrying me farther away. I was lucky people on a passing boat spotted me.

The terror I felt that day on the water comes back to me now. Mathias and I are thousands of kilometers out from Cancer, so far away that the full shape of our Crab constellation is visible. I've never seen the real thing before. I've never been this far from home.

We're sealed in the nose of a bullet-shaped craft, shooting toward Gemini, our nearest neighbor. I just hope we get there in time.

Now that we're alone in the sky, I decide to activate the black opal. I need Ophiuchus to see I've left Cancer. If he's going to attack me, better he do it here.

My muscles are clenched so tight, they ache. I need to program an escape capsule for Mathias to ensure he'll survive this—only I've never programmed anything in my life. I'll just have to shove him into a capsule when Ophiuchus shows up and trust that Mathias can take it from there.

The rounded front nose of the bullet-ship is capped in thick, diamond-hard glass, creating a fishbowl at the bow, and that's where I'm floating in midair and peering into Space, like a damselfish confronting infinity. Behind me, Mathias is monitoring an arc of control screens at the helm. Now and then, he glances up, and our eyes meet. He looks pale and tired.

I'm too nervous to be tired. My black opal is clipped to a peg so it can't float free, and its ovoid hologram of starry light fills the ship's glass nose with its radiant map of the universe. Just beyond the glass, the real universe cradles our ship.

Like most spacecraft, this ship has handrails and safety belts for use in zero gravity, and Mathias has his legs hooked around the pilot's seat while he works. Meanwhile, I float free on my back, stargazing.

I deliberately slow my breaths and relax my muscles, trying to open my inner eye. The hologram shimmers over the black fabric of my space suit, dappling my body with stars. For the past hour, I've been focusing on the region of the Thirteenth House.

"What do you see?" asks Mathias.

I rub my eyes. "Nothing so far."

Mathias is programming the ship's shield to defend us. Deep Space is full of hazards—pirates, foreign surveillance drones, cosmic radiation, stray junk, and debris. He says if we're threatened, this bullet-ship will fly faster than a Capricorn can think—and it even has a cloaking veil. He was surprised he could hack the controls, considering the sophistication of the computer system.

"We're entering the Double," says Mathias from the helm. "Have you planned what you'll tell them?"

"No clue." I float upright and stretch my spine, staring out at real Space through the ship's nose. "Apparently I'm no good at this."

"Actually, you can be pretty forceful sometimes."

Still facing away from him, I say, "I haven't convinced you."

He doesn't speak for so long that I worry I've offended him. "Rho." At the sound of his low baritone, I turn to find him floating just a few feet behind me. "I listen to everything you say."

"That's not it," I say, shaking my head. I struggle with the words. I want to tell him I know he's loyal and will always support me, but his allegiance only makes things worse. If sense of duty, and not trust, is what compels him to follow me, then I'm forcing his free will—and how is that better?

But I can't say any of it. Sometimes Mathias makes me so angry that I'll revert into a toddler who can't form sentences. I wonder if it's because we stayed silent for so many years that now we don't know how to talk to each other.

"I need to keep looking, he could have attacked already," I mumble, floating back to the Ephemeris. Our silence stretches longer, and soon Mathias is programming protections at the helm again, and I'm scanning the black opal's imitation Space.

The engines emit a quiet hum, and the piloting screens flicker soft blue light. The map revolves above me hypnotically, and after a while, I give up. Ochus isn't coming.

"My lady."

My head jerks up, and I nearly do a somersault in midair.

There's a guy with white-streaked blond hair and large green eyes coasting into our ship's glass nose. His expensive suit bears the Libran coat of arms.

"What . . . what are you doing here?" I ask, reaching out to touch Hysan Dax, to see if he's real. When my hand is in front of him, he holds it and kisses my skin again. An Abyssthe-like rush shoots up my veins.

"Happy to already be of service."

Mathias eases in front of me, shielding my body with his. He's holding some kind of device in his palm, oval-shaped and silver bright. A *weapon?*

"I scanned this ship," he says in a clipped, military voice, pointing the device at Hysan. "How did you stow away?"

"You misunderstand." Hysan's face is still pleasant, but his eyes harden when they land on Mathias. "You're on *my* ship."

Mathias draws himself up, ramrod straight in midair. "Emergency requisition. You were notified to vacate."

Hysan's centaur smile widens. "*Equinox* is a Libran emissary ship. You can't confiscate diplomatic property."

"By galactic law, this ship is under emergency orders from the Cancrian Zodai Guard." Mathias bites off his words in sharp, precise syllables. "Please get to your capsule, and we'll launch you in any direction you choose."

"Or maybe I'd prefer to launch you." The pleasantness in Hysan's face flashes dangerously. A different expression rises to the surface, a counterbalance to his charm.

I've never seen Mathias lose his composure, but a muscle in his cheek is quivering. I use the handrail to pull myself between them. "Hysan, we're sorry we took your ship. We're on an emergency mission, and I hate that in our haste we've put you in danger. *Please* get in your capsule, and we'll return your ship to you when we're done."

I swallow, thinking of darker outcomes. "Or Cancer will send you an IOU."

Hysan bursts into laughter, and his return to good humor is so genuine that he seems to radiate warmth. "An IOU," he repeats, his cheeks still dimpled and his eyes looking at me in a way I've never been looked at before. Like I'm someone who might amaze him.

Then he turns to the screen on the wall nearest him, presses a few buttons, and suddenly my hand is heavy with gravity, and my feet hit the ground—as does Mathias's Wave, my boots, and Mathias himself.

"Simulation gravity," says Hysan, shrugging. "Makes things easier."

Mathias stands and brushes himself off. He definitely looks impressed, even if he'll never admit it out loud.

I cross my arms and stare at Hysan. "Where have you been this whole time? We've been flying for hours."

He punches in a few more keys on the screen. "I was asleep in my cabin when I awoke to find you stealing my personal transport." He turns to Mathias. "You now have access to the full navigation controls, by the way."

Mathias spins around to the holographic control panel, and ten new screens pop up beside the five he was staring at, each one offering myriad more options. The screens have strange headings, like *'Nox's Brain Powers, Recovery Requires Review,* and *Shielding from Shadows.*

While an entranced Mathias scrolls through the settings, I start to speak in a whisper so only Hysan can hear me. "This ship seems too advanced for Mathias to have broken through its security as quickly as he did."

Hysan's green gaze grows so soft, I can almost feel its touch. "What are you saying, my lady?"

A moment ago, I wanted his attention. But now that he's right here—so close he takes up most of my view—I wish he'd look anywhere else. "I-I think you knew we were coming aboard, and you gave us permission."

In the corner of his right iris, I spy a small, star-shaped bloom of gold among the green. I've heard about this—it's the Libran version of a Wave, called a Scan. Librans use it to scan new information into a special storage space in their minds. It's housed in a small chip that's implanted in their brains when they turn twelve. They can also use it to send each other messages or review stored information.

"I told you I'd be at your service," he whispers. "Always."

"Always is a long time."

"Wisely observed, my lady."

I laugh. "I guess you better start calling me Rho."

"We're approaching planet Argyr now," announces Mathias, his voice cold. I feel my cheeks go pink as I meet his disapproving stare.

"Argyr?" asks Hysan. "That morass of debauchery? We can't take Lady Rho—"

Whatever Hysan says next is drowned by a low, thin wail coming from my Ephemeris. I whip around, and so does Hysan. A fiery, invisible pulse buzzes through my cells—just like the night of our concert on Elara—and the unnatural squeal of the black opal scrapes my eardrums.

Mathias leaps over to catch me as I cover my head and crumple. "Rho, what's wrong?"

"Don't you hear it?" I shout. The pain makes my jaw clench, and I can no longer speak. Beside me, Hysan is also clutching his head, wincing on the ground. He hears it, so why doesn't Mathias?

Suddenly our ship makes a violent turn and starts zigzagging back and forth, flinging us into the walls and each other. The accelerating engines howl, and when the whining dials back, Hysan and I lift our heads. He flies to the control screens. "*Equinox*, report!"

When the ship's brain starts blinking data, Mathias joins him at the helm, and I grab the black opal and head for the jettison tube. The Ephemeris flares through my fingers in bright searing rays, the Psynergy trying to break through from the other side. Its heat stings my hand.

Hysan calls out, "What kind of attack is this? I see no missiles!"

I keep pulling myself along the rail toward the jettison tube, but the ship's veering so erratically, it's hard to move. Suddenly the hot black opal slips from my hand, and the Ephemeris blossoms outward again to its full ovoid shape.

From its center, Ochus's inky eyes stare back at me.

14

COLORLESS, TRANSLUCENT, OCHUS SHIFTS FROM one grotesque form to another, billowing tall and thin like a wraith carved from ice, fracturing into particles and just as quickly reforming.

I told you what I would do if you spoke of me.

Phantom fingers whisper over my face. I try to push Ochus away, but my hands pass through his hazy form. How can he touch me when I can't touch him?

"Rho!" shouts Mathias. "What's happening?"

On some level, I'm aware Mathias has seized my body. I even hear the anxiety in his voice. And somewhere behind him, Hysan is barking commands to his ship.

But I feel removed from all that. Ochus holds my attention. *Murderer!* I lash out, trying to punch him, but again my hands pass right through.

His fingers cinch around my neck. *Ah, such passion. Delightful. Do you feel my touch? Am I real?*

I twist and kick, but he holds me tight. The more I struggle, the more his fingers bruise my throat.

You will not stop me. You're out of time. He grips me harder, cutting off my air. Black spots start to crowd my vision. Desperately, I sweep my hands around, searching for the black opal.

Hysan seems to guess my thought because I see his hazy form through the monster, and he puts the stone in my hand. As soon as I touch its hidden key, the Ephemeris shuts down, and the ice man vanishes.

I cough and gag, then inhale long raking gulps of air. Mathias is holding me and massaging deeply into my skin, trying to help my circulation. Hysan rushes back to the controls.

The ship is jerking through Space. We're still under attack. "Mathias, I'm okay, go help him," I gasp.

"Right."

He joins Hysan at the controls while I drag myself toward the jettison tube to get rid of the black opal. Twice Ochus has used it to find me, and I never want to see that face again. As the ship careens forward, I open the tube.

Hysan runs over to me. "What are you doing?"

"I have to ditch this opal."

He seizes my wrist. "No, you don't realize what it is."

The ship starts talking, and Hysan sails back to the helm. He speaks to *Equinox* in terse phrases, more like a seasoned Zodai Guard than a diplomatic envoy. "'*Nox!* Engage all shields. Run progress scans. Activate maximum protections, and switch to energy-conservation mode."

Before I can toss the stone, I hear the crackling whir of the shield generator, and every opening in the hull seals itself, including the jettison tube. I clutch the opal tight. We're veiled, hidden from view, only a faint mirage in the night-black void. . . . No ordinary eyes can see us. But are we concealed from Ophiuchus?

Tension closes like a fist in my chest. The ship stops rolling, and for a full minute, we hold steady on course. I can almost hear *Equinox*'s artificial brain ticking and waiting for the next attack. My hand cramps from gripping the rail as we wait through another taut five minutes.

"Setting new course," says Hysan, breaking the silence. We do an abrupt ninety-degree turn that hurls all three of us sideways, and the ship thrusts off at top speed, going anywhere but here.

Mathias rushes over to me, concern written across his face. I've never seen him frightened like this. "Rho, I thought you were having a seizure."

"Ochus tried to strangle me." Now that it's over, I realize I'm still weak from the encounter.

Mathias turns even whiter. "What are you talking about?"

"You didn't see him?"

"I didn't see anyone." He slides his thumb over my neck, but oddly, my throat doesn't hurt anymore. "No bruises . . . do you feel pain?"

"No," I mutter, the thoughts in my head growing fuzzy from his touch. He's never been so openly affectionate with me before.

I've only gotten to known Mathias this last week, but when he's around, my heart acts like this ship fighting off a Psy attack—its beat bounces all over my rib cage, and I can't decipher the melody. Each time I try to figure out my feelings, I come up against the same wall: I admire him . . . I'm attracted to him . . . I like him . . . and *wall*.

I can't go deeper than that.

Still gripping the black opal, I say, "Let's not use this Ephemeris again." Ophiuchus knows I've left Oceon 6 now. That's all I needed.

"I'm sorry," whispers Mathias. "Sorry I didn't protect you."

His apology haunts me long after he returns to the helm. He asks forgiveness for pain he didn't cause, but he's fine with under-valuing what's in my head. He thinks failing to save me is worse than not trusting me. I've just found the wall: Mathias doesn't see me as someone with insights to offer—he sees me as a little sister who can't be left alone.

While he and Hysan work together at the screens, I sit near the nose looking out, trying to think of more important things. Like how the Helios I'm going to earn the Houses' trust when I can't even earn my friends'.

We change course repeatedly, but there are no more attacks. "Your veil worked remarkably well." The sound of my voice is strange even to me after so much silence.

"Of course it did," says Hysan, his cocky smirk never far from reach. He slides his hand across the console, beaming. "Can this day get any better? 'Nox and I get shelled by invisible bombs, right after a beautiful pirate steals our heart."

"I'm flattered," says Mathias. How can they joke when Ophiuchus is so strong, and we have no way of defeating him?

Hysan stares into my face like he's reading it. "What weapon can attack through the Psy?"

His words startle me. "Did you see him, too?"

"Who?" Hysan reaches for my black opal.

I draw away, gripping it tight. "If we use this, he'll find us again."

"He?" Hysan frowns. "I think you have more to tell me."

I zip the opal into my pocket, next to my Wave. Again, I probe my throat for nonexistent bruises. "Have you heard of Ophiuchus?"

Surprisingly, Hysan has heard the theory of a Thirteenth House. He says the secret society 13 has a strong base on Libra. Among my friends, I'm usually the one who knows the most facts about our universe. Yet for all the knowledge Mom drilled into me, she never mentioned anything about another House in the Zodiac.

When I explain how I saw Ochus in the Ephemeris, and how he's responsible for the recent disasters in our world and the attack on our moons, I begin to see why I've continuously failed to convince Mathias. It isn't easy to convey the terror I felt in the ice man's presence when all I have are words.

As I speak, Mathias busies himself at the screens, but Hysan pays close attention. Instead of mocking my story, he seems to be giving it earnest thought. When I finish, he says, "Early astrologers said the first Guardians could project an alternate node of their being through the Ephemeris, because they themselves were once objects represented there."

Mathias grimaces at his screens. "That's just a theory; no one knows if they actually spoke that way."

Hysan looks only at me. "Even so, it fits what you're describing."

"But then . . . you believe me?" My voice is so small it probably undermines any credibility I have, but I don't care. I haven't registered anything beyond the fact that Hysan hasn't laughed or scowled at me yet.

Slight lines form on Hysan's face, framing his confusion. "My lady, why in the Zodiac would I not?"

The ship seems to grow smaller the longer the conversation stays suspended. While Hysan tries to figure out what he missed, Mathias avoids my gaze.

Hysan didn't jump to doubt. He just met me, and still it came easier to him to trust me than not.

"Have you shared your findings with the Psy?" asks Hysan.

"I can't. Ochus is in there listening."

"Let's not take irrational leaps, Rho," says Mathias, and I can tell by the red splotches on his face that he's struggling to keep his emotions in check. "I know it's not what you want to hear, but I'm not the only one who can't accept your theory. Reasonable people don't believe in Ophiuchus."

I want to shake him, but instead I cross my arms and glare. "Hysan believes me."

Mathias's jaw shakes dangerously, and he finally snaps at me. "Really, Rho? He's just a kid!"

I don't say anything in response.

A kid. Hysan is my age, if not a year or two older. *A kid. A kid. A kid.* I say the phrase so many times in my head that it starts to sound like a tune. In that tune lies the truth of how Mathias sees me: He treats me like his kid sister because to him that's who I am. *A kid.*

Hysan's voice cuts through the dead space. "Maybe 'Nox can convince your . . ." He looks to Mathias like he's searching for the right word. *"Lady of Robes?"*

Mathias glares at him, and Hysan calls up a holographic log. "'Nox has Psynergy sensors that can detect a Psy attack."

Mathias studies the arcane column of symbols. After scrolling for several seconds, he frowns. "I'm not denying there's been Psy interference or that someone isn't after Rho. I just don't think we're blaming the right person."

I wall off my annoyance with Mathias. Something else is bothering me—how we got away. Shutting off the Ephemeris got rid of Ochus's form, but how did the veil shake off the Psy attack on the ship? "You have a Psy shield," I blurt, looking to Hysan for confirmation.

He nods. *"How?"* I ask, awed.

"'Nox and I like to invent things," he mutters, growing distracted by something on a screen.

His green-gold eyes start to wane, as if his attention were literally fading from the present moment. But before I can press Hysan, Mathias injects in a suspicious voice, "It's unusual for a diplomat to carry such a specialized shield."

"I like my privacy."

There's a finality in Hysan's tone that makes me drop the subject. I'm glad to know the three of us are protected, but Ophiuchus could use a Psy attack to hit Virgo or Gemini at any time, in any way, from anywhere. This trip is feeling more hopeless by the moment.

"I'll have to convince the Houses to cut off communications with the Psy . . . somehow," I muse.

"Your enemy attacked our ship because he means to silence you," says Hysan, frowning, piecing together what he can.

"We can still turn back," offers Mathias.

"No, we can't. Not when the Houses are at risk." If Mathias actually believed me, he'd understand.

"What Houses?" asks Hysan.

"All of them. Virgo and Gemini will be next."

Hysan listens without moving, then turns and speaks to his ship. "*'Nox*, set an immediate course for Libra."

Mathias instantly countermands the order. "Gemini's our destination."

"My duty is to warn my own House about this threat," says Hysan, rounding on him.

Mathias draws himself erect. "And Gemini gets no warning?"

In a low voice, I say, "Hysan." At the sound of his name, he turns and looks at me. "I need to warn Gemini and Virgo. They're in the most danger right now. After that, we can go to Libra. Okay?"

His chin tips up, and I realize his pride is so great he might disagree.

Instead, he bends forward in a low bow. "As you wish, my lady."

15

TO SETTLE MY MIND, Hysan locks my black opal and our three Rings in his strongbox. We even drop in my Wave with the tutorial Ephemeris, to be extra safe.

It seems impossible, but Ophiuchus has discovered how to bend Psynergy to his will, so we're shutting ourselves off from everything that could tether us to the Psy. I even make Hysan and Mathias promise to avoid sending or receiving holograms, at least for now. So we're flying dark. And with no news from the outside world, worry is starting to infect my every thought.

Our zigzag flight during the attack took us far out from Gemini, but we're speeding back, and the constellation already fills our view. Even now I can't forget Mom's drills on the Double.

House Gemini has two colonized planets. The largest one, Hydragyr, is an airless cratered rock, but its mountains hold a trove of rare metals. The smaller planet, Argyr, has been terraformed to support a vast forest. The chief point Mom drummed into me was that Gemini is a House divided. The rich live in splendor on Argyr, while the vast majority of Geminin work in beryllium mines deep under the surface of Hydragyr.

Mathias is in his cabin napping; he and Hysan are taking turns at the helm. "Do you need a break?" I ask Hysan.

"No, but your company would be nice."

I sit beside him and stare at the screens. *'Nox's Brain Powers* has a litany of settings for the ship's artificial brain. *Shielding from Shadows* lists the various veils available, including those of the Psy variety.

"He doesn't believe you," says Hysan, as though we've been carrying on a conversation this whole time.

"Mathias?" I ask. "No. Neither do the rest of my Advisors. Right now, my only supporters are my best friend, Nishiko, who's a Sagittarian, and you, a Libran. The only people I can't convince are my own."

"The most crucial truths are always rejected before they're accepted," he says, gazing out at Space. "It's one of our greatest human flaws: arrogance. We look up and dare to assume we know, when the universe is unknowable." The words sound like they're coming from a deeper place than usual. "In my experience, it's better to keep an open mind and judge without prejudice . . . whenever I can."

There's an invitation in Hysan's voice to get to know him better . . . and the more he shares, the more I want to learn about him. I know I should leave my wall up, at least until he's revealed more about himself, but it's hard keeping my distance when every time he gets close, I find myself wanting to get closer.

"How very Libran of you," I say, pointing to the heading on one of the monitors. "I like your House's *Recovery-Requires-Review* approach."

"Always nice to meet a fan."

Librans are known for their pursuit of justice, and they believe education is the best path to achieving it. To recover from any blow or overcome any challenge, they recommend reviewing all information available and studying all of one's options, as an antidote to snap judgments and rash actions. "Do you know this one, too?" he asks.

A hologram beams out from the gold bloom on Hysan's iris. The text he's projecting is a children's morality tale from Libra.

> *When the letters of the alphabet began disappearing, word spread there was a murderer among their ranks. They agreed every letter with a sharp edge on its body was a suspect. This ruled out O, who was asked to be the judge. He put each letter on trial and eventually blamed X, who had the most violent appearance and the worst disposition of them all. The real killer went free.*
>
> *It was the eraser.*

For the Librans, the villain in the story is O because he judged without knowing all the facts. From this tale, students are supposed to list all the things O did wrong as a judge. They can say he didn't canvass broadly enough for suspects, or that he didn't widen his worldview to account for all possibilities, or anything else that comes to mind.

The point isn't the answer—it's for Libran children to brainstorm as many potential factors in a given situation, in the hopes of broadening their outlook and instilling objectivity as an early value.

"O . . . for Ophiuchus," says Hysan, shutting down the hologram. "I wonder why he's been biding his time, and why he's coming out of hiding now."

I know I should be relieved Hysan trusts me—and I am—but there's something strange about how easily he's accepted my story when compared to everyone else's reactions. "How did you get to be a diplomatic envoy at such a young age?" I ask.

"That's funny." But for the first time, he's not smiling. "I didn't peg you as someone who would ask that question."

His eyes seem to darken during moments when he's most present, but when his mind clouds over with other thoughts, like now, the green fades until his irises become as elusive as air. We're quiet again, and I realize he's touchier about his age than I am.

"You've been to Gemini before?" I ask, determined to keep the tone lighter from now on. There's enough tension on this ship already.

"Unfortunately," he says, his eyes still distant.

"Can you tell me about its Guardians?"

He nods. "'*Nox*, show us the Twins." A small holo-map of the Double constellation spins in the air above the helm. "Gemini's two Guardians are brother Caaseum and sister Rubidum, and they're at least three centuries old—but when you see them, you'll think they're twelve-year-olds. They use appalling procedures to maintain their youth."

"Three centuries? How can anyone live that long?" My mother told me about the Twins, and we touched on them at the Academy, but only very peripherally. Like every House, Gemini guards its secrets jealously, so they don't share all the details of their major discoveries.

"In the early days, Gemini led the Zodiac in scientific and humanitarian achievements," says Hysan. "They imagined solutions for every problem, and they brought a lot of those solutions to life. Then their House discovered cell regeneration, and holding on to youth became a Geminin obsession. Lots of aristocrats do it, but few take it to the Twins's extreme. The cost is beyond imagining, and so is the pain."

"How long can they live that way?"

"The longest anyone's lasted is about three hundred and fifty years. The Geminin Guardians are probably reaching their end."

Goosebumps ripple up my arms. The thought of living long enough to watch my family and friends die around me is depressing and lonely in a way that no other companionship could fix.

Hysan scans the blinking messages on the *Shielding from Shadows* screen. As he clicks through the entries, I ask, "How did you design a shield that repels Psynergy?"

He keeps studying the controls, looking preoccupied. Another screen blinks new data, and he speaks quietly to his ship. To me, he says, "We're about to land. Better alert your watchdog."

"He's my Advisor," I say defensively.

He hands me two metallic devices. "Take these collars. There's one for each of you."

"What do they do?"

"They're cloaking veils that project a mirage of invisibility. We should all wear them when we disembark until we're sure it's safe."

Before I can ask more questions, he turns and starts a long conversation with his ship, so I wend my way forward to reach the front tip of the nose. Ahead of us, the smaller Geminin planet, Argyr, shines like a green melon. When we get there, I'll have to explain my theory about Ophiuchus again, the theory Mathias still won't accept.

I peer through the glass, and the cold black eternity of Space makes me sad. I miss the Blue Planet. "Every world is beautiful from a distance," says Mathias, coming up beside me.

The sound of his musical voice still jostles my heart, though I'm not sure how I feel about him anymore. If he could be the guy with the soft eyes all the time, it'd be different. But I can't reconcile the person who swore his loyalty to me on his Mother's life—who risked his own life setting out on this mission—with the Mathias who distrusts me.

"What are those?" he asks, pointing to the thin metal collars.

After I explain, we put them on. "All this stealth technology," he whispers. "I suspect your Libran may be involved in espionage."

"*Espionage?*"

"Every House engages in it," he says, still whispering like Hysan can hear us. "Even Cancer has a secret service."

"We do?" It's hard to imagine Cancrian spies. We're not very good liars. "Well, aren't you glad this ship is veiled?" The question comes out like a challenge, and I realize I'm being as defensive of Hysan as I was of Mathias earlier.

"Of course," he says, forgetting to keep his voice down. "If it hadn't—if the shield hadn't shut down the Psy attack . . ."

He moves closer, and the raw look from earlier comes over his features. Seeing how much he cares about me makes my heart pump at hyperspeed. If he would just trust me in equal measure, things could be different.

Trust . . . the word reminds me there's something I haven't told Mathias yet. And it's time I confide in him fully—after all, even without believing, he's come this far.

"Mathias, I've put you in more danger than you know by letting you join me on this trip." I hesitate a moment, then I confess. "I didn't tell you earlier, but Ochus threatened to kill me if I spoke of him. In fact, if I do exactly what I'm doing now—warn the other Guardians—he pretty much guaranteed it."

Mathias blanches. "You predicted the attack on the ship? And you chose to do this anyway?"

"To warn the other Houses," I say, nodding. "Otherwise they'll be unprepared . . . like we were."

The mysterious expression that comes over him is like the one he wore when I mastered the Ring. "You're a truer Cancrian than I realized, Rho." Even though it's a compliment, his severe tone makes it sound like a criticism.

Crius and Agatha may disagree with me, but they stopped questioning my qualifications for Guardian when I passed their test.

Sometimes I feel like Mathias is still evaluating my candidacy.

"I'm sorry I didn't tell you about the risk sooner," I say.

He sighs, softness coming to the surface of his midnight-blue eyes. "I might not have believed you."

The ship rolls to the left, and we both reach out for the handrail. There's a change in the atmosphere, like we've just crossed an invisible barrier.

Real gravity is weightier than the ship's imitation brand, and our muscles grow heavier. I feel every part of my body, like I'm becoming more alive by the second. It's my first time on an alien world.

"Entering orbit," announces Hysan from the helm. "When we land, stay alert. . . . This is a place where nothing is as it seems."

16

AFTER STUDYING THE PLANET'S TERRAIN, Hysan decides
to dock in a wooded park outside the capital city. No one will see
our ship, he says, thanks to the cloaking veil. Argyr is a lush garden
planet with plenty of breathable air and decent atmospheric pressure, so we won't need compression suits. It's also massive enough
to exert a reasonable level of gravity.

I change into the Zodai suit Lola and Leyla made me, with the
four silver moons on the sleeve. Before leaving the ship, Hysan
activates our veil collars. The collars are networked, which enables
us to see each other, but to anyone else, we're invisible.

When the outer hatch opens, we're embraced in a warm bath
of humidity, and the first thing I notice is the sweet smell of the
air. I step onto loamy earth, birdsong echoing through a grove of
enormous tree trunks. Our Cancrian trees are mere reeds compared
to these giants.

"Let's be quick." Hysan sets off at a fast trot. He's lighter and thinner than Mathias, and he runs impressively fast in his expensive boots. The forest gives way to a belt of meadowland circling the capital city. We sprint single file through feathery, knee-high grasses, and when we draw close enough to see the buildings, I have to stop and shade my eyes.

Every surface ripples with stripes of color. Orange, blue, green, white, purple, brown—the color bands swirl in sinuous patterns over the rounded domes.

"Like it's made of rainbows," I say, repeating what I used to tell Mom when she'd show me pictures.

"It's agate," says Hysan, "mined from their other planet and transported at tremendous cost."

Mathias puts on a pair of lightweight field glasses and scans the east and west. He's holding that silver oval thing that may be a weapon, and when we take off running through the grass again, he stays close beside me.

The buildings are shaped like globes, with fanciful cupolas bulging in all directions. Windows bubble outward, gleaming in the sunlight. The city has no wall, no apparent defenses, and since we're invisible, it's easy to walk in. I think about our own unfortified islands, and I wonder how often Hysan, or other veiled travelers like him, has wandered unseen through our villages, spying on us.

With a shudder, I glance up at the sky. Does Ochus already have us in his sights?

Hysan winds us deeper into the city, through a warren of curving lanes, where we constantly dodge little kids on skates and hover-skis. From my lessons, I already knew the people of Gemini have coffee-colored eyes and lustrous tawny skin, ranging from salmon pink to deep burnt orange. What I didn't know was how bizarre it would be to walk through a world overrun with children.

In the shops and residences, I glimpse adults working as salespeople and household servants, but the streets are filled with kids, and their formfitting suits gleam in metallic patterns of brass, nickel, and platinum with accents of glittering jet. They're so androgynous it's hard to tell girls from boys.

Soon, we arrive at a broad plaza, dazzlingly white, where hundreds of small, elaborately dressed Geminin dash about, all wearing thick sunglasses and interacting with unseen people and things.

"This plaza is Gemini's Imaginarium." As Hysan explains, I remember. "People come here to interact with their own imaginations. When you're wearing the glasses, anything you envision in your mind becomes real . . . but only to you."

His words pull on my memories of Gemini, until it feels as though I've lugged Mom's lessons up from a long way down. "Holograms you can touch," I say, recalling the mnemonic I'd made up.

"The technology extends the length of the plaza, and it only works when paired with those heavyset glasses. As long as you feel the weight of the glasses on your nose, you know you're still in the Imaginarium. It's the only way to keep from going crazy."

Sounds like a protective measure that falls under the banner of *Trust Only What You Can Touch*. I scan the childlike people and realize not all of them look like they're enjoying themselves. Some are crying, others shouting, and a few are running from invisible monsters.

"There are two sides to the imagination," says Hysan, catching where my gaze has strayed.

"There are two sides to everything," I say. Only I meant every-one. Maybe I meant Mathias.

Or myself—after all, I never thought I could feel competing emotions for the same person. Or that I could be attracted to two people at the same time.

Mathias looks at me with questions in his indigo eyes. I turn away, hiding my answers.

Hysan leads us forward, toward one peculiar building, differ-ent from all the rest. Instead of a globe, this edifice is dull black and cone-shaped, sweeping upward to a sharp point. It's the tall-est building we see, so I think it must be House Gemini's royal court.

Zodai Guards in Gemini's orange-colored uniforms flank the entrance, wearing ceremonial swords, their eyes managing to look fierce despite their childlike stature. In our veils, we slip past unnoticed.

Inside, the hall is cool, dim, and quiet. Mathias puts away his field glasses but keeps the silver weapon half-concealed in his palm. He pivots and watches for danger, while Hysan strides ahead, walk-ing like he owns the place.

The vaulted ceiling echoes our footsteps, so we slow down and move quietly. We ride up a moving staircase, then dart along a bal-cony, peeking in through various doors. Images depicting aspects and characteristics from each House drown the walls and ceiling of each room, rendered in such detail that I could be persuaded this building contains the actual Zodiac—and that each of these doors opens up to our various worlds.

When I look into the room that depicts Cancer, I bite down on my inner lip to avoid crying out. The skyline over the Cancer Sea looks like it always did, our moons like four pearls on a string. The water is clean and roaring, and the pod cities light up the horizon with our gleaming, cascading buildings and sun-bleached streets. From this high up, they look like massive lily pads cradling our Cancrian communities in their palms. It's not easy closing the door on home.

"You see why I despise this place," Hysan hisses under his breath as we pass more rooms filled with children who are engaged in some version of playing, cuddling, or fussing. "These people are Gemini's leading families. Not one of them is less than a hundred years old, yet they behave like toddlers."

"They seem creative," I say. After all, we're in the land of imagination—and I've never seen anything like it.

A heavy scent hangs in the air, something fragrant and beguiling. It makes me dizzy and . . . dreamy.

"Don't breathe too deeply, my lady," says Hysan, glimpsing the change in my face. "They're using psychotropic drugs."

I wonder how I can avoid breathing.

"And before you make excuses for them," he says, "you should see the miners who pay for all this. Only the richest people can afford youth and imagination. The rest of the population ages and dies like the rest of us, and they spend their lives in the mines, unearthing the minerals that keep the rich rich. It's sick."

Hysan's right, but for a Libran, he's not being entirely fair. My mom's lessons taught me that mining is the highest-paid work on Gemini, so the mines are mostly filled with people who want to one day retire to this city and live like children again. There's a separate settlement in the caves of Gemini's other planet that's filled with people who aren't seeking an inhumanly long life. They're just normal humans who use their imaginations to build incredible cities within the rock.

We slip into another corridor, where the fragrant scent wafts from every door. Hysan stops at the entrance to a lavish room full of giggling centenarians. They're sprawled among cushions, watching a puppet show in an ornately carved theater the size of a dollhouse.

We stand at the front of the room, beside the small stage, invisibly looking out at the audience.

"There," whispers Hysan, pointing to the far back, where two especially gorgeous young people are ensconced together in a blue velvet puff pillow. They have skin as pale as the inside of a cantaloupe and curly copper hair. Their arms are draped around each other, and their cheeks rest together. I would guess they were in love, except they look exactly alike.

"Those are the Twins."

17

EMBRACED IN SIBLING AFFECTION, the Twin Guardians of Gemini look so angelic, they could be cherubs in a frieze—except for their tunnel-like eyes. Eyes so deep they're endless.

The puppet show either wraps or reaches intermission because the puppeteer scurries right past us. Everyone is applauding. "How should we introduce ourselves?" I whisper.

Hysan says, "How about we send a message requesting an audience and then reveal ourselves once they accept—"

"No more tricks." Mathias tugs at his veil collar. "How do I get this thing off?"

"We'll lose our advantage," whispers Hysan.

I shake my head. "Mathias is right. We came for their trust—how will it look if we don't give them ours?"

With a sigh, Hysan gives a quiet command. Our veils switch off, and twenty pairs of wide, coffee-brown Geminin eyes turn toward us. There's a hush, then a series of shrieks as some of them have meltdowns and others scatter away, like they're really frightened children.

"Sorry," I say feebly from the front of the room. "We . . . we apologize for our sudden appearance, but we come in friendship."

Instantly, the Twins spring up from their blue pillow. Their metallic costumes throw off brassy scintillations, and their faces shimmer with opalescent skin paint, the kind Deke's family manufactures. "Welcome!"

They speak in unison, in a cheerful singsong. "Holy Mother Rhoma, how delightful. We've been expecting you."

I freeze. "You have?"

They give a signal, and the remaining little Geminin scurry out, whispering and giggling. Arm in arm, the Twins sashay toward us, beaming. As we exchange the hand touch, one of them—the girl—says, "My name is Rubidum, and this handsome fellow is my brother, Caaseum."

Caaseum rises a few centimeters into the air and kisses my hand. I notice he's wearing levitation boots to enhance his height. "Rhoma Grace, what a privilege it must be to reign over a Cardinal House." Cardinal Houses mark the changes of the seasons, and each represents one of the four elements of life: Earth, Air, Fire, and Water. "We have so many questions for you!"

The Twins usher us off the stage and toward the pillows where they were seated. We pull over a few more, and we all sit down. The moment we're settled, I say, "I've come to warn you—"

"About an enemy as old as time," says Caaseum, nodding genially.

My eyebrows pull together in confusion. "How do you know?"

"Good Mother, why just this morning the stars showed an omen! Have you not been consulting?"

Mathias, Hysan, and I stare at him in shock. The depths of his eyes make me nervous. "You mean you've seen him?"

Caaseum shuts his eyes and presses a hand dramatically to his forehead, like a fortune-teller at a fair. "I've seen someone powerful in the Psy is challenging you, someone using a timeless weapon. That's why you've come, am I right?"

"He's going to attack your House using Dark Matter," I say firmly.

"Remarkable." Rubidium gives me a vivacious smile. "Admiral Crius said you were coming to raise relief funds, but this is much better. Tell us more. I love your accent."

Caaseum leans toward me. "Did you bring your stone with you?"

"My stone?" His change of topic addles me. "You mean my black opal? We left it on the ship."

"Black opal? Intriguing." Caaseum's eyes shine brighter. "The omen I saw was open to many interpretations. What I described is only one view. My Ephemeris may not be as precise as your stone. We should compare."

He opens his left hand, and the drawing on his palm starts to glow. The Geminin version of a Wave is a Tattoo. Each one is unique—in look and function—because every person designs and programs their own. When tiny stars spray upward from his palm, I yell, "No! Please don't use your Ephemeris!"

"Not use my Ephemeris?" He stares at me. "That's like telling a bullet-ship not to speed."

"Or telling a Sagittarian not to ask nosy questions," says Rubidum with a laugh. "Close your hand, brother. You're making our young friend uncomfortable."

"If you insist." Caaseum briefly slings his hand, and the glow in his palm vanishes.

I blink to clear my head. "Listen. Ophiuchus struck our world with a Psy attack. He made our moons collide. And your House may be next."

When they flinch back and stare at me, I launch right in, describing the Dark Matter, the pattern in the stars, and my encounters with Ochus. Next I explain the omens I saw for Houses Gemini and Virgo. "You need to build shelters. Make an evacuation plan. Ochus will show you no mercy."

"*Ochus?* Priceless. This could be an opera." Rubidum takes up a small musical instrument and rapidly plucks its strings, filling the air with melody. "My sources said your were quite a spinner of tales, and they weren't wrong."

"Tales?" I have to force myself not to shout when I say, "Twenty million of my people are dead!"

Rubidum plays more vigorously. Her fingers fly along the strings. "You want revenge."

"Absolutely," I say. "But first I want to make sure your people are safe."

"Murder and vengeance, a classic. I hear the theme song now."

"Can it, Rubi," says her brother. "Our guest is in mourning."

"I'm aware of that." Rubidum's music grows darker, stormier, and her eyes seem to hollow out like a pair of deep caves. "Revenge is a tale that never ends. It goes round and round forever, and no one finds peace." She plays a run of soft descending notes. "It's very sad, what happened to your moons, but as the years go by, you'll gain perspective on these ups and downs. No one escapes the vagaries of nature."

"Nature had nothing to do with this." I glance from one twin to the other. "Ophiuchus ravaged my world, and he'll do the same to yours."

Caaseum inches toward me. "Let's consult your black opal. I've heard fascinating reports of its powers."

"You should watch for abnormally high traces of Psynergy," I press on. "Do you have a Psy shield?"

"Never heard of such a thing." Caaseum tilts his head. "Interesting idea. A metaphysical shield."

"How would it operate?" Rubidum asks brightly.

I steal a glance at Hysan, hoping he'll speak, but he's watching me with narrowed eyes. Suddenly he breaks into a genial smile and pulls me to my feet. "This has been a charming visit, but we really should be on our way," he tells the Twins.

"Oh, don't go yet." Rubidum springs up. "You've only just arrived."

"And I have much more to tell you about your enemy." Caaseum hurdles over beside me. He's amazingly fast. "Please stay."

I hesitate. My intuition urges me to listen. Maybe he saw something that can help us. But we also need to warn Virgo as soon as possible, and we've already spent too much time here. Finally, I say, "We can spare a few more minutes."

"Ah, the omen's far too complex to cover in a few minutes." Caaseum puts a finger to his chin. "I have an idea. Why don't I come with you, and we'll discuss things along the way?"

Rubidum purses her lips. "Really, Caasy? Another junket?"

"Mother Rho and I have much to contemplate, Rubi, dear." Caaseum turns to me, and when his eyes meet mine, I don't know what to make of this strange, elderly child. His face is smooth and untouched by time, yet his eyes are eerily ancient.

"Okay," I say at last. "Come with us."

Hysan and Mathias both snap their gazes to me in alarm, but Rubidum's eyes sparkle. "In that case, enjoy your journey, brother. And try to keep your eccentricities in check." While brother and sister embrace and peck air kisses at each other, Hysan and Mathias pull me aside.

I speak first, so they're forced to listen. "I know what you're going to say, but this is our best option. It gets us back in the air fastest, it gets me the information Caaseum saw in his Ephemeris, and it gets the people of Gemini a final chance. I can use the flight time to convince Caaseum to take my warning seriously. If he believes me, he can send a message to Rubidum when we get to Virgo."

Both guys look like their resolve is crumbling in light of my reasoning. "It's Gemini's only chance," I add unnecessarily. They're not fighting me anymore.

When the siblings pull away, Rubidum takes my hands. "You're a vivid storyteller, Mother Rho, very inventive. You've totally won me over. I hope we meet again." With those words, she lifts her stringed instrument and plays a rollicking waltz. Apparently, this is how Twin Rubidum bids farewell.

We head into the corridor, now thronged by curious Geminin. Their russet heads fill the passage, and they bob up and down, trying to see us. As we weave through the crowd, Caaseum takes my elbow. "Where is your ship? I'll have a food locker delivered."

On my other side, Hysan puts his lips close to my ear. "There's something devious about the way he watches you."

When Mathias glances back and sees Hysan whispering to me, his face darkens.

The pretty little Geminin kids keep shoving against me, touching my skin with their soft searching fingers. They jam the passage, blocking our way, and the air is so thick with their cloying perfume of drugs, my head swims . . . until Mathias lifts me up in his muscular arms.

"Make way!" he booms, and the crowd parts in two halves. While the Geminin people stand back, murmuring and pointing, he carries me across the balcony, down the moving staircase, and all the way outside to the sunny Imaginarium. Even though he's doing all the work, I'm the one feeling breathless.

Unfortunately, an even larger crowd is congregating on the plaza. Hysan comes up behind us and says, "We'll have to activate the veils."

Mathias sets me down. "Where's Caaseum?" I turn to see him parading toward us, flanked by his adoring subjects. When he comes near enough, I seize his hand. "Whatever happens, hold on to me."

Hysan activates our veils, and as a collective gasp rises from the crowd, Caaseum says, "Now this is a trick I want to learn!"

Mathias wraps a protective arm around me and pushes ahead, nudging people aside so we can pass. The Geminin gripe and kick when they feel our shoves, but they can't see us. All the while, I keep a tight hold on Caaseum's wrist, dragging him along like a toy. When he realizes what's happening, he lets out a hoot of pleasure.

By the time we make it back to the ship, I feel like I haven't slept in days.

18

"I SENSED A CORRUPTED SOUL who's set his sights on you. This may hold many meanings, but of one thing I'm certain."

"Please don't keep me guessing," I say for the tenth time. Caaseum plays with me the way kids play with their food. It's infuriating.

"I wish you'd call me Caasy."

"Okay . . . Caasy. What is it you're certain of?"

The Geminin Guardian and I are in *Equinox*'s galley, talking over glass vials of hot tea. We left House Gemini an hour ago, and after a fight in which Hysan and Mathias nearly resorted to martial arts, we're traveling at top speed toward House Libra.

We had to strike this compromise because, after all, we're on Hysan's ship, and he's frantic to alert his own House. At least he trusts my warning.

He promised me the detour would be brief. Caaseum— *Caasy*—doesn't seem to care where we go. He's treating this like an adventure. Mathias is holed up in his quarters meditating, and Hysan's at the helm. This is the first moment I've had alone with Caasy.

"Dear Mother, tell me again why we can't use your black opal. I think you're overstating the risk."

"Just trust me. It's a rule."

I used to hate when people said things like that to me. But Caasy knows why we're flying dark. I've already explained our situation three times, yet he keeps going back to it. At first I thought his lapses in understanding were genuine, but now I think he's toying with me in more ways than I realized.

At least he promised not to use his Tattoo when he got on the ship, and since Hysan has the Psynergy shield up, he won't be able to access the Psy even if he tries. So far, Caasy hasn't noticed. I hope it stays that way.

"So what are you certain of?" I ask again, trying to keep my impatience from slipping out with my words. He munches on a sweet biscuit. I tug my plush yellow hood around my ears and pretend I don't want to reach out and smash that cookie in his face.

I dropped my space suit and the blue Zodai uniform in the refresher to clean them in time for our next stop. In the meantime, Hysan lent me a hooded Libran uniform. It's as soft as a blanket, and its smart fabric actually senses my body temperature and thickens when I get cold. I've never worn anything like it.

Caasy takes a sip of tea from his vial, and when he's run out of ways to drag the moment out longer, he says, "You have been singled out, but not by the one you think."

I frown. "It's Ophiuchus. Trust me. I discovered who he is, and he wants to shut me up."

"Possibly." Caasy sips more tea. "But I sense you are being deceived. That deception hangs over you larger than anything else. If it is not Ophiuchus who is deceiving you, then you must find out who is. Until then, this deception will cloud your judgment."

I think about this new piece of the puzzle, turning it around and around in my head, like I'm trying to find the right orientation to make it fit everything else I know. I'm deceived—by whom? Someone close to me?

Immediately the faces of Mathias and Hysan come to mind. I don't believe one of them is against me. They've been saving my life this whole time. I stare at the youthful old face before me, and suddenly something else occurs to me. He's been having a lot of fun at my expense; couldn't this be Caasy taking things too far?

"I don't think I'm deceived," I say decidedly.

"Of course, Mother. You wouldn't! That's how the best deceptions work!" He laughs at his own joke. Then, maybe seeing my good humor's been depleted with his games, he leans in and says, "Deception does not have to be as sinister as what you imagine. Consider this: Perhaps you are deceived in that you think Ochus is the one hunting you . . . when in fact, someone else is pulling his strings."

With that, Caasy stands up. His curls bounce like copper coils, and his chin dimples. "We'll be doing our slingshot soon, and I wouldn't dare miss it. Every close flyby of Helios gives me a sensory charge."

His words remind me of the course Hysan has charted to take us from Gemini, the Third House, to distant Libra, the Seventh. Since we're in a hurry, we'll do a slingshot around our galactic sun and use its gravity to boost our speed. Hysan says we'll cut as close as possible without setting ourselves on fire. It's unnerving—but thrilling. I can't wait to see my first close-up view of Helios.

I stay seated a while, thinking about what Caasy said. I don't like the idea of someone more powerful than Ophiuchus out there. Maybe that's not the deception.

Even though I have a ton to prepare for, I feel homesick. Stepping on foreign soil made me think of the last time I set foot on Cancer. And since I can't concentrate on anything else, I search for the thing on this ship that brings me closest to home.

Equinox is small, so I don't have far to go. "Mathias?" I knock on his round metal door. "Can we talk?"

When he opens it, he's shirtless and holding a stretch band. Droplets of sweat cling to his hair, and his chest is swelling in and out like he's been exerting himself. His body is so smooth and sculpted that soon the homesickness is replaced with fantasies of what his skin would feel like if I touched it.

When he pulls on his blue Cancrian tunic, I look up.

"I can loan you the band if you want some exercise," he offers.

"Thanks, maybe later." The way he eyes my Libran uniform makes me wish I hadn't put it on.

I edge a little farther into his cabin, which is as narrow and cramped as mine. It's chrome green, and there's a sleeping cocoon, a few storage bins, and a desk that folds down on hinges. Unlike my cabin, though, his is neat and tidy, without a single item strewn on the floor. "Caasy just told me what he saw in the stars. He says I'm being deceived somehow. He thinks someone else is pulling Ochus's strings."

"Do you believe him?" Mathias stows the stretch band.

"I don't know. I don't think he was lying when he said it."

"Well, I don't trust him." He turns around and faces me. "Or Hysan either. Although I admit we wouldn't be alive without the Libran's ship."

"Yeah, this place is starting to feel like a safe harbor." I rest my side against the wall. "I just wish I knew how the Psy shield works. Hysan won't spill."

Mathias takes a small device from his belt and waves it in a broad sweeping pattern, as if brushing away cobwebs. When he continues this strange behavior, I ask, "What are you doing?"

"Checking for eyes and ears."

"You mean Hysan may be eavesdropping?" I glance around for cameras, but of course they would be concealed. "Well, as Cancrians we have nothing to hide. Right?"

"Yes. We're not sneaks." Mathias announces this to the walls, as if the cabin itself is listening, and I have to smile. In spite of our disagreements, his Cancrian nature comforts me and reminds me of our people back home.

We head to the nose and find both Hysan and Caasy planted at the front tip, gazing at Helios. Our sun's light flickers through the glass, setting every surface aglow. At this distance, it nearly fills our view, and although the glass has automatically polarized and darkened to protect our eyes, the light is intense. The surface boils like liquid fire in hues of violet, crimson, brass, and gold, with bursts of white so extreme, my eyes sting. Around its horizon, a scarlet corona blazes like a holy crown, and here and there, super-heated jets of gas spew outward in luminous blossoming fountains.

"Hail mighty Helios, womb of heaven." Mathias murmurs the Zodai chant, and we all join in. "Star maker, heat giver, doorway from death to light. Preserve our Houses now and in the ages to come."

I study the three enraptured faces around me. It's easy to see why Helios stands at the center of all our sacred texts. The Libran Seddas. The Gemini Book of Changes. Of course our own Holy Canon. Even the famous eight-volume Covenant of Scorpio, the most secular and scientifically advanced House in the Zodiac, speaks of Almighty Helios. Many people believe our galactic sun holds the gateway to paradise, and seeing it, I understand why.

Youngest looking, but oldest by far, Caasy watches Helios with reverent adoration, like one gazing at a great beauty from afar, knowing he can never hold her.

An hour passes while we gather in the glass nose. None of us seems willing to move while the sun's still in view. Only when our transit's complete and *Equinox* hurtles away toward Libra do I settle back into my skin. The sun's behind us now, visible only in the small square frame of *Equinox*'s rearview screen.

Hysan returns to the helm, and Caasy goes back to the galley for something to eat. He says the sight of Helios always gives him an appetite.

Mathias comes over to me. "Our course is locked in. We'll be on Libra by morning."

"I thought it was farther off," I say, rubbing my neck.

"This bullet-ship has a photon pump, so we can travel at hyperspeed. And thanks to our loop around the sun, we'll go even faster." He peers over his shoulder at Hysan, then lowers his voice. "The Libran's totally unreliable. He encrypted the ship's controls and locked me out."

"That's a little paranoid."

"He's a spy. Spies don't trust anyone." Mathias's jaw tightens. "Problem is, we need him to fly us to Virgo."

"He promised he would. Let's go talk to him."

Hysan glances up from his screens as we approach, and his eyes glint with amusement. "You might as well know I overheard you."

Mathias gives him a dark scowl. "Hidden microphones?"

Hysan's centaur smile dimples his cheeks. "Truth is often overlooked for her simplicity. This cabin has excellent acoustics, and I have excellent hearing. I don't need microphones."

"Why did you encrypt the controls?" I ask.

"My lady, I assure you I meant nothing shady. This is my ship, and I'm captain here. I don't like having to give your *Advisor* explanations." The way he says Mathias's title leaves little doubt he has a different word in mind.

Before Mathias can argue, I say, "But you'll take us to Virgo, like you promised?"

Hysan steps around his screens and moves closer to me. Mathias tenses, but I see only humor in Hysan's expression. He's doing this to annoy Mathias. "Will you promise not to grill me about my Psy shield?"

I appreciate his directness, so I answer in the same spirit. "Not a chance."

Hysan laughs, and his cheer is so sincere, it relaxes me. Again I feel my skin growing warmer in his presence, like he's radiating his sunny disposition. I know it's probably the smooth-talking Libran thing, but every time we have an interaction, I'm already looking forward to the next one.

Having skirted another battle between the guys, I head to the bathroom for an ultraviolet shower, and then I change back into the plush yellow tunic. I'm so exhausted that I sleep through dinner. When I awaken, everyone but Mathias is asleep. He's out front, having discovered one of the ship's secrets by accident.

It turns out *Equinox*'s helm has a Libran teaching crown. I've heard of them but never seen one before—they're only installed on ships outfitted for long-distance travel. Librans have them for the same reason they have a Scan embedded in their eyes: They believe when you're leaving home, the most important item you can pack and take with you is your knowledge.

Mathias found out we can access it by speaking the word *tome*. At the sound of that trigger, the helm projects a horizontal ring of glittering lavender light. It's about head high and two meters in diameter, so Mathias and I can both stand inside it.

We ask it a series of questions about Psynergy, but it mostly spews back things Mathias already taught me. None of its answers help us form any theories about how the Psy attack on the ship—or moons—was possible. So after a while, I try something else.

"Tome," I say in the crown's ring of light, "how does a Psy shield work?"

This is the first time the crown has no answer. Its ethereal voice responds, "Insufficient data."

"Is Hysan Dax a spy?" asks Mathias.

"Insufficient data."

"Is the Libran censoring what you tell us?" he growls.

"Insufficient data."

I leave the circle of light. "Mathias, turn that thing off."

"Let's try another neutral question," he says. "Tome, who are the most respected experts on the Psy?"

"Good one." I go back in and watch the answer materialize inside the lavender ring. Tome displays a miniature 3-D image of a glowing spiral ladder shaped like a double helix. On its rungs stand seven shining figures. They look like tiny celestial beings on a stairway, and nametags glow over each of their heads.

On the top rung, of course, stands Empress Moira of Virgo, our Zodiac's preeminent Psy master. The image standing on the rung just below her is far too familiar. It's our own Mother Origene. I bite my lip. "This list is outdated."

When Mathias sees Origene, he sucks air through his teeth. As a member of the Royal Guard, he probably knew her better than most. On an impulse, I reach out and stroke his arm. "You miss home as much as I do," I say, halfway between question and statement.

He glances at the ladder of scholars again. "Alerting the other Houses is the honorable thing to do . . . but every hour we travel at hyperspeed, two hours pass on Cancer."

"I hate not knowing what's happening there."

"Me too." He unzips a pocket and takes out his antique Astralator. The mother-of-pearl glimmers softly in the ghostly light. After a moment, he presses it into my hand. "I want you to have this."

I jump back like he's offering me a weapon. "I couldn't. Mathias, this was your sister's. I could never take it from you."

"It's tradition for a Zodai mentor to give his student a gift when she's mastered her studies. *Mastered* is an understatement when it comes to you. So much was thrust on your shoulders . . . and you've been incredible." He takes my hand, his eyes bright in the lavender light. "The gift is traditionally an Ephemeris, but that will have to wait until we get home. For now, it would mean a lot if you'd accept this."

"Mathias," I whisper, an aching in my chest, "thank you, but it's too much."

He puts the device in my hand and closes my fingers around it, like flower petals protecting pollen. "This Astralator has been in my family for generations. It's become a good luck charm. My older sister gave it to me when I became a Zodai."

A slight crease forms between his eyebrows, and he takes his hands away, leaving the Astralator with me. "We each have our cares, Rho . . . but you and I, we can't succumb to individual grief."

Understanding what he's saying, I take the Astralator. "Spoken like a true Zodai," I whisper.

When I slip it into my pocket, I promise myself I'm just holding on to it. If Mathias feels better knowing I have it, I'll keep it for now. But I'm giving it back to him when we're home.

He combs his long fingers through his hair, looking more troubled than I've seen him. "An enemy from the Thirteenth House," he says, like he's considering my words for the first time. "It still sounds irrational, but the Psy attack on our ship was real. Something's happening that I can't explain."

"You're not alone."

"I've been trying to put it together, but nothing fits."

For a minute, we drift into our separate trains of thought. I wonder if I'm wrong to worry so much about my family and friends. My job is to protect all Cancrian people, but my brain doesn't work well with big numbers. It works well with faces. Names. Memories.

Whenever I worry about my world, I don't picture millions of unfamiliar people. I see a House of mothers, fathers, brothers, sisters, friends. Dad, Stanton, Deke, Kai, Leyla, Lola . . . those are the faces I see.

"Tome, tell us about the Guardian of Libra," says Mathias. The teaching crown's light marbles with rainbows, and images of a white-haired, cold-eyed man begin to materialize. I hear a noise behind me and turn to see Hysan.

"Busted," I whisper to Mathias.

"I see you've met Tome."

Mathias turns to Hysan. "Is that a problem?"

"If it were, you wouldn't have gained access, I assure you."

Here we go.

"Hysan, it was my idea," I say, hoping to avoid another spat. "I just wanted to prepare a little before meeting your Guardian."

"My lady, Lord Neith will be pleased. I came to tell you Libra's in sight. We'll be landing soon."

I rush forward, into the nose, to see the constellation of the Scales of Justice. Since we're travelling at hyperspeed, the nearest stars streak by like threads of light, and only the distant ones seem to hang still. For the next few minutes, I cling to the rail, watching House Libra bloom ever larger and closer.

Soon we're deep inside the constellation, and Libra's one inhabited planet, Kythera, glows like a smooth velvet ball, as lemon yellow as the Libran tunic I'm wearing. Smoky swirls and vortexes dimple the ball's surface.

Kythera is blanketed in clouds as thick as fiberglass, made of black carbon and yellow sulfuric acid. Dirty, smothering clouds. They press down on the planet below with bone-crushing weight and lock in every joule of heat. The surface weather is brutal. The acidic storms can grind away entire mountains in a single night.

That's why Librans live in flying cities. We're near enough now to see the communities floating in the cloud tops like silver bubbles. There must be hundreds. Some appear gigantic, while others are very small, and they drift on leisurely currents in the upper atmosphere. Occasionally, two of them bump together, then bounce slowly apart. Their movements are fluid, dancelike, mesmerizing. Like the orbits of the balls of light in the Ephemeris.

Libra is one of the wealthiest Houses in the galaxy. Kythera's never-ending flow of volcanic magma yields the purest industrial gemstones in the Zodiac. What's more, Librans harvest their atmospheric gases and refine them into precious high-grade fuel and plexines.

I keep watching until we enter the atmosphere, and then once again, my feet sink further into the deck, and my bones bear more of my flesh. It's nice to feel my full weight again.

Mathias says Lord Neith's court is "high church," very formal and ritualistic, and it would be a serious misstep for Cancer's Guardian to show up in a Libran uniform. I know why he's really saying it, so I go back to my quarters to change into my blue Zodai suit. The refresher has finished with it, and the fabric is crisp and fresh. I slip it on, and my fingers trace the embroidered moons on the sleeve. I miss the sisters.

I check out my reflection in the mirror and try applying makeup the way Leyla does. I don't manage nearly the effect she can, but at least I obscure the blue-black bags beneath my eyes. I add a little eyeliner and some lipstick, then I loosen my ponytail and spray one of the smoothening lotions on my curls. They lengthen and grow glossy.

When I return to the nose, Caasy is still sleeping, and we're now racing down toward the largest bubble in sight, the city Aeolus. The sphere contains breathable air, which is much lighter than the planet's dense atmosphere. Each sphere is weighted at the bottom with ballasts so it can't flip over, and the storied levels inside are oriented to the planet's surface. The uppermost level gets the most sunlight, so it houses the city's corporate farms. The lower levels recycle air, water, and waste.

"Like it?" asks Hysan. "Our airborne capital is one of the Four Marvels of the Zodiac."

"It's amazing," I say. "Is it made of glass?"

"Ceramic, actually." He slides closer to me, and for the first time I notice the cedary scent of his hair. "Transparent nanocarbon fused with silica, extremely tough. It's engineered to withstand our sulfuric atmosphere."

Mathias edges between us. "A hot air balloon. Very appropriate."

Hysan looks like he's about to say something, but when he spies the discomfort on my face, he keeps quiet. *Equinox*'s thrusters fire, and we glide low over the face of Aeolus. This close, its protective membrane is mirror-bright and pockmarked with thousands of openings, with aircraft of every size and color circling, landing, and taking off. Hysan leans over me and says, "The landing pad is through there, and that's—"

"Why are we still veiled?" snaps Mathias. "Aren't you welcome in your own home?"

Hysan gives Mathias a superior look. "Do you think I'd draw a Psy strike on my world?"

They glance at me and turn away, and my stomach flips upside down. "Yeah, I know. I'm a walking target."

The lower we glide, the denser the swarming traffic grows, and *Equinox* dodges through the jumble of vibrocopters, hover-ships, and pulse-jets. The ship makes a banking turn into a port and comes to rest, invisible to all eyes except our own. I wake up

Caasy, and once again, Hysan insists we don our collars before disembarking.

From inside Aeolus's transparent skin, the surrounding clouds look woolly green. This far above the planet's surface, gravity thins out. The walls and ceilings are made of glassy-smooth ceramic, and the floors are covered in soft, cushiony plexifoam tiles. The whole place has a light, airy feel—a wonderful change from the cramped bullet-ship. The halls, however, are crowded with Librans dressed in all the colorful plumage of tropical birds.

We've landed near a major shopping zone, and consumers rush along with mesh bags and gold-starred eyes. Vivid films blare across the walls, promoting overstuffed fruit baskets, gourmet liqueurs, and baked goods. Illuminated arrows point the way to hostess gifts, caterers, florists, and party planners, and holographic ads flit through the throngs of people, showering everyone with minute-by-minute announcements of festive new merchandise.

Hysan seems to swell with pride as he takes everything in. "I forgot it's Friday. Everyone's planning weekend dinners. Hospitality's a blood sport here."

Caasy eyes a display of feathered hats. "I don't suppose we could try a few things on?"

"There's no time," I whisper, already moving.

Caasy dawdles briefly, fingering the hats, then hurries after us. The line to enter the transportation tubes is a dense mass of bodies rather than an orderly queue, but since we're invisible, we follow Hysan's example and shove right in. Watching Hysan move, I begin to suspect this isn't the first time he's entered his city unseen.

He elbows his way through the shoppers, and though it goes against my grain, I have to do the same to keep up. The last thing I want is to lose sight of Hysan in this mob. Mathias stays close behind me, but I worry about little Caasy—until I remember he's been taking care of himself for over three centuries.

Hysan leads us to a cordoned-off area marked *Departures*, where a crowd of people stands around, waiting to catch a Flutterby. We squeeze in among them and look up—a flock of transparent tubes, each with its own pair of large flapping insect wings, is descending on us.

When a Flutterby gets close enough, Hysan shows us how to reach up and grab the plexine loops overhead. Caasy's too short, so he hangs on to Mathias's belt.

Since no one can see us, several others try to grab our loops. When a heavy man steps on my toes, I pinch him to make him move. Hysan spots me and cracks up. "You're violent."

"Yeah, so watch yourself," I say through my smile.

All at once, the Flutterbys ascend again, and I feel a thrill of fear and excitement as I realize there's no floor beneath us—just air. I feel a cool whoosh of wind pressing past us as the tube soars toward the city center. The Flutterby itself is barely visible, so it feels like we're flying on a zephyr.

Looking around, I realize everyone's blond here, whether natural or not. Yellow blond, platinum blond, silver-gray blond streaked with gold. Their eyes glisten in shades of green, gray, and quartz, like Lord Neith's, and a gold star adorns the lower corner of every right iris. They wear a variety of fashions, but they seem to prefer their primary colors—reds, yellows, and blues.

Caasy yanks Hysan's sleeve to get his attention. "I've always wanted to witness Lord Neith read the stars. After all, the Cardinal Houses have outstanding Emphemerii—and as Libra represents Air, his is bound to be extraordinary. Will you ask him to demonstrate his great skill?"

Hysan frowns. "We won't have time for that."

Caasy looks genuinely annoyed.

Three people let go of their loops and fall through the sky. I shriek and reach out to grab the closest one, but Hysan calls out, "Don't—they're fine, Rho!"

I try asking him where they went, but the air whipping through the tube has grown too loud—we're now shooting through Aeolus at tremendous speed. In a residential area, we pass towers of flat, circular apartments stacked up like porcelain platters. Abruptly, we bend around a corner, then drop down a thick ceramic deck into an industrial zone full of tanks and pipes and steamy white smoke. More layers rush by as we descend—factories, office districts, theaters, aqueducts. Through every zone, transparent tubes flap their insect wings, speeding gusts of commuters to their urgent destinations. The rapid alternating sights are making me a little seasick.

"Your Center steadies you," whispers Mathias in my ear.

I close my eyes and think of Dad and Stanton on Kalymnos, putting our sand-and-seashell bungalow back together. The picture of them safe and side by side, surrounded by the blue of the Cancer Sea, does what Mathias said it would—only ever since the attack on our moons, my protective wall has been faulty, and bad thoughts are hitching rides with the good.

I see again how Crius's face filled with fear as he interrupted the meeting with the Matriarchs to announce an emergency. Then I think of House Pisces's urgent warning, and of the feeling I had when I faced the Ephemeris and sensed the approach of more storms . . . and war.

"Almost there!" calls Hysan, and I open my eyes. Beneath us, House Libra's royal court stands next to their parliament at the city's core—a collection of spiky towers that look like sharp-edged teeth.

"Let go now!" he shouts.

"*What?*" I blurt, watching in horror as Hysan releases the plexine loop. When Mathias does the same, I let go, too.

The fall starts fast, making my stomach shoot up my throat. Twenty feet from the ground, we slow down, and I open my eyes. The four of us are dropping gently, our bodies swaying like feathers. We land in a cordoned-off area labeled *Arrivals*.

"Our seat of government," says Hysan, gesturing at the grand buildings around us.

I have to lean against the wall to catch my breath. The jam-packed tube left me feeling jostled, and one of my side pockets has ripped halfway off in the crowd. At least there are fewer people in this transportation hub.

Breezes rustle through ferny plexine trees, and water trickles down a curving plexine chute. At the far end, Zodai Guards stand at attention in their lemon-yellow uniforms, flanking a pair of tall fluted gates that lead into one of the government buildings.

They stir and squint when we pass, but they can't quite see us tiptoeing inside. The arched entrance is three stories high, and the antechamber is full of blond-bearded courtiers dressed like Hysan, in rich, stylish clothing. *"Veils off,"* murmurs Hysan.

We materialize like magic, but the few courtiers who notice us don't seem at all impressed. Compared to these platinum-blond urbanites in their fancy court suits, Mathias and I must look like peasants. Hysan, however, looks like a fish returning to its rightful school—even if he's the youngest courtier by far. I watch as he steps up to a kiosk and speaks to a female official who's working at a smart screen.

He returns a moment later, beaming. The official's expression sours when she sees him squeeze my arm. "We've been granted an audience."

19

CAASY STAMPS HIS FOOT. "Granted? *Helios, please.* When the Guardians of two Houses come calling on the same day, your man ought to damn well meet us at the front door."

Ever the diplomat, Hysan pretends not to hear. "This way." We follow him through clusters of murmuring courtiers. It seems they've just learned who we are, and they're staring, so I cover my torn pocket.

Hysan leads us through a long gallery of decorative porcelains and blown glass. Overhead, a jewel-encrusted mural depicts our Zodiac galaxy, and I lean back to locate the Fourth House. Planet Cancer's designed as a mosaic of tourmaline and lapis lazuli, circled by four opal moons. I wish we could linger, but Hysan's practically at the other end of the hall.

At last we enter the last room in the passage. The place is dim and hushed, and a number of richly dressed dignitaries sit in red velvet seats facing a stage on which stands nothing but a large white cube. The cube is about five meters tall, and its walls are smooth and glossy. Maybe it's some kind of multisided screen.

Hysan directs us to the front row, and we hear the dignitaries rustling their robes as we pass. I keep watching the cube. It's just sitting there.

Hysan leans over me and says, "I need to file my report. I won't be long."

"Can you send a message to Cancer?" I whisper.

He shakes his head. "You know a public message wouldn't be safe."

"At least try to get the latest newsfeed," I say.

"Right. I'll only be a minute." He bows to the other courtiers and hurries out.

Ten minutes pass. Then another ten. I keep shifting in my seat, glancing around, wondering how soon the next attack will come. We don't need this delay. We have to warn Virgo.

"This is outrageous," grumbles Caasy. "What happened to the famous Libran hospitality? I expected singing birds and dancing monkeys. At the very least, a bite of fried larks!"

I've never met anyone who could get so moody over missing breakfast. Mathias closes his eyes to meditate—a sensible response to having to wait. I only wish I could feel that calm. The white cube is starting to bore me . . . so much that I start to hallucinate it's moving. . . .

Until it really is.

What I took for solid white glass appears to be a trick of light. It's roiling and marbled with iridescent color . . . and now the cube looks like a block of rippling liquid. The dignitaries stir as the house lights dissolve to darkness. The cube glows brighter, and through its fluid front pane, a regal figure steps forth in a white hooded robe.

He's taller than anyone I've ever seen, and when he throws back his hood, his face has flawless golden skin and is framed with close-cropped white hair. Behind him, the cube alters from gold to violet, crimson, chrome, emerald green, and cerulean blue. The shifting light forms a prismatic halo around Lord Neith.

I have to remember to close my mouth.

"So pompous," whispers Mathias. Caasy's giggling with glee.

Neith lifts his hands in welcome, his face grave and his pale eyes glittering. "Honored guests, you grace us with your presence." The deep, sonorous bass of his voice unsettles me.

Caasy's on his feet, bobbing a bow. "Lord Neith, good to see you again."

"You as well, Twin Caaseum. To what stars must I give thanks for this charming visit?"

While Caasy chats with Lord Neith, Mathias nudges my knee. "I think it's all smoke and mirrors. They're not taking us seriously."

"I'll see if I can touch him," I whisper back.

When Lord Neith finally acknowledges me, I stand up and move closer, stretching out my arm for the hand touch. "Honored Guardian, I'm Rho Grace from Cancer."

Only after a slight hesitation does he stoop to brush his fingertips against mine. His hand is warm, and blue veins run beneath his skin. When we touch, his quartz eyes soften slightly, and I wonder if I've connected with this foreign Guardian. "Well?" whispers Mathias when I sit back down.

"Solid flesh."

Mathias doesn't seem satisfied.

"Holy Mother," booms Lord Neith, "we have watched the news of your planet with great heartache." When he pauses, I'm startled by the degree of heartfelt compassion that comes over his face— a stark change from his severe expression. "The people of Libra grieve with you."

I rise. "Thank you, Lord Neith." I launch into my story, warning about the ancient leader of the Thirteenth House. The dignitaries near us shift restlessly as I describe how the Dark Matter knotted around Virgo and Gemini. "He already smashed our moons. I think he's also behind the natural disasters of the past year, and he's going to strike again soon. You should be prepared for the worst."

When I finish, Lord Neith leans closer to me, and I catch a strong whiff of the scented lotions the Libran commuters all wear. It gives the skin special protection from Helios's rays, which can be more potent here, given Libra's heavy atmospheric gases.

"We are grateful for your concern, Mother Rho, but we have our own Zodai who have seen no cause for alarm. And now, may I offer you the hospitality of our court?"

The pleasantness of his rejection staggers me. "Please believe me," I insist. "You have to prepare."

He smiles. "Your colleague has already shared this story with us."

"You mean Hysan?"

Lord Neith pauses a moment, and I hope he's not accessing the Psy. "A juvenile named Nishiko has sent many messages. You deputized her, yes?"

Nishi. The sound of her name is like a shot of adrenaline, and I feel myself coming back to life with purpose.

Nishi hasn't given up. She's doing what I asked of her. Now I need to do my part—whatever it takes to convince the Guardians to believe me.

"We admire your good intentions," says Neith, "but the myth of Ophiuchus is a lovely work of art. And here on Libra, we deal in facts."

Behind me, the dignitaries sigh, seemingly with relief, so I twist in my seat and face them. "Please listen. The Psy weapon is real. Your own envoy knows the truth. Hysan Dax. Ask him."

"Hysan Dax," Lord Neith repeats, and the dignitaries titter. "Hysan loves his pranks. He's useful, but very green."

As the titters die down, two Zodai Guards enter through the rear doors, and Lord Neith lifts his hands. "Again, my thanks for your visit. My Guards will escort you to our banquet hall, where many in my court are eager to greet you."

I clench my fists. That's it? We came all this way, and the grandiose Lord Neith just dismisses us? And where is Hysan?

"We can't," I say. "We have to warn Virgo."

"Very well. Do come again." With a bow, he steps backward into the cube, and the liquid surface closes over him.

I turn and stomp out, too angry for good manners. I've probably broken some dire rule of state protocol, but I don't care. Mathias and Caasy follow, flanked by the Guards, and Caasy says, "I wouldn't mind a taste of fried larks. It's House Libra's signature dish. Have you ever tried it?"

Mathias touches my back. "Let's go to the banquet."

"Are you serious? We don't have time for a formal dinner."

He gives me a subtle nod, and I sense this isn't about protocol. He's up to something.

"Okay," I tell the Guards. "I guess we're hungry after all. Please lead us to the banquet."

20

OUR FOOTSTEPS ECHO AS THE Libran Guards escort us down another wide corridor glistening with plexifoam tiles. We're going to the banquet hall, though I can't imagine why. Mathias glances behind us, and so do I. The dignitaries haven't followed—we're alone with Caasy and the two Guards.

I catch Mathias's eye and notice he's clutching his silver weapon. He gives me a subtle signal with his eyes. It seems like he's telling me to hang back.

I slow down, and when I've put a little space between myself and the Guards, he moves like a bolt. He fires first at one Guard, then spins to shoot the other. His weapon discharges an arc of electricity, and I realize it's a Taser. The Guards fall unconscious, and Caasy shrieks.

"What the Helios did you do?" he asks.

"They're not injured. They'll revive soon." Mathias glances around and listens, but when no one else appears, he says, "Something's wrong here, and I want to look around. You and Rho can go on to dinner."

I square my shoulders. "Forget dinner. I'm coming with you."

Caasy rises up in his levitation boots and sputters, "I'll not be part of this. We're abusing the hospitality of this House."

"Then enjoy your meal, Guardian," says Mathias. "We'll find you when it's time to leave."

"Humph." Caasy pivots on his levitated heel and marches off like an indignant child.

Mathias seizes my hand, and we run back the way we came. When we hear footsteps, he pulls me into a shallow alcove. "Our collars," I say. "Should we veil?"

Mathias presses me farther into the shadows, and he's so close I can feel his heart pounding through his tunic. Or maybe it's mine.

"We're Cancrians," he says. "We don't use deception." The distinction strikes me as ironic since we're creeping around like a pair of thieves, but I don't argue. I'm enjoying being near him too much.

A few courtiers pass by without noticing us, and then we slip down the hallway and steal into the room where we'd been earlier. It's now dim and deserted. Onstage, the white cube looks as inert as a block of salt.

Mathias puts a finger to his lips, then pulls a thumb-sized laser torch from his belt. Its beam scintillates across the cube's white surface. The walls look like they're solid glass, but when we touch them, our hands pass right through.

Mathias turns to me with raised eyebrows. Then he steps through the wall and vanishes. I watch the surface ripple for a second. Then I follow him.

Inside, the cube is much larger than it appears, and it's empty. Mathias shines his light around the glassy walls, casting tiny rainbows everywhere. He brushes his fingers over one side, and I follow his example. It feels solid now, and I wonder how we'll get out. When I rap it with my knuckle, it rings like glass. Mathias bends to examine the floor, and I ask, "What are we looking for?"

"Smoke and mirrors," he whispers, stooping to run his hand along a seam. "*Ha.*"

He shines his light on a panel in the floor. It's so well concealed, I never would've spotted it. He pulls some kind of tool from his belt, and when he presses a tab, it fans out with a dozen blades. He uses one to pry open the panel, and a shaft of brilliant light shoots up from below.

We hear a noise, and the light shuts off. Mathias wrenches the panel wider and drops into the darkness. I ease down after him and fall to a slick, hard floor. When I stand up, Mathias flares his laser torch around the space, and the first person I see is Lord Neith.

He's sleeping under a row of lights that are now switched off. His long, golden body lies stretched on a waist-high table, and there's something funny about his nose. We step closer.

The Guardian's nose is tipped up like a hinged lid, revealing a triangle of clear plexine underneath, flecked with bits of glowing metal. "What—"

"Shh. It's a machine." Mathias dims his laser torch. It seems we've entered some kind of workspace. There's a bank of inactive smart screens, shelves of exotic gadgets, and dozens of small tools lying scattered over every surface. As his muted light plays over the room, it catches the glint of two green eyes.

"Wake up."

The room suddenly fills with soft light as screens flicker to life and gadgets begin to hum. Hysan steps forward. "So you've found my secret."

He's exchanged his court suit for gray workman's coveralls that show off the muscles in his lean build, and he's holding what looks like a stylus. Everything in here is stainless steel and spotlessly clean, even the scattered tools.

Mathias touches Neith's skin with his fingertip, and his face twists with disgust. "Kartex."

Hysan beams. "Pretty realistic, don't you think?"

"Why does an android pose as Libra's Guardian?" demands Mathias. "What are you hiding?"

"Mathias, you have no right to question me in my own House." Hysan steps closer, and his eyes flash with authority. "But since dear Rho is here, I'll tell you: I don't like living at court, so Neith stands in for me."

Mathias glowers. "Are you implying that *you* are Guardian of Libra?"

Hysan performs his low bow. "In the flesh." His gaze jumps to me. "Literally, this time."

21

I STARE AT HYSAN, completely at a loss for how to react.

For some reason, the first thing that runs through my mind is the Taboo. It's been around since the Trinary Axis, and it's pretty much the only rule the Guardians have to follow: We're forbidden from dating—or loving, or marrying, or even kissing—each other.

I shake my head, as if afraid someone might read my thoughts. I don't know why I'm even thinking of dating right now.

"I use Neith because I can't be tied down," says Hysan, looking at me as though his explanation is for my ears only. "I'm a born traveler. I must have had a Sagittarian ancestor."

"A born spy," mutters Mathias. "That android doesn't even look like you."

"Of course he doesn't. I was eleven years old when they named me Guardian. Do you think a boy could ever command respect?"

Eleven.

I've been Guardian for barely two weeks, and it feels like a year of my life has elapsed. But Hysan has already been doing this for *six years*. My eyes meet his, and we exchange a look of loneliness that no one else in the Zodiac could understand.

No one else is a teenager and a Guardian.

"How many people know about this hoax?" asks Mathias, still using a demanding tone of voice even though we're *technically* addressing the Libran Guardian in his own home.

"You do enjoy interrogating me, Cancrian."

For the second time, I glimpse the counterbalance to Hysan's good nature. The darkness beneath his light.

"How did you pull this off?" I ask, drawing Hysan's attention from his staring contest with Mathias.

"On Libra, our Guardians predict their own deaths. In their final year of life, they read the stars to find their successor. The new Guardian's identity is kept hidden until the present Guardian passes."

I remember that from my lessons with Mom. The thought of knowing the day of your own death always struck me as cold and unnatural. Now I feel like mine could be at any moment.

"When my predecessor, Lord Vaz, chose me to succeed him, he understood no one would trust a boy. That's why he and I built Neith, in secret. When the time came to name the new Guardian, he announced Neith's name. Everyone in our government just knows me as a diplomatic envoy who happens to be a distant relative of Lord Neith's."

Mathias makes a disparaging face. "This is outrageous. You deceive your own people."

Hysan's expression tightens when he turns to him. "My people are wealthy and content. They don't complain."

"Why did your android claim not to believe me?" I ask.

"That was for the jury's benefit." Seeing Mathias's confusion, Hysan explains: "A jury of at least a dozen Advisors and City Senators must be present for every meeting with our Guardian, to protect him from making rash decisions." He bends over the robot and gently tips its nose back in place. "I knew they wouldn't give their consent, so I reprogrammed Neith to begin shielding my people from Psy attacks. He's going to activate our House's veils so they'll protect our cities from the Psy whenever our sensors pick up high traces of Psynergy."

"So that's why you insisted on coming to Libra first," says Mathias.

"Of course. My people are my priority. I never joke about that." Hysan crosses the room and opens a hidden door. "Rho, let me show you something."

Mathias moves between us, but I dodge him to look inside the secret room. What I see makes me stagger.

The space is hexagonal, and all six walls are covered in artificial glass eyes of varying shapes and sizes, each with quartz irises like Neith's. The intense way they rake back and forth makes them seem alive. They're all staring at a large holographic Ephemeris that slowly rotates at the center of the room. "Shut if off!" I shout, shrinking back.

Hysan whispers a code, and the Ephemeris instantly vanishes. "It's not connected," he explains.

All the eyes turn toward me. It's one of the creepiest things I've ever seen. Mathias materializes at my side, looking as shocked as I feel.

"This is my reading room," says Hysan. "My talent for reading the stars isn't the same as yours, Rho. I rely on technology's help."

Despite all the eyes watching me, Hysan's green gaze has never felt so intense. "I'll do anything to defend my House."

Having finally met the true Hysan, I don't doubt him for a moment. I step inside the hexagonal room, and the large glassy irises follow me. "This is pretty bizarre," I admit. "How does it work?"

He flashes his crooked smile, then stoops to make a tender adjustment to one of the eyes. "Each of these oculi is a cyber-brain. They collect and analyze data from the stars, then relay information to each of our cities. They're also linked to the brains of Neith and 'Nox." He gestures to the whole room. "Thirty-six hundred brains, working around the clock. Massive parallel processing. Their findings are far more objective and extensive than a subjective human mind."

From the animation in his voice, I think technology must be his natural element. He seems as much a Scorp as a Libran.

Then again, as a kid I always felt the dividing lines between us were blurry. For example, Librans value justice, and they pursue it through education, which is essentially the dissemination of knowledge. Knowledge is a Capricorn value, and yet Librans have made knowledge necessary for obtaining justice. Hysan's just taking things a step further by using technology to amass knowledge.

"An artificial astrologer," I say, thinking how cool it is. "Did you invent this yourself?"

He shrugs, for the first time not leaping for a compliment. "I came up with the general concept when I was nine and presented it at the annual Pursuit of Justice Symposium. It's when all Libran citizens, of any age, are allowed to submit a new idea—system, invention, procedure—that furthers or improves our pursuit of justice. It's why Lord Vaz chose me."

He flashes another quick, dimpled smirk. "That and, of course, my consummate Libran nature."

"Did this contraption predict the tragedy in our House?" asks Mathias. "Did it foresee the attack on your ship?"

Hysan's sunniness fades. "No . . . it didn't. I'm not sure why."

"Not so accurate after all." Mathias scowls and strides out of the hexagonal room.

"Maybe it can't see through Dark Matter," I suggest.

Hysan stares into the eyeballs, as if deep in thought. His body grows so still and his expression so intense, I can almost feel his clever mind sorting through hypotheses and calculations. I move toward him. "Hysan, you have to tell us about your Psy shield. Can you protect the other Houses?"

"Come." He leads me back to his workroom, where he lifts a beaker containing a bluish liquid. With a pair of tongs, he scrapes some chunks of grainy sediment from the bottom and drops them into a shallow dish. "I'm making you a present, Rho. Sorry it's not finished yet."

He shows me the contents of the dish, about half a dozen tiny, round beads. As he tips the dish, they sparkle with rainbow light. "Cristobalite beads. They're still growing."

"What are they?" I ask.

"Nothing yet . . . but soon, maybe a bracelet, or whatever you like."

"You're serious?" I frown. "How about a time machine?"

He shakes his head sadly. "I'll explain later. We first need to learn more about the Psy weapon. When we reach Virgo, we'll consult Empress Moira, and then I promise you I'll do my part."

"Fine. Let's go now then."

He bows. "As you wish, my lady."

✦ ✦ ✦

The flight to Virgo will take a day at hyperspeed, and the tension on the ship is thick. Mathias and Hysan are locked in a cold war, and Caasy, who's grown bored with me since I won't show him the black opal, only eggs them on.

Back on Libra, I tried convincing Caasy to go to Gemini and protect his House, but he still wouldn't believe there was any cause for panic. When he discovered he couldn't use his Ephemeris on the ship, he became livid. Now his only entertainment is interfering with the guys.

And cooking. Turns out he's a decent chef. I only wish I had more of an appetite, but I can't stop worrying. We checked the newsfeeds before we left Hysan's court, but the commentators only talked about a new pirate attack in Space. Armed assailants hijacked a fleet of Taurian frigates and abducted all the crew members. No one knows the motive.

The only good news is that Hysan downloaded the hologram Nishi sent around to all the Houses. I'm sitting at the kitchen table, alone, projecting the message from a small device Hysan handed me.

When it starts, it looks like a recording of Drowning Diamonds performing our most popular song on campus, "Across the Zodiac." But a few seconds in, I have to rewind it to be sure of what I'm hearing.

The visuals are definitely from a performance we put on a few months ago at the university. It was our first paid gig—two Zodai instructors were getting married, and they hired us to play. But the song lyrics are not the same.

> When the Zodiac was new
> There was a thirteenth star
> The first among us knew
> But in time we forgot
>
> Now the serpent, he is back
> And we must find a way
> To push his presence out
> Or he'll be here to stay

When she gets to the chorus, Nishi belts out my name, and I cover my face with my hands, even though no one else is in here.

Trust in Guardian Rho
She's our galaxy's best chance
She'll make Ochus go
He'll forget his plans

I can't believe what Nishi's done.

Like always, she's bold and brilliant—I only wish she hadn't told the Zodiac I'm our best chance. All I've been doing is running around sounding an alarm. That's not making Ochus go. . . . It's just making a lot of noise.

I watch the film a few more times. The new lyrics are actually pretty catchy. After a while, I feel reinvigorated, and I access the ship's Tome. There must be something in here about Ophiuchus, maybe in the older stuff.

An hour later, most of what I've found says the same thing. How our early forebears believed the sun's core held a gateway to a mirror universe, one they called Empyrean. According to the scrolls, the gateway to Empyrean was cursed. If anyone tried to pass through, the two universes would collapse and annihilate each other.

To prevent a catastrophic collapse, the original Guardians sealed the gateway after the last people from Earth came through. There's evidence our ancestors colonized Aries first, before spreading to the other eleven Houses. Over the millennia, the gateway drifted into the fog of legend, and that's where our Cancrian burial tradition of ceremonially launching a body into the sun comes from.

There's no mention of the Thirteenth House. I speed through

a different text about conflicts in the Zodiac. Mostly it's the same old story about the Trinary Axis. A millennium ago, three Houses formed a conspiracy and triggered a hundred-years war that engulfed the entire galaxy. Vicious atrocities raged back and forth, all too horrible to imagine.

Since then, the Zodiac has lived in peace, and each House has evolved its own systems and traditions. Instead of watching over a mythical gateway, our Guardians now focus on reading the stars to improve the management of their worlds and promote trade. I go back to the kitchen and play the song again.

When Caasy comes in to eat something, I punch the off button so hard I slam the device on the table, like I'm killing a water-fly.

I make up an excuse to go, and as I'm leaving, I distinctly hear Caasy hum, *"Trust in Guardian Rho. . . . She's our galaxy's best chance. . . ."*

I don't play the song again.

✦ ✦ ✦

The next morning, I wake up anxious to meet Moira. As I change into my Zodai suit and fix my hair, I try to think of a more convincing way of relaying my warning. So far, I haven't been very successful.

Moira is a Guardian-empress. She rules all of Virgo. It sounds unnatural to me, since we Cancrians value consensus so much, but she's beloved on Virgo—and even among the other Houses. She's one of the most venerable Zodai in the Zodiac.

Moira's is a benevolent dictatorship. She is a passive monarch who allows her people to police themselves and only interferes when cases are brought before her.

Given their controlling natures, Virgos find it impossible to submit to someone else's command. So Moira ensures that every household has access to food, water, housing, and education, but she allows her people to make their own decisions about all other aspects of their lives. She has only two commands: Everyone must contribute in some capacity to growing grain, and no Virgo will interfere with the pursuit of happiness of any other.

I'm standing in front of the mirror, adjusting the ripped pocket of my suit so that it's not as noticeable, when there's a knock on my compartment.

"Your gentleman-in-waiting, my lady."

A smile tugs at the corners of my mouth, and as I reach for the door, I spy my expression in the mirror's reflection. I'm so startled by the sudden flush in my cheeks and brightness in my eyes that I hesitate—it's scary how someone I've just met can change so much about me, from my mood to my physical appearance.

When I open the door, Hysan scans me up and down, and a light flashes from the golden bloom in his eye.

"Did you just take a picture?"

"A remembrance of your loveliness," he says as he walks inside the cabin.

Bubbles of conflicting emotions rise within me. The feelings bump into each other like Libran cities, bouncing through my body and confusing my thoughts, as I turn to face him. "Sometimes you make it very hard for me to picture you as a Guardian."

He stands closer to me than usual, and I realize I like him best as he's dressed now, in the plain gray coveralls. It sets him apart from the stuffy members of his court.

"But I'm the perfect Libran," he says, counting off each word on his fingers. "Cordial, graceful, nonviolent, and, of course, endowed with a massive . . . *intelligence*."

We both burst into embarrassed laughter and look away. I've never met anyone like him before. Maybe that's a stupid thing to say because I've never met another Libran . . . but I have a feeling they're not all like him. The fact he was made Guardian at age eleven proves that.

"What do your parents do?" I ask.

"I'm an orphan. I never knew my parents."

It takes me a moment to react to the news. On Cancer, the Matriarchs make sure every child has a home. Growing up without parents would be awful, but to be made Guardian at eleven while forced to hide behind an android, all without a family's support . . . I can't even imagine what kind of childhood that must have been.

"I'm sorry," I murmur, instinctively reaching out to touch his arm. The moment our skin makes contact, electricity sparks through me, and I pull my hand back.

"You're sweet, my lady." Hysan leans a few microscopic degrees closer. "It really wasn't as depressing as it sounds. I was raised by our household robot, Miss Trii."

As usual, I'm not sure if Hysan is being serious. "Miss Trii?"

His eyes lose focus, like he's staring into the distance of memory. "What a terror she was . . . until I discovered how to disassemble her. Once I reverse-engineered her central processor, life was good."

I hold back laughter. "'*Nox*, Neith, Miss Trii . . . have you ever had any human friends?"

He lowers his voice and grows serious. "Just you."

The urge to laugh disappears as a stronger impulse suffocates our conversation. His eyes travel down my face, and I clear my throat. "A-are we friends?"

"I hope so," he says softly, gazing at my lips. "I would hate myself if I've done anything to put you off."

He's so close his leaf-green irises alternately swirl like air and harden into stone. I still don't know what to make of him. "Tell me why you really came to my swearing-in ceremony."

His eyes move up from my mouth to meet mine. "I guess I wanted a friend," he says, a different expression coming over him, one I don't recognize. "It's hard, being pushed into a role that defines you before you've had a chance to define yourself. I thought you'd understand."

It's only now I realize I've been avoiding being alone with him. The last time we spoke privately like this was on the way to Gemini, when he wore a similarly unprotected look on his face. I like it now as much as I did then.

"Why do you run from me?" he whispers.

Librans like to be liked, and they're good at reading faces—after all, every performer wants an engaged audience. But Hysan is so perceptive that at times it borders on clairvoyance. "I'm not running, it's just . . ."

"The Taboo?" For the first time, Hysan's face looks fully naked. There's no centaur smile or cocky expression for him to hide behind. He's . . . vulnerable. In a lower voice, he asks, "Or Mathias?"

I shake my head. "It's . . . *me*." I'm not even sure what I mean. Some days, I wake up believing I can do this . . . and other days, I still think of myself as that lonely girl in the solarium. Hysan slides my chin up with his hand, tilting my face so I'll meet his gaze.

At that exact moment, Mathias comes to my door. When he sees Hysan touching me, color drains from his features, and he marches away.

Caasy pokes his head in right after. "Breakfast, anyone?" He looks Hysan and me over, a mean smile stretching the length of his face.

"Mathias, wait!" I push past Caasy into the hall. "We weren't doing anything."

Mathias whirls around. His face is a savage white mask, and I flinch backward. "Have you forgotten the Taboo?" he thunders. "You're a Guardian. Sex between Guardians is forbidden."

Hearing the word *sex* slung out like that by Mathias embarrasses me. I don't like that he assumes he gets a say in every part of my life, and I hate feeling constantly judged by him. "We weren't . . . it was nothing like that."

He glowers at me. "Remember who you are."

Who I am. A week ago, I was an Academy Acolyte, and the only variable in my future was my admissions decision from Zodai University.

Mathias was made for this. Being a Zodai runs in his blood. He's put so much effort into his training that he graduated first in his class at the university. He was recruited into the Royal Guard at twenty-one. He *knows* who he is.

But I feel like Hysan. Before I even had a chance to figure myself out, the stars did it for me. My life is a speeding train I'm constantly racing to catch.

"I'm not sure who I am, Mathias," I say finally.

"Then let me help you." His midnight-blue eyes harden into steel. "*He's* forbidden, and *I'm* too old."

22

WE'RE APPROACHING VIRGO, and I'm locked in my cabin, mortified. I don't see how I can face Mathias or Hysan ever again.

It's only when I remind myself that my people have just suffered the worst disaster in Zodiac history and another House may be assaulted any minute that I snap out of my self-indulgent bad mood and leave the room. Fair or not, I don't get to be a girl who mopes about boys.

As I approach the front of the ship, Mathias and Hysan are shouting at each other from opposite sides of the nose, while Caasy's hanging out in the middle, sucking a grape-colored snack from a squeeze-tube, his tunnel eyes large and entranced. When I enter, they fall silent.

"There you are, *oh divine one*." Caasy ogles me in an exaggerated impression of a lovesick schoolboy. "Your heavenly splendor is blinding me, your magnificent, Motherly holiness."

Hysan and Mathias busy themselves with different screens. They set the ship down at the far end of the busy Virgo spaceport, and because we're veiled, no one bothers us.

Hysan's changed into a muted black court suit. "Time to dematerialize," he says, touching his collar.

Mathias frowns. "Why do we need veils here?"

"Do they shield us from the Psy?" I ask Hysan hopefully.

"Unfortunately, no." He lifts one shoulder. "These collars refract light. They make us invisible, nothing more."

"In that case, I won't be needing mine." Mathias yanks off his collar and drops it on the console.

I lay mine down, too. Partly because I don't like the secrecy, but mostly to make up with Mathias. Hysan just arches an eyebrow and lays his collar beside mine.

Caasy mutters, "I must update my scoreboard when we return." I shoot him a death glare so he'll can it before we get to Moira. He smiles penitently, pretending to get the message.

House Virgo's largest planet is Tethys, a massive green-and-brown sphere with much stronger gravity than I'm used to. Just walking across the landing pad is strenuous. I feel like I'm carrying another person on my back. If the atmosphere weren't so highly oxygenated, I'd be gasping for breath.

As soon as we announce ourselves to the Guards and they get word to Moira, she sends out an unmanned hover-car to take us to her capital city. Sleek burnished gold, bearing the green peridot glyph of House Virgo, the self-guided car is more magnificent than any vehicle I've ever seen on Cancer.

As we're getting in, Hysan says, "She's converted her lesser planets and moons for agriculture. Every House in the galaxy buys Virgo grain."

"Speaking of food," interjects Caasy, "we're running low. You go on ahead. I'll stay here and check the shops in the spaceport."

"You don't want to visit Moira?" I ask, surprised.

"A fine chef prefers to choose his own ingredients." He gives me a cagey smile. "Go on, please. Moira and I are not the best of friends."

He snaps a mock salute, then trundles off. He looks so innocent, a tawny cherub with bouncing curls. I wonder what he's really up to.

The rest of us climb in, and Mathias scans the interior of the car for surveillance devices. Hysan cracks a scornful smirk. "You really don't have to do that."

Mathias ignores him. "Center your mind, Rho. Say your meditation chant."

"Just leave her alone. She'll be perfect." Hysan folds his arms and keeps smiling.

Our car whisks out of the spaceport into rolling green fields. I've never seen this much tall grass in my life. So much solid land, it doesn't seem real. Our hover-car skims over the greenery, and I twist to look around. The fields stretch to every horizon.

"Where's the city?" I ask. Mathias is also craning and searching.

"It isn't far," says Hysan. "We're almost there."

Ahead, a light glints in the sky, then disappears. Odd. I stare in that direction and see another flash. "Was that an aircraft?"

Right in front of us, a wide swath of sky begins to flash and spark, from the ground all the way up to the clouds. Then our car runs straight into it.

For a moment, we seem to be sliding through the heart of a diamond.

Hysan grins at our reactions. "The city wall. Its mirage technology masks Moira's capital from uninvited guests. Without a proper key, it's impenetrable."

The mirage wall reminds me of Hysan's veil collars, and I wonder if he borrowed the technology from Moira.

As we cross out the other side, Mathias spins in his seat to keep scanning the wall, but my eyes are only for the city. It's built like a needle shooting into the sky. "It looks like sterling silver," I say.

"Osmium-iridium alloy," says Hysan. "One of the most durable metals in the galaxy. Moira designs her cities to leave maximum acreage for growing grain."

With a whoosh, our car begins to rise up the face of the needle, and all three of us move to the right side for a better view. The needle is so massive, it fills our window.

We ascend past a series of wide platforms, cantilevered out like leaves. They're parking lots for hover-cars. We don't stop, though. We're still rising, and when I look down, the distance thrills me. Up here, the needle tapers to a point at the top, and I can see the shining gold capstone at the very peak, crowned by Virgo's green peridot glyph, an emblem of connected lines representing the Triple Virgin.

We soar to the highest level, just under the capstone, where a circular port slides open, rimmed in beacon lights. No one's here to meet us, but Hysan opens the car door. "This is our stop. This private port leads directly into Moira's compound."

As soon as we step out, monitoring devices swivel from the eaves to scan us. Again the extra gravity weighs me down as we trudge through a set of sliding metal doors into a vestibule where ultraviolet spotlights rove over our bodies. "Decontamination," Hysan tells us. "Moira does all she can to protect her genetically modified wheat."

"Free shower and laundry in one," I say with a nervous laugh.

Once we're properly sanitized, we step into a long, narrow corridor lined with giant wallscreens. Holographic films balloon out from them, filling the hallway with soft, flickering color, and the competing voiceovers blend like babbling water. The overall effect is relaxing.

Slumping under my own weight, I walk through the bubbles of moving light, watching reports about weather, crop insurance, soil amendments, and off-world pests. Hysan hurries on through the next pair of doors, but I stop to watch a slow-motion capture of a swelling wheat bud. Its fine, silky threads wave like antennae.

Just as I pass the last giant screen, I glimpse my own face in the news and almost trip. My picture's floating beside the classic Capricorn depiction of a starving Ophiuchus caught in the fat coils of a snake.

The image cuts to a crowd of teenagers in Acolyte uniforms holding up posters at some kind of rally. Before I can make out what's happening, the newsfeed shifts to a revolt of immigrant Scorp workers on a Sagittarian moon.

Mathias and Hysan are waiting up ahead, so I shake off the picture and hurry to catch up. Whether or not Nishi's message is being taken seriously, at least she's channeling attention to our cause. Ophiuchus can't possibly like the spotlight, even if it hasn't officially found him yet.

Together, the three of us enter a gilded antechamber where twenty gray-haired courtiers stand in a formal receiving line. "Your welcoming committee," says Hysan.

"Don't let them scare you," whispers Mathias. "You were born for this, Rho."

I lock eyes with him, surprised to find in their blue depths that he really means it. Bolstered by Mathias's confidence, I step forward. Up close, the grim courtiers look like ordinary executives in their dark robes and tasseled caps. Olive-skinned with iron-gray hair, they have eyes the color of moss. All three men's mustaches are waxed into exaggerated curlicues at the ends, and one of the women has chartreuse freckles. They wear numerous rings on their fingers, ears, and eyebrows.

They bow as we approach, touching their hearts: a Virgo sign of friendship. My friends and I return the bow to exactly the same degree, but this ceremonial homage doesn't feel natural. I just want to touch hands and get on with it.

"Holy Mother Rhoma, you have our deepest sympathy for your troubles." The courtier with the largest tassel on his cap makes a complicated gesture, flaring the wide sleeves of his robe before offering me the hand touch. "Empress Moira has foreseen your arrival. Please be concise when you speak with her. She has little time today."

I nod, feeling more nervous than ever. The man's eyebrow ring flashes green. "The empress will receive you now. Your companions may wait here."

"But . . . they're my Advisors. I want them with me."

The head courtier bows again. "What need is there for Advisors when Guardians meet as friends?"

Hysan nudges my arm and whispers, "Moira sets the rules here."

Mathias darts forward. "I'm not leaving you."

An inner door slides open, and an attendant beckons me in. My knees feel weak. I glance back and forth between sunny Hysan and brooding Mathias. Then I smile at Mathias. "You said I was born for this."

With a quiet frown, he steps back, and I follow the attendant into Moira's chambers. The Virgo court is not the opulent palace I expected. It's more like the corporate headquarters of a major corporation.

The attendant shows me into a triangular conference room containing a small black table and six green chairs. One wall is solid glass, and when I look out, Moira's landscape spreads below like an ocean of grain.

"I suppose you didn't come for the view." I spin to see the speaker.

The woman who's entered behind me busies herself with a Perfectionary in her hands and won't meet my eyes. She wears a simple gray tunic and no ornament save the emerald pins in her hair. She's even smaller than me, and wizened. "Are you Empress Moira?"

"My schedule's quite full, so please state your business." I've never seen such wrinkled skin—she looks sun-dried.

I offer my hand for a touch, but she won't look up from her Perfectionary—the Virgos' Wave. Virgos are extremely organized, diligent, and anal-retentive. They all carry around a booklike digital device they rarely part with—it holds their schedules, notes, photographs, diary entries, everything that has any value to them—and it even has an opening for inserting samples of soil, seeds, fertilizers, etc., for analysis.

"I'm Guardian Rho from Cancer."

"Obviously." She doesn't waste words. Or facial expressions.

"Empress Moira, I've come to warn you. Our moon collision—someone deliberately set it off with a Psy weapon. Your House may be next."

At last, she looks up. She eyes me closely as we trade the hand touch. Then she sits at the table and continues browsing her Perfectionary. "Go on."

I sit down, too, and I tell her my theory that all the recent disasters have been triggered by Psy attacks from Ophiuchus.

I can't believe it's possible, but Moira becomes even more emotionless. "You speak of myth. The Zodiac holds only twelve Houses."

"Well, that's what I thought, too." Once again, I narrate my account of Ophiuchus, and even I see how meager the evidence sounds. I describe how the Dark Matter thickened around Virgo, how the entire region around her House went black, but all I have are words, ordinary words. If only I could make Moira feel the terror that shook my bones when Ochus appeared in my Ephemeris.

"He tried to kill me. He wants to silence me." I'm practically wringing my hands.

Moira keeps her eyes on her Perfectionary. When I finish my tale, she says, "We've seen your Sagittarian comrade's warnings of doom in the news. Such alarmist talk may appeal to the young, but not to me. And when I learned Hysan Dax escorted you here, I thought perhaps there was more to your story—he usually has more sense than this."

I blink. Alarmist talk?

She taps her Perfectionary. "Has any other Zodai confirmed your sighting of this alleged Dark Matter past the Twelfth House?"

I bow my head a fraction. "Not that I know of."

"And has anyone in recorded history ever witnessed a Psy attack like the one you're describing? Or seen Ophiuchus?"

"I . . . I'm not sure."

"They have not." She gives me a quick scowl, then turns away. "What's your age?"

"I'm sixteen, galactic standard. I'll be seventeen in a few . . . days." I'd gotten used to saying *weeks*.

"And how long have you trained?"

"Not long," I admit.

Moira sighs and really looks at me. "Mother Origene was my dearest friend. It pains me how your House has suffered. For these reasons, I will spare a moment to show you that there is no monster in the Psy. Afterward I hope you will return home to lead your people."

She gives a quick series of voice commands to darken the glass wall and dim the lights. A small device lowers from the ceiling. It looks like a metal spider. When I understand what it is, I gasp—it's transforming the entire conference room into an Ephemeris.

"No!" I shout.

As soon as the room is drowned in stars, Dark Matter pulses out from the heart of Virgo, and I hear a screeching noise, like the shrieking that came from my black opal. For a moment, I can only stare, petrified.

Moira stands and looks around, her gaze crinkled, as if she hears the psychic disturbance but it doesn't overpower her as it does me. "The Psy has been unsteady since the disaster on House Cancer," she murmurs, more to herself than to me.

She points to the Triple Virgin constellation. "On Virgo, as I'm sure you know, we have our own version of the Ophiuchus myth. Here, he's represented as a serpent who tempts Aeroth and Evandria, a virtuous Virgo couple who stray off the pure gardening path. He leads them into temptation. Yet in all my years as Guardian, I have never seen a shred of evidence to prove Ophiuchus is or ever was real. Now show me his Thirteenth House, if you can."

"He'll see us!" I scream, once I've regained my voice. "Please, shut this down!" I leap to my feet and reach for the projector, but it's too high.

"You're being absurd." She moves away as if I might infect her with my lunacy.

"Empress Moira, trust me. You don't want to draw his attention. He's . . ."

Moira's not listening. She's staring into her Ephemeris, transfixed.

I start to shout, "Turn it off—!"

But a voice like a hurricane is already blasting through my mind. *There you are, Empress Moira. I've long been savoring the thought of this day.*

23

THE PHANTOM BILLOWS INTO THE ROOM, a man-shaped wind devil, overturning chairs and whipping Moira's clothes. Half tempest, half glacial frost, he whirls around Moira and almost lifts her off her feet.

Whispers echo from every corner of the room, the words swimming through the air we're breathing. *Virgin Empress . . . first-order master of the Psy . . . so meticulous in all your dealings.*

"What are you?" Moira tries to push him away, but he constricts around her with suffocating force.

I've prepared some entertainment for you, Empress. Today, you will watch your House fracture and fade . . . as I watched mine.

She squirms and thrashes, her face going gray with shock.

Don't struggle so hard, teases Ochus. *I want you very much alive to see my little show.*

ZODIAC

"Let go of her!" I yell.

Ochus's stormy face shifts toward me, and his features harden to glaring ice. *It's not your turn right now.*

Moira's lips are blue. "Leave her alone!" I shout.

With a malevolent smile, he releases Moira and moves toward me. *Foolish child, you think you're brave.*

I edge backward, but he's too fast. His icy hands reach for my throat. "Get away," I moan, punching wildly.

Trust Only What You Can Touch, Acolyte, he taunts, gripping my throat. *Can you feel me? Am I trustworthy?*

My airways tighten, and the lack of oxygen rushes to my brain, making my vision blurry. I'm desperate to fight him, desperate to defend Virgo, desperate to save these people from what happened to mine.

The thought of my House focuses me in the Psy, steadying the chaos in my mind. The physical pain becomes more present, like I'm moving closer to its true source. When I'm steady enough, adrenaline and survival instinct compel me to take a swing.

At last, my fist connects with something solid and bitterly cold. I push against it, straining my mental will. His freezing skin burns my fingers.

You're stronger this time. His words fly like hailstones.

My hand starts turning black, but I manage to throw another punch, and a crack runs down his icy face. His gravelly laughter grates my ears. *Stronger, yes, but still unripe. Yet today's battle is not on water—it's on land.*

His shape dissolves and he shrinks away, retreating into the Ephemeris, until he vanishes into the region beyond Pisces. I fall to the ground, my skin still burning, as the room grows quiet.

Moira is still staring wild-eyed at the place where Ochus had been, her hair tumbling loose. I survey my aching hands, but they're undamaged. The pain wasn't real. . . . It was an illusion.

When I look at Moira again, she's giving me a long, penetrating stare. Just as she seems about to speak, we're interrupted by an ear-splitting clap of thunder. "Windows on!" she commands, pulling herself upright. "I've forecast no storms today."

As soon as the glass clears, we see a bolt of lightning streak down and singe the nearby field, followed by another bolt, and then another. Soon, lighting is forking across every visible patch of sky.

A lurid storm cloud foams directly above us, flashing ugly purple and red. It spreads wider, shading the ground below, and then an acidic rain starts to pummel the ground, burning through the green and grain like fire.

Moira turns to me in terror. "A Psy weapon? How was this hidden from me?"

"Dark Matter," I say. "Somehow, he's using Psynergy to manipulate it—"

Thunder explodes right above us, and the floor tilts. Lightning must have hit the capstone. A sconce falls off the wall, and a chair topples. Somewhere, we hear screaming. Then a crack splinters across the window, and Moira lunges to push me under the table, just milliseconds before the entire glass shatters.

With a sizzling roar, a million shards fly inward, shredding the walls, the table, the chairs, the skin of my arm. I look around and see Moira sprawled on her back, bleeding.

I rush to check her wounds. She's clutching her arm to her chest, clenching her teeth in pain. Jagged chunks of glass encrust one whole side of her body. "Help!" I shout at the top of my voice. "In here! We need a doctor!"

Moira tries to push me away. In a broken voice, she says, "I've been blind to the stars. I looked, but I didn't see. . . ."

Thunder detonates like a thousand bombs, and alarm horns blare. The head courtier charges in, and when he sees Moira, he kneels and tries to help her stand. "Talein," she says, "get to your station."

Grunting and wincing, she pushes us away and gets up without help. When she stands, her proud posture makes her seem taller than before. She plucks a shard of glass from her hip, then staggers to the gaping window frame. Outside, lightning crackles across a bruised and burning sky, and cinders gust downward, setting the grain fields on fire. In the oxygen-rich atmosphere, the flames rapidly spread. Moira doubles over and screeches, as if this is turning her soul inside out.

She catches the window frame to keep from falling, and her courtier and I run to grab her. We pick up an overturned chair and help her sit. Her eyes are squeezed tight, and one side of her face is streaming blood.

"Dear Empress." The gray-haired courtier is weeping.

"Talein." She pats his hand weakly. "I had hoped to live out my final years in peace."

Another lightning bolt strikes, and a temblor rolls through the needle, throwing us from side to side. When it's over, Moira gazes up at her courtier with a sadness that makes my chest ache. "Talein, call the rest of my Ministers. Call our fleet. We have to evacuate."

"Yes, Your Highness." The old man dips a mournful bow, then lumbers off.

The other courtiers have been waiting at the door, and when they try to crowd in, Moira motions them back. "Get to your posts. Launch our emergency plan."

"Your surgeon is coming, Highness. Let us help you," one of the women pleads.

"Help the people," she wheezes. "Get them to safety. This Cancrian girl will wait with me until the surgeon arrives."

When they're gone, I use my sleeve to dab the blood that's dripping in her eye. She's sliding out of the chair, so I kick away the broken glass and help her lie on the carpet. Blood trickles from the wounds in her side. Where's Mathias with his field-medic training? Hysan? What if they're hurt?

I can't think of them now. They're fine, they have to be. But Moira may be dying. As I dab at her wounds, she gives me a sullen glance. "Let it be. We have little time, and we must talk. I felt Ophiuchus."

Her words make me limp with relief. "So I'm not insane."

"I have no way to . . . judge that." Her voice is growing weaker. "But you were right about the Psy attack. You have a potent gift for . . . one so young."

I hold her head in my arms. "Let me help with your evacuation. Tell me what to do."

"No, you . . . have a more difficult task. You must . . . leave quickly." Her words come out as hoarse croaks, and I wonder if the glass has punctured her lung. "I didn't . . . know you at first. I have . . . long expected you."

"*Me?*"

"You must go to Aries . . . and warn the . . . Planetary Plenum."

Talking has worn her out. I gently lay her head on a chair cushion to cradle it, then stumble to the door and look for the doctor. The place seems deserted. Walls are ripped apart, furniture lies scattered, and broken glass litters the floors. There's another loud crash, and ceramic tiles rain from the ceiling.

"Mathias?" I call. "Hysan?" *Where are they?*

I can't desert Moira. My glass-riddled arm burns as I stagger back through the crunching glass. I sit beside her as a new bolt of lightning bangs into the needle somewhere below. Smoke from the burning grain rises in columns, and the air's really heating up. Soon the atmosphere will be too hot to breathe.

Moira's trying to talk again, so I lean close. "I'll speak to the other Guardians . . . as soon as I . . ."

"Save your breath."

At that moment, a young man and woman barrel in with a wheeled gurney. I back away so they can tend to Moira's wounds, and then I run to find my friends.

Hysan is lying in the antechamber with a deep gash in his thigh, and Mathias is leaning over him, pressing down on the wound with both hands to staunch the blood flow.

When he sees me coming, his face brightens. "Rho! They said you were unhurt and tending to Moira. I would've come for you, but Hysan would have bled out."

I hide my wounded arm. "Don't worry about me. What happened to Hysan?"

"Piece of metal ripped through his leg. We need a tourniquet."

Dark blood soaks Hysan's trouser leg. I kneel and stroke his damp forehead. "*Equinox* has life support," he groans.

"Lie still. This is arterial bleeding." Mathias presses down harder. "You won't make it back unless we stop it."

Hysan grits his teeth, so I spring to my feet and call for help.

"There's no one," breathes Hysan. "They've gone."

Mathias presses the wound with all his might. "Find something like a cord, a sash, anything we can tie around his leg." I start to unclasp my belt, but Mathias says, "Our belts are too thick. We need something thin and flexible enough to twist."

I look around for something better, but the antechamber's almost bare. Only one thing comes to mind. I kneel and slip Hysan's ceremonial dagger from its sheath. Neither of the guys notices.

The air is so sizzling hot, every breath burns my throat. I turn my back and strip off my uniform tunic, peeling the fabric from my bleeding right arm. I'm bare to the waist, but that can't matter right now. I clamp one end of the undamaged left sleeve in my teeth, then stretch the fabric tight and slice it off at the shoulder.

Turning back around, I hold up the sleeve to Mathias with my good arm and try using my injured one to cover my bra. "Will this work?"

Pain spasms through me, and my injured arm falls. Mathias looks up and does a double take. Hysan stares, too, and I say, "Take the damn sleeve."

Blushing, Mathias averts his gaze. "I-I can't lift my hands. You'll have to do it."

I turn around and yank my one-sleeved tunic back on, scraping the fabric over my wounded arm, regardless of the sting. Part of my bra is still showing, but I can't fix that.

I kneel on the baking-hot floor, and Mathias gives me step-by-step instructions. "Tie the sleeve around his leg, about two inches above the wound." As I slip the sleeve under Hysan's skin, he stares up at me, wincing but still trying to smile.

I cut another small square from the hem of my tunic to make a pad. Pulling the sleeve ends together over the pad, I tie half a knot, lay the jeweled hilt of Hysan's dagger across it, then do the rest of the knot. I twist the dagger until the sleeve-tourniquet tightens around Hysan's leg just enough to stop the bleeding. Finally, I secure the frayed ends of the sleeve so the tourniquet won't come loose.

"Good job," says Mathias. "You'd make a good field medic."

Hysan's skin looks ashy. "H-Healer Rho."

"We'll have to carry him," says Mathias. "Can you manage the weight?"

"Yes." Playing the drums works out my arms, so I'm strong for someone my size. I grab Hysan's ankles and lift him up.

The parking port is so full of smoke, we have to hunker low to breathe, and the heavy gravity doesn't help. By a miracle, our hover-car is still parked where we left it.

With a few awkward bumps, we manage to get Hysan inside and stretched out on the floor. Everything's hot to the touch, but when we seal the door and activate the car's cooling system, we can breathe a little easier. "How do we program this thing to take us back to the spaceport?" asks Mathias.

Hysan tries to push himself up on one elbow, but he falls back. "The panel." He points to a small metal square inset in the wall. "Color coded. Works by touch."

I jump up and tap the square, scorching my finger. A grid of diodes lights up, glowing in dozens of different colors. "What next?"

He closes his eyes. "Return trip is . . . press magenta three times."

I frown at the colored diodes. "Magenta's like purple, right?"

Hysan doesn't answer. He's passed out.

My fingertip circles over all the purplish lights. Lavender, fuchsia, burgundy, until finally I just pick one. When the hover-car lifts out of the port and sails down the needle's face, we're engulfed in pitch-black smoke. Mathias puts on his field glasses, and as he scans the scene, his square shoulders begin to sag. After a moment, he takes the glasses off.

"Can I see?" I ask.

"You might not want to."

I put on the glasses, and their enhanced optics reveal a sky transformed into a smoldering cauldron. Moira's grain fields have been reduced to charcoal, and the needle city is listing to one side. "It's going to fall," I whisper.

"Yes," says Mathias. "How did this happen?"

"Moira turned on her Ephemeris, and Ophiuchus saw us."

Mathias doesn't have a response.

We zoom over the grain fields, parting a path through dense flying ash, but apparently I picked the right shade of magenta because we're heading back the way we came. In the distance, ships are rising from the spaceport. Everyone's trying to escape. I wonder what will happen when we all fly through the burning atmosphere overhead.

Caasy.

Just as I turn to ask Mathias about him, I see the needle city collapsing. It falls straight down to the earth, and clouds of debris mushroom out from its base. I scream a sob.

Mathias takes the glasses and looks. He scans for a long time, but I don't want to see anymore. All I can do is cry.

"Ochus followed me here. Moira saw him right before the storm. I didn't imagine it. He blasted Moira's city using Psynergy."

"We don't know who's behind this," says Mathias, "but you were right about the attack on Virgo. You were right about the omen."

I rub my face. "I don't want to be right," I mumble, gazing up at the darkening sky. "Moira told me to go to the Plenum."

He wrinkles his forehead. "I'm not sure you'll be safe there. From what my parents tell me, the place is full of criminals and spies, and Guardians try to stay away."

Our car dodges through heavy traffic, and its onboard cooling system can't keep up with the rising heat. Hysan's head lolls from side to side.

"Then we better watch our backs."

Mathias lowers his head. "We have to assume this enemy will

try to assassinate you again. We'll need to take better safety precautions on Aries—physically and metaphysically."

The traffic grows thicker, and we chug to a halt, hovering over coal-black embers that were once stalks of grain. It feels like we're slow-poaching.

I can't look at Hysan. I'm worried he's lost too much blood. Every passing second seems to steal more things from him. One less breath, one less heartbeat, one less smile.

Mathias keeps checking the wound, releasing the tourniquet a bit, then retightening it. Ahead, more ships are launching. "We should help these people," I say.

"We will." He wipes sweat from his face. "*Equinox* has enough air for about ten more passengers."

When we reach the spaceport and find Hysan's ship, the smell outside is nauseating. Nobody's in sight at this end of the field, so we'll have to go to the main terminal to find our ten passengers. The question neither of us asks is how we're supposed to only help ten when there are so many who won't make it.

The bodies floating on Elara flash before my eyes. Only this time, it's Virgo's children who've been attacked.

Ophiuchus is a plague, and he won't stop spreading. Our only chance of survival is for the Houses of the Zodiac to come together. I have to plead my case to the Plenum. After what's happened here, the other Guardians have to believe me.

The launch pad radiates heat like a griddle as we carry Hysan's unconscious body from the car to the ship. At least the air in *Equinox* is cooler.

"Caasy!" I call out as we enter, but he doesn't reply.

"I'll try to locate him on his Tattoo once we have control of the ship," says Mathias.

We lay Hysan on the deck, and Mathias races to the galley to get the ship's healing kit. I keep checking the tourniquet. Hysan's skin is losing its golden color. I cushion his head on my lap and stroke his cheek. "Please hang on, Hysan. . . ."

When Mathias comes back, I ask, "Where's the life-support pod?"

"We'll find it later," he says, digging through the kit. "First, we have to wake up your Libran and get him to unlock his ship."

Mathias snaps an ampoule of wake-up gas under Hysan's nostrils, but he doesn't rouse. Outside, we hear another thundering explosion, and I readjust Hysan's head and run to the glass nose to see what's happening. "Our car just caught fire!" I yell. "The whole launch pad is melting!"

Mathias snaps a second ampoule, and Hysan opens his eyes with a groan. "Unlock your ship," says Mathias.

Hysan squints and blinks. He seems to be in a fog, so I kneel beside him and take his hand. "Please, Hysan. Please unlock *Equinox*'s controls."

"Look alive, 'Nox."

The ship's navigation screens flash on. "He's yours," breathes Hysan. "Take care of him . . . Rho." His eyes roll up and close.

"*Hysan!*" I shake him while Mathias bounds to the helm and activates the enhanced optics so he can see through the smoke.

I lower my head and press my ear to Hysan's chest to listen for a heartbeat. In my sideways vision, I see a small figure fly out from the far end of the ship.

I jerk my head up. Caasy is opening one of the ship's escape capsules.

"Caasy!" I call out.

He turns, but there's something strange about his expression. He doesn't run over to help me with Hysan. Instead, he shouts, "Fly safe, Dear Mother! I am returning to Gemini!"

We're escaping a House that's just been attacked, Hysan's limp body is sprawled on the floor, and still most surreal of all is this moment. Caasy's abandoning us.

"Please! Help me move him!" I call.

Caasy clicks a few buttons on the screen beside the capsule, and as the door is opening, he ducks in. And that's when I notice his hands. He's clutching something dark and oblong in his fingers.

"Caasy, don't!"

The door shuts behind him. There's a noise of hissing gears, and the capsule detaches from the ship, shooting up into Space.

Mother Origene's stone is gone.

24

MATHIAS CALLS OUT TO ME from the front of the ship. "I see people on the terminal roof! As soon as we land, open the hatch and help ten of them board."

I have to put Caasy and the stone out of my mind if I'm going to help.

Hysan, too.

The ship lifts off in a banking turn toward the terminal building. "Ready!" I call out, gripping the hatch release, poised for quick action.

There's a loud rolling crash, followed by a cannonade of smaller explosions. Instead of slowing, Mathias pulls up and goes faster.

"What are you doing?" I shout.

He turns to me slowly, a look of disbelief on his face. "A burning freighter just hit the terminal building." His voice shakes. "We won't find any passengers now."

I shut my eyes, unable to take it in.

I never should have come here.

◆ ◆ ◆

We abandon Virgo.

We leave without saving anyone.

Equinox's scans show a world on fire. Thick black clouds boil over the Western Hemisphere, blocking the landscape below, and orange flames geyser upward. The planet Tethys shines like brimstone.

Our ship's hull has proved impervious to the burning atmosphere, but I can't say that about the others. We've seen at least twenty ships explode and plummet. Twice, Mathias tried to dock with a burning ship to rescue the passengers, but our attempts failed. The blazing oxygen is too hot.

First Cancer. Now Virgo. Ophiuchus is exterminating the Zodiac, one House at a time. The horror is beyond understanding, but what's worse is the guilt, gnawing through my insides like hungry Maws. He was following *me*—that's how he found her. I must have brought Moira with me, somehow, to the plane where Ophiuchus can communicate.

How long before he attacks Gemini? Will Caasy take me seriously after what he witnessed on Virgo? Is that why he ran?

But why take my black opal? This whole time, I knew there was something else he wanted, an ulterior motive for tagging along with us. I should have been more protective of the stone.

I want to ask Hysan what he thinks—after all, he didn't let me jettison it from the ship the first time Ochus attacked us. But it'll have to wait until he awakens. He's still resting inside his life-support pod, having his leg repaired.

When we searched his quarters to find the pod, we discovered a number of other interesting items: a weapons cache, body armor, a case of tiny micro-cameras, tracking chips and scramblers, and, of course, the Psy-hardened strongbox that's been holding our devices, its door gaping open. From the scratch marks, it's clear Caasy jimmied the strongbox lock. That we can tell, only my black opal was missing.

For now, we're flying straight to the Planetary Plenum, despite Mathias's concerns. We're traveling at hyperspeed, hoping our fuel won't run out before we get there. Mathias has calculated the space-time relativity effect, and he says if all goes well, we'll arrive two days before this year's Plenum session winds down.

The Plenum rotates from House to House each year, and now it's at Aries, the first and oldest House. The Ariean civilization has risen and fallen many times, and these days, the newsfeeds show its main planet, Phaetonis, as a wild and rowdy place ruled by a junta of warlords. While the Plenum's there, the ambassadors have to be protected by the Ariean army, which is made up of soldiers, not Zodai.

The black market flourishes there, and local militias wrangle for territory. The universal corruption and high crime rate may explain why Aries is the most militarized House in the Zodiac—and the most impoverished.

Aries is a Cardinal House, and it represents Fire. The Ram constellation has a small sun and three settled planets, but only the planet Phaetonis has breathable atmosphere, and it's thin. Phaetonians live under domes, although walking on the surface is possible with the aid of an air mask. The planet's porous, so its gravity's weak, but at least we'll have weight again.

Mathias and I are working on my speech for the Plenum when *Equinox* informs us that the life-support pod has finished healing Hysan's leg. "I'm going to check on him," I say, rising.

Mathias stands, too. "We'll both go."

Hysan's cabin is larger and more comfortable than our spartan guest quarters. The lid of his coffin-shaped pod has already popped open, and he's inside in his boxers, apparently still asleep. His golden hair fans over his forehead, and his skin nearly glows, his leg completely healed.

Mathias throws a blanket over Hysan, covering him to his chin. "The Libran's out of danger. You should use this pod to heal your arm."

"Yeah, maybe later." I've cleaned the glass cuts, but they still sting. Even the plush yellow uniform I'm wearing feels like sandpaper against them.

But I don't want to cheat the pain. I want to feel it. I need to.

Mathias has laid out Hysan's weapons across his dressing table to ask him about them. Four plexine laser guns, a particle-beam pistol, a half dozen Tasers, a twelve-pack of nuclear grenades. Quite an arsenal for a traveling Guardian. Along with the mini-cameras and tracking bugs, I can no longer doubt our friendly Libran likes to play spy.

Hysan opens his eyes, and when they find me, I watch recognition settle on his features, curving the ends of his mouth. He sits up and throws off the blanket. Mathias impatiently hands him the pair of gray coveralls that are lying on a nearby chair.

As Hysan steps out and pulls on his clothes, he sees the weapons. He looks straight at Mathias. "I see you have no respect for private property. Not even a Guardian's."

Mathias glares right back. "At least I saved your life."

"Thanks," says Hysan, like he's forcing a word that won't roll off his tongue. "But you should have done what I asked and gone to look for Rho. She's hurt her arm, it could have been worse—"

"Shut up, both of you." I look at Hysan. "Caasy ejected himself in an escape capsule." His eyebrow shoots up, like he finds this amusing. "Right after breaking into your strongbox and taking my black opal."

Now he grows alert. He looks around eagerly for the box, and when he sees that it's been forced open, his whole demeanor changes. He becomes kind of . . . professional.

"Rho. We need to talk. Alone."

"You're dreaming," says Mathias.

"What's going on?" I ask.

"It's a . . . Guardian thing." He looks at Mathias. "I know what you're thinking, but you're wrong. Since Rho was unable to meet her predecessor, she was never told some things that a Guardian needs to know. That's all this is about."

Mathias is unmoved. "I was in Mother Origene's Royal Guard. I've told Rho everything I know."

"Yes, but there are things even Advisors are not aware of." A gleam crosses Hysan's eyes, like a new thought just swam by. "The greatest secret of the Houses is passed on from Guardian to Guardian. No one else can know. This is a truth entrusted to only one person in each House."

"That's ridiculous. Cancrian Guardians are only named after the current Guardian passes," argues Mathias.

"That's what everyone in every House *thinks*, but it's not true." Hysan sighs in frustration. "Guardians are so attuned to the Psy that they can sense when their death is near, and they prepare their successor before anything is made public. If Mother Origene had seen the Dark Matter, she would have sensed her passing. As a backup, we also leave hidden messages in our chambers that only the new Guardian can find. If Rho had been able to access Origene's residence on planet Cancer, she would have found this information."

I look from one guy to the other. I can see why Mathias is having trouble believing Hysan—this sounds strange enough to be a sneaky excuse for us to be alone.

The problem is, I don't think I'd mind being alone with Hysan. And that's why I have to insist that Mathias stay.

"Hysan, I get it. And I believe you, but at this point we don't know whom we can trust—including Guardians, since one just stole my stone. The only people we can be sure of are the three of us. We've already been trusting each other with our lives, now let's live them in the open."

When I'm finished speaking, Hysan gives me a look that expresses the opposite of Mathias's one of approval. Then he eyes

Mathias warily. "You can never speak a word of this to anyone. *Anyone.*"

"I know my duty to my Guardian, Libran," snarls Mathias.

Hysan sighs. He sits on the edge of his bed, and for the first time I notice his golden complexion hasn't fully returned. He's not altogether better. He lost a lot of blood and still seems a little weak. I perch next to him so he doesn't have to keep looking up. Mathias hangs back against the wall.

"When the original Guardians fell to mortality, they all brought one thing with them: A Talisman, each of which holds the knowledge of an aspect of humanity, giving each House a different strength."

"Cancrians are natural nurturers," I supply. "Librans are just. Aquarians, philosophers. Capricorns, wise. . . ."

He nods. "Each House excels in a different field because each Guardian guards the knowledge of a particular universal truth. This ensures we'll always be equals, and we'll always depend on each other for survival. That way no House can seize more power."

"Only the Talisman is symbolic," I say, speeding things up. Every House has its own theory for why we each evolved with different values, but the idea of a magical object is pretty popular, especially on Gemini and Sagittarius, whose people are more inclined to believe the unbelievable if the evidence fits. "It's just a way of explaining our differences."

Hysan shakes his head. "It's real."

He looks too tired and distraught to be making this up.

"*How?*" asks Mathias. "How could a *thing* contain a concept like nurturing or curiosity?"

"The secret stored in the Talisman is accessed the way you access the Psy. It doesn't simply contain words or diagrams or films—it's knowledge of the thing itself. Similar to how the communal mind creates meaning when it answers a query."

Hysan looks at me and speaks slowly now, like he's approaching our first speed bump. "Since they're made up of Psynergy, the Talismans usually double as a different device."

I know what comes next. He doesn't say it, but it's written all over his face.

I rise and walk to the other end of the room, where the strongbox is lying open and defeated. I stare hopelessly into its emptiness.

I just let the Geminin Guardian steal House Cancer's Talisman.

25

"WHAT INFORMATION HAVE YOU UNLOCKED in yours?"
For some reason, I whisper the question, as if on some level I know
it's inappropriate.

"I can't say."

"But it has to do with your Psy Shield."

He looks at me a moment before nodding. "The Talisman . . . it
doesn't give answers. It just makes concepts clearer. Based on what
it revealed to me about Psynergy, Neith and I were able to devise
the shield. On Libra, I nearly finished synthesizing cristobalite
beads that should veil people from the Psy. Individual shields."

That's the gift he was making for me, I realize. "Thank you," I
say.

He nods. "Lord Vaz and I built the Libran Talisman into this
ship. It powers *Equinox*'s brain and projects the Ephemeris you saw
back in my reading room at home."

"And now Cancer's is gone, before I could even find out what it can do." I bump my forehead on the wall, feeling every failure of my tenure as Guardian so far. "This is all my fault."

"Why don't you take a rest in the healing box?" Mathias suggests, only gentleness in his voice. "Fix your arm."

"The pod is all yours, my lady," says Hysan, rising to his feet and following Mathias out the door. "And don't worry about your Talisman. We'll get it back. We know where Caaseum lives."

✦ ✦ ✦

The ship is flying on fumes.

We're close enough that we should make it to House Aries before running out of fuel, but the timing will be tight.

The Zodai suit Lola and Leyla made me is ruined, so I have to wear the Libran uniform. To make sure Mathias doesn't flip, I salvaged the four silver moons from the blue suit and sewed them over the Libran glyph of the yellow tunic. Probably best to head him off now, before we land, so there are no disagreements when we disembark.

When I get to Mathias's door, it's ajar, and he isn't there. But Hysan is.

"What are you doing?" I ask.

He snaps his gaze to me from behind the desk and stops rifling through Mathias's gear belt. "Inspecting cargo?"

I cross my arms. He glances toward the lavatory stall, where the ultraviolet shower is humming. He's a little pink in the cheeks but otherwise unaffected by being caught. "You won't tell, will you?"

"Hysan, these are Mathias's things. This war between the two of you—"

"What about *him*? He went through my weapons—"

"Yes, and that wasn't right either. But you've been keeping a lot of secrets."

Hysan steps closer to me and lowers his voice. "I also just revealed my biggest secret to a complete stranger, my lady, and now I would like to know exactly who he is."

"Two strangers, actually. What about me?"

He turns back to the desk and replaces Mathias's things where he found them. "Rho, you're a Guardian. It's no more your fault Origene couldn't teach you than it is my fault my parents couldn't raise me. But it's still your right to know."

There's a noise from the lavatory, and we both freeze—but the UV keeps humming.

"Look, I know that was wrong, and I won't go snooping again," says Hysan, coming around the desk. "But please keep this between us. I don't want to set him off right as we've arrived."

I swallow, hard. "I don't like secrets."

"It's not like that." His eyes grow greener. "Rho, that truth was mine to protect, and I swore never to speak of it to any soul other than the next Libran Guardian. I broke my sacred oath, and I didn't do it for Mathias, or even House Cancer. I did it for *you*."

Hysan walks out of the room, leaving me alone with his secrets and my guilt.

When the shower cuts off, I flee from the cabin, easing the door closed behind me. I hate keeping things from Mathias, but I don't want to give him any more reasons to dislike Hysan. We're going to need to work together on Aries, and that can't happen if the guys are at each other's throats.

I've never felt so far from home.

✦ ✦ ✦

Night is falling when we reach Phaetonis. Sunset gives the domed capital city of Marson an amber sheen.

Equinox circles low over the spaceport just outside the city dome. The place is a fortress, bristling with laser canons, hover-drones, and radar surveillance. It's also enclosed in a high mesh fence. "I don't like this, but we need fuel," says Hysan. "We won't make it much farther."

"Is there another depot?" asks Mathias.

"Not near the city." Hysan circles again, watching the enhanced optical view on his screens. "I'll put us down as close as I can get to the fuel pumps at the edge of the port."

A vibrocopter sits on the pad beside the pumps, and two armed soldiers patrol around it, wearing dusty helmets and air masks. We watch them through *Equinox*'s glass nose while we alight on the field adjacent to the pad, as soundless and invisible as a sigh.

The soldiers whip around and point their guns at us. "Come out, and put down your weapons," they command.

I cover my mouth to imprison my scream. How can they see our ship if we're invisible?

Mathias and I look at Hysan in alarm, but he doesn't seem bothered by the guns pointed at our heads. *"Sleep,"* he whispers, and a halo of gaseous white mist spurts out from *Equinox*'s hull, showering the soldiers. Instantly, they fall like rag dolls.

I gasp, but Hysan chuckles. "They're only napping. The heat of our engines must have given us away."

When he offers us our veil collars, Mathias says, "Enough deceit."

"You're insane," says Hysan. "You don't know this world. You told Rho yourself, it's brimming with criminals and spies."

"We'll do it Mathias's way," I say, the guilt of keeping Hysan's secret still burning through me.

Hysan stows the veil collars.

Before leaving the ship, we all put on lightweight air masks. While I stand lookout, Hysan and Mathias hustle to the pumps, grab the hoses, and feed *Equinox*'s empty belly with ultracold fluid plasma. It's funny how the guys get along like dance partners when they're doing physical work.

Hysan drops some galactic gold coins by the pumps, then steals gate keys from one of the unconscious soldiers. We then set off at a flat-out run, dodging under passenger ships, hiding behind beastly ground vehicles with tires the size of small moons, and sneaking around ranks of soldiers wielding grenade launchers and rifles.

It's deep twilight now, and we're making fast time in the weaker gravity, but this spaceport looks as if it's under siege. Laser burns riddle some of the hangar walls, and the sooty blooms of recent fires stain the launch pad. Searchlights rove over the tarmac, and the high mesh fence is topped by concertina wire.

Mathias stays close beside me, Taser in hand, pivoting constantly and scanning the area with his field glasses. Hysan uses the stolen keys to exit the fenced-in spaceport through a maintenance gate, and we can't leave fast enough—until I see what lies beyond the fence.

The historic capital city of House Aries is ringed by a gargantuan slum. I'd seen pictures of the slum in our Acolyte studies, but the holographic images didn't convey the decomposing feel of death that pervades the air.

Shacks lean and tilt on mountains of rotting garbage, and the valleys in between are open sewers. Even with the air mask, the stench makes me dizzy.

Through the open doors of the shacks, we see older people silhouetted in pools of lantern light, and they're sewing, hammering, assembling electronic devices, sharpening knives. Overhead, modern pulse-trains rocket from the spaceport into the city center, skipping over the slum.

"We have to catch a train," says Hysan. "It'll take too long to cross on foot in the dark."

Mathias points to one of the massive columns supporting the elevated train track. "Maybe we can climb it."

Hysan nods, and we sprint toward the column, splashing through muck. My yellow trousers get speckled and stained. The column has a ladder bolted to its northern face, and the rungs are slimy with blue-green algae. Hysan goes first, then me, followed by Mathias. My boot soles are still warped from the heat on Tethys, and they slip and slide as I climb.

When we near the top, I feel a stitch in my side. Above me, Hysan's Scan shoots out a golden beam, and the locked access panel instantly pops open.

We climb up into the webbed steel truss that supports the train track. The build-up of static electricity here practically makes my curls stand on end.

"The closest station's that way." Hysan points. "It's an ordinary pulse-train. It runs on a current of oscillating magnetism. We'll have to crawl through this truss to reach it."

Mathias gives me water from his canteen, and I tug down my air mask to drink. "How far?" I ask.

Hysan wipes sweat from his eyes. "A kilometer or two."

There's not enough room to stand inside the truss, so we crawl along the riveted beams on all fours. Every few minutes, a train blasts over us with a deafening rumble. By the time we reach the station, our water canteens are almost empty, my eardrums feel lacerated from the train noise, and my hands are bruised from the rivets. We're all covered in slime.

Hysan unsheathes his dagger and uses its blade as a mirror to peek over the edge of the dimly lit station platform. When he gives the all clear, we scramble up, onto the platform, where it's a relief to stand upright.

Hysan surveys his grimy suit. "They'll never let us on the train looking like this."

Mathias scrapes his boot soles clean with his knife, but we're all so mud-splattered, the effort's futile. Hysan draws something from his pocket: our veil collars.

"It's your decision, Rho. Do you want to reach the Plenum or not?"

Mathias and I share a questioning glance, and without a word, we each take ours. No one seems to notice when we waver out of sight.

We slip into the first train that stops, then huddle in the aisle, trying not to bump anyone. The train has an air supply, so we stow our masks, which are now gray and damp. I can only hope the veils cover up our odor, too.

Some of the Ariean passengers around us are hooded and concealing what are obviously weapons. They look like muggers, though they're too clean to be from the slum. Their complexions range from tones of dark pink to wine, and they're all built like soldiers. Arieans are the most physically fit people in our galaxy.

No one on the train talks aloud or makes eye contact. Most people are listing to the right, enthralled by their Earpiece—a small device Arieans get pierced into their right ear when they turn seventeen, an age when every Ariean commits to two years in the army.

The Earpiece functions like a Wave, only its images aren't projected as holograms: They're screened inside the person's mind, where no one else can see them. Arieans are masters in the art of war, and troops need to communicate with each other discreetly in the field.

Mathias hands me a tiny squeeze-tube, then passes another one to Hysan. "Antiviral," he says. Holding his own gingerly by one corner, he bites off the tip between his teeth, then sucks the contents into his mouth. Hysan and I do the same. The syrup tastes like sea cherries.

It's late at night when we reach the city center, but I don't feel sleepy. My internal clock must be out of order. The enormous central train station is crowded with passengers and soldiers, all heavily armed. So far, I haven't seen any wallscreens where we might get news from home.

As we wind through the labyrinthine station, Hysan says, "We'll find sanctuary at the International Village. Every House has an embassy there."

"Let's go to Cancer's," I say, the thought of seeing my people giving me new strength.

Marson's city center is sheltered under a high-tension fabric dome, held aloft by air pressure, like a giant inflated beach ball. Buildings squat like bunkers, especially the hulking hippodrome where the Plenum meets. Soldiers in armored vehicles barrel along the dark narrow streets, billowing fumes. They stop and hassle people at random, like they're looking to pick fights. Hysan was right—I'm glad we're veiled.

When we get closer to the hippodrome, the crowd of Arieans surrounding us begins to thin. People from all over the Zodiac are here to observe the Plenum in session. I see mystics from Pisces veiled in woven silver. Dark-haired Sagittarians in levlan suits that remind me of Nishi. Olive-skinned Virgos, too, as well as blond Librans and petite pairs of Gemini. On every street corner, red-suited Ariean soldiers stand guard.

The hippodrome's been blockaded. Around us, people are

talking about a bomb threat. The ambassadors and their aides have been taken to an underground shelter while bomb squads scan the building for explosives.

Everyone seems to view this with more cynicism than shock, as if these kinds of attacks happen often at the Plenum. Suddenly I remember Mom telling me something about these sessions. She said the Plenum meetings were a waste of time because the ambassadors don't work well together. She claimed the system had been corrupted. Turf grabs. Partisan squabbling. Bribes not paid.

Apparently things have gotten worse in the decade since our lessons ended.

"I see a lot of soldiers, but where's the local Zodai Guard?" I ask Hysan.

"The Ariean Zodai were marginalized when the junta seized power. Even General Eurek is little more than a figurehead, living under house arrest. The military employs its own astrologers, and so do the warring militias."

"Can we visit Guardian Eurek?"

Hysan whispers to his Scan, and a small hologram floats before his eyes. It's a miniature figure of a plump man wearing extravagant robes trimmed in sheepskin. He looks like he was once a bodybuilder whose muscles have since melted into folds of skin from lack of use. Hysan spins the hologram so I can see the man's face.

"This is Albor Echus, the Ariean ambassador. He's more a mouthpiece for the generals. You can meet him, but General Eurek receives no one."

On Stanton's tenth birthday, the same year she left, Mom gave me a necklace. It was the only gift she ever gave me that wasn't from Dad, too. On a strand of silver seahorse hair, she had strung together twelve nar-clam pearls, each one bearing the sacred symbol of a House of the Zodiac.

"We share the same universe, but we live in different worlds," she used to often remind me.

Yet despite her insistence on the Houses' differences, I never saw the Zodiac as a collection of multicolored pearls caught in the same necklace's orbit—I saw us as *one necklace*. Each pearl has its purpose, but no one is more important than another, and every pearl is integral to the beauty of the whole, and to our calling ourselves a necklace at all.

I'm embarrassed that it's taken this trip to show me how naive that sounds. Mom was right: Every House I've visited functions as its own, separate world; even Cancer operates that way, only I never thought of it like that before. We don't generally go around thinking of ourselves as one piece of a larger whole.

But now I have to address all the Houses and find a way to convince them we *are* one necklace. Every pearl matters. What happens to one star in our universe can and *does* affect every other.

That's the advantage Ophiuchus holds over us: As long we keep on distrusting each other, we're easier to pick off, one pearl at a time.

26

WHEN WE GET TO THE VILLAGE, we have to remove our collars. The community is enclosed within a solid black fence, and guards barricade the only entrance, so we can't sneak past without alerting them.

We're immediately asked for proof of identification. An Ariean soldier holds out a small screen for our thumbprints. His colleagues scowl at the grime on our clothes.

As soon as Hysan's thumb hovers over the screen, a hologram pops up of his face, and beneath it the words *Hysan Dax, House Libra, Diplomatic Envoy.* Plus a bunch of facts like his astrological fingerprint, birthdate, schooling, and other information I can't see. Mathias goes next. *Lodestar Mathias Thais, House Cancer, Royal Advisor.* Then me. *Mother Rhoma Grace, House Cancer, Guardian.*

The soldiers look at me curiously.

"Thank you," says Hysan, reaching out to bump fists with each of them. I spy glints of gold in the soldiers' hands when they pull away, and each slips what look like galactic gold coins in their pockets. Then Hysan takes my hand and hurriedly pulls me through the entrance, Mathias following close behind.

On the other side of the wall, the International Village looks like a smaller version of our solar system. The village is round, like a clock, and divided into twelve embassies. At its center is an inter-House market with food and amenities from across the Zodiac.

The look, style, and operation of each House is so diverse that the effect is dizzying. The only thing I can compare this place to is an amusement park, where every section has a different theme. The embassies are considered sovereign territory, so they don't fall under Ariean rule.

We pop in on the Libran side. Their building is a sleek-walled, armed fortress, surrounded by surveillance cameras and Zodai from their Royal Guard. To our other side is Virgo. The round, golden embassy looks like a beehive, and its recessed entrance gives way to a colorful fruit-and-vegetable garden on its front lawn.

Mathias runs ahead, and I break into a sprint after him. We both sense the Cancer Sea's call.

We rush past Leo, an elevated theater house with live lions prowling the front—a couple of them are ripping into a hunk of raw meat—and then we see the Fourth House. The Cancrian embassy looks like an island villa: Instead of one building, we have four multi-level bungalows, each draped with airy curtains, the structures built from sand and seashells.

Like home on Kalymnos, I think with a rush of breath.

Weaving through the four bungalows, and forming a protective barrier around the whole embassy, is a wide stream of water, winding like a serpent made from the Cancer Sea. There's a plank bridging the stream, but two members of our Royal Guard are removing it for the night. I recognize their faces from Oceon 6. I sent them here the night I took my Guardian's oath.

"Westky! Bromston!" Mathias calls out to the two Lodestars, and they stop what they're doing.

"Lodestar Thais!" one shouts back, recognizing Mathias. "Are you here with Holy Mother?"

"He is," I say, running up behind Mathias, a little out of breath. A smile spreads across my face. Home, at last . . . kind of.

The Lodestars reset the plank, and the three of us cross over. The ground floor of the first bungalow is the only place with lights on, so we go inside—which is easy, since it has no doors. From a quick glance, none of the four bungalows seem to offer any privacy on the first floor. Doors and walls are only for the higher stories.

The lobby we step into is designed to be a waiting area. Half the room is decked with hammocks and rocking chairs, each equipped with an embassy Wave for checking news and sending messages. The second half is taken up by a saltwater pool for swimming.

The only person here is a man seated at an official-looking desk. When we get closer, I realize he's a hologram.

"I'm Lodestar Mathias Thais," says Mathias as we approach. "Holy Mother is with me. We are looking for Amanta and Egon Thais."

The holographic man's eyes widen. They linger on me. Then they turn to Hysan. "Who is the Libran?"

"He's—"

"Diplomatic envoy Hysan Dax," says Hysan, cutting Mathias off mid-answer.

The explanation irritates Mathias because he clarifies, "He has been chauffeuring us on our journey. Do you know where my parents are?"

The hologram nods. "I was just shutting off for the night. I'm transmitting from bungalow three. Your parents are only one floor up. I'll tell them you're here."

The hologram disappears. Just seconds later, two people run in toward us and fold Mathias up in their arms.

Hysan and I step away to give them privacy, the absence of my family suddenly hurting like real physical pain. This whole journey, I've tried to be strong, to focus on the mission, to put aside my own needs . . . but the truth is, I've never felt lonelier. Maybe I can try Waving Dad and Stanton from here. There might be a way to reach them by now.

Mathias brings his parents over to introduce me. Their eyes are rimmed red, but they smile and bow together. "Holy Mother."

"Please, you needn't bow," I say, reaching out to them for the hand touch instead. "And please, call me Rho."

It's clear Mathias gets most of his features from Amanta, his mother, who's tall, pale, and blonde. The wavy dark hair comes from his father, Egon. They seem happy beyond words to see their son . . . but there's also a deep sadness that's impossible to ignore. They've just lost their daughter in the attack.

When their eyes land on Hysan, he says, "I'm the chauffeur."

I have to look to make sure it's him speaking. There's no attempt at magic in his voice, and sunlight is even missing from his features.

He meets my gaze and tries to muster some of his usual liveliness, but it seems forced. For the first time, charm fails him. "It's late, and I should find lodging at the Libran embassy. I'll see you tomorrow, my lady."

"You can stay—"

"I shouldn't." The moment he leaves the lobby, he vanishes from sight. He must have slipped on his collar.

Mathias's parents usher us toward their private quarters. As he fills them in on the highlights of our journey, my mind lingers on Hysan. I wonder who hugged him when he had nightmares as a child. Who waits for him when he comes home from his travels. Whose faces he sees when he thinks of his people.

As Cancrians, caring after our loved ones is our top priority. When Mom left, it caused ripples through our whole community. Broken families are rare on Cancer, runaway mothers unheard of.

But I had Stanton and Dad. I can't even imagine what it'd be like to have no one.

"My parents are helping with the resettlement," Mathias tells me, after they've gone to bed. I'm staying in their guestroom, and Mathias is going to sleep in the den, but for now, we're both on the hammock in my room, talking.

"They're negotiating with other Houses for temporary housing and food. My dad's trying to establish an orphanage."

An orphanage. Is that where Hysan was raised by the robot Miss Trii? Is that where generations of Cancrian and Virgo children will be raised after Ochus's attacks?

"Rho?"

Mathias's deep, calming voice brings me back to tonight. "Sorry." I muster a small smile. "Life has been upside down for so long that things like parents and sleeping in a bedroom now feel alien."

"I know what you mean," he says, a dark lock falling into his eye. His Zodai-style haircut has grown out.

Amanta put our clothes in the refresher and lent us outfits to sleep in. I'm wearing one of Egon's old shirts—it falls a little higher than my knees, and the neckline slings across my shoulder. Mathias is in a pair of sweats and no shirt. Every time he moves, the lines of his chest and arms readjust, and I can almost see the muscles working beneath his skin.

When the impulse to touch him grows louder than my thoughts, I ask, "Can I borrow your Wave?" Mine is still locked up, in case Ophiuchus can activate the tutorial Ephemeris.

I use Mathias's Wave to try to reach Dad and Stanton, but I can't get through. I know they've most likely lost theirs, but I keep hoping I'll see them on the other end of the line. "I'll ask the embassy to try locating them tomorrow," says Mathias soothingly.

"Thanks." I Wave Nishi's Tracker next, but she doesn't answer. No one is going to rescue me from being alone with Mathias, and Mathias's muscles, and Mathias's silence.

Earlier, we took turns showering, and it was amazing to feel real water on my skin and hair again. While I dried my curls, Mathias cleaned the gunk off his boots; and now, in spite of my protests, he's doing the same with mine. He looks so serious, drawing his eyebrows together as he works bits of mud from the seams. The careful movements of his hands make me ache with guilt.

Before we got to Virgo, when he walked in on Hysan and me, he told me to remember who I am. Even though I'm still figuring it out, there are things I already know. Like I know I'm not a liar, and I don't like secrets.

I shouldn't have kept Hysan's snooping from Mathias. Not because it was a big deal—I'm sure Hysan didn't take anything— but because it's not who I am. Mathias was right to refuse the veil collars from the start of our journey. We may have to fight, but we can't lose sight of what we're fighting for.

How are we saving Cancer if we lose our Cancrian values in the process?

"Rho, about your speech to the Plenum," says Mathias, pausing to wipe the toe of my boot even though it's already clean. "Maybe you shouldn't mention Ophiuchus."

Everything down to the thoughts in my head freezes. "What do you mean?"

He turns the boot over to inspect the heel. "The ambassadors will be hard to convince. I just think you might do better by sticking to facts you can prove, for now."

The room darkens, as if someone's dimmed the lights. "You don't believe me. *Still.* After Virgo, after all you've seen."

"Make your case about the Psy attack," he says, his tone pleading. "You can prove that with the ship's log, and Moira will back you.

Why bring in a children's story when you don't have to? You know it makes people tune out."

I can't believe Mathias is asking me to lie. After everything he's said about Hysan, now he's telling me to be exactly like him. To lie to my people for their own good.

I remember the day of my swearing-in ceremony, when Nishi confronted me with her theory about Ophiuchus. I remember for a moment that I'd considered not mentioning Ochus to my Advisors so that I'd be taken seriously.

Then I remember Leyla's words and Agatha's blessing and Nishi's commitment, and I know why I can't lie: I would lose my way.

"Talk to me," whispers Mathias. "You can't just get upset when you disagree."

I want to speak, but anger is once again building up in my chest. *Mathias still doesn't trust me.* He can't vouch for my account of the truth because he didn't see all the things I saw. He didn't see the warnings for Thebe or Virgo either, and I was proven right both times . . . but still he refuses to see that I'm right about Ophiuchus.

The anger clogs my throat with a powerless fury. There's nothing I can do to prove I'm right to Mathias, short of opening my Ephemeris and calling Ochus here, right now.

"Rho." Mathias sets down my boots and kneels on the floor in front of me. "I live to serve you. You *know* that. I'm just trying to help you make a stronger case. I want the Houses on our side."

"Thank you," I say, taking his hands and pulling him up. "I just need some sleep."

"Of course, I'll go," he says, though he sounds a little sad. I feel the sadness, too—and I realize that under different circumstances, tonight could have gone another way.

"I'll be in the den if you need anything."

When Mathias leaves, I lie in the dark for a long time. It's not his fault he doesn't believe me. I know he's trying. It just goes against every grain of his nature to take something this outlandish at face value. Until now, his skepticism bothered me, but his loyalty was enough.

It's not anymore.

After everything that's happened, convincing the Houses that Ophiuchus exists is all I have left. If I don't make my case, the Zodiac is doomed. In the same way Mathias can't find a way to believe me, I'm not sure I can find a way to forgive him.

Because no matter how much we care, or how hard we try, we remain on opposite sides.

✦ ✦ ✦

The next morning, we leave the village and head to the hippodrome, where the Plenum is meeting.

The city is large, crowded, and disorganized. Yesterday's bomb threat locked everything down and caused the ambassadors to stay overnight at the shelter, so we couldn't meet with the Cancrian representative back at the embassy. We're trying to meet her now.

When we arrive, Mathias's parents have to report for their duties, but we agree to find them once we have an update. We spend an hour arguing with the clerks at the front desk who control the Plenum agenda, trying to convince them to give me a slot on today's schedule. First, they insist there's no way it can be adjusted because it's jam-packed. Once we've persuaded them our business is urgent, they claim to need a series of permissions, and they take forever getting each one.

All around us, soldiers are walking through the crowd, inspecting every questionable person and item. Yesterday's bomb scare left everyone rattled.

"Anything I can do, my lady?"

I whip around at the sound of Hysan's voice, a grin on my face. He looks like the sunrise.

Immediately, he takes charge of the situation. Though he's only seventeen, he's got all the skills of a seasoned diplomat. While he haggles with the clerks, I check out the hippodrome: It's a cube housing a giant, freestanding sphere of shining steel in its center. It looks like a small metal planet that's been hidden in a concrete box.

We're in the reception hall on the ground floor of the cube, and when I look up, I see the enormous underside of the sphere swelling overhead. Around it, a translucent pipe made of what looks like ruby glass spirals up as far as I can see, carrying people on a moving stairway up to the sphere's many levels.

"What's inside the sphere?" I whisper to Mathias.

"That's the arenasphere. When the Plenum's not here, the locals use it for holographic wrestling. It's actually a big business here."

I've seen that on my Wave before. Contestants alter their holograms to look like imaginary beasts—flying horses, gargoyles, three-headed dogs. The technology is similar to what powers the Imaginarium on Gemini.

There's a holographic newsfeed nearby, and Mathias and I sprint over to hear it. The footage is of ground fighting on the Sagittarian moon, where immigrant Scorps have turned against their Sagittarian employers, demanding the right to practice religious rituals in the workplace. Sagittarians are extremely tolerant people, which makes me wonder what kind of rituals the Scorps want to practice.

Since Sagittarius is a large constellation with many livable planets, I hope Nishi and her family are far away from the fighting. We don't hear anything about Cancer, but there's a report on the charred wasteland of Tethys in House Virgo. Where the needle city once towered, a crater now gapes like a dark wound, fringed by smoking rubble.

The fire was contained, but the sky is full of ash, shading out the sunlight, and much of the oxygen has burned away. Zodai predict a bitter winter on the planet's surface. Years of grain harvests will fail, causing universal food shortages. All survivors have been evacuated to Virgo's lesser planets, where the main problem now is overcrowding. Empress Moira remains in critical care.

Virgo's cries still echo in my head when we return to the front desk to check with Hysan.

"They've finally agreed to contact your representative. Ambassador Sirna is on her way." His verdant eyes narrow on mine. "What is it?"

"What *isn't* it?"

"We're still around to bemoan our state, my lady." His lips hitch into his crooked smirk. "So that's something." No matter how dark the circumstances, Hysan can always find the light. It's my favorite thing he does.

When she arrives, the sight of Sirna's Cancrian face warms me like a hug. She's in her thirties, with dark hair, ebony skin, and sea-blue eyes, and she's wearing Cancrian formal attire: a long, flowing skirt coupled with a coat that bears the four sacred silver moons. But up close, I realize she's not smiling. "Honored Guardian, we meet at last."

We exchange hand touches, and after I introduce my friends, she says, "Your long silence perplexes us. We don't understand your presence here when our people need you so desperately at home."

I open my mouth, but Mathias interrupts. "Ambassador, there's no place our Holy Mother would rather be than home. She's come here with an urgent message for all the Houses."

"The same message your classmate has been spreading?" Sirna's eyes sharpen. "We've seen the video she's sent to all the news outlets. We know your band is touring school campuses and using their performances as a cover to spread rumors about the childhood monster Ochus and win you more followers. Do you intend to incite hysteria? With all the suffering in our House, would you use our tragedy to promote your personal cult?"

I'm so astounded by the accusation that I can barely take my next breath, much less compose an answer. Hysan cuts in, deepening his voice with authority, "Ambassador, your Guardian will address the Plenum. Please arrange this now."

"Yes, please," I say, my voice wispy. "It's vital."

As much as Sirna might like to, an ambassador can't refuse a direct order from her Guardian. Sirna talks to the clerks, and somehow they manage to squeeze me into today's schedule. I'll speak in less than two hours. Even though we just won a small victory, it doesn't feel that way.

Once the arrangements are made, Hysan says, "I have to meet the Libran representative. I will see you at the Plenum, my lady." He bows and takes off, and I can't tell if his lack of eye contact is intentional, or if he's just preoccupied.

Sirna escorts us to her office on a lower level beneath the giant sphere. "You can wait here," she says. "I have other duties."

"What's the latest news from Cancer?" I ask.

"Worse every day." With a curt goodbye, Sirna takes off to a committee meeting, leaving me standing there, gaping at her words and easy cruelty.

Her basement office is chilly and sterile, with scarce furniture. There are two benches, a desk, and a saltwater aquarium. Two soldiers stand guard outside the door. Mathias sweeps the place for surveillance tech. "It's not secure," he whispers. "There's at least a dozen brands of spy devices in this room alone."

"So we won't talk." I watch the miniature seahorses in the aquarium, then sit down on one of Sirna's hard steel benches. "I'm going to think of what to tell the Plenum. You should find your parents and let them know where we are."

He frowns. He never smiles anymore. "I'd rather not leave you alone."

"Go," I say. "We said we'd check in with them. I'll wait until you're back to get into trouble."

With a reluctant grunt, he leaves, promising to be back right away. A little later, and with barely a sound, the door eases open, and Sirna returns, signaling silence before I can speak.

She touches a blue, clam-shaped brooch pinned on her collar, just at the base of her throat, and when it flashes, I realize it's her Wave. Next, she takes a silver ball from her sleeve and tosses it up in the air. The ball sprouts wings and flies around the room, whining like a sand flea.

"My office is always being watched," she whispers. "But this scrambler can blind prying eyes for a few minutes."

She watches the little scrambler buzz around the room. Then her quick blue eyes roll back to me. "Why did you desert our House, Guardian?"

Her question feels like a slap, and her ferocious expression makes me feel like a little girl again. "You'd better have an answer ready," she says, "because many here will ask."

I try to infuse my voice with authority, the way Hysan did when he spoke to her earlier. "You know why I've come."

"I know the ring of moon rubble has changed our ocean tides," says Sirna, almost hissing the words at me. "We're seeing massive dislocations. The marine food chain is breaking down at every level. There were further shifts to the planet's core. More tsunamis. We've had to start evacuations . . . planet-wide."

Her last word stands out in the sea of blankness of my mind.

Planet-wide.

I left Cancer to save the Zodiac . . . and now my home is dying.

"Only our largest cities are still above water. Our islands and low-lying communities have been drowned."

"W-what about my family?"

"*Your* family? I hope you're referring to the entire population, Holy Mother. As Guardian, you're Mother to *all* Cancrians, or did you forget?" She exhales loudly and stares at the scrambler, pursing her lips.

My heartbeat is suspended in her silence.

In a milder voice, she says, "Your father and brother are missing. I'm sorry, Guardian."

27

MISSING?

I'd just recovered them. I didn't even get to see them when they were found—how can they be lost again?

My heart feels like it's doubled in size, and my ribs can barely contain it. I squeeze my eyes shut to keep the tears back because I don't want to give Sirna more reasons to look down on me. But the biggest thing fueling my journey was the fact that Dad and Stanton were alive. I couldn't have found the strength to leave Cancer, to draw Ochus away, if I hadn't seen with my own eyes that my family was safe.

How can home ever be home without them?

I feel the way I did my first night on Oceon 6: bereft, Centerless, alone. Like once again, I'm being asked to give more than I have left. Only this time, it's not just Cancer at stake. It's the whole Zodiac.

"We have a larger problem," says Sirna, as though my family were just a bullet point on a long list of items. "Did Crius inform you of my duties here?"

I blink a few times, letting the pain fill me a little longer, and Nishi's words come back to me: *It's okay to feel your pain before walling it off.*

The thought of her makes me almost smile, and it reminds me that she hasn't given up. She hasn't gone home to see her family, even though there's trouble now on Sagittarius, too. She's still out there, still fighting for me. For our cause. For our world.

I can't fall apart now.

"You're our ambassador," I say, straightening in my seat, my voice steady and brisk. I haven't heard myself sound this way before. "You represent our interests at the Plenum."

Sirna seems to consider the change in me before speaking again. "Then Crius didn't tell you." She crosses her arms with a frown. "I'll have to educate you myself. But first, you'll swear *on your Mother's life* never to reveal what I'm about to say."

"I swear."

She leans close and whispers, "I oversee a group of agents in the Cancrian Secret Service. My agents have uncovered information about a clandestine army gathering on the Aeriean planet Phobos."

The thought of Cancrian spies is still more funny than interesting, and I don't have time to worry about a gang of humans speaking surreptitiously when there's an immortal Guardian bent on our destruction. "I don't know anything about an army. My goal is to warn the Plenum about Ophiuchus."

"Oh, grow up!" she shouts, springing to her feet. I jump up, too, and we both glare into each other's faces. "You'll find an army can be a hell of a lot more destructive than a children's-book monster," she growls.

"Then I hope you never have to meet that monster face to face, Ambassador."

I blast out of the room, banging the door shut behind me.

✦ ✦ ✦

Our sea is in turmoil. Our people are in exile. My brother and dad can't be found. In a daze, I wander beneath the colossal steel globe of the arenasphere, stumbling into people and kiosks.

Dozens of Ariean Acolytes race past, conducting the Plenum's urgent errands, but to me they're just shadows. Mathias would advise me not to dwell on individual grief, and yet, oddly enough, I'm thinking about my mother.

She feels more present today than she has in years. After all, she's the person who taught me to believe in my fears.

I've never told anyone, but when Mom left, I wasn't upset. I was *free*.

For Dad, the change was overnight. He was quiet to begin with, but he barely spoke again. For me, the sadness started later. First I rejected the things that reminded me of her—Yarrot, Centering, reading the stars—then I clung to them like they could bring her back.

Stanton missed her the most. She was different with him. When it came to me, she was more instructor than mother, but with

Stanton, she was a friend. She would ask him to tag along with her on errands, and she'd pull him into arguments with Dad, as if Stanton were an adult who could referee. When she would get to that point, Dad usually let her win.

After she left, Stanton began telling me stories about her, ones I hadn't heard before. His favorite was the one about Hurricane Hebe.

Mom had seen it coming in her Ephemeris, so she warned our neighbors and filled our storm cellar with bags of fresh water, dried kelp, and medical supplies. But Hebe didn't strike our atoll. It only blew a few trees down and knocked over the nar-clams. Dad teased her all day for overreacting.

Mom didn't defend herself. She was seven months pregnant with me at the time, and while Dad rescued his nar-clams, she loaded up her schooner with the supplies she'd set aside. Six-foot waves still roiled the sea, and when she placed little Stanton in the schooner's front seat, Dad railed at her and tried to stop my brother from going.

"Stanton has to come," she said. "It's fated."

So they set off to Naxos, the next nearest island, eighteen kilometers away. The stars had told her Naxos would take a direct hit, and it had. For five days, she and little Stanton helped the Naxos families dig through the ruins for survivors, and on the fifth day, Stanton wriggled down through a tiny hole into a collapsed cellar and found an infant still alive.

If it hadn't happened to my own brother, I'd never believe it.

Will fate lead someone to rescue Stanton and Dad if they're in trouble now? Or should I abandon what I'm doing and be the one who finds them? If only I could use an Ephemeris again. . . .

Through the haze of my thoughts, a recognizable figure walking toward me becomes clearer. I almost can't believe my eyes.

"*Dr. Eusta?*"

"Honored Guardian. How glad I am to have found you in time." He doesn't look glad. His beady eyes glare at me.

"What are you doing here?" When I offer a hand touch, my hand passes right through him. He's still a hologram.

"Ambassador Sirna has informed us of your plan to speak at the Plenum. You must not do this. You'll bring shame on our House."

"But, Doctor, I—"

"Cancer will be the laughingstock of the galaxy. Do our anguished people deserve such a blow?"

"And do the other Houses deserve nothing?" I ask, blood rushing to my cheeks. "I can't stand by in silence."

His face distorts with rage. "Your own House suffers grievously, and Admiral Crius commands you to return. He sent me here to bring you home."

When he shows me Crius's written order, I squint at the virtual document, confused. Crius doesn't have the authority to command me. He's my Military Advisor, so he can only overrule me in times of war, and only if he and the majority of my Advisors vote that my life is in danger. But . . . this doesn't feel right.

Dr. Eusta glances aside. "Another emergency. I must go. But hear me well, Guardian. Do not speak at the Plenum."

The doctor's hologram flashes away, and I blink as if waking from a stupor. Mathias is standing in front of me, gently shaking my arm.

"Rho, I've been searching everywhere for you. The session's beginning. We have to go in."

"Right," I say, still a bit dazed. "Did you find your parents?"

"Yes. We'll talk later. Let's hurry."

We step into the ruby-colored stair pipe, and its walls turn everything blood red. I'm still reeling from my meeting with Sirna, and the doctor's visit has not boosted my confidence—nor did Mathias's advice last night. I still have no idea what I'm going to say. I feel more uncertain of myself than ever.

Mathias guides me out of the pipe at the first level, where a round door opens for us. The vast echoing arenasphere is a hollow globe lined in dark quilted fabric like a jewel box. Tiers of sleek chrome seats ring its curved walls, and virtual screens move through the air, forming panes of flickering color.

The sphere's almost empty when we enter, and the air has an exhausted staleness. The entire upper half is one giant holo-tap. Only a few lackadaisical holo-ghosts drift under the ceiling, viewing the session like passing clouds. And as I watch them, it strikes me what felt wrong about Dr. Eusta: *He wasn't a ghost.*

How did he project his hologram all the way from Cancer without a time lag? He spoke to me as if his signal was coming from nearby.

Mathias pulls on my hand, and I have to speed up to keep pace with him as he leads us deeper into the arenasphere. For the Plenum session, the Arieans have rigged a temporary platform in the bed of the sphere, a half-moon stage facing an arc of tall gilded seats reserved for the ambassadors. When I step onto the stage, three flying micro-cameras buzz around me like gnats.

I have no idea what Nishi likes about the spotlight. Looking out at the vast arena from the stage, the only thing keeping me together is the hope of the finish line. If I can manage to convince even a few Houses of the danger we're in, we'll have allies. Then there will be others besides us on the case.

I rub my sweaty palms on my yellow suit with the glyph of the four silver moons. What a sight I must make: a girl almost too short to see over the top of the lectern, wearing a mismatched uniform. I have to stand on tiptoe to face my meager audience of only seven sleepy-eyed ambassadors and their entourage of adjuncts, Acolytes, and aides. It's the end of the day, and they look like the last thing they want to do is hear another speech.

Brick-red Albor Echus sits at the center, representing Aries. His opulent fur robes can't hide his double chins or bulging belly. Next to him is a rail-thin man with a face like a knife blade. His nameplate says he's Ambassador Charon of Scorpio. The Virgo ambassador's chair is empty, as are several others.

I spot Sirna. She's leaning back with her arms crossed under her chest, looking sullen. I should have reached out to her when I was made Guardian. There are so many things I should have done.

Crius is right to order me home. Mother Origene won people's devotion through her deeds. I've done nothing but disappear.

Mathias stands at attention in his blue Cancrian uniform near the main door. Just as I'm about to begin, Hysan makes an entrance, bumping fists and slapping backs with people from every House, looking resplendent in a charcoal-gray court suit. He winks at me, and my stomach does a small flip.

He sits behind his own Libran ambassador, a stylish, bearded blond man whose nameplate reads Ambassador Frey. Leaning forward, Hysan whispers a few words to Frey, and they smile as if they're sharing a private joke.

I take a deep breath and stammer the formal greeting Mathias taught me. "Hail, Excellencies, Most Honorable. Thank you for hearing me today."

The faces of Sirna, Dr. Eusta, and Mathias all seem to be swimming in my head, their words making me hesitate.

Am I wrong to insist on honor when we're dealing with an enemy who has none? Ophiuchus is manipulating people, pretending he doesn't exist—would it be so bad if I manipulated as well, blamed Sirna's army or some other boogeyman for the bloodshed? Isn't that the point of the children's-book monster after all—to be scapegoat for a bigger evil?

What I need is for the Zodiac to unite. Regardless of what name I give him, there's still someone out there after us, and the ship's logs documenting a Psy attack prove at least that much. When Moira awakens, she can tell them it's Ophiuchus, and I'll back her then.

"I've come to warn you," I say, a slight tremble in my voice. I clear my throat and put more force behind my words. "Every House in the Zodiac is in danger."

There's an edgy stirring in the audience, and I glance overhead, waiting for Ochus to strike. When nothing happens, I stiffen my shaky knees and start my story by counting off all the recent natural disasters in the newsfeeds, sharing my theory that they're part of a pattern, and then insisting they were triggered by someone who's manipulating Psynergy to control Dark Matter.

A louder hum of protests begins. As I watch people's faces, any words of a Thirteenth House turn to sand in my mouth.

Then I flash back to the Strider and the bubbles breaking the sea's surface. I see the gray light of Thebe flickering in the Ephemeris. If I'm not brave enough to speak now, I'll be like one of the Guardians in Mom's Ochus story—too afraid to believe in my fears.

Agatha's blessing comes back to me: *May your inner light always shine, and may it guide us through our darkest nights.*

I think this is exactly the kind of moment she was referring to. The darkness shrouding our galaxy is growing so thick, it's getting hard to tell right from wrong—even for our leaders. Agatha advised me to stay true to my Cancrian values, even—or especially—when the temptation to do what's easy over what's right feels greatest. And now I know what I've come to say.

"Some of you will not want to believe me, but I beg you to have open minds. Everything I am about to tell you can be confirmed by Empress Moira, as soon as she recovers. There is a part of our galaxy that has been hidden from us, I don't know how or for how long. The Thirteenth House isn't just a fable we tell our children—it's a real constellation, just past Pisces. A House called Ophiuchus."

The audience stirs like a nest of sea spiders, and the ambassadors whisper among themselves. But I'm not finished. "Its original

Guardian was exiled, condemned to immortality in the darkest reaches of Space. And now he's returned to the Zodiac for revenge."

I start describing how he felt solid in the Psy, and I have to raise my voice to speak over the audience. I rap the lectern with my knuckles, but no one seems to hear. Finally, Hysan stands and yells, "Quiet! Let her speak."

I catch his eye and nod my gratitude. He smiles at me, and for a moment I see the same teenage guy who was in the sea of representatives at my swearing-in ceremony. He didn't know me then, but still he had my back.

When the audience settles down, I say, "Ophiuchus must be stopped. We can only do that if we quit arguing among ourselves and come together to form a plan."

More people are entering the arenasphere now, people from all corners of the Zodiac. The seats are filling up, and the noise level rises. A dozen more tiny cameras buzz around me. Word of my speech must have spread already, so I keep talking, as loud as my lungs will allow.

"If this enemy can damage a House as wealthy and powerful as Virgo, no one's safe. Our only chance is to band together."

"Rho! Rho! Trust in Guardian Rho!"

A dozen noisy people push their way in. They look like university students, and one of them waves a holographic banner with a picture of me behind my drums. They're marching down the aisle, shouting my name.

My stomach plummets. I know the youth vote will only hurt me with these ambassadors.

Albor Echus calls for order, and a couple of soldiers force the rowdy students to leave. When the arenasphere quiets down, it takes me a minute to regain my composure.

The blade-faced man, Charon of Scorpio, lifts the long speaker's staff in his hands, signaling that he wants the floor. As he rises, a profound hush falls. He radiates a kind of magnetism even I can feel.

"My dear Rhoma." His voice has a greasy thickness. "How sweet of you to come all this way to read us stories, when your people must surely need you at home. How long have you held your position? A week?"

"Almost three, Ambassador. But we've been traveling at hyper-speed, so my calendar's a little mixed up."

"And when exactly did you complete your Zodai training?"

"In between attacks from Ophiuchus, under the training of my Guide and Advisor Lodestar Mathias Thais." I smile at him. "Anything else?"

"Yes, dear girl, there is. I'm old and a little hard of hearing, so forgive me, but did you just spend half an hour telling us your House was attacked by the boogeyman?"

People burst out laughing, and Charon's thin lips curl into a smile, his eyes far from friendly.

"I believe I said Ophiuchus."

"My dear young lady, we bow to the grief of your stricken world. How confusing this must be for one so inexperienced. No wonder you're seeing monsters under your bed."

He signals to an Acolyte, who stands and points at my head, as though he's going to shoot me with his index finger. Instead, a film beams out from his Paintbrush—a Wave-like fingertip device Scorps use for designing holographic blueprints of their latest innovations.

The film shows Cancer on the night of the Lunar Quadract. The image has the grainy grayness of footage taken through a long-range telescope lens, but the vision of our four pearl-white moons makes my chest ache.

"Please note"—Charon shines a light from his own Paintbrush to indicate our smallest moon, Thebe—"prior to the horrible incident, scientists on this Cancrian moon were experimenting with a new type of quantum fusion reactor. Let's run this video in fast-forward. Pay close attention, Excellencies."

I steel my nerves for what's coming. First, an immense explosion knocks Thebe off course. Then Thebe knocks into Galene, which smacks into Orion, which explodes against Elara, filling the sky with debris. In superfast-forward, the rubble sweeps around Cancer, forming a rocky ring, while a score of larger pieces flame down through the atmosphere, splashing into our ocean and setting off ripples of destruction. When the video ends, my cheeks are wet with tears.

Charon turns to the audience. "Now I will show you what caused this."

His Acolyte's next projection shows a star exploding at the edge of our galaxy, far out beyond Pisces. It glows like a thousand suns, expelling sharp rays of debris and hot gases.

"That is a massive hypernova in the Sufianic Clouds. Our data proves cosmic rays from that event triggered a critical overload in Cancer's quantum reactor, located on the moon Thebe. In short, this dreadful event was caused by a freak accident."

Cosmic rays from the Sufianic Clouds? Has that been the omen this whole time? Was Caasy right that I'm being deceived?

Charon gestures toward the screen. "House Scorpio tracked this event with our telescopes. Your predecessor, the honored Holy Mother Origene, must have been sleeping not to foresee it."

"How dare you," I breathe through my teeth.

Charon's smile is like a razor's edge. "Child, no one blames you for fantasizing about monsters. You're suffering post-traumatic stress. After what you've been through, who wouldn't be?"

"What about Virgo?" I snap. "Who set their planet's atmosphere on fire?"

Charon's thin-lipped smile makes the air colder. "Virgo was also experimenting with quantum fusion. Regrettably, the hypernova discharged radiation for many days."

The Acolyte in the audience screens another video, showing a satellite exploding above Tethys and lighting its upper atmosphere on fire. "That satellite housed Virgo's quantum reactor," says Charon. "The result was a storm of acid rain that washed over the planet. Empress Moira would confirm this fact if she could speak. Unfortunately, she's in a coma, but I have sworn affidavits from her own scientists."

After he shows these documents, I don't know what to say next. If I hadn't been in the room when Moira faced Ophiuchus, I would doubt everything, too.

Who's going to believe me if Moira doesn't wake up soon and set them straight?

"So you see," says Charon, "these sad events have rational

explanations. There's no grand conspiracy at work, only nature and chance."

When Charon concludes his presentation, Albor Echus rises. "Our thanks to the Eighth House for this report. I think we've heard enough."

28

I START TO OBJECT, but Hysan signals me to wait. He whispers to Ambassador Frey, who stands and takes up the speaker's staff. "Excellencies, this needs further discussion, but the hour is late. I propose that we table this item until tomorrow."

He's buying us time. The hum in the audience increases to a din of complaint, and Albor Echus says, "Must we really continue with this adolescent claptrap?"

I catch Sirna's eyes and nod, signaling her to stand and speak. She squints defiantly at me, and, with an obvious display of reluctance, she rises and says, "Excellencies, I agree with Ambassador Frey. Let us reconvene tomorrow."

Another ambassador raises a willowy white hand, signaling for attention. It's the delegate from House Aquarius. He stands to speak, though he doesn't take the speaking staff.

Ambassador Morscerta, his nameplate reads. I didn't notice him before. His alabaster-white features are narrow and elongated, and his long hair falls in a cloud of silvery waves, yet he doesn't strike me as an old man.

Actually, I can't tell his age. He has a smooth high forehead, a protruding lower lip, and small gray eyes that burn like nuclear fission. There's even a shade around him, a barely noticeable aura that shifts in and out of sight as he moves. Can he be a hologram?

When he speaks, I have to reassess everything. His silky soprano sounds way too feminine to be a man's voice. Not effeminate, not female, just different from any voice I've ever heard.

"I wish to hear more of this unusual story," purrs Morscerta. "Mother Rhoma, will you agree to meet us here tomorrow for a continuation?"

"I can be here at daybreak."

✦ ✦ ✦

By the time I reunite with Mathias and his parents, Hysan has disappeared. Sirna agrees to meet us at the embassy later.

It's been a long day, but I'm glad to be with the Thaises, heading back to their quarters. I miss being near family.

As we walk through the city streets toward the village, the high-tension fabric sky glows lead gray in the early dusk. The neighborhood around the Plenum lies quiet, thanks to new security blockades. The scene feels almost peaceful, despite the soldiers patrolling in armored cars.

Amanta wears a handsome blue cloak draped around her shoulders, and her shorter husband wears an ordinary business suit and skullcap. On the surface, Amanta and Egon seem like a mismatched couple; but the more they talk, I realize they share the same calm sensitivity and responsiveness to each other that all Cancrians value.

"Mathias tells me you're helping with the resettlement," I say. "Are you working with Admiral Crius?"

Amanta looks at me and frowns. "Crius died in the quake. We're working with Agatha and the Matriarchs now."

I stumble. "But . . . Admiral Crius ordered me home just this morning. He sent Dr. Eusta by hologram to tell me."

"You must be mistaken," she says, shaking her head. "Crius died many days ago. I'm sorry, Rho."

I almost run into a streetlamp. Was somebody masquerading as Dr. Eusta? If so, *who?* Mathias looks at me questioningly, but I shake my head, *not now.*

As we walk, Mathias occasionally scans nearby roofs and alleys through his field glasses, while Egon speaks in cool, measured phrases about the Cancrian exodus. "Most survivors have emigrated to Gemini's mining planet, Hydragyr, our nearest neighbor."

At least they've found shelter, but the image of my water-loving people entombed in the hot, dry beryllium mines of House Gemini turns my stomach. I'm about to ask how they're faring there, when Mathias shoves me to the pavement.

My hand and knee scrape the ground hard, and all I feel is Mathias's weight on me, shielding my body with his own. Through a sliver of space, I spy a particle beam cutting a bright sizzling line across the wall above us.

"The alley!" he shouts to his parents. "Take cover!"

He helps me up, and the four of us sprint into the dark narrow gap between two buildings. My heart is hammering my chest as more beams hiss around us. Mathias draws his weapon.

"What's happening?" asks Egon. "Why are they shooting?"

Amanta flares a laser torch into the depths of the alley, and we see it's a dead end. "Keep low," she says, and I notice she's also clutching a weapon in her hand.

Hot lesions slice across the walls, and shards of granite fly up. These fiery beams are meant for me. . . . Ochus must have seen my Plenum speech, and now he's fulfilling his threat.

Mathias scans the nearby roofs. We're trapped. Without thinking, I start edging toward the street. All I know is if I show myself, Mathias and his parents can get away.

I never should have dragged Mathias into this. I shouldn't have let him come on what was always a suicide mission. I won't let him—or his family—die for me.

"Keep still!" Mathias slings me around and crushes me against the wall. "I see the sniper."

Particle beams fizz into our alley, etching the pavement with flames, so we retreat farther back. Mathias keeps scanning the building across the street, and Amanta, who's also wearing field glasses, does the same. "Looks like two men, at least," she says.

She and Mathias take aim at an upper window, although the only thing I see is a dark pane of glass. Can Ochus be hiding behind that glass, looking back at me this very minute?

I could end this now. It feels like an easy solution, if only Mathias would let go of me.

"I can't get a good shot from here," he whispers, turning to Amanta. "Mother, please keep Rho safe."

"*Mathias*—" I reach out for him, but Amanta takes a firm hold of my arm. Her grip is like iron.

"I will," she says. "Do what you must."

"Mathias, *DON'T!*" I shout.

He's already scaling the alley wall. It's solid concrete, and the seams he finds to jam in his fingers and toes are almost invisible. He moves so fast, he's practically swimming.

Three stories up, Mathias fires his laser, and the window across the street shatters. Particle beams hiss back at him, cratering the wall above our heads. He ducks behind a cornice as concrete explodes around him.

I blink in the spray of dust, trying to see if he's okay. "Mathias!"

Amanta inhales sharply. "Egon, hold her," she says, passing me to her husband as if I were a bag of nar-clams.

Then she steps toward the street and starts firing her own laser at the window. Volleys sizzle back and forth, and the smell of burnt concrete sours the air. Egon holds my head against his chest, trying not to let me see.

The horrible noise builds and builds, until it's over. And then silence is worse than sound.

"They're retreating." When I hear Mathias's familiar baritone, I break loose and run to him. He drops down from the wall to the alley floor, and I see an ugly burn on his arm.

"You're hurt—"

Pulling me into a hug, he presses a hard kiss on my forehead. "Doesn't matter. You're okay."

There's a flutter overhead, and I look up to see the faint shades of three large, birdlike creatures silhouetted against the fabric sky. Mathias aims his laser, but his mother says, "It's all right. They're friends."

The bird-shaped devices glide across the street and enter the broken window, merging into darkness. Whatever they are, they seem to absorb almost every photon of light.

"Cancrian Secret Service. Ambassador Sirna sent them." Amanta parts her cloak, and in the dimness, I see she's wearing body armor underneath. She draws a fresh laser cartridge from her belt, breaks open her weapon, and reloads it.

"Holy Mother has made enemies here," she says. "We feared there might be trouble."

"It was Ophiuchus," I say.

"We'll track the shooters down. Trust me, we'll find out who did this."

Mathias steps toward her, and they press the backs of their right hands together. Such a simple ordinary gesture, and yet I can almost feel the current of emotion flowing through their touch.

"There may be other snipers." Amanta steps out to check the street, then motions us to follow. "Keep to the shadows. We'll need to hide Holy Mother in the safe house tonight."

✦ ✦ ✦

Amanta guides us to Sirna's safe house.

As soon as we enter a side door, we pass through the pale blue rays of a biometric security scan. Then she leads us down a flight of stairs, through a steel gate, and down an elevator to a deep sub-basement. After another bio scan, she opens a pair of thick, heavy doors, and we enter what feels like a vault. It's strange to see Cancrians using so much stealth technology. It's not our style.

The common room has a wallscreen, a couple of faded sofas, a kitchen alcove, and a lavatory at the back. Doors on either side lead to small bunkrooms, and in the center of the room, Sirna is waiting.

"It's good to see you unharmed, Guardian."

"I need everyone to keep their Ephemerii away from here," I announce in a loud voice. Now that I'm almost certain Ochus knows I'm on Aries, he might be able to track me down through people using the Psy near me.

"Mathias has already informed us that everywhere you enter must be kept free of devices connected to the Psy," says Sirna. "He said the people behind the attacks have been using Psynergy against you, and that's why you can't do your readings."

I look at Mathias. His father is tending to his arm. It's hard to stick to any decision I make about him. Just when I think I can't forgive him for not believing me, he goes and saves my life.

"About the troops gathering on Phobos," says Sirna, giving me the briefing she tried to give earlier, when I stormed out of her office. I wouldn't listen before, but as she shares more details, I begin to understand the wider implications. "My agents have infiltrated their subterranean camp. They call themselves the Marad, and they are being funded by someone with deep pockets."

"They're the ones who stirred up the worker revolt on the Sagittarian moon," adds Amanta, "and they may be behind . . . other terrorist attacks as well." It's clear she meant to say what happened to our moons and Virgo, but she doesn't want to contradict me publicly.

"We think they've established cells in every House," says Sirna.

"Who are they?" asks Mathias. "What do they want?"

"We don't know their objective yet. The recruits are mostly teenagers. Unemployed Scorp dropouts. Child laborers from the Geminin mines. Impoverished slum dwellers from Phaetonis. Risers from every House." Sirna touches her blue brooch and gets a faraway look, as if she's listening to a private message.

A Riser is a person born into the wrong House. It's a change that happens when a person's exterior persona conflicts so strongly with their internal identity that they begin to develop the personality and physical traits of a different House. And it can happen at any age.

Most people handle it well and either choose to stay on their home planets and continue living their lives, or move to the House that reflects their rising persona. There are rare cases where the change doesn't take well, and a Riser can have an unbalanced ratio of personality traits from their new and old Houses. Sometimes it deforms them. Sometimes it turns them into monsters.

"Are they being brainwashed?" I ask.

She drops her hand and looks me in the eye. "They're being fed, clothed, and welcomed into a group for the first time in their lives. You might call that brainwashing."

Amanta lifts off her heavy armored vest. "We count fewer than a hundred thousand troops so far, but new recruits arrive daily."

"The expense to house and train them must be substantial," says Mathias, his voice distant, like he's lost in thought. "You don't know who the backer is?"

After a moment, Sirna says, "We're trying to track the money flow. No single individual could afford so much. We suspect a wider conspiracy."

Egon finishes bandaging his son's arm. He's been quiet throughout the discussion, but now he asks, "Do you think some of the Houses might be in league, like the Trinary Axis of old?"

"That's what we fear most," whispers Sirna.

Everyone falls silent. No one wants to believe that could happen again.

Amanta drops her bulky gear belt on the floor. "Please keep this information to yourselves for now. We can't expose our covert agents in the field."

I nod and look away, wondering where Ophiuchus fits in. Could he be funding the army?

After a while, Egon switches on the wallscreen, and while they watch a newsfeed about the escalating Sagittarian conflict, Sirna steps into the kitchen alcove to put on a kettle for tea. I follow her in and lean against the cooler. "Why don't you believe me?"

She spoons tea leaves into a cast-iron pot. "Since the crash of our moons caught everyone off-guard, my agents have searched day and night for reasons. Your classmate's messages steered us to Ophiuchus. We've investigated your story."

"And?"

"And nothing. That trail is dead."

My fingers curl tightly. "You mean you can't see him."

"Guardian, use your head." Sirna lays down her spoon and faces me. "The secret army on Phobos is our real concern. Whoever's funding them almost certainly hired those snipers tonight. They're your enemy, not some *big bad* from a children's tale."

I have to struggle to stand still. Her sarcasm, like Mathias's doubt, makes me too furious to form sentences.

"Forgive me, Guardian," she says, setting out a row of teacups. "Duty demands that I speak the truth to you. Duty can be a harsh master."

"Keep looking for Ophiuchus then. That's an order."

"As you wish, Holy Mother." She gives me a curt bow. "I'll look again."

I start to leave. Then, grudgingly, I turn back. "Thanks for helping us tonight."

She pours the boiling water. "I live to serve Cancer."

✦ ✦ ✦

The safe house clock says it's early morning in the Ariean capital, two hours before the Plenum convenes. Mathias and his dad have gone up to street level to check for snipers.

Now, for the first time in weeks, I find myself in the company of only women. After living for so long with a pair of testosterone-driven males, I've almost forgotten what a feminine atmosphere feels like. Ambassador Sirna and I aren't exactly two pearls in a nar-clam, but on the surface at least, we're calm.

Amanta hums softly as she polishes my much-abused boots, while Sirna clips off the ragged ends of my fingernails. I wish they wouldn't, that they would let me take care of myself, but they insist on keeping every tradition alive, even in these times. I think that to them, letting go of the little things means we've given up the big ones.

Sirna seems slightly less hostile to me this morning. She believes some of the ambassadors plan to blindside me at the Plenum, and whatever she thinks of me personally, she won't tolerate an affront to our House. "Charon of Scorpio is stirring things up, but he's just the talking head. Someone else writes his script. We don't know who."

"Why can't I speak first thing? Ophiuchus could attack again any minute."

"I don't set the agenda." Sirna puts her nail clippers away. She's brought me a tailored azure court suit and a simple coronet with the Cancrian glyph outlined in silver. She had the coronet made overnight, and I know it's not really for me. It's to honor our House. She says the Guardian of Cancer should look the part.

I want to snap at her that I couldn't care less about clothes right now—only I remember that I don't represent just *me* anymore. I now stand for every Cancrian. So I sit still and let them dress me however they like.

The vault doors swing open, and the men come in, looking grim. "We've spoken with the local army unit," says Mathias. "They're sending us an escort."

"Have you made notes for your next speech?" Amanta asks me. "You could rehearse with us if you like."

I shake my head. "Thank you, but I don't think anyone in this room wants to hear it."

Sirna purses her lips. "I must speak the truth, Guardian. You'd be wise to retract certain points that seem . . . unreasonable. Say you were mistaken. Keep it simple."

"You mean Ochus."

Her ebony cheeks soften. "Guardian, you're so young. You've barely trained. Can you honestly say you're so certain of what you saw that you would gamble the reputation of House Cancer and let slide this opportunity to unite the Zodiac?"

A flash of heat surges up my neck, searing my cheeks, nose, and eyes, and I can feel the tantrum, the storm of tears, the meltdown I'm yearning to have at the unending injustice of it all.

I've done what they asked. I read the stars, and I swore to always act in the best interest of Cancer. That oath led me to sacrificing everything I would rather be doing—searching for my family, helping rebuild my home—and it's sent me all over the galaxy on a crazy quest that's made me the laughingstock of the Zodiac.

And now my own people want to turn me into someone I'm not.

I knew when I accepted the Guardianship that I would be giving everything up. But there are some things I have to hold on to, if only for the sake of performing my duties in this role. Integrity is one of them.

"I'm certain, Sirna."

29

WE TAKE SIRNA'S ARMORED CAR, flanked by soldiers on hover-scooters, and I feel a rush of relief when I see Hysan already waiting for us at the hippodrome.

His hair is freshly trimmed, and he's dressed more elegantly than ever. His court suit is a shade of purple so deep it's almost black. He grins at the coronet in my hair. "Lovely." Then he gives me a closer inspection. "You didn't sleep well."

"She was ambushed in the street last night by snipers," says Mathias.

Hysan's eyes grow wide. "Are you okay? What happened?"

I nod, and Mathias starts describing the attack, but he stops midsentence. At the far end of the hall, students are waving Cancrian banners and chanting my name. Fifty of them at least.

"*Rho! Rho! Rho!*" They rush toward me, snapping my picture

with their Waves and trying to touch me, until Mathias intervenes and hustles me into the ruby stair pipe.

Inside the arenasphere, hundreds of holograms drift overhead, a circus of pixilating colors. Below, the tiered seats are full. Dozens of micro-cameras swarm around us, and we swat them away as we weave through throngs of spectators toward the stage. As usual, Mathias goes first, opening a path.

When Mathias's back is turned, Hysan's hand closes around my wrist, and he pulls me away to a secluded corner of the arena.

He turns to me in the shadow of an emergency exit, where no one is close enough to hear. I sneak a glance at the crowd— Mathias is going to worry when he notices I'm missing.

"Rho, I've thought it over, and I'm going to address the Plenum today," says Hysan, speaking loudly over the arena noise. "My ambassador is already getting me a timeslot. I'm going to reveal my true identity."

My eyes feel like they're taking up my whole face. "You're going to *what?*"

"I'll tell everyone about the attack on our ship, that way there's no question about the Psy weapon. Then I'll let them know I believe you, that Ophiuchus is real, and that House Libra stands with House Cancer."

I give a kind of flying leap and hug him, and his husky laugh tickles my ear. When we pull apart, I say, "Hysan, there's going to be a lot of fallout. I mean with your people, after you reveal the truth. You said it the other day, you've broken your Guardian's oath for me—I don't want to ask you to do more."

"That's just it, though. You don't have to ask." He sweeps a curl from my face, leaving a line of heat on my skin. "I know you don't like secrecy, but it's all I've ever known. I've never had a role model like you to teach me a better way." Deep dimples form on his cheeks.

Even though I never would have believed it possible, I'm smiling, too. "I owe you."

"No, Rho. I owe you." His expression grows uncharacteristically serious, but his eyes retain all their warmth. "Ambassador Frey told me a mass of Psynergy probed four of our flying cities late last night. If you hadn't warned me, I wouldn't have known to shield them."

It takes me a moment to digest what he just said. "Then . . . we did do some good," I sputter. "This—all of this hasn't been for nothing."

Before I can clear my head, he muddles everything even more by leaning into me and laying two slow kisses on either of my cheeks. The brush of his lips against my skin makes my brain buzz.

"Those cities are home to twelve million people," he whispers, his mouth now near my ear. "I'm going to tell the whole world what you did. You'll always have House Libra's deepest gratitude."

"Rho!"

I hear Mathias's voice calling out close by, but he hasn't found us yet.

"She's here!" shouts Hysan, leading me to Mathias, while my mind races at the speed of my pulse. Just as the three of us meet, a little girl approaches and pinches my arm. I turn to look and am struck by her otherworldly, childish beauty.

She has skin as pale as the inside of a cantaloupe and curly copper hair, and she looks exactly like her thieving twin brother. "*Rubidum?*"

"What have you done to Caasy?" she asks, her tunnel-like eyes expanding. "He's so obsessed with that black opal of yours, he won't even come out to play."

"Where is he?" I snap. "I need it back!"

"Then the stars must have put you in my way." She pulls out the stone from her pocket.

I gasp, unsure if I should reach for it or toss it away. Ochus could use it.

Hysan sees what's happening, and he swipes it from her hand. "I brought something with me," he says, pulling out a velvet pouch. "It's veiled from the Psy," he explains to me before slipping the stone inside.

"Thanks," I say, amazed, as he hands me the pouch. Then I look at Rubidum. "Why did he take it?"

"He thought you were on a suicide mission," she says, shrugging as though that were the most normal kind of mission to be on. "He knew what the stone was, and he was worried you didn't, so he took it. To protect Cancer. And to play with it himself, of course." She smiles brightly. "But *mostly* so it wouldn't get lost with your bodies."

I'm not sure if I believe that's what really happened, but either way, I'm happy Rubidum had the sense to bring the stone back to me. "Where is he?" I growl.

She tilts her head and pouts. "Caasy wouldn't come with me. I had to answer the summons on my own."

I blink. "Summons?"

"Yes. Very inconvenient. I've been traveling for days. This carnival had better be worth it." She nudges against me with a wry smile. "Your song has quite the following on Gemini. I didn't know you were a drummer! We should start an intergalactic band—I hear Lord Neith has perfect pitch!"

Sirna takes my elbow and hustles me forward. "It's time." Mathias falls in line behind us.

As we pass the ambassadors' throne-like seats, I see Morscerta whispering with his aides, and again I wonder if he's a hologram. So I seize the moment to brush against his sleeve.

The touch gives me a slight static shock, and he must feel it, too, because he turns with a scowl of indignation, which quickly transforms into a gracious smile. "My lady Rhoma."

"Sorry, sir. This place is quite crowded," I say, hurrying on.

He's no hologram. His dark aura must be some sort of energy field. For personal protection or to mask his appearance, I don't know.

I glance around the audience, wondering how many other visitors are really who they seem.

Again, I climb the short run of stairs and stand alone on the half-moon stage, facing my inquisitors. Only this time, the arena is filled to capacity. My heart's beating shakes my whole frame, like it's the hiccups.

I bat the flying cameras away and try to clear my throat. Others have joined the ambassadors on the main floor, and more gilded seats have been added. One newcomer is radiant little Rubidum.

Another new arrival leaves me thunderstruck: *Lord Neith.*

Even sitting, his regal figure towers over everyone. He wears a golden court suit, and perched on his short white hair is a high-church miter bearing the Libran glyph, the Scales of Justice. His quartz-white eyes are sharp and amazingly human. Hysan sits directly behind him, and when I give him a questioning look, he merely quirks his eyebrows and shakes his head.

Ambassador Charon is whispering to an old man wearing a massive holographic crown that looks incredibly real and is engraved with a Scorpion. In fact, all six newcomers wear headdresses adorned with royal glyphs. I see Sagittarius's Archer, Leo's Lion, Pisces's Fish. Why are so many of the other Guardians at the Plenum today?

They would have to have started their trips many days ago to cover such vast distances, and no one knew I would address the Plenum before yesterday. *Right?*

The crowd quiets down, and someone's standing to speak. It's Morscerta. Next to him sits a dull-eyed boy of five or six, wearing a royal Aquarian crown twice the size of his head. Morscerta pats the child Guardian with fondness (though whether it's genuine or for show, I can't tell), then speaks in his strange, lilting voice.

"Greetings, Honored Rhoma. May I ask why my young Supreme Guardian has been summoned into your presence?"

A horrid dread makes me stagger . . . as suddenly, I realize why we're all here.

I catch hold of the lectern, and without thinking, I shout, "It's an ambush!"

The crowd erupts in angry hollering, and for the first time, I notice many of the seats are packed with wiry Scorps in dark glasses. They look surlier than everyone else, and suddenly I'm reminded of their conflict on Sagittarius.

I look around to see who else is in the audience. None of the students are here, and I can't spot a single one of the Cancrians I saw in the lobby. Someone has rigged this.

I try to speak above the noise. "There are too many Guardians· gathered in one place. We're a sitting target. We have to separate ourselves and scatter!"

Beside me, Charon lifts the speaking staff and bangs its long rod on the floor. Every voice falls silent, and he lets the tension gather. It's clear he knows how to control a crowd. For such a secular House, the Scorps seem to be carrying on a lot like zealots these days.

When he turns to me, he's smiling, but his face looks more than ever like a rapier. "Guardian, you agreed to submit to more questioning. Are you afraid we'll expose your hoax?"

I pound the lectern, knocking my coronet askew. "You have to listen. This same thing happened on Cancer. Ophiuchus struck us when nearly all our Zodai Guards were together in one place."

"Enough fantasy, child." Charon brandishes his staff. "Now. First question. Is it true you left your House in the middle of the night without informing your Matriarchs?"

I'm shaking with frustration. "Yes, but—"

"A simple yes or no is sufficient." Charon beams his greasy smile at the spectators, then rounds on me. "Is it true you and your lover stole a ship belonging to another House?"

I stare, openmouthed and mortified, but Hysan shoots to his feet and says, "I offered the lady a ride. She's no thief."

Charon wheels around and points his staff at Hysan. "Guards, escort this heckler from the Plenum."

"Wait a minute," starts Hysan—but four soldiers materialize from the crowd and Taser him. My horrified scream is drowned by the hooting and clapping from the Scorps in the audience.

"*Stop!*" I yell as the soldiers bundle Hysan's limp body toward the exit. I look to Sirna for help, but her seat is empty. Mathias seems to have vanished, too, and Lord Neith sits so completely motionless, I wonder if he's been switched off. Sirna was right—the ambassadors blindsided us. I led us right into a trap.

Charon reads from a screen floating in front of him. "Admiral Crius informed your people that you were raising disaster relief funds. Did you raise one single coin to aid your House?"

I bow my head. "No."

"Louder, please."

"*No, I did not.*"

"Is it true," says Charon, "that you crept into House Gemini masked in a cloaking veil?"

"I can testify to that." Rubidum hops to her feet. "Rho materialized in our playroom like a magician. Such a theatrical entrance. She's a queen of melodrama."

After her brother's treachery, I shouldn't be surprised she's contributing to my humiliation. I'd thought since she brought me the stone, that she'd had a change of heart. But I was wrong.

Her Guardian tiara flashes golden reflections as she climbs up in her chair and stands to face the audience. "Rho isn't malicious, fellow Excellencies. She's simply blinded by anger over the death of her friends. Revenge is a tale without end, I warned her."

"A tale without end," the audience echoes, as if this phrase explains everything.

She resumes her seat and Charon gives her a bow. "Our thanks for your testimony, honored Rubidum." He looks now to the row of seats where Hysan was just sitting. "And, Lord Neith, did this girl not use the same devious veil to invade your House as well?"

After a slight delay, Neith lifts his chin. "Insufficient data."

I hold my breath, as my heart counts off the seconds of silence that follow Neith's declaration. I have to do something—I can't let them expose Hysan's secret like this—

"It appears the Guardian of Libra has been napping." Charon turns to the audience with a mocking sneer.

I hold my exhale until the crowd explodes in guffaws, and the threat is over.

It takes a minute for Charon to settle everyone down, and I keep glancing up at the ceiling, imagining ways Ochus might attack us. The Dark Matter has set off explosions, burned the atmosphere with acidic rain . . . what else can he do with it?

I search for Mathias again but find no sight of him.

"Final question," Charon booms, making me jump. "We know from eyewitnesses that you were visiting Empress Moira when her orbiting lab exploded. Is it true you fled in your stolen ship without offering a ride to a single man, woman, or child?"

My feet go numb, followed by my legs, stomach, chest, until my whole being is submerged in an inability to feel. It's like even my body is jumping ship and abandoning me. I let those people die. I brought Ophiuchus to them, and then I didn't save a single soul.

"It's true."

Now the crowd noise grows to a clamor, and I feel tears welling up. Once more, Morscerta rises to his feet and takes the speaking staff. Beneath his courteous manner, he has a potency that commands attention, and the arenasphere falls so abruptly quiet, I hear myself breathing.

"Guardians, Excellencies, this whimsical episode has clearly charmed us." Again, the Aquarian's silken voice startles me. "But on this last day of our session, let us settle down and turn to more serious topics before we close."

When the others nod assent, Morscerta speaks to me in a sweet, almost tender tone. "Rhoma Grace, thank you for your fascinating comments. You are dismissed."

He bangs the staff on the floor, and the subject is closed.

30

MY FRIENDS ARE ON THE STREET, waiting behind a barricade—Hysan, Sirna, and all three Thaises. Hysan's still a little woozy from the Taser sting, and Egon is keeping him steady. I run up to him. "Are you okay?"

"Never been Tasered before," he says, smiling lazily. "It was *electric*."

We've all been banned from the Plenum, and soldiers are guarding the entrance to make sure we stay out. There's no sign of the students who welcomed me before. I take off my coronet and give it back to Sirna. "Keep this safe."

She accepts it with a solemn nod, and while Mathias scans the nearby buildings with his field glasses, she whispers to her brooch to call the car.

"I'm sorry I wasn't there, Rho," says Mathias, coming up beside me. "They tricked me with an urgent call from Agatha, then wouldn't let me back in."

"It's okay." Ochus seems to be doing everything he can to isolate me.

People from the audience are starting to come out. They're all Scorps, and soon one of them spots me. *"There she is."*

Hysan draws a pistol, and Mathias steps in front of me as the Scorps yell insults. When they move toward us, Mathias fires a blue-white arc of electricity from his Taser.

The men fall back a few steps, out of range, but they don't leave. Hysan pulls my veil collar from his tunic and fastens it around my neck, activating it. And I disappear.

The Scorps encircle us, and Mathias and Hysan fire their weapons to hold the crowd back, both guns set to stun. After two tense minutes, Sirna's car arrives, and we jump in.

"Guardian, our safe house might no longer be secure," she says as soon as we're all inside and I've taken off the collar. "We need to find a new place."

"She can stay at the Libran embassy," offers Hysan. "They won't think to look for her there."

"Thank you," I say.

Mathias turns quickly. "No. We don't know who's trustworthy—"

"Rho can trust House Libra," says Hysan, glaring.

To my surprise, Sirna says, "The Guardian has made her choice. We each have our duty."

I study Sirna's inscrutable face. Is she taking my side? Or hoping I'll be eliminated from her list of nuisances?

When we get to the village, we group together outside the Libran embassy. "I'll make sure you all have access to visit Rho at any time," says Hysan, his eyes on Mathias. "You're welcome to spend the night here as well."

Mathias looks taken aback by Hysan's generosity. But instead of answering him, he turns to me. "I'm going to help the Royal Guard while you get settled in. I'll swing by soon."

Sirna gives me a quick bow, though I still can't read her expression. "The Plenum has insulted our House. This will be rectified."

"I hope so," I say.

She and the Thaises wait to leave until Hysan and I step inside the Libran embassy. Given the degree of surveillance technology and armed Zodai surrounding the starscraper, I'm expecting to encounter a series of metal doors and biometric body scans inside. Instead, we walk into a creaky wooden courtroom.

A white-wigged judge towers above us on a high bench, the Scales of Justice hanging over his head. Beside him is a rickety witness stand, and to the far left are twelve teenagers, squirming in squeaky seats and arching their necks in our direction.

On Cancer, House-wide trials require one juror from each of the Twelve Matriarchies. In the Zodiac, galaxy-wide cases require one juror from each House. The teens in this jury box look like Acolytes from the Libran Academy.

"State your case," says the judge, his voice a low drawl.

"Hysan Dax, your honor, diplomatic envoy, representing Holy Mother Rhoma Grace, Guardian of the Fourth House, Cancer. She is being pursued by unknown assailants and has come here seeking refuge. I would like to grant her ladyship our Libran sanctuary."

I stare at Hysan in bewilderment. He grins and wriggles his eyebrows back.

"That sounds rather reasonable," says the judge. He turns to the jury. "What say you?"

The twelve teens—who have been staring at me with wide eyes—now turn to each other and form a circle, whispering in discussion. Almost immediately, a holographic question beams up from the jury box: *"Why are assailants chasing the Cancrian Guardian?"*

"Because she speaks the truth about a monster the Zodiac does not want to believe in," says Hysan, winking at me. "They cannot judge her fairly because they will not accept the possibility of her story's veracity. As we Librans know, those who think only in straight lines cannot see around a curve."

A moment later, the teens disband and sit forward again. "Have you reached your verdict?" asks the judge, sounding bored.

"We have, your honor," says the Acolyte closest to the high bench. "We believe the Cancrian Guardian should be granted sanctuary until her peers can embrace the plausibility of a wider worldview. Yet we would also remind Lady Rho that when we open our minds too wide, we risk closing them."

"Very good." The judge bangs his gavel. "Next!"

Hysan leads me through a small side door, and we step into a brightly lit hallway. The whole time, I'm staring at him in wonder. *"That's* your top-notch security? I'll be safe because your junior jury will rule against my would-be assassins?"

"If you saw all that security outside, would you really try to breach this place?" He laughs at the expression on my face. "If it makes you feel better, you were scanned the moment you walked through the door. All your information—name, astrological fingerprint, House, records, it was all processed. And the Knights outside are real Zodai."

Knight is the Libran word for Lodestar. "Then what's the trial for?" I ask, as we approach a pair of double doors at the end of the passage.

He freezes just shy of opening them and looks at me with concern. "*Fun*, my lady—though I'm seriously starting to wonder whether Cancrians are familiar with the concept."

When our eyes meet, I sense more than fun behind the centaur smile. There's a kind of serenity that's surfaced in his stare, as though he's close to the thing that anchors him—his Center.

A courtroom symbolizes a quest that is sacred to Hysan and his people: The pursuit of justice. Librans draw strength from this pursuit the way we Cancrians draw strength from the Cancer Sea, the nurturing Mother of all life on our planet.

Being in this place with him, I understand why Hysan's dedication to our mission hasn't wavered, even when he's never been under any obligation to come. Beyond just believing Ophiuchus is real, Hysan shares my need for *justice*.

"Fun sounds fun." As soon as I say the words, I cringe at how stupid they sound.

He chuckles softly. His hand is on the doorknob, but he still hasn't opened it. Though neither of us moves, the space between us seems to shrink.

I feel his green gaze and golden glow heating my skin, and as he pushes open the double doors, I realize my dark mood is lifting, burning up in his radiant light. "Welcome to your Libran sanctuary."

I step over the threshold, and Libra's shocked me again. Their embassy is a ritzy, dichromatic hotel. The marble walls are white and the floor is black. There are bellhops (in black) and valets (in white) everywhere we look. The high-ranking Libran officials are in yellow, so they're easy to spot. The lobby is a vast circular room that spans the height of the building, and the higher stories spiral up. All around us, help desks outline the room's perimeter.

It's probably the tallest embassy in the village, except for the Aquarian one. The upper floors ripple up in rings, about twenty stories high. We step into a humongous elevator, and Hysan tells the operator, "Penthouse suite."

We immediately shoot up to the top floor, where I only see one door. "Will I need a map?"

A glint crosses Hysan's eyes. He swipes an access card, and the door swings open on its own into a vast . . . workshop.

Long, flat tables fill the floor, their surfaces covered in all kinds of tools and machinery. Cabinets along the walls are brimming over with gadgets and electronic trinkets, and the glowing holograms of hundreds of measurements and equations crowd every particle of the room's air.

"Since I'm always traveling, I like to keep workstations on every House . . . in case Neith or 'Nox need a tune-up." I notice his gray coveralls hanging on a peg near the door. "The shield is up, so no one can access the Psy from here."

"Thanks." I step through floating words and numbers. "Where do you sleep?"

He leads me to a door at the far end of the workspace. On its other side is a lavish suite decorated in the dichromatic style of the lobby. The floor is checkered with black-and-white marble, the furniture is black levlan, and the tables are crystal. There's an expansive living room, a reading room, a kitchen, a dining area, a series of bedrooms and bathrooms, and a balcony that wraps around the whole space.

"Anything I can get you?" asks Hysan, opening his arms wide, as though the whole world were at his reach.

"The news," I say, thinking of Ochus. I need to know if he's attacked again.

Hysan nods and turns on the wallscreen, muting the audio. I wait for him to sit, and then I take the other end of the couch, careful to keep a cushion between us.

We watch the images from Sagittarius for a while. Next there's a quick report on the surge in hate crimes against Risers on Aries, Leo, and Aquarius. Historically, there's been a stigma around them, and they're one of the few social groups that still faces prejudice in the Zodiac, even if it's unpopular in most Houses to adopt that standpoint.

No updates on Cancer. No bombs at the Plenum. No attack on Gemini. This is torture, just blindly waiting for Ochus's next move. "What do we do now, Hysan?"

"We keep fighting, of course," he says, looking from the screen to me.

"Mathias doesn't believe me." I know Hysan isn't the best person to discuss Mathias with, but I need to talk to someone. I've never been so confused . . . or alone.

"I'm sorry, Rho."

"After everything Charon said at the Plenum, and those photos and the documents he showed . . . I can't blame him. Or Sirna, or any of them. I wish *I* could not believe me. If I could lie to myself, or question my memory . . . but my memory never lets me forget." The last part comes out bitter, so I clear my throat and look away.

"I believe you."

When I turn to meet his gaze, my inhale sounds like a whispered breath. Hysan has slid closer, onto the cushion between us, but he doesn't cross the dividing line.

"Why?" I ask, even though it's dumb to question one of your only followers.

"I trust you," he says simply, and I see no evidence of game-playing in his face. "I may not have your natural ability to read the stars, but I'm a natural at reading people." He takes my hand, and as his warmth seeps into my skin, I feel a flicker of hope. "I'm sorry I couldn't speak today. I should have tried yesterday."

"They wouldn't have listened. I just wish I could at least convince my friends. After everything the three of us have been though, why can't Mathias trust me? Why does he need proof?"

Hysan's eyes grow soft with sympathy, and the golden star in his right iris shines brighter than before. "Shall I quote that line about people who think in straight lines, or have you already committed it to your infallible memory, my lady?"

I want to laugh and kiss him at the same time. And then just the thought of doing either of those things makes me want to jump and run away.

I've never felt further from myself in my life—from home, from my family, from the person I was before this began. As Hysan starts to lean a little closer, I grasp for conversation. "Why haven't you been around much these days?"

His expressive eyes grow darker, becoming more present, as if every atom of his being were pouring itself into this moment. "I didn't mean to desert you, my lady." His face still seems to be coming closer, until his features blur in front of me, and I can almost feel his lips brush mine as they shape his next words. "But I'd rather not say."

I pull away, hurt. "*Another* secret, after what you told me today at the arena?"

His golden brow wrinkles, like he's considering my point, and then his expression clears. "Okay." He moves in for my mouth again, and the cedary scent of his hair and the sweetness of his breath tempt me closer. "The truth is, I don't know what it's like to introduce my parents to the girl of my dreams . . . but it didn't feel fair to ruin it for Mathias."

The feelings for Hysan that I've been suppressing seem to burst through my chest, and I press my mouth into his. My heart is fluttering with so many nerves that I'm worried it'll fly up my throat and escape my body—

Then the door to the suite clicks open.

31

WE FLY APART AS MATHIAS walks in from the workroom.

"Everything's quiet outside," he announces when he sees us. "I think we'll be safe for the night."

Hysan and I are at opposite ends of the couch, pretending we've been watching the news. My pulse pounds so loudly in my head, I'm worried it will betray me when Mathias sits on the cushion between us. "Thanks for leaving me a key at the front desk," he says to Hysan.

"No problem."

"I would have been here sooner, but your jury made me recount our whole journey. They were . . . interesting."

He places a bag of food on the table, and his elbow brushes mine—but I can't meet his eyes. "They said I could enter because saving your life on Virgo instead of looking for Rho proved I trust only what I can touch. Then they advised me not to live life so literally."

Hysan smiles indulgently. "Ah, they're good kids," he says, carrying over a carafe of water and three glasses from a corner table.

Mathias passes each of us a box of Cancrian rolls, probably from the village market, but I'm thinking of the warning Hysan's jury gave me. "What did your good kids mean when they said, *When we open our minds too wide, we risk closing them?*"

"It's a popular Libran line," says Hysan, setting our drinks down on the crystal table. "It means even open-minded people can become narrow minded when they refuse to consider other arguments."

Mathias bites into a sushi roll stuffed with crabmeat. "I've been thinking about where to go next. We shouldn't linger on Phaetonis." I feel his stare on the side of my head, and suddenly parched, I take a sip of water. "The largest Cancrian settlement is on House Gemini, which is where the embassy thinks your family might be."

The muted screen on the wall shows images from the Plenum. There are shots of my Cancrian supporters, of the Scorps that heckled me, and then there I am. Looking like a little kid on a big stage, performing for a group of disappointed adults.

Ochus was right. I'm no threat to him, just as he predicted on our first meeting. After all, who's better at reading the stars than a former star himself?

The reporter gives my full name, age, and status as an Academy Acolyte. Turns out I'm one of the youngest Guardians in centuries. Only the six-year-old Aquarian is younger, but his title is only symbolic because his regents do the actual work. On Aquarius, being Guardian is a birthright, so the lineage is determined by blood. Often, their House's best star reader will actually be the Guardian's senior Advisor and not the Guardian himself. Obviously, the reporter doesn't know about Hysan.

Next the video shows soldiers throwing me out of the hippodrome. I glower at the screen, and a new thought stirs through my mind. "Rubidum said she was summoned to the Plenum days ago, before we even arrived."

"Same with Neith." Hysan spears a bite of crab with his chopsticks. "It doesn't make sense."

"You didn't know your android would be here?" asks Mathias.

"Total surprise. Neith thought I was the one who summoned him. He's very intelligent, but he can be naive. He didn't think to consult me before he left for Aries."

Mathias sets down his empty sushi box. "Why call so many Guardians to the Plenum?"

It sounds like something the same person who doctored Dr. Eusta's appearance would do—*Ochus*. Who else could pull off such a massive forgery?

"At first, I thought he wanted to target us with one blow," I say, continuing my inner thoughts aloud, "but that's not it."

"No, he would've struck by now," agrees Hysan.

"Maybe Ochus wanted the Guardians to see Charon's false evidence firsthand," I muse, thinking back to my own decision to deliver my warning in person and not by hologram. "To match what I'm doing . . . you know, to *really* ruin my credibility."

"Of course," says Hysan, nodding, "he's making his lies more believable. *Trust Only What You Can Touch.*"

I rub my head. "Ochus must have foreseen that I would come to the Plenum, and he wanted to discredit me. The only good news is he's still afraid of me, at least enough to put some effort into defeating me, so there must be a move we can still make, something that still worries him. We just haven't thought of it."

"Your questioning way of getting around a problem is very Sagittarian," says Hysan, following my reasoning so closely he's abandoned his food.

I beam at him. "My best friend must've rubbed off on me." Suddenly hungry for the first time all day, I take a bite of my Cancrian roll. The taste of fresh crab reminds me startlingly of Cancer, and I savor the meat's buttery softness in my mouth, especially after so many compressed Space meals.

Mathias stands up and crosses to the balcony's open doorway, looking out at the surrounding village. "We should get away from this place. Help our people back home."

I swallow, the food suddenly tasteless, and push away the rest of my meal. *"Home?"*

Even just saying the word, I realize no place in the Zodiac offers real shelter from Ophiuchus. Whether he attacks today or tomorrow, there's no doubt he'll slaughter more of us soon. "As long as the Guardians are here," I say, "I'm going to stay and keep trying to convince them."

Mathias rounds on me. "Rho, you can't be serious. Do you have a death wish?"

"I swore to protect Cancer," I say, rising to my feet, too. "This is me upholding that oath, whether you understand it or not."

He shakes his head. "You've done your best. You've given enough."

"Thanks for your help, but making speeches is *not* my best." I start pacing up and down the living room to work off my frustration with him. "My best is reading the Ephemeris, which I can't do, because Ophiuchus will use it against me. So I'm blind, and I'm powerless, but I'm still the only one who knows the *truth*. I can't turn away from that."

"How will you convince them, Rho?" asks Mathias, planting himself in front of me to block my pacing. "You've already tried twice, and both times they've shut you down. There's nothing more you can say or do because there's no *proof*—"

"Then I have to go to the Thirteenth House." The realization comes to me as I speak the words. Avoiding his eyes, I say, "I have to get proof that Ophiuchus is real."

"No." Mathias stares at me in alarmed disbelief. "Rho, you're the Guardian of Cancer, your people need you."

I turn away from him and face Hysan, who's watching us from the couch. "I need another huge favor." His attentive and still stance reminds me of the jurors downstairs. "Could you program *'Nox* to fly me to the Thirteenth House?"

"There is no Thirteenth House," interjects Mathias. "That's only a legend."

"Fine," I say, still staring at Hysan and refusing to see Mathias. "Then Hysan, could you program your ship to take me to the Sufianic Clouds?"

He nods. "I'll fly you myself."

"Rho, you're tired," says Mathias, softening his tone and trying a new approach now that we're two against one. "You need sleep. Tomorrow everything will—"

"Mathias, you have so little confidence in me." I walk around him and start pacing again, too agitated to slow down. "Ochus is real, and he's hiding somewhere, maybe in his House. I'll find him, or I'll find proof the Thirteenth House exists, or I'll find something to corroborate my story and redeem Cancer's reputation and rally the galaxy against him. Something people can *touch*."

Hysan stands. "Rho's right. It's not just about Cancer anymore. Everyone in the Zodiac is a target as long as the Houses refuse to protect their people from Ophiuchus."

Mathias reaches for me, but I dodge out of his way. "Rho, please," he says, following me to the far end of the room, his midnight-blue eyes sparkling. "I'm just asking you to be reasonable about this."

"I'm sick of reason," I say, glaring at him. "Go to Gemini if you want. I'm going to find Ochus."

Pain cracks Mathias's face, and he whispers, "You know I'll never leave you."

Someone knocks loudly on the suite's door.

Adrenaline drowns the guilt and anger twisting my gut, as Mathias motions me into a bedroom and draws his weapon. He follows Hysan to the workspace to see who's here, and seconds later they return with Ambassador Sirna. "Where's Mother Rho?"

I edge out of the bedroom, and as soon as she sees me, she says, "We've received a report that your brother is alive. Injured, but alive."

Stanton's okay. Blood rushes into my chest, and I reach for the doorjamb to steady myself, emotions crashing over me like ocean waves.

"The grid is down again, but I'll let you know as soon as we can put you in touch," she says, her dark face creased with concern.

My brother survived. I can barely let myself believe it. I'm so relieved, I might finally sleep tonight—except she didn't mention Dad. Is that because there's no update on him yet, or—

"I have other news. Charon was bribed to denounce you, and I can verify it." She touches her brooch, and holographic screens of data begin to beam out. Hysan shuts the curtains, and the facts and figures flare brighter in the darkness.

"We analyzed Charon's so-called scientific evidence," she says, as more screens fill the living room. "We knew the explosion on Thebe originated in the quantum reactor, but the cosmic rays he alleges are complete fabrications." The first few holograms are now spreading to other rooms of the suite.

"Then what caused the reactor to explode?" asks Mathias. He's investigating an image taller than him that shows our four moons at the time of the attack.

"I went back through the logs from that night." Sirna points to a screen floating near the kitchen, a spreadsheet of numbers, and smiles at me. "You ordered me to look again. I've just found unmistakable traces of a Psy attack."

Hysan looks over Sirna's spreadsheet, then turns to me. "Rho—with this proof, plus 'Nox's logs, the Plenum will have to believe there's a Psy weapon out there."

He's right . . . even if they don't think it's Ophiuchus using the Dark Matter, they'll know it's a powerful Zodai who can manipulate Psynergy. It's a start. "Why didn't anyone else bother to fact-check?" I ask Sirna. "There must be more data."

She shakes her head. "Psynergy fluctuations are easy to miss if you're not looking specifically for them. No manmade sensors detect them permanently because their traces in the Psy disappear so quickly. We see only the faint trails they leave in the matrix of space-time."

I steal a glance at Hysan, but he doesn't mention his shield. He's trusted me this far, so I stay quiet and trust his silence. Mathias is still poring over the data, combing fingers through his wavy hair.

I know this doesn't change his stance. He already believed in the Psy attack because he saw the ship's logs. What I can't convince him of—or anyone else—is the perpetrator. At least revealing Charon's deceit will convince the ambassadors not to trust him. Then maybe, like Hysan said to his jury downstairs, I can finally get my fair hearing at the Plenum.

"Who bribed Charon to lie?" asks Mathias.

"We're still investigating," says Sirna, tapping off a few of the holograms to make room for new ones. "We believe it may be the same conspirators who are funding the troops on Phobos. We've infiltrated a network of spies that stretches all across the galaxy."

Sirna's Wave beams out a new screen. It's Charon's financial records, and there are a series of anonymous lump-sum payments with date-stamps going back several weeks. "This plan has been long in the making," she says.

My intuition stirs. "Does anyone have a galactic calendar?"

Sirna whispers, and a wheel-shaped holographic calendar joins the others hovering through the suite. I spin it with my fingertip, mentally translating local dates into galactic standard. "I knew it! The first bribe was date-stamped the same night I saw Ochus."

Mathias double-checks my dates. "Rho's correct."

"Ochus foresaw my trip to the Plenum that very day," I say, aghast at what that means.

Hysan whistles. "A first-order clairvoyant," he says, voicing my fear. "Your *boogeyman* has skill."

"He's behind everything," I say, thinking of all the violence in the news lately. "The army, the civil unrest, all of it!"

Mathias cuts through the wheel-shaped calendar and faces me. "Rho, you're leaping to conclusions."

"Then I'll find *proof*—"

"Our first priority," says Hysan, walking up to us and playing referee this time, "is debunking Charon's lies." He turns to Sirna. "Can you present your findings while the Guardians are still here?"

She shakes her head. "Not the details about the army, not while our agents are still undercover. We need to collect more information."

"Agreed," says Hysan, "but the bribes and Charon's trickery— you can reveal that at least?"

"Yes, only . . ." Sirna folds her hands and crosses a blue holo-gram. "If I do it, I'll expose our covert operations at the Plenum. Someone else will have to."

Hysan looks to me. "I have a feeling Lord Neith will take up this cause."

✦ ✦ ✦

Sirna stays up late with us, drinking black tea and talking about the secret army on Phobos. We gather in the reading room, which is a staple of Libran homes. Holographic booktitles line every inch of wall space, dozens of mismatched plushy pillows pool in the middle of the floor, and every text—whether fiction or non—explores the theme of justice. To read one, Hysan just has to Scan the booktitle, and its holographic pages unfold before him. The rest of us can do the same thing with our Waves.

The cushions are arranged around a crystal tabletop that's embedded into the marble floor, where Sirna set down a tea tray and some snacks. I'm relieved she and I are finally friends, but I spend the whole night watching her face, wondering if she knows anything about Dad.

Both she and Mathias insist that I take time to reconsider my plan of flying to the Thirteenth House. To convince me, Sirna shares more classified documents. It turns out Ophiuchus has been looked into before, and not that far back.

"Seventy-seven years ago," she starts, sitting upright in her body-massaging pillow, "our Mother Origene's predecessor, Mother Crae, saw a disturbing omen in the vicinity of the Sufianic Clouds. Although Crae didn't describe it in detail, she did appoint a panel of our leading Zodai to reexamine the folklore. In the process, a scholar named Yosme traveled to House Aries to study the earliest version of the myth. Yosme unearthed another scroll written in an older, more archaic language. He translated it as *The Chronicles of Hebitsukai-Za, the Serpent Bearer*."

"So does that mean . . . Za and Ophiuchus are the same person?" I ask, nestling into my clump of fluffy, oversized cushions.

"The two legends were too similar to be coincidence. The *Hebitsukai-Za* scroll was a major scientific find."

"Why has no one heard of this Hebitsukai-Za before?" asks Mathias. He's lying on his back on the hard marble floor. He says the firmness helps for Yarrot.

"The report was buried," says Sirna, cradling her teacup. Hysan, who's in a nook of the room reviewing holographic books, now turns to her with rapt attention.

"Mother Crae feared that certain new details in the Za account were too alarming to make public. So Yosme's report was sent into deep archive, and after Mother Crae's death, it was forgotten. We only found it by scouring the history files and searching for the extra-encrypted documents, the ones that don't appear on a search unless you know exactly what you're looking for. We had to break into our own security system to access the master list, and that's where we found this report."

"What are the alarming new details?" I ask, hugging my knees.

"They have to do with time." Sirna Waves Yosme's book of the myth of Hebitsukai-Za over our heads, and the four of us lie on our backs and look up, reading the text and reviewing its images.

The first picture shows travelers from another universe passing through a time warp to settle our Zodiac Galaxy. Hebitsukai-Za was the last in the group to traverse the time warp, and when he emerged, his body was entwined in the ropey coils of an enormous worm that was biting its own tail, simultaneously devouring itself and growing longer. This worm was Time.

Passing through the time warp had altered the laws of physics and created an unstable leak between the old universe and our own. The two universes were in imminent danger of sliding together and collapsing. So the terrified travelers sealed off the time warp, but only after Za had brought the time-worm through.

The book's images mesmerize me. They show how the worm could turn its head both forward and back, thus ruling the direction of time. Recognizing what chaos this might cause, the travelers tried to kill the worm, and by accident, they bludgeoned Za to death. But the worm needed a host, so it reversed time and resurrected Za.

When the book ends, a new image rotates in the air. "This is the glyph of the mythical House Ophiuchus," says Sirna.

I study the familiar staff entwined by two serpents, the emblem we call the Caduceus, or healer's wand.

"Now look at this one," she says. A second emblem materializes next to the first. This one shows a stylized outline of a man trapped in the coils of a single giant worm biting its own tail. When Sirna overlays the two images, the resemblance is too strong to miss.

"Myths speak to us through metaphor," says Hysan.

"I don't know what it adds up to," says Sirna, shutting off the holograms. "It's only legend."

"Maybe nothing," says Mathias.

"Or maybe everything," I mutter, my inner sense foaming with possibilities.

On a sudden impulse, I sit up and say, "Sirna, could you call up 'Beware Ochus'?" When the holographic poem hovers above us, I read it out loud and linger on the line A *wound even time could not mend*. All these references to time . . . are they just coincidence, or could they be clues?

Before Sirna leaves, I find an excuse to pull her into the privacy of a bedroom. As soon as we enter, she lowers her gaze, and I realize she knows what I'm going to ask.

And I already know her answer.

32

"WE DON'T KNOW WITH ABSOLUTE CERTAINTY...."

"But you're pretty sure," I whisper, dropping onto the bed and clutching my chest. She doesn't say anything, so I look up. From the expression on her face, I know Dad's gone.

I turn away, staring at the floor but not seeing it.

I don't feel pain.

I don't feel anything.

Yet.

"I'm sorry if I've been rude to you," says Sirna, her voice constricted. "I've misjudged you, Guardian." She draws something small and shiny from her pocket.

"Mother Origene gave me this. . . . Now I'd like it to be yours. Please wear it always to honor our House." She opens her hand and a thin gold chain dangles out. On it hangs a simple pendant holding a single rose-colored nar-clam pearl.

Like the ones on the necklace Mom made me . . . the one I lost on Elara.

That day, Stanton was bitten by the Maw, and we rushed him to the healers, who did what they could for him. . . . But no one could say with certainty if he would ever wake up. Stanton was out for five hours, and Mom and I spent every one of those three hundred minutes trying to find his fate in the Ephemeris.

But it was Dad—not the stars—who kept Stanton safe. He sucked the poison from his wound after the attack, and while Mom and I were off predicting if my brother still had a future, Dad was caring for Stanton in the present. He sat beside him and held his hand all five hours.

Whenever I've thought of that day, Mom's stood out in my memory as having saved us. She killed the sea snake. So why am I only seeing the true hero now, when it's too late?

"Please promise me you'll never take it off," says Sirna, pulling me out of my sink-sand past and clasping the gold chain around my neck. "Let it bring Cancer to you, wherever your travels lead."

✦ ✦ ✦

I wish Sirna a tender goodbye, and after she leaves, Mathias tells Hysan he needs to talk to me privately. I can barely speak, but he thinks it's because of what happened at the Plenum and where I plan to go tomorrow.

I can't tell him or Hysan about Dad. That would make it too real.

"Please, Rho." It's Mathias in the room with me instead of Sirna, but my eyes keep finding the same spot of the floor, like I can't stop reliving the realization of Dad's death.

"It's my duty to raise objections. I'm just trying to help you think clearly."

"I know," I manage to say. "I'm just tired."

His baritone grows gentler. "I'm going to do some scouting tonight with my mom, see if I can find out who's after you. I'll be back in the morning. Just try to get some sleep . . . and think things over."

"I'm leaving tomorrow to find Ophiuchus," I say in a dead voice.

Mathias goes without answering.

When I'm alone, I strip off my clothes and step inside the shower. Once the water is scaldingly hot, I sit on the tile floor, huddled against the wall, and I let the sticky steam fill me with something—*anything* but this awful, gaping, deadly absence.

I rub Sirna's rose pearl between my fingers, thinking of Dad. The last time we saw each other, I was on vacation from the Academy, a year and a half ago. Stanton was home, too, and it was almost like going back to when we were kids, and the three of us lived together. Mom's ghost still haunted the bungalow's darkest corners, but mostly she was gone, and we had a great visit.

The last day of vacation, I helped Dad clean our old schooner. I told him about starting a band with my best friends Nishiko and Deke, and we even talked about my plans after the Academy. It was the closest he and I had come to a real conversation in years.

There's so much I wish I'd told him. The tears flood my eyes all of a sudden, one for every truth, story, and feeling I should have shared with him—all the unsaid things I kept stuffed inside my shell.

I should have told him why I left home. I should have asked how he felt after Mom took off. I should have admitted I was angry with her, but that I was angry with him, too—for not protecting me from her mania.

Everything pours out from me in sobs that shake my chest and scrape my throat, like my memories and emotions are trying to claw their way to my surface.

By the time I turn the faucet off, my eyes feel desiccated and my fingers look shriveled. I slip into a cottony white robe and sit in front of the mirror, passing a brush through my wet hair, staring into my dull and deadened eyes. Their pale green reminds me of the bioluminescent microbes that glow in the inner lagoon where Dad keeps his nar-clam beds.

Where Dad *kept* his nar-clam beds.

My exhalation gets caught in my throat and won't come out. Just like my brain won't accept this nightmare as my new reality. Dad can't be gone.

Suddenly, I hear drumming in the distance. No—*knocking*. It sounds faint and far off, like it's coming from somewhere in my head.

Then I realize someone is at my door.

My face comes back into focus in the mirror. Enough time has passed that my hair is dry. Since I've been brushing it nonstop, it's almost straight. I have no idea how long I've been sitting here, thinking of Dad. Of our home on Cancer. Of everything I've already lost.

So what's the harm in one more gamble—one last trip into Space?

"Rho? Everything okay?"

Hysan's voice wraps around my soul like a blanket, and I feel myself pulling out of this stupor, peeking out from my shell. This cold aloneness isn't what I need right now. I need warmth.

"Come in," I say, tucking the pearl necklace under my robe and cinching the belt tighter.

"I brought you something to sleep in," he says, stopping short when he sees me. "Your hair . . . I like it."

"Thanks," I say, taking the sleeping shirt and stretchy pants he hands me. He's wearing his gray coveralls again, and there's a stylus in one of the pockets, like he's been working.

"Room service will bring you anything you need—toothbrush, food, clothes. Just tell the wallscreen what you want, any time." He's silent a moment, then turns to leave.

"Will you stay with me awhile, or do you have somewhere to be?"

My whisper hangs in the dimly lit room, the words so low I'm worried he didn't hear them.

"Somewhere is where you are, my lady."

His voice is like a caress; it brushes softly down my spine, until every knotted nerve within me begins to loosen and liquefy. Until all my body wants to do is finally let go. I'm tired of holding on so tight when everything has already fallen apart.

"Can room service bring us any Abyssthe?" I ask when he's

in front of me again. "Or that Geminin drug?" I'm only half joking.

Hysan frowns as he registers the heaviness in my gaze. "What's happened? Something's changed from before."

"My heart stopped beating," I gasp between waves of emotion, "and I can't feel anything anymore." I won't tell him I'm an orphan now, like him. I won't say those words yet.

Instead, I move closer, until all that's between us is the lumpy knot of my robe, pressing against my waist.

"You be my drug then," I say, looking into those green eyes. "Make me feel something . . . while we still can."

"You're sure?" he whispers, his breath soft against my skin. He combs his fingers through my hair. "You're not afraid?"

"Of you?"

"Of crossing a line. I don't want you to do something you'll regret." His stare scans my face like a laser, and I wonder if I even need to speak my answer, or if he's already found it.

"I don't have many lines left to cross," I whisper. "And this one hardly seems like the worst."

My friends on Elara are gone. Millions more Cancrians have died since. Virgos, too. Dad, Mathias's sister, Deke's sisters, Kai's parents . . . I can't stop any of it. Ochus is too powerful to avoid or defeat, and he's bound to destroy me, too.

After all, I'm at the top of his death list. Any moment I'm going to go like the rest of them, and I've barely lived. My world's axis is off-kilter, and I can't set it right.

Other than Nishi, I've never cared for anything or anyone that wasn't Cancrian before. Hysan is wrong for me in so many ways—the Taboo, the innate differences between us, the timing. And, of course, Mathias. But that's how I know this is right. Because it isn't something I *should* or *need* to do—for the first time since becoming Guardian, I'm doing something I *want*.

Fingers shaking, I clumsily undo the knot around my robe, until the white belt falls limp on either side. The robe's curtains sway a little, leaving the slightest sliver of space between them.

Hysan plants his hands on my hips, but he doesn't remove my robe. Instead, he leans in until my eyes naturally close, and I feel his lips brush mine. "I'll do anything you want," he whispers, his voice husky. "You set the rules."

My heart's beating too quickly to speak again.

What a strange way to discover I'm still alive.

I dated a little at the Academy—but I've never been kissed like this before. When Hysan's mouth meets mine, it's like he's discovered a new flavor, something foreign and delicate, and he's savoring the taste. His lips are gentle and curious, yet experienced, and the more carefully he kisses me, the stronger my desire for him builds.

I shiver when his hands slip beneath the robe and trace my hipbones. His fingers feel light and velvety on my skin, and I gasp as they travel up my sides, curving in with my waist and grazing the sides of my breasts. When he reaches my shoulders, his hands slide down along my arms, shedding off the white robe entirely.

It falls to a soft heap on the floor, leaving me naked, save for the necklace Sirna gave me. I've never stood like this in front of a boy before. I feel every cell in me constricting with shame and fear, my face burning what must be a brilliant crabshell red, and I get the urge to cover myself back up—

"You're so beautiful, Rho," whispers Hysan, touching the pearl on my necklace, cutting off my thoughts. I forget to be self-conscious when I see the openness in his face. He's vulnerable, too.

"I've never met anyone like you," he murmurs into my neck, "and I'm crazy about you."

A shot of something new spikes my blood. In this moment, I don't feel like a girl or a Guardian or a teenager or an Acolyte or like any person I've been before.

For the first time, I feel like a woman.

I never even knew there was a difference.

Hysan takes off his gray coveralls, removes a wrapper from a pocket, and then eases me onto the bed. The sight of protection suddenly makes what's happening real.

As I lie back, his hands come down on either side of me, and his arm muscles bulge as his body presses down. I couldn't be more aware that the only clothes between us are his boxers.

"Hysan . . ."

He looks at me, his messy hair falling over his golden face and soft eyes. "Rho, we can stop if you'd like—"

"I don't want to stop," I say, pulling him closer. "I just wanted you to know," I breathe into his ear, "I like you, too."

His cheek curves against mine. Then our mouths crash together again, and for a night, he makes me forget the burning hole in my chest.

33

WHEN I WAKE UP THE NEXT MORNING, I immediately feel different. For starters, I've never slept naked before.

I've also never woken up expecting to see a guy in my bed. But when I look over to Hysan's side, I'm alone.

I stay under the covers as the air grows brighter, my emotions a jumbled mass of confusion. I don't know how to feel. Dad is a wound that will never heal, and the devastation of his death weighs on me like a cloak that will stay fastened forever.

And yet when I think of Hysan, my body feels sensitive and light, producing echoes of new sensations he introduced me to last night. My curves feel new to me today. Experiencing my body through Hysan's hands and lips gave new meaning to every part, and I feel more connected to myself than ever before.

Maybe I should regret last night, but I don't. My old self wouldn't have done this, but that girl is gone. So is that life, the one where I consulted an Ephemeris daily, the one where the stars and I shared our secrets.

Ochus has cut me off from that life. From my future. My *family*. And last night, Hysan gave me a good memory, one that's all mine, one I can take with me when I meet my fate. When I set off to find Ochus.

For now, I can't think beyond that. So I change into the unused sleeping outfit Hysan brought me and pad into the living room.

"Morning," says Mathias.

As soon as I see him, needles of guilt stab my insides.

"Did you sleep well?"

His scrutiny makes me turn to hide my face. "I did, thanks. Any news?"

"I saved you some breakfast," he says, still watching me. Does he suspect anything, or is he just being Mathias?

He's cleaning his silver Taser, and he looks like he hasn't slept yet. There's a small nick in the cleft of his chin from shaving.

"Where's Hysan?"

Mathias pours me a cup of tea, and I feel like a traitor. "Just picking out which dress to wear. He's going to visit his android this morning."

"I'm going, too."

"That's not a good idea."

I grab a roll from the bread basket beside him to avoid answering, just as Mathias pulls something from his pocket and places it on the table in front of me. "Happy birthday, Rho."

The sight of the small green package fills me with nostalgia. *Sugared seaweed.* "Dad and I ate this all the time at home," I whisper, choking back a wave of sadness so Mathias won't know the pain his gift caused.

"It's almost impossible to find off-planet," he says. "I thought it'd be a welcome reminder of Cancer."

"Thanks," I say, pulling him into a hug, mostly to hide my face. But guilt twists my gut, and I pull away quickly. I didn't even realize it was my birthday—that I was seventeen—when I woke up this morning.

We split the box of seaweed between us silently, and then he turns on the news. When Hysan comes in, I'm glad to see he's wearing the gray coveralls again. We give each other shy nods, and I hope Mathias is too distracted to notice my awkward blush.

"Morning, my lady." Before Hysan can say more, we hear the door to the suite clicking open.

Mathias grabs his weapon and slips through to the workspace, returning instantly with Lord Neith, whose stern eyes soften with affection when he sees Hysan. "Father," he says, opening his arms.

I watch, entranced, as Hysan embraces the towering android. Neith pulls out a smart screen from his pocket and calls up some data to share with Hysan. The hologram's reflected light glimmers across his perfect Kartex face and makes his white hair glisten.

While they work, I step onto the balcony and look over the railing. Far below, armored cars rove the streets like tiny beach beetles. Drab sunlight filters through the planet's fabric sky, and the black wall ringing the village casts gray shadows.

Mathias joins me. "Bleak, isn't it? I'll be glad to leave this place."

"Are you still planning to go to Gemini to live in an underground mine?"

"Our people are there." His handsome features catch the sun's dim rays, and I'm struck by his quiet poise, the way I was five years ago when I first saw him doing Yarrot. "I still believe in my heart that Cancer will recover."

Then I admit something I didn't expect to share: "I've known this whole time you'd make a better Guardian."

Mathias looks at me long and hard before speaking. "At first, I couldn't understand why they chose someone so young and . . . untrained." He leans his broad chest against the railing, still absorbing me in his indigo gaze. "But those were the wrong things to focus on. Your talent is raw, but you have more discipline and determination than anyone I know." His musical voice dips, like he's embarrassed to be speaking so openly. "You're an everlasting flame that can't be put out."

I used to wonder what he saw when he looked at me—a little girl or a grown woman. For too long, he made me feel like the former. And at best, something in between the two. But for the first time, Mathias's words make me feel big instead of small.

"You're also the bravest, kindest, and most selfless person I know," he says, his expression lightening. When the lines fade from his face, he looks like he's shed off years. "You're pure Cancrian, through and through."

Even as his words make my heart soar, the guilt eats away at my stomach. Just when I get Mathias's respect, I'm no longer worthy of it. Hysan isn't alone in keeping secrets anymore.

"Thank you, Mathias." Guilt makes my gaze too heavy to meet his. "I hope that means you're not going to fight me on going to find Ochus, or proof of his existence."

When I sneak a glance, the lines on his face have resurfaced. "No one has ever come back from the Sufianic Clouds, Rho. The person behind all this—Ochus, as you call him—manipulates Psynergy in ways no Zodai ever has, or can even fathom. You've had less practice than most and don't know your full strength yet."

It's the first time he's said the name Ochus aloud, and even though it wasn't an endorsement, at least he's accepting the *possibility*. He's showing me he's trying. He wants me to meet him halfway.

Only I can't. I've committed to this mission, and I have to see it through. "I'm going, Mathias. I'm just asking you not to try to stop me."

"Then let's at least consult Psy experts and learn as much as we can about how whoever's doing this is doing this—how we can fight him before we act—"

"That's a good idea," I say, the pieces coming together in my mind to form a plan. "While Hysan and I get proof that Ochus is real, you and Sirna and the others can start gathering information on how we can use the Psy to defeat him. Then we can appeal to the other Guardians again, only this time we'll have *proof* and a *plan*."

He shakes his head and rubs his eyes, like I'm a hyperactive toddler who's testing his patience. Like I'm once again small. "Rho, I don't think you should travel there without more information. If you insist on going, we'll need to consult the rest of your Advisors first."

"If I'm an everlasting flame, why do you keep underestimating me?"

Hysan snickers behind us. "*Classic.*"

"What is?" growls Mathias.

"Prejudice of the old against the young."

Mathias looks torn between expressing his anger verbally and using his fists. He takes an unsteady breath, then walks back inside without another word.

Alone with Hysan, I suddenly feel new to the Zodiac. We smile at each other as he edges closer, and side by side we look out at the city, our fingers lacing together on the railing.

Police sirens echo from far off, and in the distance we hear artillery fire. Thin gray light leaks through the fabric sky. "Happy birthday, my lady," he says, handing me a small box. I open it to find a Crab-shaped pin made of turquoise cristobalite beads. The color of the Cancer Sea.

It's my very own Psy shield.

"Thank you," I say, clipping it on my sleeping shirt. The Crab shines like a reminder of home. "How'd you know it was today?"

"Saw it as the soldiers scanned our thumbprints when we got here." He admires the pin on me, then says, "Neith convinced the ambassadors to extend their session so he can speak. He's very persuasive. He learned from a master, you know."

"A humble one."

"And that's just one of my *many* sterling qualities." Hysan slides his thumb up and down my little finger.

"How long is the trip to the Sufianic Clouds?" I ask.

"Four days, maybe. We'll need to stay invisible the whole time, since Ophiuchus could have eyes everywhere."

I peer at the many windows overlooking our balcony and shiver. "Let's go inside."

In the living room, Mathias is standing rigid and white-faced, staring at the wallscreen. He turns to me, his expression blank.

For a moment, I think he overheard Hysan and me, or he saw us holding hands. Then I catch a glimpse of the bloodshed on the news.

"Gemini's capital has just been obliterated."

34

THE PLANET ARGYR HAS BEEN RAZED. Images on the wallscreen show devastation beyond understanding. The rainbow buildings flattened. The Imaginarium smashed. Small Geminin bodies burned to cinders.

Caasy didn't come to the Plenum. Was he at the royal court where we first saw him? Did he survive?

I'm sitting on the sofa, between Mathias and Hysan, biting my nails as the newscast unfolds. The images are so grisly that I want to cover my face, but I force myself to keep watching. Behind us, Neith stands like a monument.

The total destruction of the city has been confirmed. A passing cruiser recorded an immense mushroom cloud rising over Gemini's capital, and the authorities are blaming an accident at the nuclear plant. But that doesn't explain why the entire planet is wobbling on its axis.

Will it crash into its neighbor, Hydragyr, where so many of my own people have settled?

"Ochus," I hiss.

"Rho," says Mathias, the word insignificant compared to the way it's delivered—with the voice of one who's been blind.

There's a pounding on the door, and Lord Neith briefly looks toward it. "An agent of the Cancrian Secret Service wishes to join us," he tells Hysan. "Shall I allow it?"

Hysan nods, and when the door clicks open, the person who enters the living room is Amanta Thais. "Mom," says Mathias, pulling her in for a hug. "You've seen the news?"

"Yes. Sirna sent me," she says, panning her gaze across us and pausing in surprise on the Libran Guardian's face.

"Charon will claim more cosmic rays." I feel myself shaking in the Zodiac's instability. Any planet could be next. "We have to move our people again. Is someone arranging that?"

"Advisor Agatha has taken charge," says Amanta, speaking with quiet urgency and looking from Lord Neith to me. "Two Guardians dead in one month. Another comatose. People are beginning to panic."

"The Plenum session has been extended," announces Neith. "I shall address them in an hour."

"Sirna wants Rho there, too," says Amanta. "This time, she thinks the ambassadors may listen."

"Can I tell them about the secret army?" I ask.

"Not yet," says Amanta, "not until we learn who's recruiting them."

Amanta is needed back at the hippodrome immediately, so we

agree to meet her there. The four of us leave as soon as Hysan and I are dressed. On the street, he turns and speaks a soft word to Neith. Abruptly, the golden android sets off toward the Plenum, running faster than I expected, given his refined manners and regal composure.

Hysan smiles with pride. "It's quicker to travel alone than in a group. He knows what to say once he gets to the Plenum."

In case my protestors are waiting for me, we use the veil collars and sprint down the street, trailing far behind Neith. As always, the area around the hippodrome is jammed with visitors from every House, including the rowdy students with banners. This time, their numbers have swollen.

We sneak past the soldiers, and when we enter the arenasphere, the ambassadors and visiting Guardians have already taken their places in their gilded seats. Except today, the makeup has changed.

Overhead, holograms of every color jam the upper half of the sphere, blinking pixilated flashes where they overlap. Micro-cameras hover as thick as smoke. Down below, tawny Geminin have taken over one full section of seats, and I also see many more Virgos than before, plus Taurians, Leos, Sagittarians, even Cancrians. In fact, all the Houses are represented in this crowd.

Many of them are young, student-aged. Surely that's Nishi's doing. Lord Neith stands at center stage, holding the speaker's staff and scrolling Sirna's data on four large holographic screens that float through the sphere, proving beyond a doubt that the cosmic ray story was a deliberate lie. Cameras alight on his arms, and he ignores them.

We haven't unveiled yet, but Neith sees us at once and motions us forward. Hysan gestures for me to go first, and this time, instead of hanging back and guarding the door, Mathias comes with me.

The three of us mount the stage, but Hysan whispers that we shouldn't unveil. "Wait till they beg for you, Rho."

"Beg for me?"

With a mischievous look, he nods toward the audience, then leans to whisper in my ear. "Someone sent Ambassador Sirna's data to news stations across the galaxy. I can't imagine who. And by the way, that's your *second* birthday gift, my lady."

I stare at him with wide eyes, not believing what I'm hearing. "Are you still going to tell the other Houses about Psy shields?"

He flashes his crooked smile. "Patience. That's number three."

I'm about to hug him when Charon shoots to his feet and tries to take the staff from Neith. We watch him struggle, but Neith wins easily. "I will not yield the floor to you, sir."

The students pelt Charon with wadded scraps of food and trash until he's forced to take a seat. Members of the Scorpio Royal Guard remove him from the proceedings, and cheers break out among the audience.

"I think you'll yield to me, Lord Neith." Solemn little Rubidum rises to her feet. "My brother's been vaporized. That gives me all the grounds I need to address this gathering."

Under our veils, the three of us trade somber looks. Caasy's gone.

I think back to his warning that I'm being deceived. Was he seeing Charon's actions? Or was he foreshadowing his own theft of my black opal just to mess with me?

"Rubi, Rubi, Rubi!"

Rubidum smiles, though tears streak her opalescent face paint. "Let her speak," I whisper, and Hysan nods at Neith.

Neith bows and gestures for her to take the floor. She climbs onstage, passing close by us without noticing. The speaker's staff is too long for her to hold upright, so she grips its head and lets the tail end rest at an angle on the floor.

"Fellow Guardians, you know me. For three hundred years, my brother and I have seen plagues, floods, famines, disasters of every kind. The Taurian mudslides, the Piscene drought, the Leonine fires—we watched them with troubled hearts. Yet until today, we assumed these events were normal, cyclical, beyond anyone's control."

She pauses to dab a tear, and the audience murmurs.

"But now, friends, we've seen atrocities without equal. Three Houses laid to waste in one month. Three Guardians struck down. Origene's dead, Moira's a vegetable, and my brother . . ." She sniffles and wipes another tear.

Then she aims her staff at the audience with a look of blood thirst. "We have to stop denying the truth. Someone's orchestrating this. Whose House will be next? Yours? Yours?"

People shrink back in their seats as she points. "Not one of us is safe while the monster lives. We know his name. What is it?"

"Ophiuchus!" the Geminin group yells. And just like that, the people of Gemini are believers.

"Yes, *Ophiuchus!*" Rubidum moves across the stage like a tragic actor, dragging the end of the staff. "Behold his work."

Near the front of the crowd, a Geminin stands and beams images from the Tattoo on his palm to the virtual screens: gruesome videos from Argyr's burn wards of the injured and the dying. Their agony silences everyone.

Rubidum lifts her head. "Mother Rhoma Grace warned my brother and me about Ophiuchus. I was a fool not to listen then, but now I say this butcher must die."

"Kill the butcher! Kill the butcher!"

The chant echoes through the Geminin group. Then, to my amazement, it spreads like fire through the entire crowd.

I can't believe how fast terror can turn the tide of public opinion. Suddenly everyone believes in the boogeyman.

"He can strike anywhere, anytime!" Rubidum shouts above the noise. "He'll destroy us all unless we act. We cannot sit still."

When the frenzy reaches a crescendo, Rubidum drops the staff with a clatter and raises both hands to the sky. "Friends, we were wrong to ban Rho Grace from this Plenum. She was the only one who foresaw this foe. We need her on our side."

The students begin to chant my name, and to my shock, over half the audience joins in. Overhead, the holograms echo the chant like crashing cymbals.

"Rho! Rho! Rho!"

I was willing to sacrifice my life just to convince the Zodiac of Ophiuchus's existence. Now that they believe, I should be thrilled . . . only I'm not. Something about this feels wrong.

Reason hasn't converted them—the fervor of the room has.

Albor Echus begs for order, swinging his robes of fur, and

Neith pounds the lectern with his fist. "Shall we call back Mother Rho?"

"Yes!" the people thunder. "Call her back! Bring back Mother Rho!"

"Now," whispers Hysan. "Unveil."

All three of us switch off our collars, and when we pop into view, the audience's reaction makes me lightheaded.

Our magic trick has them on their feet, giving us a rousing standing ovation, and from all over the arenasphere micro-cameras zoom toward me. The colors and lights and flashes and shouts and sounds—it's all overwhelming.

Small arms embrace me. I look down and see Rubidum. "We're placing our faith in you, Rho. Bring this monster to justice."

Now I realize what a grave mistake I've made.

I let these people believe I'm more than a whistleblower—that I actually have a plan for defeating someone who can turn our own particles of air against us.

I'm not in the military. I'm not a qualified Zodai. I can't lead an army. As the cheers rise louder, Neith hands me the speaker's staff. But for the first time, I have no idea what to say.

My speeches never went beyond pleas to unify the Houses . . . and now it's done. I've accomplished what I set out to do—I've sounded the alarm, the very thing Ochus threatened to kill me for attempting. The whole point of joining forces with the other Houses was so I could share the quest for justice—not *lead* it.

At my silence, Rubidum raises her voice. "House Gemini will outfit forty war ships to crush the butcher. Who'll join me?"

Ear-splitting cheers erupt from the audience.

"We will!" shouts the amber-eyed Guardian of Sagittarius. I remember her face from the newsfeeds two years ago, when she was named Guardian at just twenty-one years old. "We'll send tankers."

"Capricorn will send arks," their ambassador announces.

The Taurian Guardian shouts, "We'll supply weapons!"

War ships? Ammunition? Is that what we need?

There's no stopping the spread of battle frenzy now. Leo's Leader—who was once the most famous leading man in Zodiac cinema until the stars chose him to lead—pumps his fist in the air. "Our House will send a cruiser!"

When Lord Neith takes up the staff again, he says, "House Libra will provide Psy shields for every ship. The enemy will never see us coming."

With a broad sweep of his hand, he tosses hundreds of cristo-balite beads into the air. People in the audience fight each other to catch them. He tosses more and more, making sure to shower the Guardians and ambassadors. "Personal shields. Contact the Libran embassy for more," he booms, tossing another handful.

So this is how Hysan kept his promise. A bead bounces off my shoulder, and I scoop it up. "Brilliant," I tell him. Hysan's lips hitch up in a subdued smile.

Neith empties his pouch and flings the last handful of beads into the air. "We're manufacturing more, enough for every House."

Now all the Guardians, ambassadors, and aides-de-camp are moving their lips furiously, speaking through the Psy. If Ochus hasn't noticed us yet, he must surely hear this buzz now. He'll know we're coming. We'll have to be stealthy in our planning.

Before I know what I'm doing, I'm addressing the crowd. "Fellow Guardians, every House is a target." The whole arenasphere goes silent.

"Please take these shields and hurry home to defend your planets. Charge your Zodai to watch the stars. Go over emergency procedures with your people. And above all, open the lines of communication with the other Houses."

Everyone looks around, like they're just noticing their neighbors. The audience looks like a color-coded population map: Most wear their House colors and sit only with their own.

"We are each other's best chance against Ophiuchus. He's worked hard to keep hidden and has gone to great lengths to keep you from believing my words. He wants us divided. It's worked for him before. I want to read you something, a Cancrian children's classic. It's called 'Beware Ochus'."

The Cancrians in the crowd cheer as from memory, I recite:

> *Once upon a Guardian Star,*
> *When the Zodiac was new,*
> *A Serpent stole in from afar,*
> *And trouble began to brew.*
>
> *Twelve Houses fell in disarray,*
> *Until the Snake drew their focus.*
> *Their discord he promised to allay,*
> *He told them his true name was Ochus.*

Trust in him the Houses did,
But cross them he would in the end.
Their greatest magic Ochus hid,
A wound even time could not mend.

Now we guard against his return,
For before setting off he did warn us,
To one day see our Zodiac burn,
So now we must all Beware Ochus.

By the second verse, holographic versions of the poem fill the arenasphere, and everyone is reading out loud with me. When we've reached the end, I say, "Making us turn against each other worked for him in the past, but it won't anymore."

Voices shout in approval. "Each of us excels at a different skill that ensures our universe's survival. We were meant to use our abilities together, as a unit, not to distrust each other and keep secrets. Ophiuchus knows how strong we are when we work together. That's why he'd do anything to keep us apart. Let's show him he's right to fear a united Zodiac."

A slow storm of applause begins to build. "Let's show him that together, we're undefeatable."

The crowd is on their feet, and there's no calming them now. I don't know where the strength came from. It was like my nurturing instinct, my impulse to protect my home and loved ones, just extended to the entire Zodiac.

Watching us, I realized how vulnerable we are, how disconnected, and I saw something I could do to help. So I just . . . acted.

Even though I'm Guardian, I've never considered myself a leader. I thought that in order to lead, you first had to have a plan. But sometimes leading is about keeping people together when there is no plan. When there's only the will to survive in the face of invincible evil.

Hysan reels me in for a tight hug. "Rho Grace, Guardian of the Zodiac," he says, surreptitiously kissing my cheek. "You're a star."

Mathias reaches for me next, but just then Rubidum grabs my hand and whirls me around to face the audience again. "*Trust in Guardian Rho!*" they chant.

She raises a fistful of beads and shouts above the noise. "I nominate Rho Grace to lead our armada!"

The audience roars its approval. Alarmed, I pull away and shake my head in refusal, even wave my arms.

But nobody wants to see it. They've already decided.

"Let us elect Mother Rho by acclamation!" joins in Neith.

I turn and see Mathias behind me. "Mathias, make this stop. I can't lead an *armada*. I barely even know what that is!"

He offers me his arm, and I hold on. "They're panicked," he says. "They're not thinking." His bicep hardens under my hand.

"Whose idea was this?" I ask Hysan when he comes over.

"Don't you see what's happened? You've given everyone hope, Rho," he says, his face shining with light. "You've been Guardian of Cancer three weeks, and you've done what no one's been able to do in centuries—you brought the Zodiac together."

He wraps my hand in both of his, and on my other side, Mathias tenses. "I've known since I first saw you at your swearing-in, and I've felt it these past few weeks in your presence, watching you with leaders from every House: Your light blazes too bright to be contained in one constellation."

His eyes have never been bigger or greener. "You're destined to be a guiding star not of one world, but all of them. If not you, *who?*"

Albor Echus stands and calls for order. The ambassadors must have finished their discussion. "The Plenum has voted. We appoint Holy Mother Rhoma Grace of the Fourth House to lead our united fleet."

The faces in the audience shine starry bright. My breathing races, and I feel dizzy. I steal a sideways look at Mathias. He and I are the only people onstage who aren't smiling.

I stare at the audience again. I was willing to give my life to stop Ochus. I can't hold back now.

"I accept."

35

AN ARMADA, IT TURNS OUT, is a fleet of warships.

I have to learn these things quickly because the strategizing begins right after the vote, when I'm swept off the stage by Ambassador Morscerta and whisked into a meeting with all the Guardians and ambassadors. They debate for eleven straight hours, dividing responsibilities among the Houses and nominating Zodai to lead the various charges. Just like my meetings on Oceon 6, I mainly spend the time listening and answering questions.

The next few days are a blur of these gatherings, sometimes with everyone at the hippodrome, sometimes with the Lodestars at the embassy, sometimes with other ambassadors at the village. Sirna moved me into one of the bungalows, so I only see Mathias and Hysan for small snippets of time—a quick bite here, a joint meeting there—but mostly, we're each working on our own tasks. Hysan's outsourced the production of Psy shields to a factory on Aries, and he's now pulling on his vast network of people he's met in his travels across the solar system to raise resources fast. Meanwhile, Mathias is training our Lodestars for combat.

Early on it becomes clear that my function as the armada's leader is to be more mascot than mastermind—and I'm not complaining. I'm relieved there are better-suited people at the helm, but I wish the twelve Admirals would invite me to their military meetings about the operation. Every time I ask to attend, they insist I focus on the metaphysical battle—my part—and leave the physical one to them. I know they're probably right, but I just want to be sure we're ready.

Ochus must know we have a plan, and he's already proven he's an extraordinary seer. Even if we're veiled from him, I want to know we've thought through every possibility.

◆ ◆ ◆

The night before we launch our attack, the ambassadors plan a universal celebration in the village. It's a revival of the Helios's Halo festival.

The festival is an old Zodiac tradition from before the Trinary Axis. The Houses used to come together to celebrate the Zodiac's top star, Helios, on the one day a year her flames were predicted to burn brightest. The celebration took place at night, under a ghostly sun: The day's light would linger long after sunset, forming a phantom ring where it once shone, an effect dubbed Helios's Halo.

No one's seen Helios's Halo since the final festival. Even though it's obvious why the Guardians stopped celebrating it, no one knows why the actual effect stopped happening, not even Capricorn's scientists. Piscenes believe Helios is punishing us for our divisiveness. While getting ready for the festival, I ask Sirna what she thinks.

She pauses painting my lips, letting her sea-blue gaze drift, and says, "I think it's because we don't look up as much as we used to." I ponder what that means while she and Amanta finish styling me to their liking.

By the time they deem me ready, the festival has been under way for an hour. I walk outdoors and see people and holo-ghosts packing the village streets, gathering in front of every embassy, sitting at round tables, dancing, talking, eating, and mingling. The intermarket in the main square has been converted into a free food zone, and the line of people waiting winds around the whole village.

I keep to the bungalow's shadow and cast my gaze across the black-walled enclosure, trying to spot Hysan or Mathias in the crowd. I hope they have an easier time recognizing me than I do.

Amanta styled my hair in an updo, leaving just a few curls free to frame my face, and Sirna added the silver Cancrian coronet. The dress she picked out for me is a sapphire sheet of satin that curves around my shape like cascading water. It falls a few inches above my knees, and the back dips down to my waist, revealing the slope of my spine.

"Trust in Guardian Rho" by Drowning Diamonds begins blasting from a holographic screen, and I see some university students petting Leo's lions start cheering and belting the lyrics. Watching the video of my band performing on campus makes me think of the Lunar Quadract. I can almost remember taking Abyssthe, setting up my drums, goofing around with my friends . . . but the memory is nebulous, like it's underwater, along with everything else I've lost.

The Rho I was then feels inaccessible to me now.

I hear soft steps behind me and turn to see Mathias. His eyes travel up to mine, and I realize he was studying the slip of my back. Awkwardness reddens his cheeks, then spreads to mine, too.

"You look like home," he says, offering me his arm.

When he's close, I catch a hint of sweet-smelling liqueur in his breath. The sight of his fresh trimmed hair and royal blue suit takes me back to the moment before my swearing-in ceremony, when my first crush finally noticed me. It's hard to recall the innocence of that feeling when we're no longer those same people. "So do you," I say, looping my arm through his.

This is the first non-war-related moment we've had, and my body's already reminding me that I haven't told him about Hysan yet. Thoughts of battle kept my guilt at bay before, but now the old squirm in my stomach has resurfaced.

We cross the plank to join the rest of the festival, and I peer out at the faces, searching for Hysan's. The crowd is in the high hundreds, and bodies continue to pour out from every embassy. I've never heard of the Houses coming together like this in recent history.

"If the stars had shown me this picture a week ago," I say, "I wouldn't have believed them."

Mathias furrows his brow as we orbit the crowd. "On the other hand, if they showed you an immortal mythical monster bent on the Zodiac's destruction . . ."

I laugh, and after the past few days, the reflex feels foreign. "Did you just make a *joke?*" I ask in awe. He cracks a toothy smile that fills his whole face with light, and now I come to a complete stop. "Lodestar Mathias Thais, is that a *smile?*"

His shoulders curve in a little—his stiff stance noticeably looser tonight—and his sweet-scented breath sweeps my skin. "Catch me on a week when we're not about to be mass murdered, and I might surprise you."

His indigo eyes are bright and closer to me than usual. Being friendly with Mathias should feel soothing, not unsettling— yet somehow my feelings for him seemed clearer when we were arguing.

We get jostled by the growing crowd, and Mathias steers me clear of their foot-stomping and elbow-jabbing. The village keeps filling up with more people, and just like when the Cancer Sea's tide rises, we're forced to seek higher ground. Wherever we go, I scan the surrounding faces for Hysan.

The Piscene embassy is on a hill, so we climb up to join the sparser groups gathering on its front lawn. The embassy—a crystal temple with curving corners—is lit up and teeming with people inside. Through its semitransparent walls, their bodies look like shadows.

Now that we have a relative bit of privacy, Mathias gently releases my arm and turns to face me. "Could we . . . talk?"

There's a quiver in his question that's an off-key note in his musical voice. The sound sings to something deep within me, and I realize whatever's weighing down Mathias, I can't hear it until I've come clean about Hysan. I don't want to lie to him, not ever again, and especially not about this.

"I think we should," I say quickly, before I can think the words over too much. "But I need to tell you something first."

A Piscene Acolyte in a floor-length silver veil approaches us with a tray of hot pink drinks. She doesn't even look at me after she's seen Mathias. "Seaberry liqueur?" she asks him.

He shakes his head. Instead of leaving, she sidles closer and jingles a pocket within her veil. It makes a tinkling noise like glass bottles touching. "Or perhaps you'd prefer some Kappa-Opioid . . . ?"

"Kappa *what*?" I ask, adding volume to my voice to prove my presence.

"Not that junk again, Pisces!"

A brusque Taurian Acolyte in an olive green Academy uniform storms over and yanks on the girl's arm. Hot pink liqueur dribbles down the side of the flute glasses on her tray. "Do you even realize who you're offering drugs to, Spacey?"

"It's *Lacey*," snaps the Piscene girl, wrenching her arm free. "I've told you so ten times, Taurian! And it's *not* a drug, it's a pathway to the stars—"

"Will you two cut it out already," says an Aquarian Acolyte holding an empty tray. She looks at Mathias and me, on the verge of apologizing for her companions—and then squeals instead.

"Mother Rho!"

Before I can react, she snaps a picture of me with her Philosopher's Stone. "I'm Mallie. It's an honor to meet you."

"Nice to meet—"

"Oh, my Helios!" cries out Lacey, cutting me off and coming closer to inspect my features. "It's *you*! I can't believe I'm meeting you!"

"I *told* you," says the Taurian, rolling her eyes. She turns to me, and in an all-business tone that matches her competitive stare, she says, "Hello Holy Mother, I'm Fraxel Finnigan, of House Taurus." She checks out Mathias next. "And *you* are?"

"Blessed Empyrean, are all Taurians as rude as you?" asks Lacey. She sets down her tray of pink drinks, then faces Fraxel, hands planted on her hips.

"We're not rude, we're efficient. Maybe if you people pulled your head down from Space and actually took an interest in the tangible world around you—"

"What was it like facing him?"

Mallie's large, glassy eyes reflect the Cancrian glyph of my crown. Even though her voice is soft, her question is loud enough to quiet the other girls. All three faces turn to me.

"Terrifying," I admit, stealing a look at Mathias, who's heard me tell this story more times than anyone. He seems distracted, and I wonder if he's thinking about the talk we almost had. "It's like fighting a solid person who can wield the power of wind, ice, and fire, and you have no way to defend yourself . . . because you can't touch him back."

Mallie holds her hand to her chest, turning the Philosopher's Stone between her fingers. The device is encased in a lead pendant that hangs from a silver chain around her neck, and its design varies according to clan. Mallie's pendant is shaped like an owl. "How did you survive?" she whispers.

"Luck," I admit, thinking back to each time I faced Ochus. If I hadn't been able to close the black opal or rip off the Ring—or if Ochus hadn't decided destroying Virgo took priority over me—I wouldn't be here right now. The knowledge fills me with a sense of doom, the kind I get in the Ephemeris when I sense an opposition in the stars. I have *no idea* how to survive this.

"How did it feel . . . knowing you were going to die?"

The Aquarian and Piscene stare at Fraxel. Even she seems surprised to hear herself ask a question more appropriate to the spiritual and philosophical realms.

"Lonely," I admit. "Not in the moment I was facing him— when you're fighting for your life, adrenaline numbs a lot of those thoughts." I feel the full force of Mathias's stare on me now, but I don't look back. "It's not even death that's lonely. . . . I think it's surviving. Because afterwards, you realize you did die—the person you were before is gone—and while everyone around you is pressing onward, you're learning to become a person all over again."

A couple of drunken Capricorns—one tall, one short—bump into Lacey, and she stumbles on her long veil, knocking over the glasses. "I *knew* that was going to happen!" gripes Fraxel, ducking to help Lacey clean up. Then, in a more muted tone, she says, "I need to check in at my embassy, so I can return your tray if you want."

"Thanks," says Lacey. She holds up her palm to press with Fraxel's just as the Taurian sticks out her arm for a handshake.

"On Taurus, we shake," says Fraxel, squeezing Lacey's hand in demonstration.

"We press palms," says Lacey, showing her how.

A strange understanding seems to pass between them, and with a jolt, I realize that in ordinary times, they never would have had this chance to meet. It saddens me to think of the price we've paid for this moment—the Cancrians, Virgos, and Geminin who had to give their lives for the Zodiac to come together.

As Fraxel wends her way to the Taurian embassy, ripples in the crowd push us farther up the hill. The four of us search the street below for the source of the commotion: The Arieans have erected a ring for holographic wrestling.

A couple of Ariean fighters step inside in red uniforms, wearing protective gear and helmets. The first man's body flickers, like he's transforming from human to hologram, and then I gasp as his image morphs and expands into a ten-foot tall snake-like creature with rippling arms and huge fangs. The second man becomes a lizard monster with talons and a lethal stinger on his tail. Both are imaginary versions of Ophiuchus.

The referee whistles, and the match begins. The avatars are projected by the men's helmets and contained within the ring, so if either fighter steps out, they automatically revert to looking human. The lizard monster stabs at the snake creature with his stinger. The snake slithers away just in time and surprises the lizard by striking back immediately and sinking its fangs in its tail.

A wave of cheers drowns the lizard's cry of agony, and then there's another round of roars as the lizard retaliates by digging its talons into the snake's arm.

"Look up!" shouts Lacey.

I turn my head to the night sky, and Rubidum and a team of Dreamcasters—Geminin Zodai—are standing on the peak of the Aquarian embassy, high above the village. They're using their Tattoos to draw delicately detailed designs in the stars.

Shining above me now, in stunning clarity, are Cancer's four moons. Mathias and I catch each other's eye but don't speak. Then the picture changes to Virgo's needle city, to Gemini's capital, to Helios. . . .

I've never seen anything like this before—the Houses of the Zodiac partying together, showing off for each other, sharing their tricks. For the first time, I see what a united Zodiac could look like—and I finally understand the full scope of what I'm fighting for.

This is about more than stopping Ophiuchus and bringing him to justice. It's about our universe, and the kind of place we want it to be. We become our best selves when we're around the other Houses: Nishi has made me more inquisitive of the world around me, and Hysan has helped me find my confidence. There's a reason Helios binds our Houses together—we're meant to learn from each other, not about each other. To speak to each other, not of each other. We're not Cancrians and Librans and Arieans and Scorps and Geminin and Piscenes and Capricorns and Sagittarians and Virgos and Leos and Aquarians and Taurians—we're the *Zodiac*.

My heels are making my ankles sting, so I lean against Mathias's bicep, linking our arms. He, Lacey, and Mallie are alternating between watching the sights above and the fight below, but I'm gazing at the crowd, a rainbow of colors that's no longer segregated but blended. Then a familiar voice floats from nearby, and at last my eyes find the ones they've been looking for.

Hysan is twenty feet away, talking to a gaggle of university students from various Houses, most of them holding pink drinks. The group looks spellbound by him, and I try to hear what he's telling them. But I can't make out the words.

After a minute, there's an outburst of laughter from the students, and one of the girls—a Libran—slaps his arm playfully. Hysan says something else and flashes his centaur smile. Even from this distance, it tickles my skin.

The holographic wrestlers take a break, and now that people have stopped shouting, I can hear Hysan's voice. It sounds like he's telling a joke.

"After creating the first human," says Hysan, his green gaze dancing with every person in the group, "Helios gave the Guardians a chance to make an adjustment to man—one wish, effective the moment it's made. Aries was up first. He gave us super strength." An Ariean girl in a skintight red dress whistles. "Taurus removed our need to sleep. Gemini imbued us with magical powers. Cancer made sure love would always guide us." He pauses and casts his gaze around for a quick moment, and I wonder if he could be searching for me.

When he starts again, he speeds through his list, and the students cheer him on as he goes: "Leo got rid of our inhibitions"—two Leos slap hands—"Virgo made us flawless, Scorpio gave us mental control over technology, Sagittarius gave humans the power to teleport, Capricorn made our brains bigger, Aquarius lengthened our lifespans, and Pisces gifted everyone with a pure soul."

When Hysan finally takes a breath, the group applauds. The hungry look on some of the girls' faces makes my stomach sear with jealousy. I've been watching the Libran girl, and she's brushed her arm against his too many times not to be intentional.

"Only Libra's Guardian was left, and for his wish, he asked that human lives be *fair*." Laughter erupts from half the group. "And that's why instead of being gods, you're listening to me tell this joke." The rest of them are now laughing, too. It's the first time I'm seeing Hysan on his own.

I longingly watched Mathias for years before we ever spoke, but Hysan I've only known as mine. I don't know him when he's not with me.

The Libran girl, who looks to be about twenty and has silky blonde hair, invites the others back to the embassy. "We can get room service," I hear her say, and even though she's addressing everyone, she's only looking at Hysan.

The group welcomes her proposal with drunken excitement, and every organ within me seems to crumble, until all that's left is my shell. She's beautiful, older than me, and doubtlessly more experienced—of course Hysan is interested.

When he leans into her ear to whisper something, my insides wring with despair. I just accepted the charge to lead our universe in a war against an eternal star, and I can't even compete with this mortal girl.

But then Hysan pulls away, and the girl's smile is gone.

As I'm watching, he casts his gaze around again, and I realize that his manner is so courteous, I didn't notice it before—but he's actually been searching the crowd often. And this time when he looks, he sees me.

He excuses himself from the group and cuts over to where I'm standing. The Libran girl's gaze lingers after him, her expression sulky.

Mathias looks down from the images of Guardians Origene and Caaseum in the sky. He spies Hysan's approach, and his arm muscle tightens under my hand.

When he's only a couple feet away, I feel Hysan taking in every part of me, even though his eyes never pull away from mine. He reaches for my free hand, and my blood bubbles where his lips touch my skin. "I missed you," he says, holding my fingers a moment too long.

"This is Mallie and Lacey," says Mathias loudly, forcing Hysan to turn away from me.

After they introduce themselves, Mallie says, "We should resume our drink service." Her glassy eyes reflect my coronet again. "Good fortune, Guardian," she says, bowing. "May you lead us to victory against Thirteen."

"It was wonderful meeting all of you," says Lacey, also bowing. She seems about to speak to Mathias before leaving, but Mallie pulls her by the elbow and says, *"That's Rho's boyfriend."* Then she looks back at the three of us and waves, dragging a mortified Lacey with her.

Hysan, Mathias, and I stand around in silence, and too late, I realize I should have corrected her.

"Can I get you anything, Rho?" asks Mathias, his mood suddenly improved.

Hysan won't meet my gaze, and it hits me I'm still holding onto Mathias—that I've been holding onto him since Hysan arrived.

"I think I should go, as well," says Hysan, his tone still amiable but his sunny glow dimming. "Since we're taking off tomorrow morning, and there's much to—"

"No, don't," I say, afraid to lose him again in this crowd. I hate all these secrets and mixed messages, but my window for a heart-to-heart with Mathias is gone, so I'll need to find another moment. But I have to explain myself to Hysan now. "I think I could use a glass of water."

Immediately, Mathias sets out to find me one, and as soon as I'm alone with Hysan, I say, "I'm sorry, I haven't had a chance to tell him yet, and—"

Hysan shakes his head. "I don't want to pressure you, Rho. It's just sometimes I don't know how you feel, and he can be so possessive of you—"

"Like the Libran girl with you?" When I hear how jealous I sound, I wish I hadn't spoken, but now that I have, I can't stop. "I just feel like there's so much we don't know about each other. I mean . . . how do I know that you don't have a girlfriend on every House?"

He laughs, startling me. "You could brand me as yours if it pleases you." He touches his forehead. "Perhaps a tattoo here. . . . What do you think of *Property of Rho Grace?* Too subtle?"

I laugh too, then I grow flustered, caught in the current of my emotions, and he interlocks his fingers with mine. "If you don't already know how I feel about you, I'm failing as a communicator."

I feel the warmth of his touch and blow out a hard breath, releasing my tension. "It's not you . . . it's *everything.*"

"I'm not going anywhere, Rho," he says, his voice now completely serious. "As long as you want me here, I'm here. If you want to wait to tell Mathias until later, when this is over, I'll understand."

I wish I could kiss him, but Mathias is returning. I wish I knew there was a later, that we'll still be around when this is over.

But for the first time in the Zodiac, no one knows what's coming tomorrow.

36

THE FESTIVAL ENDS CLOSE TO DAWN, when a couple of rowdy Leos sneak the embassy's lions into the wrestling ring and try turning them into holographic fighters.

A few hours later, the Zodiac goes to war.

Hysan, Mathias, and I are stationed on the cruiser *Firebird*, our flagship. The fleet is accelerating across the galaxy to the place where the vision used to appear to me in the Ephemeris. We're taking a convoluted route known only to a few senior officers, and our whole armada is shielded, veiled, and running silent. Hopefully it's enough to keep Ochus from finding us.

Even though the three of us are on the same ship, we barely have time to talk amid all the preparations. Mathias is on the hangar deck, teaching people how to pilot the skiffs; Hysan is one of his students. After four days of flying, we're now only hours away from the thirteenth constellation.

Since we're maintaining radio silence, we can't get fresh news from home, and I'm anxious. The last thing we learned before setting off is that Gemini's devastated planet just missed colliding with its neighbor, so our refugee camp is safe for now. But I have no idea if another world has been ravaged, or if the army hiding on Phobos has made a move yet.

"Have you ever seen a ship this majestic?" Admiral Horace Ignus of Leo spreads his arms wide. He and I just finished reviewing my part of the plan so that things can go smoothly when it's time.

He's a loud, expansive man, with a broad Leonine face and thick brown beard. When I first stepped aboard, he had his orchestra play a fanfare and greeted me with a kiss on each cheek. "Welcome, little lady," he said. "Have no fears while you're aboard the *Firebird*." As if this were a pleasure cruise, not a battleship.

"Admiral, I was hoping to hear more about the battle strategy—"

"We've got that pretty much under control, darlin'. Trust me, we'll nail that murderin' sonofabitch." He's condescending, but like most Leos, he has a good sense of humor, so it's hard not to like him. "You just keep your eye on the metaphysical stuff and leave the physical work to us."

All I know of our battle plan is that it's what Ignus calls a *feint*. In sea sports, it's when you pretend to go one way, and while your opponent's distracted, your teammates go another. But since I don't play sports, I don't know how often it works. All I know is that without Hysan's shields, we wouldn't stand a chance.

The *Firebird* is a long black cylinder with fake gravity like *Equinox*. Behind us, more than two hundred other vessels trail through the sky, and unlike *Firebird* and *'Nox*, few of them were built for speed. Gawky freighters, leisurely yachts, sluggish galleons and arks—they string out like clumsy runners at a marathon.

All twelve Houses sent spacecraft to fight Ophiuchus. Even Cancer managed to supply a barge. Scorpio contributed a squadron of sloops, even though Charon is under investigation by the Plenum. House Virgo provided mirage veils to cloak every ship from view. Sirna is stationed on the Ariean destroyer *Xitium*, which flies just off our starboard flank, and Lord Neith is piloting *'Nox* on our port side. Rubidum's somewhere behind us, steering a neutron zeppelin.

On Phaetonis, the Ariean generals converted a chemical plant for mass production of Psy shields, and now every vessel in our fleet carries a full-size facsimile of Hysan's veil. Since we're flying silent, ship-to-ship communications are tricky. Sometimes we shuttle back and forth, but mostly we use blinking signal lamps. Our entire success rests on a surprise attack.

"I just think if I knew more," I tell Ignus as we walk together, "maybe I could help, based on what I learned from my previous encounters with Ophiuchus."

He gazes down at me with a look of grandfatherly patience. "Little Mother, you worry too much."

While Ignus goes to the bridge, I head to the forward observatory, going over what I know of the plan in my mind. First, we'll zigzag through the Kyros Belt, a broad band of ice in the Fish constellation of House Pisces. The Kyros Belt will conceal our stop at a Piscene space station orbiting planet Ichthys. That's where we'll load up on fuel. We'll need a lot of fuel to reach the Thirteenth House.

Then, heavily veiled, we'll pass through Ochus's wall of Dark Matter. When we're within visual range, we'll lower our Psy shields, and every Zodai in our fleet will read the patterns of his constellation to find him. We'll need to be incredibly fast, since shields down means he'll be able to attack us. Once we find Ochus's base, the feint comes in.

I'm the feint.

Ignus has given me a Wasp gunship with a high-resolution Ephemeris onboard, and I'll fly it far from the fleet. When we find him, I'll lower my Psy shield and open an Ephemeris to attract Ochus's attention.

The instant he attacks me, my Psy shield will switch on and keep me safe . . . I hope. And while Ochus is distracted, the fleet will move close enough to destroy his headquarters. Then, as Rubidum says, "We'll incinerate the butcher." But I also know I could be incinerated in the process.

I sent Nishi and Deke encrypted messages before leaving the embassy. In Nishi's, after thanking her a million times for everything—above all, for being the best friend imaginable—I included a letter for Stanton. I asked her to track him down and deliver it if I don't return.

Mathias finds me in the forward observatory. "The enemy knows we're coming," he says, storming over in a bad mood. "This armada's too big to hide."

I recite the facts Admiral Ignus used to ease my own worries.

"We're invisible, and we change our heading every few hours. He can't possibly know our exact location."

Mathias adjusts the telescope lens and looks through it. He stays glued to the eyepiece, and I can't read his expression. His stretches of silence are more maddening than his outbursts.

"Our Zodai are already watching for ambushes," I insist. "We'll do lots of reconnaissance before we strike."

Sirna's still worried about the secret army on Phobos, but that's not what troubles me most. I'm worried we've been at peace for so long that our Houses have forgotten the art of war.

Except for the five Ariean destroyers, none of our vessels were designed to carry weapons, and other than the Arieans, our crews have no experience in battle. *Combat* is just a word from the history files for most of us here. The older men like Ignus are almost giddy. They don't seem to understand there's a chance we won't come back from this.

I plop onto a stool while Mathias recalibrates the lens array, and numbers fly across his control screen as the telescope refocuses. He's working harder than anyone, training new skiff pilots en route and instructing the ship's crew in martial arts. We all have to be ready for anything—no one knows what's behind Ochus's wall of Dark Matter.

I run fingers through my curls, wondering what critical factor I've missed. I can't fight the bad feeling that keeps creeping up my neck, no matter how many times I try to shake it off. "Ophiuchus is just one House, and we're twelve. We've got the numbers. Everyone believes we can do this."

"Well then, if everyone believes, we'll definitely win," he says flatly.

I stare at him. "What is it?"

He finally faces me, and his eyes shine with more passion than his voice betrays. "They're asking too much of you, Rho. They're using you like bait."

Now I'm the one to look away. "Mathias, I launched this voyage. These people trust me. You want to turn back?"

"Of course not. We're committed now." He rises from his scope and moves toward me. "I'm having your Wasp armor-plated."

"Thank you," I say, even though we both know physical armor won't hold off a Psy attack.

"I'll be with you every step," he murmurs, looking like he wants to say more.

He thinks he's going to pilot my Wasp, but I've already decided there's no way. I'm not going to let him die with me. He already came aboard *Equinox* without knowing the full risk, and he could have died too many times. I have to return him to Amanta and Egon. Mathias has to get home.

I nod and try to smile. "The plan will work. It has to."

He studies my forehead, my mouth, my chin. I can't read his expression. "When was the last time you had a decent meal?"

"I ate some breakfast." Actually, I had a tube of fortified energy paste, but it counts. "I'm going to get ready for my meeting with the Psy experts."

Mathias and I agreed that I would consult the foremost Psy scholars in our fleet while we're on our way to see whether they can help me defend myself in the Psy, if I'm forced to fight Ochus.

One of the three notables is Chronicler Yuu, a Capricorn. The second is a Piscene mystic, Disciple Psamathe, and the third is a Virgo I met during our visit. Moira's gray-haired courtier, Talein.

"Eat a little more," Mathias calls on my way out.

37

VERY SOON NOW, WE'LL BE entering the Kyros Belt. Our scans show the ice field glittering in the distance like a fine mist.

Blinking signal lamps are not the speediest way to communicate, especially when the signals have to be relayed through the fleet from ship to ship, so it will take more than one galactic hour to shuttle Yuu, Psamathe, and Talein aboard *Firebird* for our meeting.

While I wait, I run through the pilot training course Ignus gave me on my Wave. I decided to bring it with me, since the Psy shield will protect us from Ophiuchus accessing the tutorial Ephemeris.

After a bit, I start to space out and watch the Leonine mechanics armor my Wasp gunship. They're covering the side and rear windows with thick plates of tungsten carbide, while a guy named Peero tells an awful joke about a Capricorn who was reading an instruction manual for how to lose his virginity. Leos have always had little love for Capricorns.

This training course makes steering a Wasp look easy, though the sight of the ship makes me claustrophobic.

"Would you like to help?" a girl named Cendia asks. I instantly like her wide, friendly face. She keeps her thick mane of brown hair tied in a topknot, and her arms are covered in artistic tattoos. "You can hold this panel while I weld the seam."

"Sure," I say, glad for a chance to do something.

Hanging out with the mechanics helps me relax. They're only a couple of years older than me, and their rowdy good humor reminds me of the dining hall at the Academy. When Cendia and I lift the panel into place over the window, I lean against it to keep it from slipping.

"You're all right, lady," she says. "All the other Guardians are, like, senior citizens."

"You're screwing up the seam," says a short guy with a button nose and a space between his front teeth. He's Foth, the chief mechanic. When he jerks the welder out of Cendia's hands and starts re-welding her seam, she rolls her eyes. "There's only one correct way to weld a reliable seam in tungsten carbide," he says, lengthening his neck and trying his best to look down his stubby nose at us.

Cendia goes at her seam again, and when Foth steps away to revamp someone else's work, she whispers, "He's bossy, but he knows how to weld."

"Your seam looks fine to me."

"Yeah, not your usual shabby mess," says Peero, joining us.

"Shut up, you." She elbows him. "You'll make us look bad in front of Holy Mother Rho."

Peero grins at me. His chin whiskers are dyed in stripes of red, yellow, and blue. "You won't fire us, will you, Mother? We're making you bulletproof against Ocú."

"Sack man," Cendia explains, even though I already know. "That's what we call him in our House. He comes at Winter Solstice with a sack over his shoulder to kidnap bad children."

"Yeah, and he eats 'em." Peero chomps his teeth and pretends to bite Cendia. She laughs and swats him away. Then she and I set the next panel into place.

Someone comes up behind me and lifts the weight from my hands. "Hysan," I say, my smile burning through my cheeks.

He's clipped his blond hair in a new military style and traded in his court suits for the simple gray coveralls he's most comfortable in. "Your watchdog paid me a compliment this morning," he says, offering me his arm after he's helped Cendia in my stead. "He said I aced my pilot's test."

"I hope you didn't cheat," I say, linking my hand through.

"Me, use trickery?" He fakes a wounded look that makes me laugh out loud. Then he turns and kisses Cendia's hand and bows elaborately to the other mechanics. "Excellencies."

Cendia looks up at him adoringly. "Your Psy shield is genius. I can't wait to study it when we get back."

Hysan tries not to look too pleased. "Can't take all the credit, of course. My android helped."

Looking away from a befuddled Cendia, he pulls me along the corridor and says, "Ignus wants you on the bridge. Your first guest arrived."

"I'm not sure about this meeting," I say as we walk to the forward section. "Come with me?"

He bows his head. "I live to serve, my queen."

I start to laugh again, and Hysan pulls me into a lavatory stall. "What are you doing?" I whisper as he locks the door behind us. The space is so small we're squeezed together.

"Serving you," he whispers, pressing me into the wall. "We won't keep your Psy scholars waiting . . . too long." When his lips meet mine, thoughts of everything else disappear.

Even with a perfect memory, my fantasies couldn't recreate the real feeling of kissing Hysan. His mouth is so sure of itself that I let him lead, and when his lips grow more insistent, my every limb starts to go limp.

"And one more thing," says Hysan, after he's pulled away. He takes some freeze-dried fruit from his pocket. "You can't defeat Ochus on an empty stomach."

While I eat, we walk to the ship's forward section, and Hysan bends my ear about the skiff he's been learning to pilot. I love seeing him so animated.

"It handles like an extension of my mind. Whatever I want it to do, it *knows*. I just wish I'd invented it myself," he says ruefully, a faint wrinkle forming on his forehead. "I'm building my own when we get home."

"*Home.*" I repeat the word, unsure what it means.

"The galaxy is your home now, Rho." He squeezes my hand. "Every House will welcome your return—Libra first and foremost."

Even though no place will ever replace Cancer, his optimism is as contagious as Mathias's doubt. Only optimism does more to lift my spirits.

When Hysan and I enter the chartroom, we find a Piscene woman in a floor-length silver veil gazing up at what looks like an Ephemeris. I almost shriek, until I realize it's a simple 3-D atlas of our galaxy projected from the ceiling. It reflects only telescope views and physical data, not Psynergy.

The woman turns at our approach and gives a deep bow, dropping to one knee. The veil shrouds her completely, falling in fluid silver folds that outline her willowy form.

"Disciple Psamathe?" I ask, copying her bow. "Thank you for coming."

She has trouble getting back to her feet, so Hysan assists her. Her voice sounds elderly and weak, as if her lungs have to labor to push the air out. "The chains of fate bind us all." She extends a palm through a hidden slit in her veil, and we touch. "I've long foreseen this meeting—and its outcome."

Hysan also touches her palm. "A good outcome, I trust."

She doesn't answer that. She simply turns her attention back to the galactic atlas.

I circle the chart table to face her. "If you already know how this ends, madame, you can save us a lot of time."

"Events will unfold as they must," she says mysteriously.

Hysan and I trade round-eyed looks, and he silently mouths, "Spooky."

Admiral Ignus sticks his head in and says, "Two more guests for your séance."

Moira's chief courtier shuffles through the hatch, looking much older than I remember him. His hair is the same gray and his skin dull olive, but his face has a bashed-in look, and his body is bent. Behind Talein, a small, ruddy man enters with his hands in his pockets. Chronicler Yuu of Capricorn wears a basic black robe, and around his neck hangs a heavy chain bearing a large medallion. His close-set eyes are as black as obsidian.

"Minister Talein, Chronicler Yuu, welcome." We exchange formal hand touches all around, and Hysan offers tea, which everyone refuses. When we gather at the chart table and face each other through the twinkling atlas, I feel an ominous air settling over us.

Psamathe parts her veil to reveal a face as gray and gnarled as driftwood. She peers up into the atlas, so I follow her gaze to the tiny smudge of light beyond Pisces, just a puff of glowing dust veiled in Dark Matter. The Sufianic Clouds.

They're so distant, they often twinkle out of sight for minutes at a time, and on Cancer our telescopes can't see them. House Pisces, in the constellation of the Fish, orbits closer to the cloud mass. Maybe Psamathe has seen more. "Has anyone been to the Sufianic Clouds?" I ask.

Psamathe clears her throat. "Our House has sent three manned missions. None returned."

Just what I needed to hear.

"Capricorn has sent unmanned drones," says Yuu. "We were more practical."

While Psamathe coughs, I ask, "What did you find?"

"Nothing of value."

"What we really need," I say, growing annoyed, "is a good physical sketch of the constellation. You know, the size? How many planets and moons? Do you have anything like that?"

The mystic rears up as if I've offended her. "Such minutiae I leave to astronomers."

Yuu's smile is brief and mocking. "Seems they've drawn a blank as well."

Talein reaches up into the atlas and slides his finger across the Sufianic Clouds, enlarging the zone until it fills the entire area above our heads. Even at highest magnification, it's no more distinct than before.

"Ophiuchus hides behind Dark Matter," I say. "That's why no other Guardians see him. Do any of you know how Dark Matter is related to Psynergy?"

"Psynergy will not be imprisoned by mere language," says Psamathe.

Yuu's laughter is dry. "People who speak in riddles are usually hiding ignorance."

I want to scream, but I swallow the urge. To my surprise, something Admiral Ignus keeps saying calms me down. "Look, we have two battles ahead. One's in the physical world, and the admirals will handle that. The other's in the metaphysical realm, the realm of Psy. That's where I need your help."

I go through the story again, covering every detail about the ice man, hoping one of these experts will pick up on something new. "I need advice on manipulating Psynergy so that I can fight him back in the Psy."

I wait to hear their ideas. Seconds pass. Mechanical vibrations hum through the deck, and muffled voices waft in from the bridge. Someone's tapping their foot very fast under the table. It's me.

"Anything?" I search their faces. "Even a hunch?"

Hysan gives me a comical look. "Maybe we should hold hands and pray to the spirits?"

Talein keeps his head down and fusses with his beaded cuffs. "You can use Morphinan," he mumbles.

Psamathe speaks in a pitying tone. "Do Virgos still resort to that sorcerer's brew? House Pisces prefers the elixir of the stars, Kappa-Opioid."

Yuu says, "We smoke herbs."

Hysan rises. "Okay, well, thanks a lot."

"No, wait," I say, the image of a frothing black tonic forming in my mind. "You mean like Abyssthe?"

I think back to when I faced Ochus on Virgo. It was the first time I managed to touch him. I replay the memory in my mind, trying to pinpoint what changed to give me newfound strength, enough to match Ochus for a moment.

Cancer.

The thought of home helped me become more Centered. What I need to fight Ochus in the Psy is to Center myself as deeply as possible and to stay there long enough to fully project myself in the astral plane and match his strength.

Abyssthe is the key.

✦ ✦ ✦

Hysan manages to get some Abyssthe from a passenger on one of the other ships in our fleet. It's strongest when first taken, so I'm going to drink it as soon as I sense Ochus.

While Hysan transfers ships to get the tonic, I'm in the forward observatory, looking through the telescope. Beside me, Mathias fine-tunes the optics so I can see more clearly. We're now approaching our fuel stop at the Piscene space station. It looks like a lacy hexagonal snowflake drifting above planet Ichthys. Through a misty shroud of fumes, the planet shines like polished glass.

Ichthys is an ice world, sheathed in glaciers of frozen ammonia and methane. It's seventeen times more massive than Cancer, so its surface gravity would flatten a human to a crusty smear of frost. The Piscene people use drones to harvest the planet's meager resources, while they live on their five minor planetoids, practicing spiritual devotion and seeking tranquility.

When I straighten up from the eyepiece and arch my aching spine, Mathias massages my shoulders. "You're in knots, Rho. Want to take a break and do some Yarrot?"

He's been coaching me to toughen up my core. The abdominals hold the body in place, he says, so the spirit can wander. He could be part Aquarian—I didn't realize what a philosopher he was until I started taking his martial arts class.

"Sure, let's go through some poses," I say.

We lie on our backs, side by side on the observatory deck. Stretching our arms overhead, we grasp the telescope's framework to brace ourselves. Then we twist through the motions of all twelve poses, fluidly blending them into a single choreography that Mathias has been teaching as a warm-up for the martial arts lessons. After going through the whole thing three times, as slowly and painfully as possible, we drop to the floor and lie on our backs, breathing rapidly.

"Mathias," I say after a while, "when the time comes for me to fly that Wasp, you won't fight me, will you?"

His lips tighten. "I'll be right beside you."

I feel my chin trembling. "I may not seem like it later, but right now, I know I can do it."

He rolls onto his side and leans over me. I look up into his smooth, pale face, and I remember our last lesson on Oceon 6, when he taught me how to use the Ring. I blacked out, and he caught my fall.

I close my eyes, and I'm startled to feel his touch. His hand massages the furrow in my brow, smoothening the crease that's been there a few days. Then his finger glides down my nose and over my mouth.

He slows down on my bottom lip, and then continues down my chin, throat, and along the centerline of my chest, stopping at my navel. His touch sets my nerves on fire.

"I shouldn't have said I was too old," he whispers, and I open my eyes to his midnight-blue orbs. "This whole time, I was too closed-minded to give you the trust I already knew you deserved. It was easier to make excuses, to look for reasons and flaws, than to just admit the simple truth."

I start to sit up, and so does he. My pulse is racing, and I don't know if I want to hear what's coming next or interrupt him now. But as soon as we're face to face, he says, "I'm in love with you."

Then he does what I never expected him to do.

He kisses me.

My hands shoot up to stop him, but when our mouths come together, I realize how much and how long I've wanted this. The instant our lips touch, it's an explosion. Hysan's kisses have a progressive build, but Mathias kisses me with a passionate desperation that comes from somewhere so deep, it takes my breath away.

Instead of pushing him off, my hands press into his hard chest, feeling the strength I've waited so long to touch.

When we pull away, his breathing is shallow. As my heart calms down, my mind turns to chaos. I'm too overcome by everything to think—about Hysan, about the future, about what I should say.

"I'm sorry for taking the liberty," he says. "I've been wanting to do that since the solarium."

"Me too," I admit before I can stop myself. My heart is pounding, like it's determined to make every beat count. Mathias and Hysan are night and day—and yet I've fallen for them both.

The only thing I can do now is be honest. I reach for Mathias's hand, and his fingers close around mine. "Mathias—"

"I know you've been upset with me, Rho, but please don't ever doubt my faith in you. You're a natural leader. I should have told you that a long time ago." His voice is lush and soothing, and the blue of his eyes is soft. "I've made a lot of mistakes the past few weeks, but believe me, all I've ever wanted to do is help you." Then he adds with a wistful smile, "Well, that's not *all* I've wanted."

A million different emotions course through me, and I don't know how I feel about Mathias or Hysan. All I know is that I need to come clean with both of them. "I need to tell you something—"

We fly off the deck and bash against the telescope housing, as an explosion hits the side of the ship. We've lost our gravity.

Screams pierce the air. Everything and everyone goes flying as the ship shakes violently, under attack.

Mathias reaches out for me, but we're too far. He digs his nails in the walls, pulling himself closer to me. I hold onto the telescope housing, stretching my free arm out as far as I can.

The moment our hands connect, the lights go out, and we're in total darkness.

38

FOR TEN SECONDS, WE'RE BLIND, until *Firebird*'s battery backups kick in. The emergency lighting blinks on with a dull green buzz.

"We need to get to the bridge," says Mathias, pulling me along with him. When another explosion hammers our ship, the deck pitches up at us, and I knock against it with outstretched hands to cushion the blow. Mathias clutches me, and we pull ourselves toward the bridge, hand over hand.

The bridge is in turmoil. Screens, charts, empty cups, and bright splashes of tea rocket through the air like missiles. *Firebird* is not equipped for zero gravity. There are no handrails or footrails. Crewmen cling to whatever they can find.

"Admiral, what's happening?" I yell through the chaos.

Ignus grapples his seat in both arms while his legs fly up and swing out of control. "Our antimatter engine imploded. Don't ask me how."

Lord Neith appears on the largest view screen. "Psynergy attack," he reports. He's calling from *Equinox*, breaking radio silence, but what does that matter now? Ochus found us.

"What happened to the shields?" I start to ask, but then I realize the question's moot. I have to get to my Wasp and draw the monster's attention away from the fleet. I may be too late, but I have to try.

Mathias must be thinking the same thing, because he grabs me around the waist and heads toward the tube leading to the hangar deck. Bouncing from one surface to another, he has to shove me along, kicking against the walls. The ship reels in a nauseating spiral, and soon I'm going to throw up the fruit Hysan gave me. I wish I could find him to know he's okay. I don't want to leave without saying goodbye.

All the skiffs and gunships are lashed down in the hangar. Hand tools zoom around us, clanging against metal walls, smashing windshields, and even hitting people. We dodge and swim through the mayhem, kicking off whatever surfaces we can find to navigate.

A massive cable comes snaking toward us, and Mathias lunges to shield me. After he's knocked it out of the way, we reach my Wasp. It's near the stern airlock, and it looks intact. Mathias gives me a push. "Get in. Get your suit on."

I ricochet into the Wasp and bounce against the console. I don't need a compression suit in here because the cabin will be pressurized when I launch. Mathias is being overcautious. Still, I do as I'm told and struggle into the tight-fitting suit while he goes to open the airlock.

At last, *Firebird* stops tumbling, and we stabilize. But the power's still out, and we're weightless. Mathias has to wrench the stern airlock open by hand, and I notice his uniform's torn at the front. That cable must've struck his chest.

I pull myself out to see if he's okay—and then I'm standing on my head, hanging onto the lashing, as every movable object goes flying up to the ceiling.

Our ship's in free fall.

I hang on with all my strength, and so does Mathias. We must be caught in the gravitational pull of planet Ichthys. Tools, broken glass, and bodies lie plastered against the hangar ceiling, and I clench my jaw to hold back a scream—Cendia's up there, twisted among the wreckage. Peero too. They look unconscious, or worse.

The ship pitches over into a nosedive, and the tools make a loud racket, rolling upward to the stern. The airlock's uphill from me now, and even with Mathias's brawn, we're not strong enough to push the Wasp up that far. I can't even undo the lashing, or she'll tumble away and crash.

"Mother Rho! Use the windlass. I can show you."

It's the chief mechanic, Foth. He's bleeding from cuts on his face and arms, pulling himself along the steep deck with something heavy slung on his belt. Straps and pulleys—it's a block and tackle. Foth climbs into the airlock and hooks one of the pulleys to a flange, then he reels a strap down toward me, and Mathias and I attach it to my Wasp.

Firebird starts rumbling, jerking back and forth. Every loose screw vibrates, and my teeth knock together. "We must be entering the Piscene atmosphere," shouts Mathias. "Get in and stay in." He boosts me into the Wasp, and for once I have no problem following his orders.

Through the Wasp's open hatch, I see Foth drop out of the airlock and sail toward a large steel spool with a crank at either side. It must be the windlass. It's as tall as he is, and he has to squeeze inside to hook the other end of the pulley strap to its spindle.

When he tries to turn the crank, the ship's motion tosses him away. He tries again, and Mathias rushes to help. The ship trembles more erratically, but other mechanics crawl out of the shadows. They brace themselves around the crank handles and strain to turn them. A second later, the ship's thruster engines fire, and we swoop upward. Ignus must have regained control of the helm.

Every loose item drops to the deck. I can't look at Cendia and Peero's bodies, fearing the worst.

As soon as our trajectory levels out, Mathias counts off, and the crew pulls together, hoisting the Wasp a meter along the deck. In rhythmic jerks, the Wasp shudders into the airlock with me inside.

Now I know what to do. This is my task, my risk. I won't let Mathias die with me.

I've scouted this airlock and planned every step in my mind, though I didn't picture doing this without power. But I have to act fast.

While the others are locking down the windlass, I propel myself out of the Wasp and throw all my weight against the airlock's inner door, trying to get it closed. When Mathias sees what I'm doing, he bellows for me to stop.

"I'm coming with you, Rho!" He races toward me, howling my name. "Don't do this! I'm begging you!"

"Fly your skiff!" I yell back. "This is my job!"

I try again to close the airlock, as Mathias bounds toward me, his eyes bright with urgency. He leaps over a fallen truss. It looks like he's trying to tell me something, but I can't hear through the roar.

Finally, the airlock door slides shut, and I slam the manual seal. Mathias's fists thud against the door, making me feel wretched. I try to wall out the sounds as I climb back into the Wasp.

Trembling, I jerk off my clumsy compression gloves to start the ignition and release the brake. I tap the controls in the proper sequence, glad I studied again today. Then Mathias's voice reaches me through the radio.

"Don't leave without me. Please."

"I'm sorry, Mathias. I've made mistakes, too—huge ones—but taking you with me would be the worst by far." I suck in a shaky breath. "It was my choice to fight Ophiuchus, not yours. Try to remember what you said to me when I went in to meet Moira . . . and find that trust in me again. I'll come back to you."

Then I fire my laser gun and blast away the outer door, expelling air and hurling my Wasp end over end toward the stars.

39

ONCE MY WASP STABILIZES, it's easy to see the damage to *Firebird*'s hull.

She's rising above the ashy upper layers of the clouds surrounding Ichthys, and three full sections of her underside have been blown away. She looks like a gutted whale. I'm amazed she's even still flying.

Ignus is steering her toward the space station that's just emerging over the planet's horizon. Its spinning hexagon gleams snow-white. *Firebird* just has to stay aloft long enough to dock.

The Ariean destroyer *Xitium* flies close by, escorting her toward the station. *Firebird*'s crew must need help, so I'm glad they'll have friends close at hand.

Equinox zigzags around the two larger vessels like a mosquito, and its evasive maneuvers tell me it's still dodging Psynergy. The attack isn't over.

I watch for the skiffs. They should be launching soon. Our fleet stretches tens of thousands of kilometers through the sky, so I use the Wasp's optic scanner to find the other ships.

At first, I can't make sense of the screen display. It looks as if hundreds of new vessels have joined us. This can't be right.

Hot, sweaty hair falls in my eyes. I slap it away. Hands trembling, I fiddle with the controls. When I get a clear image, I realize the blips aren't vessels—they're chunks of wreckage.

Understanding shoots through me like a Taser: Our whole fleet is gone. Ochus has already destroyed them with Dark Matter.

I radio the *Firebird*'s bridge. No answer. I try optic, infrared, microwave. My Ring is long gone, so I can't fuse with the Psy. Finally, I radio *Equinox*. Lord Neith comes on the radio. "Wasp W4A, identify your operator."

With a blast of light, my Wasp scans my retina, then answers automatically. "Rhoma Grace, Guardian of the Fourth House."

That's great. Bet Ochus can see me now. I grip my armrests and try not to snap. "Lord Neith, what happened to the Psy shields?"

A familiar voice joins our conversation. "Ambassador Sirna here. *Xitium*'s cristobalite bead has ruptured from within. We suspect sabotage." She sounds breathless, as if she's been running upstairs.

But . . . sabotage? *All* our shields? How could this happen?

"My shield is functional," Neith reports. "*Xitium*, stay in my shadow."

I notice something spewing out of *Firebird*'s port flank. Wreckage? Bodies?

I aim the scanner, and I'm relieved to see a dozen skiffs zooming my way. Hysan and Mathias made it out. They'll be fine. It's time for me to clear out. I set a course straight for the Sufianic Clouds.

"Rho, slow down. I'll escort you." It's Hysan. He's calling from one of the skiffs.

"Stay and protect the fleet, Hysan. Please stick to the plan. Trust me." I shut off the radio before Mathias calls, too.

My Wasp's hydrogen powertrain was engineered for speed, and no skiff can catch up with me. All I have to do is put a decent amount of space between the fleet and myself. Ten minutes at hyperspeed should do it.

Sailing outbound toward the galaxy's edge, I feel a burst of adrenaline. This is my fate. I'm not a fighter, and I don't invent things, but in the Ephemeris, I grow powerful. Even though it means meeting Ochus, part of me is thrilled to be returning to the astral realm, where I feel closest to the soul of the Zodiac.

My Wasp zooms lightning fast, and my fingers tingle with energy. After ten minutes, I lower my shield and flip on the Wasp's Ephemeris. Let's see if Ochus finds me as tempting a target as I hope he does.

This onboard Ephemeris is designed as a crystal ball mounted on my console, but something's wrong with it. It won't light up.

I toggle the digital switch off and on. Nothing. I command the Wasp to turn it on. My console talks back. "Please provide the encryption key."

Admiral Ignus didn't have time to unlock it. How am I supposed to distract Ochus now?

I aim my optic scanner back toward the fleet. *Firebird*'s closing in on the space station, but she's skimming through the planet's upper clouds, losing altitude fast. *Xitium*'s beside her, and *Equinox* buzzes around them both, diving in and out of the atmosphere to shield them. Farther out, the skiffs fly in echelon formation, probably waiting to retrieve escape pods, should the need arise.

I get on the radio and try calling Ignus again, and when that doesn't work, I hail the skiffs. "My Ephemeris is locked. Does anyone know the key?"

Hysan answers. "Sorry, Rho. Ignus didn't trust me with his secrets."

"What about Mathias? He's piloting one of the skiffs, right?"

"No, he's not with us. I haven't heard from him or anyone on *Firebird*. Their transceivers are down."

Mathias is still on board?

"Hysan, can you signal them with your running lights?"

"I'll try."

My scan shows one of the skiffs leaving formation and swooping down toward the gutted flagship. He's going to position himself in front of the bridge, where Ignus can't miss his blinking lights. I ease forward in my seat, watching the scanner screen, hoping to see more skiffs leaving the flagship.

Sirna comes on the radio again. "Mother Rho, where's your Ring? Mathias is trying to speak to you through the Psy."

I twist my Ringless finger. "I don't have it. I never took it with me from the strongbox. What's he saying?"

Hysan's still twenty kilometers out when *Firebird*'s gutted belly starts shooting sparks. It's hitting the planet's denser methane clouds, building up friction. I cover my mouth as I realize what's happening: The cruiser's breaking in two.

Sirna comes back on the radio. "He says . . . *You were born for this. I should have told you every day.*"

I want to look away from the blazing ship, but I can't. The bow section noses upward, bounces and rolls, then bursts into flames. The fire dies almost at once, but debris flies against *Xitium*, knocking her off course.

Equinox shoots into the clear, and so does Hysan's skiff, just as the stern half of the cruiser skitters into a spin, flaring streaks of burning fuel. Fire engulfs it. Mathias was near the stern when I left him.

Shaking, I grab the radio mike. "Hysan, do you see any more skiffs? Or escape pods?"

"I don't, Rho." His voice grows quiet. "I'm sorry."

The stern breaks into a thousand pieces, and their fiery trails streak downward through the clouds. In seconds, the fires snuff out. The Piscene atmosphere holds too little oxygen to keep a flame alive.

"Look again, Hysan!" I scream at the radio mike.

Mathias can't be dead.

At first, no one responds. All I can hear is a rhythmic rush of noise . . . then I realize I'm hyperventilating.

"Someone do something!" I shout.

Lord Neith replies. "Scans show no survivors."

Sirna adds in a somber whisper, "Their voices have fallen silent in the Psy."

40

MATHIAS.

I grip the view screen with such force, the plexine housing creaks.

For an instant, I consider turning my Wasp around and diving into those methane clouds to find him. I almost do it.

My hand's on the tiller, ready to make the turn. "Mathias," I whisper, closing my eyes. I was scared, too. It was easier to focus on the things that stood between us—his doubt, our disagreements, the age difference—than explore how I truly felt about him.

I loved him my entire adolescence.

I love him still.

Sirna hails me from the Ariean destroyer. "Guardian, stay on course. I'm trying to find the encryption key you need."

On course?

What course?

My hand falls off the tiller, and I let my body sag loose and weightless in the seat belt. Colors fade to gray. Losing consciousness would be a relief.

"Alert," announces Lord Neith. "Psynergy attack incoming. *Xitium*, you're the target."

No.

Not Sirna, too.

I sight the Ariean ship through my scanner and see a burst of wreckage rising from the weapons array mounted on her hull. The destroyer's engines fire.

She's taking evasive action, and *Equinox* circles her like a tiny dune spider wrapping a fat beetle in silk. *Xitium*'s fast; they have a chance. They're going into orbit, probably to gain more speed. As they dip behind the planet, I lose sight of them.

I draw a sharp intake of breath. "Hysan, stay with them," I whisper.

"I will," he says, his voice low and grave. "Are you all right?"

Am I all right?

Mathias's baritone breathes through my memory. His words warn me to be cautious, to think my plans through, to gather more information before pushing ahead. "I've been so blind."

The moment I say it, I'm reminded they're the same words Moira spoke when Ochus attacked. Only in my case, it's not stars I misread, but hearts. My own and Mathias's.

We were too stubborn to give each other a chance, and now I'll never know what that kiss truly meant . . . for either of us.

I slam the Wasp's console with my fist. "Take me to the Sufianic Clouds. Maximum speed."

Acceleration pushes me back in my seat, and I rocket out of the Kyros Belt toward the Thirteenth House. What's my plan now? Shoot Ochus with my laser? Dive-bomb him like a suicide pilot?

Reckless adrenaline fuels me now, not logic—until another memory jerks my head around.

My Wave.

I unzip my compression suit and pull it out from my pocket. I call up the tutorial Ephemeris. The star map swells out of my palm-size screen, small and low resolution.

"Face me, coward!" I yell at the small flickering orb of starlight. "Come on!"

All I see is the clam in my hand, the whirling map, the chaos of overlapping patterns half-hidden in Dark Matter. In a fit of rage, I hurl the Wave against the side of the Wasp, cracking its golden shell.

I didn't stand a chance anyway. I never got the Abyssthe from Hysan.

A prickle spreads through the back of my skull, and I know what's happening before I hear him. Ochus is calling me.

I reach back to retrieve my Wave. Swelling from the cracked screen, the small holographic map stutters like a lopsided clock. My fit of temper broke it.

Vicious laughter grates my ears. *How droll. You struggle with the most basic skills. I wonder, will you ever understand your own gift?*

There he is, swelling out of the cracked Ephemeris. He looks different, grainier, like a blast of cold sleet. *Ask me your questions, little girl. I know you're dying to.* How is Dark Matter ruled by Psynergy? *Ask me.*

I swipe at his eyes. *This is for Mathias!*

He shifts aside with ease. *Keep trying. Everything is Psynergy. This universe is a figment. And I'm the supreme illusionist.*

If I'm going to meet him on his plane, I need to Center myself. I stare at the faint lights of the Ephemeris and immediately find the one I'm looking for. The place that gives me peace and power, the home that will always be my soul.

I open myself up to Psynergy from Cancer, only instead of using it to read the stars, I pull on it to feed my presence on the astral plane. And as the star map swells in size, I feel my surroundings changing, until I'm no longer trapped within my body on the Wasp—rather, I'm facing Ochus in the wind tunnel where I first met him, the slipstream in Space where he's been hiding.

That's right, little crab . . . crawl out from your shell, he teases. *Let's see how strong that inner flame is.*

I root myself more firmly in my Center—breathing deeper, feeling Cancer, tapping into my innermost voice. Ochus's icy form swells before me, and I reach into my store of Psynergy. This time when I strike, my hands close on something solid.

He feels like icy bone, and he's freezing my skin. My palms blister and blacken, but I know the pain isn't real. Ochus tries to move away, but I grit my teeth and hold tighter. I've got him.

Then the bone melts in my hands, and I'm grasping empty air.

Behind you, he says, taunting me. *Don't give up yet. You're doing so well. But you are going to have to be stronger than that.*

The effort of Centering myself so deeply leaves me weaker than before. I see him rising over me, a gruesome carcass of ice, and I ask, *Why are you doing this?*

I was a healer once. I restored life with these hands. His fists grow to the size of small moons. *I was beloved . . . and then I was punished for it.*

He swings at me with one of the chilly fists, and I close my eyes, steadying myself in my Center, until I feel control of the Psynergy surrounding me. When I look again, time has elongated between us, stretching his punch so that his fist is still inches from my face.

Dodging it, I say, *So now you punish innocent people in return?*

He stumbles when his fist doesn't connect with anything, and then he glares at me, his fists shrinking back down. *You made me what I am. You and all the Guardians. You twisted my miracle into everlasting bondage.* His primordial eyes burn at me through the ice. *You can't conceive the torture I have endured, the unbearable solitude of my exile, desolation without end.*

His body twists and deforms as he moves, and to my surprise, it looks like he's suffering genuine distress. *You are the strongest of the twelve, but even you can't kill me. Each time we meet, I hope.*

You hope? I ask. *That I'll kill you?*

End my torment, yes. He disintegrates as he speaks, and his icy form evaporates. For an instant, I almost pity him. Then he rematerializes and with a mocking hiss says, *I dare you.*

His eyes flare blacker than pure Space—like Dark Matter itself. He swells into a giant ice wraith, and reflected in his glassy stare are the faces of his victims. Mathias. My father. My friends. I force myself to remain still.

Fight me! he roars.

All I want is to batter his desiccated corpse with every fiber I possess. But instinct warns me that's useless, so I hold steady. I need to regain my strength in the Psy, so I play his psychological game.

Besides, as long as he's with me, he's not sending Psynergy strikes on the rest of the armada. I won't survive this, but maybe I can buy Hysan and Sirna a chance to escape.

Ophiuchus, I want to set you free.

Do you? How kind you are. He morphs into a blast of needle-sharp sleet that cuts into my face. I turn aside, and a spray of red droplets trails me. The sting is agony, and I clench my muscles tight, struggling to keep sane through the pain.

Then I hear him cough. I look over, and now he's stooped and gaunt, an old broken man, half-eaten by time.

Even though I loathe him, even though his thirst for slaughter revolts me, the wetness of that cough and the droop of his crippled spine tug at my compassion. And for a fleeting instant, I actually feel the visceral agony of his never-ending death in life.

How old are you?

Ah, now you begin to understand. His eyes grow dull, and his long, bony arm stretches to point toward Helios. *Ask the Lord of Light what eons I have endured.*

The cuts on my face throb, and a bloody film swirls in the air around my head. Ochus withers away, then reforms. *When I was a young man, I was as fresh and idealistic as you are now. I was an alchemist, striving to heal the sick and find a cure for death. I dreamed of a never-ending galaxy as the highest blessing mankind might achieve.* He eases into a new position, grimacing as if his tortured body might break. *Now I know. Immortality is hell.*

Then let me help you die, I offer too eagerly.

Halt. I can't move. He's trapped me in a coat of ice. His laugh blasts through my frozen bones, and then he says, *You think this is real? How easily you fall for my cunning. I have no wish to die, mortal!*

When he morphs back into a man's shape, he's larger, stronger, more heavily muscled in rippling ice. I can't believe I tried to help him.

Paralyzed, my hatred comes raging back. I strain to break free and strike him, but his iceberg of Psynergy holds me rigid.

Are you comfortable, little girl? You look quite fetching in your glossy new skin. His booming laughter vibrates in my ears. *Why should I wish for death when the glory of my House will soon be restored? You read the prediction written in the stars. I will endure any torment to get what's been promised to me.*

I jerk and wrench, but I can't escape. I can't even speak.

You have amused me long enough, child. Let's end this battle.

He's going to kill me now. When he raises his hand for the deathblow, I stare at him through the glaze of my frozen blood. I see the murder in his eyes.

"Cancer sustains you." Mathias's words whisper through my mind, and I sink into my Center. There, I pull on Cancer's Psynergy with everything I've got, until time lengthens again, only now it's moving so slow, it's practically stopped.

Light waves bend, and Space curls in on itself. Milliseconds stretch toward infinity, and my breathing slows. My muscles relax.

I've never experienced life like this before—it's as if time is a rubber band being stretched to its limit—and I'm seeing every particle that makes up every instant of our existence.

Somehow, it transforms into my own timeline, and I think about how strange my life has been. The one thing I knew for certain growing up was that I loved Cancer—and that I left it. The one person I never wanted to be like was Mom, then I followed her footsteps and abandoned Dad and Stanton. The first guy I ever fell for was a university student whom I watched silently for years, loved silently for weeks, and then let die in silence, without giving either of us a chance to say our goodbyes. I was in too much of a hurry to reach my own death.

Everything starts to connect in the air around me, as though a new Ephemeris were swelling out, only it's a map of my life and how it's led me to this moment, my death.

Time is three-dimensional, and it forms its own galaxy of lights and connectors, not like the music of the stars, but more like a brain's neuron network. Only it's never-ending and ever-expanding, like our universe. As it rotates round and round, the image of a worm eating itself comes to mind.

Everything is connected, cyclical, eternal. Time, Space, Ophiuchus. And somehow I understand what integral element the Thirteenth House brought to the Zodiac. The thing missing from our galaxy today.

Unity.

At Helios's Halo, I felt something electric in the air, something I've never felt before. It's not just our trust that Ophiuchus stole from us—there's something more powerful he took, something we glimpsed for a minute that night, when we came together.

It's hope.

And in a universe of people that spend their *todays* searching for *tomorrows*, hope is the most powerful weapon you can have.

Ophiuchus was supposed to bind our solar system together. His defection left us imbalanced and broken. Fighting him will require a force of souls from more than just House Cancer.

I'll need to fuse with Psynergy from the whole Zodiac.

41

SOMEHOW, OCHUS'S ARM IS STILL SWINGING. I dig deeper into my Center, staring into the blinking lights of the twelve constellations, until I'm fusing with the Psynergy flowing from the whole solar system.

I'm borrowing psychic energy from people all over, the way Ochus does, so my pulling tugs on his own store of Psynergy, and his fist falls.

What is this? he demands. *You can't do this!*

We wrestle for power, each of us gaining and losing physical strength. Ochus has an easier time retaining his hold on this dimension, and I don't have Abyssthe, or even my Ring, to help. All I have is me—so it's a good thing I'm an *everlasting flame*.

I keep holding on, knowing it's only a matter of time until Ochus's gradual change comes over him—the burden of time—and he grows old. When eventually he curves into his hunched form, he lets go. He can't defeat me in this shape.

So. You have won a round. Perhaps you will even become a worthy opponent in time. His body grows less visible every moment, but his black-hole eyes remain dark, churning in midair.

This game never ends, but you have earned a respite. House Cancer has nothing further to fear from me.

I glare at him. *You've already destroyed it. What about the other Houses?*

Hear me well, child. This game never ends. *I serve a master who has more surprises in store.*

He wheezes a fading laugh. Then he blows me a kiss. A sharp, white-hot kiss of pure Psynergy.

I dodge, but the poison dart burns a glancing blow across my neck, etching my skin like acid.

Remember me, he says, vanishing.

I feel myself plummeting downward through burning gases and dust, flailing my arms, and then solidifying into a mass of pain. My head smacks the deck of the Wasp, and I touch the throbbing wound on my neck.

As soon as I look up, my Wasp's mechanical voice chirps. "Warning. Hydrogen leak."

I look around. I'm alone in Space.

"Passenger eject," says the voice. "Eject urgently."

The console buzzes with emergency messages. My Wasp's powertrain is about to rupture.

On autopilot, I zip my suit up all the way and put my helmet back on, wincing from the pain in my hands. Then I cinch the belt tight and speak the final command.

With a detonating crack, my cabin capsule separates from the engine assembly and tumbles away. Soon the orange flash of the rupturing powertrain spins across my porthole like an angry sun. The capsule has no navigation, so I can't direct it. I just turn over and over on end, until—

Thump.

I'm caught in the claws of a grappling arm, which has appeared out of nowhere. I'm not spinning anymore, so I watch the arm haul me in, holding my breath, unsure who's got me.

And then a much smaller ship coasts into view. A skiff, its lights blinking.

Tears fill my eyes. It's Hysan.

✦ ✦ ✦

As soon as my capsule's inside the *Xitium*'s bay, Hysan's skiff glides in and docks, and Sirna pries open my hatch. When she sees my face, her helmet shield rests against mine, and I hear her voice. "Praise Helios, you're alive."

Hysan springs out of his skiff and lifts me from the capsule, clasping me in his arms. The outer bay doors shut, and the three of us cycle through an airlock to the ship's interior. We rip off our helmets. "How did you find me?"

Sirna touches a spot at the center of my chest. "I've followed all your movements, Guardian. The pearl I gave you is a tracker."

Spyware? She lied to me? I look up at her, the indignation building in my chest—and when I see the expression of exhaustion and determination on her face, I realize I should be grateful. She saved my life. "Thank you."

We've entered what looks like a metal shop. Shears, rollers, punchers, and drills are clamped to the walls, and two uniformed soldiers wield a plasma cutter to slice a sheet of steel. The air smells of ozone. "They're making repairs to the ship," says Sirna. "Let's stay out of their way."

I peel off the constricting gloves, wincing.

"Rho, your hands," says Hysan, gingerly holding my wrists so he can survey the damage without inflicting more, then examining the rest of me. "Your neck, too."

"Frostbite," I say. "Ophiuchus. He injured me with Psynergy."

"How is that possible?" asks Sirna.

Hysan wraps me in his arms again. "I'm so relieved you're okay," he says, his voice husky. "We should get you into a life-support pod and heal your hands."

We weave along a narrow passage cluttered with crates of food, water, and gear lashed to the walls. The *Xitium's* a large ship, but its neutron drive and weapons take up most of its volume, and the spaces left over for humans are dim and cramped.

On the bridge, I greet the Ariean Captain Marq, a dark, leathery man built like a boulder. At the start of this mission, Marq seemed enthusiastic, but now when I thank him for rescuing me, he examines me with bloodshot eyes.

"Guardian," he snarls, making my title sound like an insult. "The shields your colleague provided were worthless. Our ships are rupturing from the inside out. Reactor meltdowns, fires in munitions bays, unexplained hull breaches. We're in full retreat."

"The shields were obviously sabotaged," says Hysan, iciness in his tone. He glares at the captain. "Rho had nothing to do with that."

Marq's maroon cheeks flush a deeper shade. "Go with your ambassador, *Guardian*. We have enough to do."

Sirna hurries me out of Captain Marq's sight. "The Arieans have lost many comrades," she whispers.

"They don't want me on board, do they?"

Sirna sighs. "Marq gave me a stateroom. You can stay with me." We skulk away from the bridge, and when soldiers meet us in the passageway, they glare.

"Where's Rubi?"

Sirna's face falls. "We lost contact."

"Rho, I'm going to check with Neith, and then I'll come find you," says Hysan. He kisses my cheek before hurrying down the corridor.

Sirna's stateroom is narrow and barren. She offers me a squeeze-tube of salmon roe. "Protein," she says. "Eat as much as you can. You'll need strength."

She activates her Wave and calls up a scanner view of the fleet, then enhances the image with false color to make the ships easier to identify. Over half our vessels have been destroyed. Sirna magnifies the view of a wrecked pleasure yacht, and I bite my lip until I taste metal. "Those drifting particles, are they . . . bodies?"

Sirna nods and closes her eyes. "The Capricorns were assisting a disabled freighter when their steering went out. Head-on collision."

She tells me our ships have scattered all over the sky, and every vessel still under power is limping back to its home world. Only two of the five Ariean destroyers survived. When Sirna shows me the latest casualty figures, the air in my lungs turns to sand.

I choke out a cough, shut my eyes tight, and see Mathias standing before me, ramrod straight in his dark blue uniform, strong and serene, only twenty-two years old.

How is it possible I'm still alive? It wasn't supposed to end like this.

"Rho." Sirna takes my wounded hands in her own. Her expression's sober, weary. "There's something else you need to know. The Marad has come out of hiding. While we've been away, they joined the conflict on the Sagittarian moon. They're arming the rebels, threatening to invade the planet below. We think they have hadron bombs. It seems what the army was waiting on . . . was for us to go."

"You mean—this was a distraction?" I blurt. "*Ochus* used a feint?"

Sirna sighs. "We're all in the dark here, Rho. But right now, we're going back to Phaetonis. You've been summoned."

✦ ✦ ✦

Right now is a relative term in Space travel. Lightspeed and relativity, time warps, wormholes. Ochus's game is far more complex than I thought. He didn't just manipulate Psynergy—he manipulated *us*.

He turned our own tactic against us.

Caasy's warning echoes through my mind. He was right: I was deceived. Maybe I still am.

Time is my enemy now. We'll need four galactic days to reach Phaetonis, and waiting is torture. I've been forced to spend the first eighteen hours cooped up in a life-support pod getting my hands repaired. Apparently, Psy wounds take longer to heal than normal injuries.

But time can be an ally, too. My long hours alone in the healing pod have given me a chance to mull things over. In particular, something Ochus said: *Why should I wish for death when the glory of my House will soon be restored? You read the prediction written in the stars.*

I think back to the vision I was seeing in the Ephemeris all along, past the Twelfth House. The smoldering mass where the constellation Ophiuchus used to be.

It wasn't just appearing to me—it was doing more: It was warping the other constellations out of shape. Like they were making room for something.

The Thirteenth House is coming back.

✦ ✦ ✦

When I leave the pod, it's late. The ship's bell just rang twelve chimes, and the interior lights have been turned low. Sirna's working an extra shift.

In her room, I pull up some research on one of the ship's screens, looking for clues about the Dark Matter. I still don't understand how Ophiuchus was able to destroy our planets with Psynergy—or how he managed to take out most of our fleet.

It turns out our own Holy Mother Origene delivered a lecture on metaphysical time, speculating that it might be reversible, asserting that time is nothing but a mental construct we create to make sense of the physical world. Theoretically, we should be able to travel through time in all directions, even sideways. She was running tests to confirm this theory when she died.

Empress Moira, still in a coma, was also doing work on metaphysical time. She believed that since time has neither beginning nor end, it must be linked in a smooth, continuous circle. In that case, we probably travel through the same points in time repeatedly.

I think about the vision of time I saw in the Ephemeris. It fits both theories.

But if Origene and Moira were both running active experiments on metaphysical time . . . that must be why they both built the quantum fusion reactors. They were collaborating. Were they on the trail of the time-worm? Could that be why Ochus awoke?

There's a knock on the door. "My lady?"

"Come in."

When Hysan walks inside, the first thing I want is to feel his arms around me and his mouth on mine, to be embraced in his warmth and light. But as soon as the impulse manifests, a competing one is born. A faction of dissent—the part of me that can't let Mathias go.

Thanks to Hysan's keen people-reading skills, it's hard to take him by surprise. "What is it?" he asks, standing at the foot of the cocoon where I'm sitting.

I look down at the screen in my lap and shut it off. "I can't."

Hysan perches on the edge of the bed, leaving space between us. "I'm sorry he's gone, Rho. He deserved better."

Tears start running down my cheeks, and I'm helpless to stop them. "I . . . I closed the airlock door on him," I say through the sobs—sobs that rattle my ribs and break my bones and stab my soul. "I didn't let him come—I left him on that—I—I killed him."

Hysan crushes me to his chest, and I crumble there, shaking and screaming and slobbering, and I can't stop. Then I start to worry I'll never stop.

The tears can never end. Dad and Mathias are gone. Cancer is barely hanging on. And for some reason, I'm still here.

"You were protecting him." Hysan kisses my hair and strokes my back. "He had a way out, Rho. He had a skiff, and he was the best pilot of us all. If he didn't leave, it's because he was helping others, and he didn't want to abandon them. Like you, he chose to do the honorable thing. Don't take that from him."

I really love the fairness of the Libran outlook. Or maybe it's just Hysan. His special way of seeing the world makes me want to experience life through his eyes.

Our past and personalities couldn't be more different, and yet everything about him resonates with me on a level that feels soul-deep. Mathias I'd been sure I liked since I was twelve . . . but Hysan was a complete surprise. Even now, I feel the same electric chemistry his closeness always produces. Any time we're in the same room, there's a magnetic pull between us, and my blood craves the Abyssthe-like buzz of his touch. Like he's a real drug.

"There's something else," I say, pulling away from his hold and forcing myself to put more room between us. "Before the attack. Mathias and I . . . kissed."

Hysan doesn't react. He doesn't move away or get angry, he just stares at me in silence.

"And I realized I have feelings for you both. I always have. And now . . . I can't do this. With you."

He nods. Even though he's not emotional, I know he's hurt because he's retreating. His eyes are dimming, growing as light as air, until he's so far removed from this moment that the only visible part of his right iris is the golden star.

He takes my hand and brings it to his lips. He presses his mouth to my skin and whispers, "At your service, my lady."

When he gets to the doorway, he says, "My skiff's been repaired. I'm leaving to help with the rescue. Take care of yourself, Rho."

Without waiting for a response, he leaves.

42

WHEN WE LAND ON PHAETONIS, a full military motorcade squires us into the city from the spaceport. Captain Marq rides with us.

I expect to be taken to the hippodrome, so I'm surprised when we head into the international village. Today, it's completely void of people, and leftover glasses and trinkets from the festival still litter the ground. My chest hurts just thinking of the night of Helios's Halo, back when we had a tomorrow to fight for. When the Houses were friends. When Mathias smiled.

A special session has been convened to hear my report of what happened in the Wasp, and I've memorized what I'll say. I'm going to share that Ophiuchus has a master—like Caasy predicted—and I'll tell them about his plan to bring back the Thirteenth House.

I cross the plank into the Cancrian embassy, following Sirna. I'm relieved not to be in the arenasphere facing the Plenum for this report. After everything that's happened, home is the only place I want to be.

Sirna walks ahead and leads me to the second bungalow, the only one I haven't visited yet. The lobby is an open sandbox, filled with hammocks and embassy Waves for guests. The roof is an aquarium, housing various varieties of fish, seahorses, crabs, sea snakes, and even sharks. Sirna and I head straight to the top story—a vast, open-air ballroom.

The floor beneath us is the aquarium, and I realize it must span the entire height of the bungalow. The heavy fabric sky of Phaetonis hangs over us as Sirna walks off to her seat at the long table facing me, and then I'm left alone, staring at Guardians and ambassadors from the twelve houses.

There's no audience today. No soldiers, no cameras, no holo-ghosts. Just all the representatives who are still alive to attend.

Everyone is glaring at me. My eyes land on blade-faced Charon, who rises. I thought he'd been suspended.

I give Sirna a questioning nod, but she lowers her eyes. *What's going on?*

"Rhoma Grace." Charon's voice thunders through the quiet, and I flinch. "You have been charged with cowardice. How do you plea?"

Cowardice. The word echoes tauntingly in my ears, the way *treason* did, when Admiral Crius accused Mom. None of this makes any sense. *I'm on trial?* I thought I was here to give a report on Ophiuchus.

I catch Sirna watching me, so I lift my chin, determined to act with honor. "Ophiuchus outmaneuvered us, but—"

Charon bangs his fist on the table. The silence that follows has an echoing quality. "Guilty . . . or not guilty?"

I open my mouth, but I don't know how to answer. My warnings launched the armada. They trusted me. I led them.

But it was Ochus who did the slaughtering.

Ochus.

When I fail to answer, Charon bangs his fist again. "Did you not claim that your Psy shields would protect our ships from your boogeyman?"

"The shields worked, but they were sabota—"

"Yes or no!" shouts Charon. "Did you not deliberately lead our fleet into the perilous Kyros Belt, the most dangerous part of Zodiac Space, an ice field you knew would claim most of our ships?"

"No! That's not what happened. Admiral Ignus did a stellar job of leading us through the ice."

Angry conversations rustle down the table, and Charon says, "Perhaps the admiral will testify." He looks around the room, smug and confident. I'm sure he knows what happened to Ignus. Sirna told me he went down with his ship.

"Admiral Ignus died a hero," I say. "He and all the others. Someone betrayed us."

"Yes. Someone did. You." Charon points at my chest. "You breached our trust, Rhoma. You weren't ready to be a leader; you were a child seeking fame. That's why the first thing you did after you were sworn in was run away. Not that it's entirely your fault—your Cancrian mother didn't set the best example.

You then commanded your bandmate—a Sagittarian not subject to your control—to continue spreading your rumors and win you more fans. In the meantime, you and your lover stole a ship from House Libra—again, not in your Cancrian jurisdiction—and shortly thereafter you wormed your way before us and manipulated the Plenum into following you on a dangerous and doomed mission that you were always planning to survive, *alone*. We were all just part of your path to Zodiac fame, and you never cared who you hurt, did you? Not even your Guide, Lodestar Mathias Thais."

Hearing Mathias's name, I feel paralyzed. There's a deadly, booming silence that follows Charon's accusation, and it feels like it's radiating from inside me. I don't even hear my heartbeats or breaths. There's just a vacuum where life had been.

"I'm a Cancrian," I say, my voice low and shaking, "a *nurturer*. What you're suggesting, it isn't in my soul."

"Isn't it true the original plan was for Mathias to pilot your Wasp?" asks Charon, and I gasp. "Yet you went around his back to Admiral Ignus for an instructional program so you could fly it yourself. You'd been planning to abandon him all along." His voice is no longer loud or impassioned, simply factual. He knows he's won.

"Why . . . would I hurt Mathias?" I ask, my voice nearly gone.

"Because if he came with you, he would learn the truth—that there is no Ophiuchus. *Admit your treason, child.*"

"Objection." Sirna's on her feet. "This girl stands accused of cowardice, not treason." Even though she's defending me, she still won't look at me.

"Fine," says Charon. "We have heard enough. The defendant has admitted her guilt. Excellencies, what say you?"

"No, I haven't—"

"We of Aries find the defendant guilty."

Charon nods. "How says the Second House?"

"Guilty," rumbles the Taurian.

"How says the Third House?"

The diminutive ambassador from Gemini hops up into her chair, reminding me of poor, lost Rubidum. "The Third House says guilty."

Charon calls the Fourth House to vote, and now it's Sirna's turn. Sirna at least will stay loyal. She stands, and her voice rings low but clear. "House Cancer votes guilty."

I freeze, stunned, while the rest of the Houses continue to vote. It's unanimous. Albor Echus reads my sentence. "Rhoma Grace, you have been found guilty and are forever banned from this Plenum."

None of this makes sense. They asked me to lead the armada—I wasn't even allowed in on the strategy meetings—and now I'm the only one to blame?

I stare at the glass beneath me, and for a moment I wish it would break so I could just return to the Sea and be done with breathing. Then I think of Mathias, and I push that wish away.

Sirna rises and solemnly walks up to me. I think she's finally going to explain what's happening, but instead she removes the Cancrian coronet she herself placed on my head this morning. I watch her in bewildered confusion, and then my brain kicks in, and I understand what's happening.

A Guardian can only be sworn in on her own House's soil—
that's why we had the salt water at my ceremony—and the same
goes for stripping a Guardian of her power. They couldn't do it at
the hippodrome. . . . It'd have to be done at the embassy.

Sirna clears her throat and speaks loud and clearly across the
roofless room. "You are hereby stripped of your title as Guardian of
the Fourth House."

43

THE VERY LODESTARS I SENT here now hustle me out of the embassy, alone, and escort me across the plank. Then they turn me loose on the streets of the village.

I don't know where to go. For the first time, I'm on my own. I have no faithful protector, no safe house, no embassy to run to. I don't even know how I'm going to get off this planet.

I amble dazedly around, like I'm in a stupor. After weeks of racing forward at breakneck speed, I'm done. My services aren't needed anymore.

I watch the world around me as though I'm not part of it. I don't feel like I'm part of anything anymore.

I was deceived after all. Mathias warned me to slow down and think things through, but I couldn't see past my own obsession. And now I've lost both him and Hysan—and the respect of our entire solar system.

Suddenly I realize people have started to trickle out from embassies. Mostly Acolytes and university students—those who didn't set out in the armada. When they see me, they point and come closer.

Something moldy explodes on my head, and immediately more vegetables start flying toward me. The crowd converges around, calling me filthy names that bleed into each other. *Traitor! Murderer! Coward!*

They throw their dead at me, too. My *husband*, my *father*, my *sister*, my *friend*, my *daughter*—everyone lost someone. And like the Plenum, they too need someone to blame. War leaves all kinds of wreckage.

I recognize one of the faces among them—Lacey, the Piscene from Helios's Halo. Her face is splotchy and wet with tears. "You were supposed to save us," she says through her sobs.

A thrown flute glass shatters and slices a cut across my cheek. Fighting tears and covering my face, I drop to my knees, as the circle closes around me. I wonder if the same people who chanted my name to lead them days ago will now rip me to shreds.

Suddenly an air horn blares. "Stand back," says a man's voice. "Clear the area."

I raise my head. My attackers are retreating, but no soldiers are in sight.

People stumble backward, shielding their faces, and a few of them fall to the ground. I hear slaps and punches, but I can't figure out what's happening—until an invisible hand grips my upper arm and lifts me to my feet.

"Your veil, my lady."

A collar slips around my throat, and a golden figure appears before my eyes.

Hysan came back.

"We're invisible now. Let's get out of here."

He takes my hand and hurries me through the crowd, shoving people aside. As soon as we leave the village, we race toward the train station.

The city around me is brimming with energy, but I can't access it. I feel as though I'm watching and hearing through a glass wall, unable to cross over and join reality. Only when we're seated inside a train car do I manage to catch my breath. "Thank you," I say, feeling too fragile to say more.

He frowns and touches my cheek. "You're hurt."

The cut throbs, but it's minor. "Why are you here, Hysan?"

Dimples half mark his cheeks, like his smile is only halfway back. "You're not an easy girl to forget." He wraps my hand in his. "Plus, you're my only real human friend."

He makes it hard not to stop everything and kiss him sometimes. "How did you get here so fast?"

"*Equinox.*" His eyes glitter. "We've been traveling at hyperspeed ever since Ambassador Frey contacted us."

"Frey voted to expel me."

"He had no choice. He and Sirna struck a deal to keep you out of prison."

We steal into the spaceport, and as before, *Equinox* is parked at the far edge of the vibrocopter pad, veiled from view. Hysan assures me *Equinox*'s Psy shield remains intact, thanks to his Talisman.

When we climb aboard the ship, two people are waiting for us—
or rather, one person and an android.

Lord Neith sits at the helm, playing digital mah-jongg with
'Nox, while a little girl watches and suggests moves. It's *Rubidum*.

"Rubi! You made it!"

When I leap to hug her, she fends me off. "Ugh. What's that
muck on your clothes?"

I step back so I won't drip on her. "Your zeppelin came through
okay?"

She twitches her nose at the smell. "No, our fuel tanks exploded,
but the honorable Lord Neith saved me. Whoever designed my
escape pod needs a brain transplant." She rips a few cristobalite
beads off her tunic and flings them at the wall. "The worst is, we
fell into a trap of our own making."

"You trusted a seventeen-year-old," I say.

Hysan puffs out his cheeks. "My Psy shields were flawless. I
tested them myself."

"Hysan, I wasn't referring to you. Ochus warned me the very
first time I saw him that people would never believe me. And
everything I've done to prove him wrong has only worked in his
favor. Now the whole Zodiac thinks I'm a coward. They actually
think I meant for things to work out this way."

"You can't take the blame alone, Rho." Rubidum tears off
another bead. "We all allowed rage to blind us."

"I guess I can cross off politics from my future."

She and I laugh weakly, but Hysan looks at me steadily, his
sunny gaze trapping me in its beam. "The stars picked you, Rho.

Humans—in their infinite injustice—have wronged you, but you'll find your rightful place again. Your light shines too brightly not to be a beacon for others."

✦ ✦ ✦

I head to my usual cabin to clean up. With Hysan nearby, I almost feel like I'll pull through . . . but my guilt makes it hard to spend a lot of time in his presence.

The moment I'm alone, all the words Charon flung at me at the embassy seem to fill the room, and I curl up in a corner of the floor, trying to escape them. But maybe I am a coward.

I didn't tell Mathias about Ochus's death threat before we left Oceon 6. I didn't tell him about Hysan. I couldn't even express my feelings or hear about his.

I just shut the door on him. I abandoned Mathias. Like I abandoned Dad and Stanton. And the people of Virgo. I don't know what light Hysan and Agatha can possibly see in me, when all I seem to bring people is darkness.

When I finally get up to drop my suit in the refresher, I shake out the pockets. Mathias's Astralator falls out.

I pick it up, running my fingers along the slippery mother-of-pearl. This belongs with his parents, not me.

Poor Amanta and Egon. Like Hysan and me, they're orphans, but in a different, far worse way.

I spend a long time in the ultraviolet shower, letting the light singe away every trace of dirt. The wound on my cheek stings, so I hold my face close to the UV faucet to sterilize the germs. When I step out of the stall, Sirna's waiting.

"Rho. I wish I could have taken your place up there." She holds out a fresh Cancrian uniform tailored to my size. "Forgive me for not warning you. It was part of our agreement with Charon."

I take her outstretched hands. "Duty's a harsh master," I say, repeating her words. "But I'm not a Lodestar. I don't have a right to wear that."

"It'll do for now." She helps me slip it on. "Events had to play out this way. If we'd pushed back too hard, Charon would have engineered something worse than expulsion. Try to understand."

I touch the Royal Guard glyph on my pocket, the three golden stars. Like the ones on Mathias's suit.

"I'm not giving up, Sirna. I just . . . need time to think and get ready."

"Rho, you've done plenty."

I gaze into Sirna's sea-blue eyes. "Agatha will be interim Guardian until a new one is selected. She's the most senior Advisor. Watch over her."

Sirna gives a solemn nod. "Of course we will. I must return to the embassy, but I wanted to bid you farewell first. Take care of yourself."

"You too." We hug, and she turns to go—then I remember the Astralator. "Wait, Sirna. Could you take something back to the Thaises?"

Her expression falls with sadness as I hold out the Astralator. "It was Mathias's . . . and his sister's before that."

She stares at it but doesn't accept. "We mustn't interfere with the wishes of those who have gone. Mathias wanted you to have this. His parents have other things to remember him by. . . . This is yours."

◆ ◆ ◆

When Sirna leaves to resume her role at the Plenum, Rubidum refuses to go, and I'm glad. She's two hundred and eighty years older than me, but she feels like my kid sister, and now we're both homeless.

Neith and Hysan man the helm, and as *Equinox* lifts off and climbs away from House Aries, I watch the planet Phaetonis disappear without regret. Far in the distant sky, unknown stars circle beyond our galaxy, spreading outward without end.

I can't fathom infinity. Telescopes see only so far, and even the Ephemeris reveals no more than our visible universe. No ship will ever travel fast enough to reach the edge of Space. Anything might lurk out there. Anything is possible.

Even Empyrean.

Rubidum comes up beside me. "See something?"

"Just thinking."

She presses her forehead to the glass. "Scientists say that somewhere in the universe, every event under the sun repeats itself an infinite number of times in every possible variation."

"I like that." Could it be that somewhere beyond our sight, Mathias still lives, and another, better Rho Grace still swims in a sapphire sea?

Rubidum nudges my arm. "Your fans will set you up as a martyr. You'll be more famous than ever. That's what I foresee."

"You got that from the stars?"

"Yes. I'm not a Guardian for nothing. Hysan's right, you know. You *are* the true Mother of Cancer. The stars haven't pointed to another."

I frown. "What do you mean?"

"Your Lodestars haven't located new astrological fingerprints as Potentials to replace you."

A far more terrible theory forms in my mind: Maybe Cancer doesn't have a new Guardian because Cancer is gone forever.

But I can't think that way.

"I need more training, Rubi." I hug my knees to my chest. "I have a ton of stuff to learn." Even as I speak, my eyes sting at the memory of Mathias's advice.

Hysan comes up behind us. "So where to?"

"The moons of Aquarius have stellar ski spas," says Rubidum. "Or we might try sun-sailing on planet Leo."

"I'd like to find my brother," I say, even though I know it's selfish. "He's probably in the refugee camp on Hydragyr."

"House Gemini." Rubidum turns to the glass and squints in the direction of her world. Her red-rimmed eyes remind me of the people in her court, so lively and creative, now burnt to ash. "I've been dreading the sight, but . . . yes, I believe it's time to return."

"Gemini?" Hysan twists his lips like he's tasting vinegar. "Neith, my liege, the ladies have decided. Set a course for the Third House."

44

HOUSE GEMINI IS FAR ACROSS the ecliptic from Aries, so *Equinox* will make another slingshot loop around the sun to boost our speed. We're on our way now, and I'm in my cabin, thinking of Mathias.

"Rho? Are you awake?" Rubidum's calling from the other side of the door. "There's something Hysan thought you'd want to see."

Equinox's nose has already darkened and polarized when I come in, and my companions are near the curved glass, admiring our sun. I come to rest between them, and when I bump Hysan's shoulder, he smiles.

"Light of the sun be with you," he says, an oddly antiquated greeting.

"And with you," I answer in kind.

We turn toward the golden fire, which is nearly out of range. "Now look to the right." Hysan points to a blue jewel in the sky.

I widen my eyes. It's Cancer.

She's glowing as bright blue as ever, ringed now by a necklace of moon stones. It reminds me of the pearl necklace Mom gave me, uniting each of the House's sacred symbols.

Unity. Ophiuchus. *The irony.*

Now, when I've lost everything and almost everyone, I feel truly naked for the first time. I have no place in the world, and the world has no place to offer me. I'm free . . . and just *me.*

Only I don't know this me. I've never been her before. In a way, she can be a clean slate. The choice Crius once told me I had, many lifetimes ago. And the only thing I know about this new me is that the Cancer Sea runs through these veins, and this heart belts out a Cancrian tune.

The one truth I've always retained—the part of me that's never faded and has gotten me through the worst—is my identity as a Cancrian. Charon challenged my very nature when he stood over the Cancer Sea and accused me of cowardice. But he doesn't understand me because the lens he views me through is narrow.

I think back to Hysan's jury, warning me against becoming so stubbornly set on Ochus—I was so focused on rallying others to my cause against the Thirteenth Guardian that I refused to see the army's threat or entertain other points of view. It's the same with Charon—he can only see me from the outside, through his Scorpion eyes.

The more we close off to the other Houses, the smaller our worlds grow. Even our worldviews begin to shrink. That's why I have to save my world. Even though people go, Cancer can't. Like Leyla and Sirna said, it has to live on.

Hysan said I'm the person the stars chose to safeguard our House, so that's what I'll do, in whatever ways I can. Only it's not just Cancer that's home anymore. It's the Zodiac.

I'm trying to view our solar system the way Hysan sees it, as an extension of my home, a place full of intrigue and adventure and interesting people. Like him, I want to be a citizen of the galaxy, not just one planet. For now, though, land and oxygen would be good. And some familiar faces.

A new home for the new me. A home I will defend with my dying breath. Because the threat is still out there. The master and Ochus and the army.

I've been Guardian, so I've seen how things work at the top. And I've realized it's always hard to effect change, whether you're starting at a position of power or doing it from the ground up. Either way, you're facing opposition—other people's and your own—and you always have to fight hard.

So I'm going to keep doing what I do best: Reading the stars. I'll go wherever help is needed. And I'll use every free minute I have to hunt down the people responsible.

The ones who stole my home, my dad, and Mathias from me.

Just as Cancer's moving out of view, I turn to my friends. "Let's lower the shield and ping Cancer. Someone may still be there."

I've started wearing my Ring again. I'm not hiding anymore. If Ochus wants another fight, I can touch him now. I'll fight him into eternity.

Cancer's power grid is still down, so we call to my home planet through the communal mind of the Psy. My friends hover near the helm, and we meditate in silence, waiting. Many intellects whisper through the Psy, but no voice arises from planet Cancer. After twenty minutes without a response, I hang my head.

Next we Wave the refugee camp deep under the surface of the Geminin planet Hydragyr. Given that holograms travel at the speed of light, there's an eight-minute time delay. The first person to answer is Nishiko.

Since my Wave is scuffed and dented, and one corner has melted, Hysan transfers the image to the view screen, and the sight of Nishi's familiar cinnamon-brown face brings the first real smile to my face, softening muscles I didn't realize I'd been clenching.

"I've been watching for you, Rho. We knew you'd find us."

We speak to each other like holo-ghosts, with long, tedious lags punctuating our talk. "Nishi, you're still with the refugees? I thought you'd gone home."

She lifts her chin and smiles. "I've got reasons for staying."

Lady Agatha joins our conversation. "Blessed Mother," she says. I start to protest, but she can't hear me yet. "The people call me Guardian, but we Cancrians know our true protector."

At length, I answer, "Thank you for your blessing, Agatha. It kept me steady."

After eight minutes, a new face pops up on the screen, and he's laughing. "Don't tell me you've got religion, Rho."

"Deke! It's so good to see you."

Another wait. Then he says, "Would you believe I'm farming mushrooms now? You'll love my fungus sushi."

On the screen, Nishiko squeezes next to Deke, and when she slides her arm around his waist, he doesn't push her away. "Your people are making a home here, Rho. They're building up your House again. You'll like this place."

A dark, dry beryllium mine deep inside an airless planet?

Yes, if my people are there, I'll like it.

I introduce Hysan and Rubidum, and in slow, halting time lags, we talk for an hour. My Cancrian friends have dozens of questions because they didn't believe the newsfeeds out of Phaetonis. I try to clear up some mysteries, but most of my story will have to wait until we arrive.

Before we break off, I ask, "Do you know where my brother is?"

Their expressions dim. Agatha says, "We haven't heard from your family, Mother. We believe they perished at sea."

"But I thought . . ." My voice dies. My mind is caving in.

Rubidum comes closer and caresses me. "It's terrible to lose a brother. I know."

Hysan pulls me into his chest, and I hide my face in his coveralls, inhaling his cedary scent, wishing the agony would end. Every day, another knife wound.

I could survive any loss . . . but not Stanton. I fought and survived for nothing.

"Your family's in the Cancer Sea," Deke says after eight minutes. "They would've wanted that."

I can't speak.

Hysan tells Agatha when to expect our arrival, and she gives him the landing coordinates. Nishiko and Deke promise a big homecoming celebration, complete with fungus sushi, and we end the call.

When it's over, we all stand around in silence. They're waiting for me to react, but I can barely take another breath, much less speak.

My Wave starts humming again. Maybe they mixed up the coordinates and are calling with a correction. I don't move to get it, so Hysan opens the clamshell.

A voice shoots out, but no image. "Rho, can . . . hear me?"

The voice is so familiar it pierces through my numbness.

"Stanton?" I look around desperately, wondering if the others can hear it, or if I've lost my mind.

"That's an optic signal," says Hysan, handing me the Wave. "Speak as close to the device as you can."

I hold it up to my mouth. "Stanton, this is Rho. Where are you?"

When he doesn't answer, I turn to Hysan. "Are you sure this thing's working?"

"The signals travel by optic beam. Give it time."

We wait four electrifying minutes before the next signal arrives. We hear a burst of static, then a voice. ". . . is Stanton Gr . . . calling Mother Rho. We're in . . . observatory on Mount Pellanesus . . . see a ship. Is it you?"

"Yes, it's me! Stanton, you're alive. We're coming!"

Again, we wait, only this time my heart is racing with hope, not dread. Hysan links my Wave to *Equinox*'s screen and hits some keys. When the next signal arrives, we can see Stanton's face.

". . . about four weeks. The Belger family's with me . . . two hundred others. We've taken over the observa . . . rigged up a link . . . fishnets . . . they've been . . . and Dad . . . with his nar-clams. He died in the . . . creatures he loved . . . are you coming?"

Stanton appears to be standing on a mountainside, buffeted by gale-force winds. Leaves and bits of scrap fly past, and behind him, a dish-shaped optical link sways back and forth, pixilating his image in and out of view.

I turn to Hysan. "Can we land there?"

He confers with *Equinox*, then nods. "Heavy storm activity, but we'll get through. If the terrain's too rough, we'll hover."

The first good feeling I've felt in a long time washes over me, and it's so new it hurts. If this is selfish, I don't care. I'm not Guardian anymore—I can think about myself and my family again.

Ochus has taken my dad, my home, and Mathias from me. As Guardian, I needed people's support to fight back. As a person, I can do what I want.

After I've reunited with my brother, I'm going after the Thirteenth Guardian.

Ochus is going to pay.

I swear it on my Mother's life.

◆ ◆ ◆

THE END OF BOOK ONE

◆ ◆ ◆

ACKNOWLEDGMENTS

Like the Zodiac Universe, my life is populated with diversely talented people who often—sometimes unknowingly—donate a piece of their power to me when I most need it. I am so, so lucky to have these *Lodestars* watching over me.

Thank You:

To Liz Tingue—for this chance, and for being equally fabulous as an editor and a friend

To Ben Schrank, Casey McIntyre, Laura Arnold, Marissa Grossman, and the rest of the Razorbill team—for the most amazing publishing experience I could have ever dreamt up . . . and I've been dreaming about this since I was nine

To Vanessa Han and Kristin Smith—for the coolest cover ever

To Jay Asher—for your out-of-this-world friendship and generosity, and for introducing me to Laura

aura Rennert—for believing in me, for your brilliant
ce, and for all our adventures to come

Will Frank—for always, *always* being there and never, *ever*
ing me give up

To Nicole Maggi, Lizzie Andrews, Anne Van, and *Scribblers*—
for your friendship, for all you've taught me, and for taking the
journey together . . . Nicole, our twin brains giving birth to twin
books must've been written in the stars

To my friends and family, across this Blue Planet—for helping
me up again every time I've fallen, and for filling my world with
wonder and love

To the readers—for giving Rho a chance and blasting into
Space with her

A los Bebos—*por ser los mejores abuelos y seres humanos del mundo,
los extraño con locura*

To Russell Chadwick, the perfect Libran—for always inspiring
me, and for being my best friend, my proofreader, and the Light of
every day

To Meli—for being more than a sister . . . you're my best friend,
my role model, and the love of my life

A *Papá*—*por siempre apoyarme y nunca dudarme y sobre todo por
enseñarme a soñar*

And to Mom—for being my first reader and fan, the best Mom
in any galaxy, and the Guardian of our House . . . *sos la mejor
mamá del universo.*

TURN THE PAGE FOR
A SNEAK PEEK OF

BEWARE THE 13TH SIGN

WANDERING
STAR

A ZODIAC NOVEL

ROMINA RUSSELL

THE BREATHTAKING SECOND BOOK IN

THE ZODIAC SERIES

1

TWELVE FLAGS, EACH BEARING THE symbol of a Zodiac House, lie in tatters before me, on a barren field that extends endlessly in every direction.

I can just make out a crest neatly sewn beneath each House name—a dark blue Crab, a royal purple Lion, an inky black Scorpion. Caked in blood and grime, the defeated fabrics sprawl across the lifeless land like corpses from a forgotten battle.

There are no sounds; nothing moves in the dusty distance. Even the sky is devoid of expression—it's just a constant colorless expanse. But the stillness in the air is far from calm. It feels like the day is holding its breath.

I turn in a small circle to survey my surroundings, and in the eastern distance I see a steep hill that's the only disruption to the flat landscape. I concentrate hard on the hill, envisioning myself cresting it to survey the valley below, and soon my view begins to transform. As the vast valley sharpens into focus, I choke on a horrified gasp—

Thousands of dead bodies litter the powdery earth below, their uniforms a rainbow of colors. Like a gruesome quilt made from people parts.

I slump to the floor, nearly crushing the glass orb in my hand, and shut my eyes, forgetting that nightmares thrive in darkness. Corpses crowd my view in here, too.

Hundreds of frozen Cancrian teens in flashy suits float through the black space of my mind, forever suspended there. I shake my head, and the vision flips to Virgo's ships going up in flames, the air almost thick with the stench of burning flesh and metal.

Then the tiny burned bodies of the once-lively Geminin people.

The wreckage of vessels from what was once our united armada.

I suck in a ragged breath as the next picture forms: the familiar wavy black locks, alabaster face, indigo blue—

My eyes snap open, and I squeeze the glowing glass orb in my fist. The valley of bodies vanishes as the sights and sounds of reality rush into my head, as if I've just broken the sea's surface after a deep dive.

The barren field has transformed back into a large, sterile room lined with floor-to-ceiling shelves that house hundreds of thousands of identical glass orbs. They're called Snow Globes, and each one stores a re-creation of a moment in time.

I replace the memory I was just reviewing in its spot on the shelf:

House Capricorn

Trinary Axis

Sage Huxler's recollections

After a moment, the orb's white light dims out.

I've been coming to Membrex 1206 for two weeks, combing through House Capricorn's memories of the Trinary Axis, searching for answers to any of my millions of questions. I'm desperate for any signs that could lead me to Ophiuchus, or help us defeat the Marad, or bring back hope to the Zodiac.

So far, I've found none of the above.

My Wave buzzes on the table, and I snap it open, anxious for news. A twenty-year-old guy with my identical blond curls, sun-kissed skin, and pale green eyes beams his hologram into the room.

"Rho—where are you?"

Stanton looks confusedly at the Membrex (a room outfitted with the technology to unlock Snow Globes) surrounding us. He's wearing his wet suit and squinting against Helios's rays, so he must still be at the beach helping out.

"I'm in the Zodiax . . . just looking something up."

I haven't told my brother what I'm really up to here—deep within the earth of House Capricorn's sole planet, Tierre—while he volunteers at the Cancrian settlement on the surface. "Any sign of his ship yet?" I ask before I can stop myself.

"Like I told you twelve times this hour, I'll let you know when he's here. You shouldn't worry so much." Stanton looks like he wants to say more, but he glances off to the side, to something happening on the beach. "Gotta go; last ark of the day's just dropped off more crates. When are you heading over?"

"On my way." Capricorns have been shuttling our people back and forth from here to Cancer on their arks, braving the planet's stormy surface to save our world's wildlife. The Cancrians on the settlement have been helping our species adapt to Tierre's smaller ocean.

Stanton's hologram winks out, and I pull up the ledger on my Wave where I've been keeping track of the Snow Globes I've examined, and input today's updates. To exit the room, I pass through a biometric body scan that ensures the only memories I'm taking with me are my own.

Out in the dimly lit passage, I brush my hand along the smooth stone wall until my fingers close on a square metal latch. I pull on it to open a hidden door, and when I slip through, the ground falls away.

My stomach tickles as I glide down a steep, narrow tube that shoots me out onto the springy floor of a train platform. Its bounciness reminds me of my drum mat, except this one's riddled with rows of symmetrical circles that light up either red or green, depending on whether that spot on the train is available.

I stand inside one of the green circles, and almost immediately there's a rush of wind and the hissing of pistons beneath my feet— then the circle I'm standing on opens.

A gust of air pressure sucks me down, and I've tapped into the Vein, the train system that tunnels through the Zodiax.

"*Zodiac art from the first millennium,*" announces a cool female voice. I grab onto the handrail above me as the wind changes direction, and a stray curl falls into my face as we shoot upward.

The Zodiax is an underground vault that contains what the Tenth House calls a *treasure trove of truths*: the collective wisdom of the Zodiac. Down here, there are museums, galleries, theaters,

Membrexes, auditoriums, restaurants, reading rooms, research labs, hotels, shopping malls, and more. When Mom described it to me once, she said the Zodiax is like a brain, and the Vein is its neuron network, zooming people around as fast as firing synapses, its route mapped by subject matter rather than geography.

A couple of Capricorn women in black robes share my compartment—one is tall with dark features, the other short with a ruddy complexion. We slow down for half a moment at "*Notable Zodai from this century*," and the smaller woman is sucked up to a train platform.

"*Surface, Cancrian settlement.*"

I click a button on the handrail and let go. I'm blown up to the bouncy bed of another train station, and biometric body scans search me again as I leave the Zodiax.

Outside, I instinctively raise a hand to shield my eyes from Helios's light. Echoing silence is instantly replaced with the sounds of crashing waves and animal calls and distant conversations. As my vision adjusts, I make out herds of seagoats (House Capricorn's sacred symbol) feeding and roughhousing at the water's edge, and long-bodied terrasaurs flicking in and out of the rocks along the seashore, their scaly skin shiny in the daylight. High above us, horned hawks flap across the sun-bleached sky, circling the air in hopes of picking off the pocket pigs feeding in the weeds.

Tierre is the largest inhabited planet in our galaxy, and it has a single massive landmass, Verity. Up ahead, the planet's pink sand beach spills into the blue of its ocean, and behind me, wild forests grow right up to the ridges of volcanoes, giving way in the distance to snowcapped mountains that pierce the sky. The view is occasionally interrupted by the long neck of a fluffy giraffe reaching up for a fresh tree leaf.

This place is a land lover's paradise—which makes sense, given that Capricorn is a Cardinal House, representing the element Earth. People here live in modest homes on vast plots of land with multiple pets that live free-range.

Cancer's colony is being built along Verity's western coastline, our people predictably opting to settle near our preferred cardinal element, Water. As I walk into our settlement, clusters of Cancrians are working on their respective tasks. Some are building pink sand-and-seashell bungalows, some are chopping seafood for sushi on flat stones, and some—including Stanton—are knee-deep in the ocean wearing wet suits, tending to the newly arrived species. As I walk past each group of people, they don't stare anymore. Not like they did at first.

A month ago, the Cancrians I met on Gemini insisted on my innocence and vowed the other Houses wouldn't get away with this insult to Cancer. Then three weeks ago, we came to Capricorn, and the Cancrians here have barely spoken to me. Their glares and pointed silence have made it clear they're not interested in my political failings—their sole concern is saving what's left of our world.

I wade toward Stanton through a shallow sea of crawling hook-crabs, miniature sea horses, schools of flashing changelings (blue fish that turn red when they sense danger), and a few just-released baby crab-sharks. My brother is with Aryll, a seventeen-year-old

Cancrian who came here with us from Gemini. They're in the process of releasing another school of changelings into the ocean.

Rather than disturb them, I hang back and scour the sky for the telltale metallic glint of an approaching spaceship. It's getting close to sunset. He should be here by now.

"You look nice today," says Stanton, spotting me. Only he says it less like a compliment and more like a question. His gaze searches my turquoise dress for clues before landing back on the water.

Aryll turns, and his electric-blue eye roves over my outfit; a gray patch covers the spot where his left eye used to be. He flashes me a boyish smile before rearranging his expression into a Stanton-like look of disapproval. Even though I know he cares for us both, he takes my brother's side on pretty much everything.

"It doesn't matter, I can still help you guys." I come closer, letting the bottom of my dress get wet to show Stanton I'm not fussy.

"Rho, don't," he says with a bite of impatience. "We're nearly finished. Just hang back."

I do as my brother says, watching as he and Aryll set the fish free. The changelings look radioactive, their fiery bodies staining the blue water red, but soon their coloring begins to cool, and they disappear into the ocean's depths. Changelings, being small and low-maintenance, have had the easiest time adapting to Capricorn so far.

Stanton opens up the last closed crate floating beside him, and he and Aryll start releasing hookcrabs into the ocean. "That's good, but watch for its pincers," says Stanton, deftly taking the crab from Aryll before it snaps his finger off.

When he talks to Aryll, my brother sounds different than when he addresses me. With Aryll, his voice dips lower, adopting a comforting tone that's painfully familiar. "See this part of the shell back here, where it curves in a little?" Aryll nods obediently. "That's always the best place to grip them."

Stanton's words sweep me back to Kalymnos, where I learned how to handle the hookcrabs that constantly clawed at our narclams, and I realize who my brother is acting like. He's being *Dad*.

It shouldn't bother me. After all that's happened, I should be mature and understanding and compassionate. I should be grateful my brother's alive at all. Some people lost everything.

Aryll was at school on a Cancrian pod city when pieces of our moons started shooting through our planet's atmosphere. The explosion took out his left eye. By the time he made it home, his whole family and house had drowned in the Cancer Sea. Like Stanton, he was herded together with other survivors and transported to House Gemini's planet Hydragyr.

Then Ophiuchus attacked Gemini.

Earthquakes ransacked the rocky planet right as the Cancrian settlement was being built. Stanton was ushering a family to safety when he lost his balance and slipped off the rock face. Aryll caught him just as he was going over.

He saved my brother's life.

"We're going to change," Stanton calls out as he and Aryll duck behind a privacy curtain to shed their wet suits.

I study the horizon again for a sign of the ship I've been anxiously awaiting all day. Ophiuchus hasn't destroyed another planet since Argyr, but the Marad attacks a different House every week. The army has also been linked to pirate ships that have been intercepting travelers and inter-House supply shipments all across the galaxy. Zodai on every House are cautioning citizens to avoid Space travel, encouraging us to travel by holo-ghost whenever possible.

What if something's happened? How will I know? Maybe I should try his Ring, just in case—

"There!" shouts Aryll, his red hair flickering like fire under Helios's rays. He points to a dot in the sky.

My heart skips several beats as the dot zooms closer, sunlight catching its gleaming surface. The ship grows bigger on its approach, until the full form of the familiar bullet-shaped craft is visible.

Hysan is here at last.